ANGELINA

THE DEAD REALM BOOK 1

JOEL SHEPHERD

Trade Paperback Edition

Angelina: The Dead Realm, Book 1. Copyright © 2023, Joel Shepherd

ISBN: 978-0-6457812-0-5

Cover and Interior Design by G&S Cover Design Studio
https://www.gscoverdesignstudio.com/

Cover Model;
Karina Bik
https://www.instagram.com/karinabnyc/

Joel Shepherd
www.joelshepherd.com

ACKNOWLEDGMENTS

With thanks to Nora Deschmann, Kathy Bernardi and Marco Calcara for help with the Italian.

Yes, that is the amazing Karina Bik on the cover. If you haven't heard of her yet, don't worry, you will.

https://www.instagram.com/karinabnyc/

"In the world of science, all myths, legends and fairy tales are assumed to be false until proven otherwise. In the world of magic, the opposite is true."

—High Councillor Elena Davidovich,
Remarks to the 821st General Session
of the High Council of Magic, 1957

"Oh Ashkir, greatest of all magicians! What cruel secrets did you take to your grave?"

—Unknown
Latin inscription, dated to
1065 AD, Constantinople.

CHAPTER ONE

Angelina has come to New York to kill a man. Normally this would be simple enough. But the man she intends to kill is Eli Leventhal, one of the two most powerful magicians in the world. Rumour has it that Leventhal is more than two thousand years old. In those two thousand years, a lot of people have tried to kill him, but Leventhal is still here.

No matter. Ange likes a challenge.

It is her first time in New York. She strolls down Broadway in her long black coat and tall boots. It's just after ten on a Tuesday night, and the theatres are emptying, tourists and locals thronging the sidewalks in search of a cab, the subway, or coffee and a slice of cheesecake. Broadway restaurants are still open and busy with customers. Even in London, Ange's previous haunt, things would be starting to close by now… on a Tuesday, anyhow. Ange admires a city that never sleeps. Sleeping makes you vulnerable. New York is ever vigilant.

Two strolling cops pay no attention to the sword in her belt. They are shroud-blind, of course. It is the oldest magic, that separates the magical world from the non-magical. The magicians who created it say it is for the latter's protection. Like everything from the mouths of magicians, Ange thinks that's rubbish. The magical class do everything to please themselves. They regard non-magical folk as eagles regard ants. Or mice.

But the shroud is useful for finding out who's who. Ange stops at a pedestrian crossing, at the back of the waiting crowd. A few people look at her, but that's mostly because she's tall. Over six foot, and taller in boots. She's no goth, despite the black hair and black leather. Her North Italian skin is not pale enough, nor does she bother with the makeup. The last few days, in fact, she's been more concerned with staying warm, and not falling to her death in the Atlantic while sleeping, than what she looks like in the mirror.

There. A woman across the pedestrian crossing spots her. Her eyes widen, and she changes her mind, and crosses the adjoining street instead. Ange watches her go, and perceives only a faint tingle. Like a breath of wind on her lips on a winter's night... but it is early October, and winter is still months away. The crossing signal changes, and they walk, Ange at the rear. Passing her, a man in a suit gives her a dark stare... a strong tingle, and Ange reaches casually to her hip, and the hilt of her sword. The man hurries on. Ulani have been unpopular with magicians for a thousand years. It is an unpopularity born of terror. Word will now spread, of the new Ulani in town. But Eli Leventhal is not a man to be killed by tricks. He'll know that she's here, and that suits Ange fine.

Ahead she sees the brilliant light and commotion of Times Square, and turns right to avoid it. All that glitz and crowds, it's not her style, and it won't give her what she's looking for.

There are dives in every big city, if you have the sense to find them. Out along Tenth Avenue, near the Hudson, Ange strolls past old brick walls, warehouses not yet torn down for development. A doorway, apparently locked with no inviting signs, but Ange gets a tingle of a different sort, and pushes inside. Within, cold bricks and a low overhead — old buildings are hell on tall people. She ducks beneath, and into a bar. It's ugly and makeshift, with just a few patrons at rickety wooden tables. There are newspapers on the floor. To soak up the blood.

Red eyes glow at her. A flash of sharp teeth, a quickly hidden rodent's tail. Ah New York, Ange thinks drily. Like every other great city — where there are magicians, there are the underworld. She leans on the bar, and a fat, hairy man in a greasy singlet glowers at her, polishing glasses from filthy to merely smudged.

"Hello," she says, and her accent is elegant Italian smoothed by English vowels. Five years, she's been in London. Five years, until Lacey died. Until Leventhal murdered her. "Who's the master in this place?"

"Mid-Town ain't got no master," growls the barkeep. "Where you from?"

Ange smiles. Not too smart, no. Fancy not recognising an Ulani, when face to face with one? "Milan," she says. "Via London. Come on, every vampire dive in a big city has a magister watching over you. Who do you serve?"

"You got ID?" asks the barkeep.

"You seriously think I'd drink what you're serving?" The stench of rat blood is strong. Masters don't like the patrons eating the local population, but every master needs minions. Most can provide better than rats, though. Maybe the barkeep is telling the truth.

"You want information?" says the barkeep. "No ID, no info."

Ange pulls her sword from her belt, and places it on the bar. It's a beauty, a Japanese katana, sharp enough to cut you just by looking at it. "Here's my ID," she says. "So who *is* the nearest master?"

"Leventhal," grumbles the barkeep. "Leventhal is master in all Mid-Town here. But we don't serve him."

A good thing to be said of Leventhal. Ange doesn't like it. "You tell him I'm here," she says. "You spread the word. Angelina Donati, that's my name. He'll have heard of me. I'm Ulani."

"No such thing in New York," growls a new voice from a doorway. Ange looks, and there's two of them there, emerging from a back room. Bigger than the usual vamps. He's got something heavy and sharp under his coat. Perhaps an axe. The tingle gets stronger. This one is unpleasant.

"Fresh blood," says his friend, similarly big and armed. "Better than rats."

"You should know better than to walk through strange doorways in a new city, girl," says the barkeep, still polishing. About them, the bar patrons are stirring, arising with hungry snarls. Ange sighs.

One of the vamps charges. Ange removes his head in a beautiful, effortless pivot. And observes them all with raised eyebrows, questioning. Is that it? The vamps back away, bloodshot eyes wide as fear battles with diseased insanity.

The big new arrival with the axe roars and charges. Ange steps back as his huge swing splinters the bar, but now the axe sticks. His friend has two big knives, and lashes with one. Ange ducks beneath, and cuts through his middle. He falls, as the axe man struggles to pull his weapon from the bar. Ange kills him too, and sidesteps to avoid the mess all over the floor. These are very good boots.

The vampires scatter, like cockroaches in the kitchen when someone turns on the light. Ange picks up the severed head, and tosses it to the stunned barkeep.

"Send Leventhal that," she suggests, making her way around the mess, and back to the door. "Angelina Donati. My friends call me Ange. The ones Leventhal hasn't murdered yet."

The next morning, Ange descends to the hotel lobby, and decides against the restaurant there. It's too expensive and glitzy. She recalls childhood breakfasts in Milan, chocolate milk and a pastry before running to school along cobbled laneways, dodging noisy scooters, delivery vans and cyclists. She hasn't lived in Milan for five years, but those childhood memories are a part of her. You can't know a city by eating breakfast behind double glazed windows from a menu.

She walks the sidewalk amid busy Manhattan foot traffic on a bright and sunny morning, past honking cabs and delivery vans. She pauses at a news stand, searching for a paper. Starace always read the Libero, in Milan. In London she'd read the Telegraph, not that English papers are ever better than pig swill, but because somehow the rustle of freshly printed paper made the coffee taste better.

Ange notices the girl in line before her. She's small and dark haired, perhaps Chinese... it's not so easy to tell because she wears dark glasses. Secured to her wrist by a loop is a wooden cane, different from the white ones used by the visually impaired, but clearly used the same way. But she is selecting papers and magazines as though she can see them all. And then, of course, comes the tingle.

"Oh, and I'll take this Cosmo too," says the girl. Her accent is all New York American — a local, then.

"How can you tell which is which?" Ange asks her. She doesn't like magicians, as a rule, and being Ulani they mostly don't like her back. But that doesn't stop her from being curious when she sees something interesting.

"From the smell," the girl says brightly. "I'm not sure if they perfume them on purpose, but it sure smells that way. Each one is slightly different." She leans in conspiratorially. "Plus I can see just a little bit."

The stall owner wraps the magazines and two newspapers for her. "You're certainly buying a lot for someone who can only see a little bit," Ange observes.

"They're for the office," the girl says airily, collecting her parcel with thanks. "When it gets boring we do a lot of reading. You have an interesting couple of accents, where are you from?"

"Milan via London," says Ange.

"Oh, glamorous. You're very tall, are you a model? I mean, as well as being an Ulani?"

Ange smiles. Well, she *did* get the tingle. And a smart, well-dressed girl like this isn't going to be like those dumb oafs in the bar last night.

Before she can reply, the girl sticks out a hand. "I'm Meisha. Meisha Wing. Have you had breakfast yet?"

They eat at a spectacular delicatessen. It's nearly a supermarket, with everything from fresh bread to cheeses to pastrami and hams, hot food and cold, to go or to stay. This morning it's crazy crowded, and office workers jostle amidst yells for orders and the jingle of the cash register. Ange has a roll, a fruit salad and a black coffee that's not quite Milano standard, but close. Meisha has a bagel stuffed with everything, and a cappuccino with extra froth. Ange keeps the sword on her knees, so it won't get snagged by the people brushing past, to whom it is of course invisible.

"It's a lovely sword, by the way," Meisha says approvingly. "Japanese?"

"U-huh." Ange nods, her mouth full. "Old tradition. Japanese swords good for Ulani style."

"Hmm," says Meisha. "And of course being Ulani, you're almost immune to magic."

"Why?" Ange says warily. "Want to try a spell on me?"

Meisha smiles. "Oh, I'm not that good."

"You know what I think? I think you can't see anything at all. I think everything you 'see' is magic." It would explain the odd strength of the tingle she gets from Meisha. "And if you can do that, you're a lot better than 'not that good'."

"Wow," says Meisha. "You can tell all that? You're right, I'm blind from birth. If I weren't born with the gift, my life would be very dark."

She takes off her glasses. She's quite pretty, Ange thinks. Early to mid-twenties, as much as that means anything, with magicians. Her eyes don't appear damaged, but they are unfocused, not fixing on any single point. It's much less disconcerting to talk to her once she's put her glasses back on.

Meisha must surely have some important job to go to, because Ange reckons anyone with a thousand dollar Armani handbag must be doing okay. But Meisha is happy to eat slowly and talk. Ange can't recall the last time she met any magician she liked this much. Meisha's parents are both doctors, and she grew up somewhat well off in Queens. Both parents are passives, not magicians, but Meisha's greater gift was considered a blessing, given her disability, and quickly she was teamed with a magic tutor. To hear Meisha tell it, her childhood was endless training, to nurture her gift on top of the school grades that successful Chinese parents demanded of their only daughter.

Ange tells her of Milan, of Starace rescuing her from the orphanage, and the adopted family of other Ulani pupils. Of little money but lots of kids and food, of games in the streets, of climbing rooftops at night and going to the dangerous places where regular kids never dared, but Ulani brats with trainee swords might venture on a bet.

"Sounds amazing," Meisha says, with more sincerity than Ange has ever heard any magician use about Ulani. "It's sad you have no immediate family, but with so many adopted family… and I mean the way Italians do family."

"It had its moments," Ange concedes. For a moment, she picks at her fruit salad. "But the Ulani have a hierarchy. Some kids thought they were better than other kids, because of their patrons. There was bullying, and fights."

"Oh," says Meisha. "Is that why you ran away to London?"

Not really. But Ange isn't about to share that right now. She nods. "When I was twelve. Five years ago."

"Wow, how did you survive on your own in London at twelve?"

"There's a lot of work for Ulani if you know where to look," Ange assures her. "And quite a few resident Ulani, not like here. They looked after me, and helped me get an education of sorts. I never really had a single home, but for a street kid I sure made a lot of money."

Meisha nods. "Lots of money dealing with Togova that go bad."

"It's not only Togova that go bad," Ange mutters.

The two great alliances of wizardry, the Togova and the Shtaal. Each comprises many old houses and types. And each is headed by a Grand Magister. Both of the world's two remaining Grand Magisters live here, in New York, within miles of each other. One is Eli Leventhal. The other is now known to the non-magical world as Samuel Riley, though his real name is far older. He's the Mayor of New York.

For the first time, Meisha's pleasant expression thins. "You think Togova and Shtaal alliances are the same thing?"

"Of course they're not the same," says Ange. She stabs her fruit salad. "The Shtaal are just no better."

"Really," says Meisha, with heavy irony. "Tell me, which side finds room for vampire covens? Lycanthropes? Transfiguration experiments?"

"All of them, at one time or other," Ange retorts, and murders a piece of pineapple with her fork. "All the houses. The alliances have always shifted, at different times they've all been friends or enemies…"

"Yes, right now, Angelina," Meisha says impatiently. "Right now is what counts, not a thousand years in the past. In the past there were hundreds of Grand Magisters and things were more fluid, but now we've only two, and that makes two big alliances. Ulani spend half their time killing what the Togova set loose on the world, and you really think the Togova no worse?"

"Eli Leventhal killed my friend Lacey," Ange snaps. Meisha gazes somewhere past her. Ange wonders vaguely what she's perceiving. Some kind of magical sight?

"How?" Meisha asks.

"We were at a pub together in Oxford." Ange stares at the window, at

7

pedestrians and traffic. "Lacey studied literature there. I'd travel up to see her on weekends, or she'd come down. We'd talk about books."

"She wasn't gifted?"

"A passive," says Ange. "Tenth Realm as far as anyone knew. I was homeschooled by a friend of local Ulani. I paid him, and he took regular students at the same time. One of them was Lacey. She sucked at math." A faint smile, remembering. "I'm pretty good at it. I was thirteen, she was fourteen. We studied together, I helped her maths, and she helped my English. We got along.

"Two weeks ago, I received this note from a visiting German professor. Magician, of course. The foreign magicians aren't so scared of me in London, they know I'm on the outs with the Ulani in Milan, I get invited out quite a bit. A chance to study the enemy, I suppose."

"Not all magicians think the Ulani are the enemy," says Meisha. "I don't."

"You should," says Ange. "We think you are." Meisha says nothing. "But Lacey loves this stuff, so I invite her to come along. And no sooner have we sat down with our host, than Leventhal's thugs burst in and trash the place. They were after our host, the German professor, I think. He escaped. But they hit Lacey instead."

Meisha's breath catches, as though somehow, she's just seen something incredibly sad. She reaches tentatively, and puts a hand on Ange's arm. Ange wonders how she does it so accurately. "I'm so sorry Ange."

"The pub burned down," Ange says bleakly. "It was all electricity and shockwaves, they were there to kill. They knew a civilian was there, they're magicians, they had to know. They didn't care. She was just collateral to them." She sips coffee. "And now they're just collateral to me."

"How do you know they were Leventhal's?"

"They announced themselves," says Ange, with a dark blaze of temper. "On the way in. The German professor ran away, they chased, and I was left holding Lacey. Watching her die. Leventhal's orders, his responsibility. Grand Magisters don't care about the little people who get in their way. I'll make him care, just once before I kill him."

"Ange, Eli heads a very large alliance. He can't be held responsible for every action by every person in it."

Ange frowns. Eli? Who on earth calls Grand Magisters by their first names? And suddenly it dawns on her — Meisha's strange but undeniable powers, her evident status, her confidence. Her odd ability to just *happen* to contrive this meeting, in a city of so many millions, with perhaps the only Ulani in town.

"You *work* for him, don't you!"

Meisha sighs. "Ange. Please, try to understand…"

"I could kill you right now," Ange says coldly. "You couldn't stop me."

"I know I couldn't," Meisha says sadly. "But I'm not scared of you Ange. I think you're a scared and angry girl who a lot of bad things have happened to. But I like you. You won't hurt me."

"Don't be so sure." It upsets her that she didn't see this earlier. Her instincts are usually better than this.

"Ange," Meisha tries again, "I'm sorry about your friend. I've lost friends too."

"Did you avenge them?"

Meisha gazes, a blank, dark glasses stare. "One or two, yes."

"Then you'll know what I have to do next."

Ange downs the last of her coffee, pushes to her feet, and strides out to the street.

CHAPTER TWO

Ange's first step in her grand strategy to kill Eli Leventhal is to find a good bookstore, get a coffee, and sit to read by a window. And Manhattan is the right place to do that.

Mostly, she knows she needs to be visible. Wizards hate threats, and bold, visible threats most of all. Soon enough, Leventhal will come after her, and then she'll learn some things. She's not vulnerable to magic, so there's not much he can do to her directly… though indirect magic is always a concern. Magic works by manipulating the environment, so while a spell cast directly at her might only blur her vision, the same spell knocking a wall down on her head will still kill her if the wall is big enough. Ulani powers mean speed and strength, warrior powers, and an immunity to direct magic. But aside from that, Ange is just a seventeen-year-old girl with an axe to grind.

Of course, she thinks as she sits before big windows above the sidewalk and flicks through the latest Stephen King, Leventhal could always hire someone to use a gun and make it simple. But wizards have reputations to worry about. In the old days, they'd seek power in kings' courts. Today, they still seek power, but in corporate boardrooms, or political office. Killing enemies with magic keeps that whole messy murder business on the magical side of the shroud, where there are no laws but the laws magicians make to govern themselves — a joke masquerading as justice, all of them. But use a gun, and the shroud-blind cops will notice, and then they'll have courts and media, because the shroud won't block people seeing a gun, and asking who fired it.

Plus it just looks bad among the magical class. The magician who has to use technology to solve his problems. Like a racecar driver caught driving a hatchback, or a supermodel wearing cheap pumps from the thrift shop. Magicians are fickle, and reputations can only take so much punishment.

A young man interrupts her reading — short hair, expensive suit. He sits opposite her, briefcase on the table beside her coffee. "You know," he says, "I'd have thought someone in your line of work would see so much horror they wouldn't need to read King."

Ange gets a very strong tingle from this man, the unpleasant kind. "Fuck off," she tells him.

He smiles. "Well that's no way for a bella signiorina to speak to new acquaintances…"

Ange hurls her coffee cup at his face. It passes straight through, a flash of smoke as he teleports, and reappears in a neighbouring chair. The coffee cup smashes against a bookcase, with a noise that makes many in the book shop look. That, and the man who instantly teleported from one chair to another in their midst. It's always interesting to see how the shroud rearranges such events in people's minds. Ange watches, as soon enough they resume previous readings and conversations, as though nothing has happened. Which, in their minds, it has.

"Here," says the teleporting man, writing on the back of a business card. He flicks it at her, with magic-assisted accuracy. Ange snaps it from the air before it takes her eye out. On one side, his details — Mathew Palmino, Assistant Chief of Staff. Mayor's office. As she suspected, one of Mayor Riley's flunkies.

Yuck. Togova Alliance, a most unpleasant tingle. Ange recalls what Meisha said about Togova, and wrinkles her nose in displeasure.

On the back of the card, he's written a mobile number, and an address. Not his.

"Leventhal wants this guy," says Palmino. "He's coming for him. You want Leventhal, you find this guy."

"Leventhal will come for me," Ange says sullenly, returning attention to her book. "I've challenged him."

Palmino grins. "Oh honey. You're so precious, you don't know how it works, do you? That's right, all the Grand Magisters in Europe killed each other last century so you've never met one before... look, Leventhal isn't coming for you. You could dance stark naked on the sidewalk outside his office and he wouldn't come for you. I might, but he won't." A grin, at his own great humour. "He doesn't care, babe. He's Eli Leventhal. You're nothing."

"If I'm nothing," says Ange, "why are you here?"

"Making mischief," says Palmino. Which Ange thinks is probably the truth. "Again, if you really want Leventhal, you find this guy." Pointing to the card. "And hey, if you get bored with revenge and want a good time in New York, call me instead." He grins, gets up from his chair, and walks to the table for his briefcase. Ange pushes it off, and it falls on the floor. Palmino sighs, bends to pick it up, and leaves with a wink.

Ange waits all morning, then gets lunch at a sushi bar. Leventhal does not show, nor any more flunkies, from Togova or Shtaal. Frustrated, and in need of exercise, she goes back to her hotel room, passing first by one of Mid-Town's many soaring office towers. Atop the tower, in neon letters, 'Leventhal Holdings'. Somewhere up there is the man himself. He'll come and go by chauffeur driven car, from the big carpark below, but Ange does not want to ambush him here — he'll be heavily guarded by all sorts, and she'll have to kill lots of them. Meisha has shown her that not all who work for him are bad people, just naive and misguided. She's here to kill Leventhal, and that's all.

Normally she'd go jogging outside, but today she runs on a hotel treadmill, with a view of Mid-Town towers and Marilyn Manson on her headphones, her sword hanging over the treadmill hand grips. Then a shower, a walk, and dinner, all in Mid-Town vicinity, but nothing. In the late evening, she trudges through gleaming lights and busy sidewalks to Central Park, and eventually finds an open grassy field, skirted by trees. There's no one here, and anyway, her friend is shroud-shielded by his very nature. Invisible to all but those meant to see.

She sits on the grass to watch the wall of neon towers rising above the dark trees, and hears a rush of wings. The soft bound of big feet, and the rustle of folding leather. Gia's big head slides in beside her, muzzle resting on her lap as he curls in behind, his long tail appearing on her other side. His muzzle is heavy, and she scratches where he likes it.

"Oh Gia, I don't know," she sighs. "Should I trust a Togova?" The dragon snorts, a blast of hot breath on her legs. "I know, sounds stupid when I say it. Meisha's right about what they're like. She's just blind about her own side."

Gia knows what she's talking about. Dragons just do, with some people, no one knows how. A kind of telepathy, maybe, Gia just knows what Ange is doing and hearing. Provided he gives a crap — if she'd been off shopping, likely he'd give her a total blank.

She pulls out the card that Palmino gave her, and rechecks the address on her smart phone. Gia observes the bright screen with distaste, one reptilian eye narrowing. "I know," she apologises. "Sorry."

The address again, on the New York map. It's in Queens. She considers the mobile number.

"You don't mind hanging around here?" she asks Gia. "Are you playing nice with the American dragons?" He snorts, and lifts his head to watch some people walk around the perimeter of the park, talking. Unaware that the girl sitting in the middle of the grass is accompanied by a thirty foot dragon, who is looking at them.

Ange worries that Gia might get bored, but he shows no sign of it now. Usually he'll let her know. Having him volunteer to come certainly saved her a plane ticket, and kept her from being alone in a strange city. Gia isn't bothered that she's here to kill someone. Most dragons are indifferent to people, making her and Gia's friendship a rare one. But as friendly as they can sometimes be, to some humans at least, they're not by nature a peaceful species.

She spots blood on a protruding fang, half the size of her forearm. "What have you been eating? Cows?" He puts his muzzle back on her lap, looking content. That means well fed, and cows are his favorite. "Well just remember to spread your kills out a bit, or else some farmer with the gift will wait for you one night with a rifle. You're in America now, everyone has guns." Gia makes a deep rumble in his throat, that she can feel like drums beating through her legs. "And no, you're not allowed to eat farmers. Not after that last one. I know he was Togova, but you promised."

It's cold at 7:30am, and Ange sits at a bus stop in Queens with no interest in the bus. Several houses up is the address Mathew Palmino gave her. It's a narrow, wooden, two-storey house in a street full of narrow, wooden, two-storey houses. Little porches, short driveways, American flags. Now it's bustling with early morning traffic, cars revving clouds of steam as they emerge from their garages, or people walking to the nearest subway station.

The door of the target house opens, and a teenage boy exits. He's shouldering a school bag, wears a tracksuit and runners, and carries a basketball. He shouts goodbye to someone inside, and takes off running up the sidewalk. Ange follows. Her boots aren't really made for it, but she's worn them in nicely, and they'll do. He stops at a corner store, and Ange waits by a tree across the street, as traffic roars on the larger road. Then he emerges with a soft drink and energy bar, and resumes running.

It's only another five minutes to the school. Ange leans against a tree and watches as the boy puts his bag and drink beneath a basketball hoop, and begins to dribble and shoot behind the tall wire fence. It's not even eight o'clock, and obviously he's risen early just for this, with his woollen cap pulled low, breath frosting in the mid-Autumn light. He's quite good too, Ange thinks, watching him drop shot after shot, with an easy, practised action.

After a few minutes she crosses the road, and goes through the gate in the fence. "Hello!" she calls cheerfully, and the boy looks. There are advantages to not being shy. 'Unshy', Lacey once called her, since 'extrovert' doesn't fit a girl who doesn't like many people. "Care for a game?"

The boy looks surprised, and takes a few seconds to look her over as she approaches. He shoots, knocks it down, then grabs the ball and tosses it to her. Ange catches easily. "Sure," he says with a smile. "You play? You look like you play."

"Yeah I play." Ange tosses the ball from hand to hand, and turns up her Italian accent several notches. "I'm from Italy, I'm visiting friends. But I haven't played a game in weeks, I get... how do you say? Withdrawal?"

The boy laughs easily. It's a nice laugh. He's damn cute, actually — about the same height as her, slim, but strong looking. His face is lean, features dark, and his teeth kind of perfect. Ange shoots, and misses on purpose, as the boy jumps to grab the rebound. "Ooo! Not bad, you've got a good shot."

"Bit rusty," says Ange, making a face.

"You gonna play in those?" He points to her boots. "You'll slip."

"Let's see how I go." The boy makes a post move, and puts in a baby skyhook. Bounces and tosses it to Ange.

"What's your name? That's a real nice accent."

"Angelina," says Ange, dribbling from one hand to the other. The sword is still at her hip — getting it off in the presence of someone who can't see it always takes some finesse. She gets no tingle from this guy. So what does Leventhal want with him? "What's yours?"

"Jamie." And he points at her, with cheerful warning. "But never James."

"What's wrong with James? James is fine." She shoots, and this time knocks it in.

"Sweet!" He catches and throws it back to her. "Like I said, that's a nice action."

She'd been planning to miss the next shot, she's not here to draw suspicious attention to herself. But being praised by a handsome boy feels nice, so somehow the next shot goes in as well.

"You don't play professionally in Italy or something, do you?"

Ange grins. "No, just on the street, and at school. I play with the boys though, so I'm not bad."

They chat and shoot for a while. He's lived in Queens since he was twelve, before that he was in Boston. His parents are divorced, and he hasn't seen his dad since they moved to New York. His mum works as a nurse in a local hospital. She doesn't make a lot of money. After school, when he's not shooting hoops, Jamie works at a car garage, and knew how to strip an engine at age ten. And he's known how to steal one from about the same age, he adds with mischief. Not that he ever has, of course.

"No brothers or sisters?" Ange asks. She started this conversation looking for a connection to Leventhal, but now she's just enjoying it. Two new people she likes, in two days! It's a record. She hopes Jamie doesn't turn out to be a disappointment like Meisha.

Jamie doesn't reply, and bounces the ball hard several times. "So what about you?" he changes the subject. "Milan, tell me what Milan's like."

"You ever been to Italy?"

He shakes his head. "Never been overseas. Pretty pathetic, huh?"

Ange makes a face. "America's a long trip, and travel's expensive. I've known Italians who haven't been outside of Italy. *That's* pathetic, with all of Europe just next door."

"Wow, really?" He shoots, and drops it in. "If I lived in Italy I'd buy some cheap bomb of a bike and go riding around. Everything's so close."

"You like motorbikes?"

"Hell yeah, first thing I learned to fix. Mum won't let me buy one though. Guess that'll have to wait until I move out." He tosses her the ball as she steps back to the three point line. "So Milan! You keep distracting me, what are you doing in Milan? Still at school?"

"Actually I'm studying in Oxford," Ange lies. She doesn't like lying, but it's an occupational hazard, and a habit with anyone on the other side of the shroud. And it's a double lie too, because not only is she not studying at Oxford, at seventeen she's not old enough for university anyhow. "That's in England." She shoots, and misses.

Jamie grabs the rebound. "Yeah I know." He fakes, then goes up for the layup. He's looked distracted since she asked him if he had a brother or sister. No longer smiling so much. Ange decides to take a risk.

"I came here because my friend died," she says. "Her name was Lacey. She was my best friend, so I..." she takes a deep breath, to compose herself. That part isn't acting. Jamie watches, concerned. "I have friends out here, and I needed a break. I had to get away, you know?"

Jamie nods. "Yeah," he says slowly. "Yeah, I know. How did she die?"

"It was an accident. A stupid thing. I don't have many friends, so..." She swallows hard. Her hand goes to her necklace. She wears two, a cross and a peace sign. The peace sign is Lacey's, a little joke between them, a gift from a gentle, happy girl to one who carries a sword and trains to kill.

"Yeah." Jamie exhales. Kids are arriving now, rowdy boys and girls with school bags. Talking on phones, laughing in small groups. "I lost my sister in a car crash. Two years ago. We were twins." He looks at Ange, and his dark eyes are clouded. "Her name was Tori."

And suddenly Ange senses it — a massive tingle, like a jolt of electricity, running pins and needles up her back. She's good at hiding it now, and glances about, surreptitiously. One of the other kids? But they're too far away. "So you've no one else?" she asks

"My mum," says Jamie. "That's it."

"I'm sorry."

"Hey," he says, with forced cheerfulness. He spreads his arms wide, ball in one hand. "What'cha gonna do?" And jumps for a fadeaway. Misses.

Ange collects the bouncing ball. The tingle had to come from Jamie, she decides. Which is just the strangest thing, because before, she could have sworn he had no magical ability at all. And still he shows no sign that he's noticed her sword. Is he just pretending? "Hey, I'm going to be here a few weeks, I think. You want to grab a drink after school?"

"You know you have to be twenty-one to drink here?"

"A coffee," she amends. Whether he leads her to Leventhal or not, this is a puzzle worth exploring. "Here, give me your number, just in case, but if I don't call I'll be here... when do you finish? Three?"

"Uh, yeah." He inputs into her phone. He's not all that fast, Ange notes. Super-social teens with lots of friends are lightning fast with phones. Jamie's not. "Three." He finishes, and hands it back to her, looking slightly amazed. Is that because he thinks he's struck gold, Ange wonders? Most boys in her experience haven't been that thrilled to get a date with a black-wearing, basketball-playing giant. "Say, how old are you, anyway?"

"Eighteen," she lies. "You?"

"Seventeen. Finish school next year!" He gives a little air-punch in triumph. Ange laughs. "You know, it's so nice to talk to a girl my own height. I can actually look at you, you know?"

"You're the first boy in years who's liked my height."

"Oh don't give me that," Jamie teases. "Look at your legs, every boy likes long legs."

"Rubbish," says Ange, smiling. "Boys say I look like a spider, I gave them arachnophobia."

"How tall are you?"

"Tall." She snatches the ball from him, and jumps for the same fall-away that he missed before. And hits it, and keeps walking, because it's such a cool exit. "See you at three, Jamie!"

"Oh come on," he calls after her, "*how* tall?"

"Taller than a flamingo in heels!"

"Sure, but not as tall as a giraffe on stilts?" Ange grins, walking away. "Wear some better shoes next time! We'll play a proper game!"

"You might regret that!" As she reaches the gate, and trots onto the sidewalk.

"I don't think I will," he replies.

The moment the bell sounds, Jamie is out the class door and down the hall, headed for the courts. Once there, amidst the crowds of departing kids, he looks at his phone for the time. It's four past three. The tall girl with that crazy Italian hair is nowhere to be seen. He takes his ball, and begins shooting. And double and triple checks that the phone's ringer is up loud.

Some passing kids look at him, and make remarks. Jamie ignores them, or tries to. He has a few friends here, but not many. He wishes he could go back to Boston, where he had more friends, but his mother's work won't allow it. And since Tori died... well, Tori was the popular one. After she died, a few of her friends had been nice to him for a bit. But that faded when he hadn't given them anything back. For most of the last two years, he's been wanting to be alone. Except for today, when a girl who understands what it's like to be strange made him hope that maybe he doesn't *have* to be lonely all the time.

"Hey Old MacDonald," says a voice, and Jamie misses his next shot. The ball bounces to the new arrivals — it's Danny Green, with his two sidekicks, who go by Bubbles and Shorty. All kind of tall and strong, all with baggy pants and torn jeans. Danny scoops up the ball, tossing it from hand to hand. "You keep practising like that, you're gonna make the NBA man. Seriously."

Bubbles and Shorty laugh, unpleasantly. Jamie's heart rate accelerates. Getting bullied isn't the thing that hurts — it's how much you hate yourself afterwards for not fighting back. He's not looking forward to it. "Come on man," he says, trying to keep it cool. Forcing a smile. "Give me the ball back."

"Come and get it, boy," says Danny. He begins dribbling, fast and aggressive. He's good, as tall as Jamie but much broader. He likes to boast how these days he's training Mixed Martial Arts as well. "Come on J-Mac! Come and get it!"

It's tempting. Jamie knows he shouldn't. He knows what will happen. But the ball's right there, bouncing on one of Danny's hands, then the other. Jamie lashes, and Danny switches real fast. He lashes again, and Danny dribbles between his legs, and shoulder charges… and with a thud, Jamie finds himself on his back.

Danny and his friends laugh. And Danny bounces the ball off Jamie's head, hard. "Oww!" More laughter.

The passing kids just watch. In the movies there's always someone who sticks up for the kid being bullied. Always some kind-hearted soul who steps forward and bravely says 'leave him alone!'. But in the real world, no one ever does.

"Hey!" It's a man's voice. Danny and his friends look, and Jamie cranes his neck to see. It takes him a moment to recognise the newcomer. It's Andrew Crosby, who prefers 'Croz', he's a part of the school mentor program — it's something set up by the Leventhal Institute, mentors for teens in the city area. He's striding fast, looking mean, a young black man in an expensive suit, a gold watch on one wrist.

"Hey man look, it's the mentor dude!" Bubbles laughs. "Nice threads man, does Donald Trump know you're stealing his wardrobe?"

Croz doesn't slow down. Danny puts out a hand to stop him, and Croz does something fast, then Danny's on the ground, his arm twisted awkwardly behind him, Croz threatening to twist the wrist even more.

"A real man doesn't need three," says Croz, with real menace. Bubbles and Shorty back away, eyes wide. "Now you little boys need to go home to your mommies, and wonder why you'll never be real men. The answer might save you."

He lets Danny go. Danny scrambles up, shaken, and tries to think of some witty comeback that might save the day. Croz steps suddenly toward him, and Danny flinches and ducks. And then, realising there is no comeback from that humiliation, gathers his buddies and leaves, fast.

Croz turns to Jamie, who has climbed awkwardly back to his feet. "Hey thanks man," says Jamie, trying to turn it into a joke. "I was just about to kick their asses myself, but you know, help's always welcome."

Croz holds up his hands. "No need to feel bad, if you're gonna fight back against three, you have to be trained. No one's ever trained you."

"Yeah, like holy crap man! Where did you learn to do that stuff?" Jamie doesn't know Croz that well, just that once a month he'll call in, talk to some boys after school, give some career advice, shoot some hoops. He's real strange for a top executive though — still barely past his mid-twenties, he's Eli Leventhal's personal assistant, and pulls down some enormous salary. And if that weren't enough, he's got the cross-over dribble from hell, and is built like an athlete. Somehow this fighting stuff doesn't surprise Jamie at all.

"I had a good teacher," says Croz, tugging his suit back into place. "I'll tell you someday, but now, I want to take you to meet someone."

"Meet someone?" Jamie looks around. "Man, I was waiting for this... this really nice girl? And she said she'd meet me here at three, and it's..."

Croz looks at his watch. "It's twenty past. I'd say she's late."

"Yeah, but Croz, she's really worth waiting for."

Croz gives a sly smile. "Really?" Jamie nods, sheepishly. "Why's that?"

"Well she's weird, you know? Like me." Croz wants more. Jamie grins. "Italian girl, black leather and boots, very tall. Good baller, we shot hoops and talked, just this morning."

"She hot?"

At six-foot-plus? "Yeah," says Jamie, with increasing confidence. "Yeah she is."

Croz clicks his fingers. "I know her. That's Angelina Donati."

Jamie blinks at him. "Angelina, yeah... who, I mean how? You know her?"

"Yeah, she's new in town, right? Let's say she caught my attention. Look, she's late, so it's her fault, right?"

"Well yeah, but..."

"Buddy I can get you her number, trust me." Croz puts an arm around Jamie's shoulders, grabbing up his school bag with the other hand, and steers him to the gate. "I'll even put in a good word for you, say I abducted you, I'll even take you guys out on a date in my car. Have you seen my car?"

Croz's car is a Ferrari SF90 Stradale. It's in the school parking lot, and has attracted a small crowd of students, and a few teachers. It might as well be a bright red alien spaceship amongst the other cars, a crazy-looking thing, a bullet on wheels, all engine, exhausts and sleek, sleek lines.

Jamie holds his incredulity until he's inside, with the crowd looking on enviously. Then Croz starts the engine with a roar like an avalanche, and Jamie starts laughing.

"Dude!" he says, as they leave the parking lot and onto the road. "This is the fastest roadcar ever made! How do you get one of these?"

"Study hard," says Croz, "and when someone offers you a lot of money, take it." He gives the engine a rev, and it feels like they're barely moving, despite sitting right on the speed limit. "Worth it for some girl, huh?"

"Well, the whole point of having a car like this is to *get* girls," Jamie reasons. "So I think you might be putting the cart before the horse, here."

"My friend," says Croz, "here's a bit of that manly advice the nice ladies at the school said I should keep to myself. Girls will come and go. But a great car is forever."

Croz drives them to Greenwich Village in southern Manhattan Island, and parks the car outside an old iron-facade building, not far from Broadway. Two guys in suits stand by the door, beside one of the fancy fashion showrooms that is all the Village seems to consist of these days.

"Are you taking me clothes shopping?" Jamie asks quizzically, eyeing the rows of designer suits before Croz takes them up a side stairway. "Because, like, I appreciate the thought... but that stuff's not really me. I mean, not that I don't like what you're wearing, what you're wearing is great, it's just that you can pull it off, because you're kinda... well, *you*."

Croz trots up several flights, past hallways that lead to apartment doors. There's no shopping here, and Jamie is feeling a little... not concerned, just anxious. This is pretty weird, Andrew Crosby is obviously a pretty serious guy, with his car and his threads and combat moves. And this is one of the most expensive parts of New York.

"Croz. Hey, Croz? Where are we going?"

"Just up here. It's a surprise."

On the fifth floor they exit beside a large door, with more men in suits standing outside. Like they're guarding it. Jamie sees earpieces, like they're Secret Service or something. Within a jacket as he passes, he glimpses a gun, in a shoulder holster. What the hell?

Beyond the door is a big, expensive apartment. There is an open kitchen at the far end, and a big living room, wide screen TV, and fancy windows overlooking the fashion district outside. Jamie stares, gazing around, wondering how many lifetimes he'd have to work in the garage to afford a year's rent in this place.

When he's finished turning, he finds that the man and woman waiting on stools by the kitchen bench have risen to greet him.

"Jamie!" says the man. "Welcome. Good to see you." He's an older guy, smallish with salt-grey hair, but with a strong, lean face and lively eyes. And he looks kind of familiar. Jamie frowns, trying to figure where he's seen him before, and looks at the girl. She wears big dark sunglasses and holds a wooden cane with a white ball on the tip... which means she's blind, he guesses. She seems to be Asian, but it's not immediately obvious behind those glasses.

Croz goes to the older man and whispers something in his ear — Jamie overhears the word 'girl', and 'waiting'. He's telling him about Angelina? To fix up his broken date, really?

"Do I know you?" asks Jamie. "Because the whole mentoring thing said I'd get introduced to some people, but..."

The old man smiles. "The mentoring thing, indeed. Do you know who runs it?"

Jamie frowns. "Well yeah. It's a Leventhal thing."

"Jamie," says Croz, with a smile. "This is Eli Leventhal. My boss."

Jamie stares at the old man. Then grins, about to protest that it's a joke… then stares again. Such a familiar face. Eli Leventhal? Eli Leventhal is just about the richest man in New York, he belongs in Mid-Town with the tall towers and Central Park… and suddenly he's recognising, from photos in the Wall Street Journal, from brief interviews in the business section at the end of the TV news and all that stuff Jamie's rarely paid attention to. *That's* why he looks familiar. This is Eli Leventhal himself.

"No way!" says Jamie, staring.

"Yes way," says Leventhal. "And this is one of my best young lawyers, Meisha Wing."

"Hello Jamie," says the blind girl. And Jamie hears something in her voice, that sounds like… emotion? Like something between grief and pleasure, held back with difficulty. Croz gives her a quick look, then strides to a big kitchen cabinet.

"Would you like a drink Jamie?" Croz asks. Inside the cabinet is every form of alcohol ever invented, stacked to the ceiling. "I'm sure we've got some ginger beer in here somewhere."

"That… that would be great, thanks." He stares at them all, brow furrowed. "Look, I'm sorry to be so blunt… but this is all very strange. Why am I here?"

"Dear Jamie," says Leventhal, almost sadly. "Always to the point. I'll tell you. Please, take a seat."

They head for the chairs, and Jamie settles into one. "What is this place, do you live here? Are those really bodyguards outside?"

"Well, guards," Leventhal concedes. "Bodyguards… if you like. I own this place, yes, though I don't often live here. Do you like it?"

"Sure." Jamie stares around. "So, I guess you'd own this whole building, then?"

"This whole street."

"Oh. Right." He accepts the drink Croz brings him. "Thanks. You wouldn't want to spike me some of the real stuff, huh? I feel like I might need it." Croz just smiles, and settles into his own chair. Jamie sips, nervously.

"Jamie," says Leventhal, "I don't wish to do this to you, but I must. Circumstances have changed, and our present arrangement cannot continue. There is too much at stake." Jamie just stares at him, not knowing what the hell to say. "You used to work for me. You don't remember it, because the shroud prevents you from remembering. You used to be on my side of the shroud. Our side. The magical side. But then disaster, and in your grief, I agreed in a fit of soft headedness to let you drift across the boundary, and forget."

Jamie's bewilderment is interrupted by a flash of deja-vu so powerful it stuns him. He stares about him, at the faces before him. New faces... but not new. He *knows* these people! He knows them so well... but how can he, if he's only just met them?

Leventhal leans forward in his chair, hands clasped on his tall, oddly shaped walking cane. "This is difficult for you Jamie, but you must listen. You are a magician. One of the most powerful young magicians I've ever seen. I do my philanthropic work with schools partly because it is my responsibility as a wealthy man, and partly because of my passion for education. But also, I do it to find and track promising young magicians like you, before others can get to them."

"Now just... just wait a..." but Jamie's interruption breaks off in another fit of deja-vu. This one *hurts,* a giant, throbbing headache in his temple, and he gasps.

"But of course," Leventhal continues, "with you, I did not merely find one magician, I found two. And Tori, I found first. Twins, sharing powers, are a rare thing indeed, so I arranged for your mother to get a job here in New York, and you moved down with her. For a while, you and Tori were my brightest pupils. But Mayor Riley found you, and perhaps sensed the danger that you posed to him. And Tori, that dearest girl and friend to all here, was killed."

Meisha wipes at her eyes beneath her glasses. Jamie stares at her, and sees flashes of memory — Tori sitting at a desk covered with books, opposite Meisha, who is studying. He and Tori ice skating in Central Park, with Croz. Croz isn't very good, and keeps falling, to Tori's amusement as she skates circles about him. Tori sitting opposite Leventhal, barely fourteen with her hair in braids, taking turns to knock a soft drink can back and forth across the room with mere gestures from their fingers.

"Tori was killed in a car crash!" Jamie rasps. His head is throbbing like it's about to explode. "She was... it was upstate, and..."

"The shroud makes you see things that are not true," Leventhal continues. "Normally a natural magician such as yourself will see past it, but when I sent you across the boundary, your magical skills vanished with your invulnerability to the shroud. And it has consumed you, as is its design, and written all trace of magic from your mind. But now, I bring those memories back, and your powers will come with it, in time."

More images flash, seared onto Jamie's mind as though with a hot brand. He hisses and yells at the pain of it, hands to his head.

"Eli!" cries Meisha. "Eli don't do this to him! He's just a boy!"

"He is an asset," says Leventhal, sombrely. "And such a valuable asset, I cannot let go to waste."

"Yeah," says a female voice outside the doors. "You're a real charmer."

The doors smash open, and the body of one of the guards outside thumps limply to the floor.

Croz swears, and rushes the doors bare handed. "Croz, no!" shouts Meisha, and Croz reappears as fast as he vanishes, skidding across the floor to lie limp. A girl steps after him, long legs in high boots and a black coat. The sword at her hip is still sheathed, and she cracks the knuckles on one hand, pausing to look down at Croz.

"Che bella macchina," she tells him, with Italian approval. *Nice car.*

"Eli, she's got a bike," says Meisha, now on her feet, as is Leventhal.

"I know. Croz was followed."

"I sensed nothing!" Meisha protests. "You mean even *you* felt nothing?"

Jamie staggers to his feet, trying to keep his balance as his head throbs. "Angelina?"

Ange draws the sword in a smooth move, and points it dangerously at Leventhal. "What are you doing to him?" she demands, furiously. "You remove whatever spell you have on him right now!"

"I am," says Leventhal. "Removing it causes pain. There is no other way."

"Jamie," says the girl, dark eyes burning, "you come over here with me. You keep away from this monster. I'm going to slay him."

"Ange no!" shouts Meisha. "You've got it all wrong! Eli's the good guy!"

"He murdered my friend!" Ange yells, her sword blade trembling. "He didn't have the courage to do it with his own hand, but he ordered it done!"

"Young girl, we are at war!" Leventhal says sternly. "Innocents have died in war since its invention!"

"Then it's about time the guilty died too!" Ange snarls, and leaps forward. Blue light leaps from Meisha's cane, and Ange simply blocks it, one hand raised as bolts of lightning flash away, then bounce straight back at Meisha. Leventhal blocks with a wave of his staff, and Meisha stumbles and falls, as electricity explodes about the room, lighting wallpaper and wood panelling, showering sparks from a chandelier.

Ange comes past the chairs, and suddenly Jamie feels the room tip, as though the far wall is 'down', and he's flailing for balance. He hits the ground and stays there, as Ange crouches, a hand to the ground to steady herself. She grits her teeth and lunges forward once more, but an impossible wind whips her coat and hair, driving her back.

"Your magic does not work on me!" she yells. "No magic does!" She closes, step after fighting step, as magazines, cushions, and anything not tied down blasts about the room in a swirling mini-tornado.

"I am leader of the Shtaal Alliance," says Leventhal, eyes narrowed and staff presented. "I am founder of the High Council, wielder of the laws, and the last of the true Grand Magisters of old. There is no power in this world that my magic cannot bend."

Jamie's ears pop, a painful pressure, and suddenly it's hard to breathe. Then a powerful thunderclap, and he covers his head as furniture goes flying. Gasping, he can breathe again, and looks up to find windows shattered, and car alarms howling in the street outside. Nearby lies Ange, eyes closed and unmoving. Jamie scrambles to her, and listens to her breathing.

"She's alive!" he announces.

"Not for long," says Croz, dragging himself painfully to his feet, and pulling a gun from his jacket.

"No!" shouts Leventhal, rising with Meisha, pressing her cane into her hand.

"You're not going to do this to me again!" Croz retorts, standing over Ange and Jamie, the pistol levelled at her head. "Some things you can't negotiate with! Some things you just gotta kill!"

"The girl lives," says Leventhal, walking through the ruined room.

27

"Mr Crosby!" He levels his staff at Croz's chest. Not a threat, but a firm warning nonetheless, tapping him twice with a challenge to meet his eyes.

Croz does so. And finds that Leventhal's stare is impossible to match. "This one," Croz mutters, "I just know I'm going to regret." He pockets his pistol, and kicks Ange's sword away.

"Eli?" Meisha says shakily. "What is she? Why couldn't you feel her coming? And why did she just presume she can take on a Grand Magister and win? Even Starace wouldn't try it."

Leventhal gazes at the fallen girl for a long moment. "When she wakes up," he says finally, "we'll ask her."

CHAPTER THREE

Ange awakes, and realises that she's alive. It surprises her. Given that she evidently lost in her battle against Eli Leventhal, and those who try to kill Grand Magisters and fail, rarely live. Except to demonstrate some gruesome punishment.

She looks around. She's in a very nice bedroom, with wide windows that overlook Central Park from about thirty floors up. Good Lord. With that view, the bedroom alone must be worth a million. The rest of the apartment, God knows. There is nice furniture, and some paintings. The sheets are silky soft. She stretches, and feels sore, some nasty bruises restricting her muscles. But far more healthy than she's any right to be. To her right, away from the windows, a painting easel, and a stool. Has someone been painting her?

Eli Leventhal emerges from the adjoining corridor. Ange stares. He's wearing an old T-shirt, baggy pants and slippers, while sipping some coffee. In his other hand, a plate with a hot bagel, buttered. He shuffles to a chair beyond the foot of the bed by the windows, and sits, appearing more interested in the view than her. He looks like any other old man eating breakfast in the morning. Grand Magisters are supposed to have more ego than this.

"How are you feeling?" he breaks the silence. "A bit sore, yes?" She's supposed to kill him. She remembers Lacey's blackened face, lying dead in the Oxford pub. Only now she recalls that Lacey never wanted to kill anyone. Rarely even got angry, in fact. Her hand finds the peace symbol, still about her neck. The white witch and the dark witch, Lacey sometimes called the pair they made, jokingly. Even though female magicians are rarely called witches. The women who use magic find it annoying.

Ange examines new bruises on her arm.

"Well," says Leventhal, "you're better than you'd be if I'd let Mr Crosby put a bullet in your head."

Ange's fingers find the slim metal collar at her throat, under the two chains. She feels around to the back, but it has no clasp. There's no sign that it will come apart. Her heart accelerates. "What the hell is this?"

"That, dear girl, is a collar." He rests his plate on the side table, and pulls a copy of the New York Times onto his lap. "The function of which you're about to discover."

"Get it off me!" Now the fury is back. How dare he collar her like some tame animal? She throws the sheets aside to leap at him, and is abruptly immobilised, all her muscles convulsing uncontrollably. It's definitely coming from the collar, and she flails at it, frantically. It's not exactly painful, but it's a horrid sensation, having no control of her body. And then she can move, and breathe again unhindered. She gasps.

"It only does that when you try to hurt me, or someone else in my organisation," says Leventhal, not looking up from his paper. "Otherwise you'll barely notice it's there. And it does make a charming fashion accessory."

"You son of a…!" and suddenly she's convulsing again.

"This can go on all day," Leventhal says mildly, turning a page. "Until you decide to grow up a little, and control your emotions. You tried to kill a Grand Magister. I'm sure your knowledge of House Law is not so vague that you're not aware of what I *could* do to you, should I choose. But the laws do require a punishment of some sort, especially as the entire magical world knows you came here to kill me, thanks to you telling everyone you met on the street. And so I must show them that you failed… and yet, I am merciful."

Ange gasps, released from the collar once more, staring at the ceiling. "Yeah," she rasps. "You're a real nice guy."

Leventhal makes a considering face. "Sometimes. But it's not about what I want. It's about what people expect. I must show them I'm in charge, or they will doubt."

"Gia!" Ange yells at the ceiling. "Gia, get in here and rip his head off!" Leventhal frowns, putting the paper down. And looks at the ceiling, then out the window. "Gia!"

There is nothing. No rush of wings, no breaking of glass as he crashes through the window. She can't sense him the way he can sense her, but there's always a tingle. A delicious tingle, like a cool wind on a hot day. Or like the time that nice boy kissed her at the Seven Dials, after they'd gone to see The Lion King with Lacey and her then-boyfriend. A thrill up her spine. But now, nothing.

Suddenly she's in tears. Gia's abandoned her. Lacey's dead. She's left the only home she's ever had and come across the North Atlantic to a foreign place to kill a man it turns out she just can't kill. And probably never could. She's an idiot, she realises, staring at the ceiling as tears fill her eyes, and roll down her temples to the pillow. A stupid, teenage idiot. Like Starace said she was, after she left. And maybe she even got Lacey killed, going to meet with that stupid Uri Menkel, who she *knew* was Togova and not a nice guy, but it's sometimes irresistable fun to play with the darkness, like some kids drink too much, or party too hard, or drive too fast with their newly won licences. And then they get dead, like Lacey.

"Angelina," says Leventhal, and his voice is almost kindly. Though not entirely, because she did try to kill him again just now. "I know you find this hard to believe, but you're safe here. Or as safe as I am. I am not the bloodthirsty monster that you no doubt believe all Grand Magisters are. All magicians, probably, given how Starace teaches his apprentices. You loved your friend, and that speaks well of you. If I had my choice, neither I nor anyone associated with me would ever kill anyone. But that is not the world we live in, Angelina. Which you know better than most."

"How does your magic work on me?" she asks. "Ulani are immune."

"Not from indirect magic," says Leventhal, returning attention to his paper. "That boast has cost many Ulani their lives, gravity…"

"…is not a magical force," Ange finishes. She heard that truism so often in Milan she was bored with it by age ten. She points to the collar around her neck. "This is not indirect. It shouldn't affect me, but it does. Like your shockwave or whatever it was last night. Why did it work?"

"We all have our secrets, Angelina. This is mine." He turns a page. "Good lord, would you look at those Mets."

"That's not good enough," Ange says stubbornly. "You've just disproved everything I was taught as an Ulani. We were created to fight magic, to use magical power against magicians. We are the antithesis. And now you've shown it's all nonsense."

"Not *all* nonsense," says Leventhal. "It's true nearly all of the time. But what works against all other magicians, will not necessarily work against me. There is a reason I am Grand Magister, Angelina. You might have thought on that before you came all this way to kill me."

"I did," Ange says sullenly. "I thought it was just that you hadn't met *me* yet."

Leventhal actually smiles, quite broadly. "Good answer," he says. "Arrogant, stupid and wrong, but good." Ange realises that since her collar convulsions, she's now lying with nothing to cover her, and is wearing only a silk pink nightie. At her height, that leaves a lot of bare leg, but Leventhal's not looking. She pulls the sheets up once more.

"You're not as powerful as you think," she says. "You haven't killed Mayor Riley yet."

"And that proves I'm not powerful? On the contrary, the fact that he hasn't killed *me* yet proves that I am just as powerful as I think. Mayor Riley is phenomenally powerful. He is the main reason why the world has gone from seven Grand Magisters just a hundred years ago, to two today. But he hasn't killed me, and not for want of trying. No others can say the same."

"You're all the same," Ange mutters. "All you bigshot wizards."

"Really?" Leventhal says tiredly. "You're going to throw that teenager's wisdom at me? I've been alive a very long time, Angelina. I was alive a long time before this city, this entire nation, ever existed. I can tell you with certainty, we are *not* all the same, magicians like anyone else. My current Alliance, the one you call Shtaal, may not be perfect, and God knows I'm not perfect either. But if you can't see the difference between me and that murdering villain in the Mayor's residence, then there is truly no hope for you."

"You only care about power, just like him. You kill innocent people to get power, just like him."

"And do you think dear Pope Serguis the Third had humanity's best interests in mind when he ordered the creation of the Ulani in the year nine hundred and seven?" Leventhal asks, eyebrows raised. "Dear Serguis, a truly villainous man, had both his predecessors killed. No, he was alarmed at all these magicians running around threatening his power, so he bought a few of them with gold and founded an army of papal assassins to protect the church from unGodly magic. Assassins like you."

"And then we rebelled!" Ange retorts. It's the simplest history lesson to an Ulani, the one they're taught first as children. "We wouldn't serve the popes, and we've never served anyone since!"

"Yes, after two centuries of doing exactly that, until my old friend Pope Callixtus the Second told you to go on the Second Crusade to Jerusalem, and your dear rulers decided they'd rather stay in Europe and kill wizards than go to Jerusalem and kill Muslims." He barely looks up from his paper. "Of course, for European Ulani, wizards were somewhat easier to kill than Muslims, and far more profitable. Ulani have been running a great European protection racket against wizards for centuries. And once the wizards began paying you money in exchange for their lives, life became far too comfortable for you to uproot and head for Middle Eastern deserts in search of God." With dry irony. "As though God has ever been of interest to Ulani. Or to Popes."

Ange scowls at him. Her history isn't so good that she can get into an argument with a man who was probably *there*, when it happened. She's only seventeen, and her schooling has been erratic, at best.

"The point, Angelina, is that all the world runs on power, whether you like it or not. Always has, always will. Now you can detest all who wield power, and hold them responsible for every terrible thing that power does, but you'll ultimately end up hating everyone and everything, because all humans lust power in one form or other. Like Mayor Riley, living in his Mayor's Residence down the road. He didn't go there for the view, trust me." He gazes out the window, at the spectacular view of his very own.

"I'm not interested in your battles," says Ange. "I'm going back to London."

Leventhal's eyebrows arch in surprise. "Dear girl, you don't seem to understand. The collar symbolises *servitium*. Service. A bondage of debt, that shall remain until paid off in full."

Ange stares at him, disbelieving. "You're joking."

"Do I look like I'm joking? You now work for me. Should you refuse, I can give the collar an operational range that can limit your movement to a single room or less. And your opinion on the matter is irrelevant."

The collar immobilises Ange in mid-lunge, and she falls from the bed to the floor with a thud.

"You know," says Leventhal, sipping coffee as she writhes on the floor, "they do these sorts of experiments on monkeys. The monkeys learn faster."

After breakfast, Meisha arrives. She enters the bedroom, holding a Starbucks, and finds Ange doing exercises in her underwear.

"I don't suppose you could go back to bed for a while?" Meisha suggests, taking a seat behind the easel and painting. "You had a lovely pose while you were sleeping."

"Well I'm not sleeping now am I?" Ange snaps, doing crunches on her back, arms and legs reaching.

"In fact," says Meisha, "when you were sleeping, for a moment there you were almost sweet."

Ange scowls, now sweating. The secret to muscle-control, she's discovered, is having muscles that are worth controlling. She'd never been much of a sporty girl until she grew a bit, but getting beaten up by other Ulani kids had become tiresome fast. Now she can't go a day without proper exercise or she'll get that nasty, cold-melty feeling in her muscles.

Meisha begins arranging her paints and brushes. Ange watches between exercises. "What are you painting?" she asks.

"You," says Meisha.

"No, I mean *what* are you painting. If you're not painting what you see?"

"Come." Meisha beckons to her. Ange gets up and goes, wondering how Meisha can be so at ease with her. They fought just last night, and while Ange couldn't kill Leventhal, she was not at all bothered by Meisha.

But Meisha seems unafraid. Then she recalls what Leventhal just told her — the collar will protect *any* member of his organisation, including Meisha.

Scowling harder, she stands by Meisha's shoulder and looks at the canvas. It's abstract, colours and shapes all combining at odd angles. But if she squints, she can see that some of the colours on the painting, and the colours in the room beyond, roughly match up. The brightness of the windows. The pink silk of the bed.

"You see this?" she asks Meisha.

"Well I'm not sure," Meisha says. "Given I can't actually see what I've painted." Ange nearly smiles. It *is* quite a conundrum. "But it feels right. I can make out shapes and textures. But I don't see them, I kind of... *feel* them. It's hard to explain." The pink of the bed has a shape on it. Ange makes out the curve of a female hip. Outstretched fingers. Glimpses, nothing whole.

"It's nice," she admits. "The colours are amazing."

"Colours are emotions," says Meisha. "Or states of mind. I can see them."

"There's lots of orange here," Ange observes.

"Orange is melancholy."

"Really?"

Meisha nods. "Or that's how I see it. Anger is red."

"Obviously."

"Longing is violet. Happiness is blue... though of course, there are all different shades. Pregnancy is gold."

"Pregnancy is an emotion?"

"Certainly," says Meisha, feeling her brush tips with her fingers. "A pregnant woman has a colour all of her own, it shades everything."

"I like black," says Ange, with dark amusement. "What's black?"

Meisha looks a little uncomfortable. "I'd rather not talk about black. All the people you hit last night are fine, by the way. In case you're wondering."

"Of course they are," Ange retorts. "I'm not an amateur and I wasn't trying to hurt them. I just needed them to stop moving for a little."

"Though I'd stay clear of Croz if I were you. He's not happy with you."

Ange puts her towel on the bed before sitting, and gives her a blank look. "Andrew Crosby. The guy with the Ferrari. He's Eli's personal assistant."

Ange frowns. "But he's not a magician, he's a receptor. Magicians always choose other magicians for assistants or apprentices."

"Not Eli." There are three types of magical people. Magicians, who can use magic and cast spells. Receptors, who receive the powers from one of the magical realms, and who gain powers but can't use spells. And passives, who are on the magical side of the shroud, but gain no powers at all. "One of Eli's schools found him in Chicago, in a very bad neighbourhood. His parents weren't magical, father was dead, mother a drug addict, she lost custody after her fourth overdose in two years. Eli put him in boarding school then business school here at Columbia, and he just aced everything. He's quite brilliant, he could have gotten a job at any Fortune 500 company he wanted, but Eli offered to make him his personal assistant and he took it."

"Not many big magicians would trust a receptor for an assistant," Ange remarks.

"True" Meisha agrees. "But Eli's very particular about who he trusts with power in his organisation. He trusts Croz. And Croz is pretty dangerous in a fight, and magic-resistant like you, so other magicians aren't always prepared to handle him."

"He wasn't so tough last night," says Ange with a smirk.

"Yes, because like most tough young men, he never expects to get beaten up by a girl. Overconfidence is a killer." She wets her brush, and dabs at the canvas. And purses her lips, considering. "You know most people would be thrilled to work for Eli. Everyone's going to be so jealous of you, people struggle all their careers just to get his attention. And now you're in the inner circle."

"I'm a prisoner," Ange retorts. "You can dress it up all you like, but this collar may as well have a chain leading straight to Leventhal's hand."

"You *did* try to kill him," Meisha reasons. Ange snorts, and runs a hand through her sweaty hair. "Look, Ange, you're young, you're beautiful, you're about to be somewhat wealthy, and for the time being at least, you're living in New York City and working for one of the most powerful and influential men alive. You could try looking on the bright side, you know. Most people don't have it so good."

"Let's start with beautiful," Ange growls. "I stopped growing at sixteen. You know what it's like to be six foot one at sixteen? Five-nine at thirteen?" Meisha sighs. "Of course you don't, you're a midget. They called me mostro gigante, giant freak. No boys would date me, I was bigger than every boy my age. I had my first kiss last year. From an *older* boy, who was six-four and not insecure like all these *little* boys."

"Is that when you started wearing black?" Meisha asks, with a hint of amusement. "And boots to make yourself even taller?"

"Yes," says Ange, uncomfortable that Meisha seems to understand. She's so used to self-righteous defiance, she's not used to people 'getting it'. "Because fuck them."

"I learned to juggle," says Meisha. "Using knives. Just to freak everyone out."

Ange nearly smiles. And forces it back. She's trying to be angry, and Meisha's not helping. "And now you're telling me to be grateful I've just been recruited into the front line of a war, where life expectancy is… what? Ten years? Five?"

That subdues Meisha. "Depends. Some grow old. Not many though."

"Right. Grand Magisters grow old. Everyone else does the dying for them."

"It's not Eli's fault he's so powerful."

"Nothing's ever the Grand Magisters' fault," Ange retorts. "People just accept it, and everyone goes on dying. Like that poor boy, Jamie. He wanted out. Who the hell is Leventhal to decide he has to come and die in his war?"

Meisha stirs her paintbrush absently on the palate. "You want to know about Jamie?" she says quietly. "Let me tell you about Jamie."

The guard at the door of the hospital ward gives Ange a considerable tingly-sense as she passes. The ward is expensive, a single with a great view from ten floors up, flat screen TV, big comfortable bed. All expenses paid by Eli Leventhal — the one big perk of being in sworn service to a magical house. Any house would do, but to a Grand Magister's house, even better. The downside to sworn service, of course, is that now other houses can invent reasons to kill you. Not that they don't kill the unsworn also, accidentally or otherwise. But that can get messy, with the High Council and all, and even Grand Magisters don't want to run afoul of that old magic.

Jamie sits upright in his hospital bed, and gazes out the window. He's hooked up to machines, watching his vitals — apparently being pulled one way or the other across the shroud boundary can cause all kinds of nasty side effects, so they've put him in here to watch, just in case his heart suddenly stops. Ange takes off her sword before she sits alongside, and hangs it on the chair. Jamie looks, and smiles wryly.

"Nice sword," he says.

"You can see it now."

Jamie nods. "Yeah." The smile fades, and he looks back out the window, out across upper east side, toward northern Central Park. "Nice collar too."

"No," Ange bites out. "It's not." But there's no amusement in Jamie's tone. No teasing. He just looks sad. Nothing like the happy boy shooting hoops at his school. "I didn't know it was possible to take a magician and drag him back across the shroud."

"Yeah. Usually it's not. But Eli's got powers. Crazy powers, like nothing else in the world." He takes a deep breath. "Well. Except for Mayor Riley."

"You made him do it? You made him put you on the other side?" She doesn't really know why it matters to her. These are magicians, and she's got no time for magicians. Usually they run a mile at the sight of her. But Jamie's different. He didn't ask to be one, and he's tried to leave them, to forget that life and start anew. Only to be dragged back across to this side of the shroud, and made to remember everything he'd been trying to forget.

"Who told you?" Jamie says darkly.

"Meisha."

"Meisha," Jamie murmurs, the temper fleeing from his voice. "Meisha's nice. She was Tori's friend first, Tori's best friend. Tori was like her little sister. Tori would hang with her when Meisha was studying law, hang out in the students dorms with the big kids. Made her feel special." He glances at Ange. "Eli recruited Meisha too you know. He gets the kids first, usually in their early teens." A dry smile. "With you, he's a little late. I guess he doesn't have much sway with the Ulani."

"He insists he's no monster," says Ange, leaning elbows on knees to look at him closely. "But he recruits children to his war, and they die."

Jamie nods. "Yeah. He does. But I mean, it's not his fault."

"Porca miseria," Ange mutters, exasperated. "Not you too."

"No it's true. If you're born with real powers, I mean the serious kind, someone will find you. Shtaal or Togova, you can't hide from them. Even the middle powers, the Asian and African schools and families, they all owe allegiance to Shtaal or Togova. They'll get you, and then either Eli or Riley will."

"You're defending him!" Ange accuses him angrily. "Why?"

Jamie gives her a very meaningful look under his brows. He doesn't look like a kid any longer. "Because better Eli than Riley. *Trust* me. I've seen it."

Ange takes a deep breath to calm herself. She hates that no one agrees with her on this point. Of course she knows what they're talking about, she's seen the Togova, and she's seen all the blood and nastiness. The evil, yes, she can't deny it. But too many people who hate the Togova, then fall blindly in love with the Shtaal. And that gets them killed, and others, just as fast. Some people love to follow. She'll never follow. The Ulani trained her to be an assassin, and predators shouldn't act like sheep.

"You know there didn't used to be a war," Jamie offers. "Eli's always been a peacemaker. He founded the High Council, he wrote half its laws. For centuries he's been trying to keep the peace, to make people work by rules."

"So did Riley, once," Ange retorts. "So what?"

"So Eli stayed the course. Riley didn't."

"That's the best you can say about him?"

Jamie shrugs. "Over two thousand years, it's not a bad thing to say. The guy's persistent."

"How did Tori die?" Ange asks. "Meisha wouldn't say."

Jamie says nothing. He just looks out the window, with the far away look of memories returning. Painful memories. His eyes fill with tears. Suddenly Ange regrets the question. She's being insensitive again, she's been accused of it before.

She reaches, and grasps his hand. "I'm sorry," she says softly. "I shouldn't have asked."

Jamie sighs, and wipes his eyes. He glances aside, at a half-eaten sandwich on the bedside table. "Dude," he says, "I'd kill for a pizza. The food here is crap."

He picks up the sandwich, and covers it between his hands. Ange feels a very sharp tingle, a twinge between her shoulder blades. She feels a little heat on her face, and smoke rises between Jamie's hands. He removes them, and the sandwich is toasted, the bread blackened and crispy. He bites it, and makes a half-and-half, not-so-bad face.

"So you really are a magician," Ange observes.

"It's coming back," Jamie admits around his mouthful. "I prefer 'wizard', though. Got more of a ring to it."

"Yes, well you can't, because then the women get called witches, and they hate that."

"Screw 'em," says Jamie. "Besides, what do *you* care what they think? I'm a wizard, deal with it." He means it lightly, and glances at Ange. She's not smiling. Just watching him, like a cat watches a mouse. "And you're a wizard-killer. Huh." He thinks about this conundrum for a moment. Then offers her a bite of his lunch. "Sandwich?"

"Not in a million years," Ange replies.

Jamie lowers the sandwich. "Oh." His face falls. "I just thought... well, you know, we're gonna be seeing a bit of each other now. Both working for Eli. So just because a thousand years of history says we ought to be mortal enemies, that doesn't mean..."

Ange points to his sandwich. "It's got pickles in it," she says. "I hate pickles. Not in a million years." Jamie looks at the sandwich, surprised. Then grins, crookedly. Reluctantly, Ange smiles back. "What's it like, being on the other side of the shroud?"

Jamie shrugs, still chewing. "I dunno. It doesn't feel like anything. I guess... it's a bit like a dream. I mean, you wake from a dream, and it's only then you realise that everything was weird, you know? While you're dreaming, even the weirdest stuff seems normal."

"I suppose I just can't imagine not knowing that magic is real," says Ange.

"What's your first memory of magic?" Jamie challenges her.

Ange smiles. "I was four. I was brought up in an orphanage, I never knew my parents. One day I was playing with the other kids, when something big and hairy jumped on the playground wall and ran along it. Then it jumped off. I think it was a werewolf, but none of the other kids saw it, just me. And I was screaming, 'look at that big hairy wolf!'"

Jamie laughs. "In Italian though."

"Naturalmente. And most of the sisters thought I was crazy. Except for one sister, who'd also seen it. She made a telephone call, and some Ulani came and got me. And realised I was Third Realm, which is rare, and perfect for them." She shrugs. "Two weeks later, they did the ceremony, I was Ulani. I've been one ever since."

"I was six," says Jamie. "We had a tree house in our yard, in Boston. And one day Tori told me she had a surprise for me, and I had to swear I wouldn't tell anyone. And we went out to the tree house, and she showed me she could make a light. Just above her hand, you know? A basic illumination spell, not bad for a six-year-old though. Then she made my Batman figure fly.

"I thought she was tricking me, you know? I mean, I wouldn't be the first kid to be fooled by his mean sister, right? But she wasn't, it was... it was real magic." He puts a hand to his head, as though dazed by the memory. "Magic used to be so much fun. Where did that go, huh?"

"Yeah," Ange says sadly. "When you're a kid, everything's a game. Sword fighting used to be a game. We used to have these huge fights with training sticks, we'd end up bruised and bloody but it was all stupid kids' fun. It never occurred to me what hitting someone with a real sword would actually be like until I did it."

"How old were you then?"

"First *thing?*" she says. "Twelve. It was a vampire, they don't count."

"You killed your first vampire at *twelve?*"

"Vermin," Ange says dismissively. "It's like killing flies. First *person?* Fifteen." Jamie is staring at her, quite disconcerted. "You've never killed someone?" He shakes his head. "Don't worry. The one I killed was torturing innocent people at the time. I don't just do it for fun."

"Oh yeah," says Jamie. "I know the ones you're talking about. If he was torturing innocent people, you're allowed to enjoy it a little bit."

Ange considers him for a long moment. Well fancy that, she thinks. A magician who's on her wavelength. She didn't think it was possible. "So when did Leventhal discover you?" she asks.

"He didn't," says Jamie. "He discovered Tori. For a few years I thought Tori was the only magical one. I mean, we figured out I had some ability because I could see her magic. Mum couldn't, Tori could make Batman fly straight past her nose, and she wouldn't blink. Only magic people can see magic, so I figured I had to be magical too — I didn't know what a passive was, I thought if you could see it, you had to be able to do it, right?

"And so I'd go out to the tree house every day and I'd try and try to make something happen. But nothing did. Until one day, I was daydreaming in class, and… Jacinta Reed." He grins at the memory. "She was this really snotty girl, Tori hated her. Rich parents, lots of friends, mean to all of them. I was daydreaming about flying — you know, I like airplanes. I was thinking of two fighter planes having this dogfight, and… the next thing, I look up and Jacinta Reed's desk is six feet off the ground.

"And I look at Tori, and Tori's staring at me like… 'it's not me!' And as soon as I realised it was me, the desk falls from the sky with a crash, and all the class is stunned because the shroud can't just make up some reason for a desk to levitate. And in thirty seconds more of course they've all forgotten it. But Tori and me got in trouble for giggling and laughing all lesson, 'cause suddenly Tori's like, 'my twin's a magician too!'… damn, she was so excited."

Jamie's story trails away, and he gazes out the window. There's so much love in his eyes when he speaks of his sister. And now, once more, it turns to pain.

"And then Eli," Jamie continues, "Eli found Tori mostly, I was the bonus magician, she was still so much stronger. And he arranged for Mum to get a job at a hospital here, and Tori and me went to school here, and we got tutored by Eli's folks and Leventhal Holdings became like a second home…"

Ange feels an odd tingling, a prickling on her nose and cheeks. She half rises from her chair, looking about the hospital room… and suddenly an oncoming rush of tingles hits her like a bucket of cold water. "Teleport incoming! Watch out!"

A flash of dark smoke and rippling flame past the end of Jamie's bed, and a man is there, a dark coat, black hair and staff. He aims the staff at Jamie. "Angelina no!" Jamie yells as she leaps onto the bed, ripping her sword from its sheath. The electrical blast hits her with a numbing jolt and pain, and the smell of singed leather, and bolts deflect and crack about the room. The caster ducks in astonishment, then raises his staff for protection as she jumps off the bed. Her sword goes through his staff, shoulder and chest, and he's dead before she pulls it out.

"Son of a bitch!" says Jamie, crouched in bed and staring. "How did you... are you okay? That was ten thousand volts, you should be dead!"

As crashes, yells and magical eruptions sound in the hallway outside. "Let's go!" shouts Ange, impatiently. "If they're teleporting they must be close, this was a setup!"

Jamie scrambles out of bed wearing hospital pyjamas, and goes to a clothes drawer, but the dead magician's body is blocking it. And he notices his bare feet are now sticky from the blood all over the floor. "Oh you're *kidding* me!"

"Jamie!"

"I'm not going out there in pyjamas!" He crouches to pull open the clothes drawer. Ange grabs his arm.

"I will put you over my shoulder," she warns him.

"I'd like you see you try... hey!" As Ange yanks him toward her, drives her shoulder into his midriff, and carries him like a sack of potatoes. "Ange! Put me...ow!" As she goes shoulder first through the ward doors and into the hallway... and is immediately knocked off her feet by a flying chair.

"Merda!" She hits the floor against a wall, finding herself in a crossfire between the Leventhal guard behind her, and an attacker ahead, who are between them filling the hall with electrical bolts, flying projectiles and bursts of flame. Annoyed, she gets up and walks purposely toward the attacker — another man, in torn jeans and a flannel shirt, this time with a wand. He hits her with more electricity, but this time she has her sword ready, and the bolts deflect, spraying about the walls. Alarmed, he sends a small bolt of fire her way, which erupts into a large ball of fire just short of her, but Ange simply closes her eyes and it dissipates with nothing more than a rush of heat. Alarmed some more, the magician backs up, and with a flick of his wand sends a hallway gurney flying at her. Ange leaps and spins past it — magical fire and electricity can't hurt her, but flying objects hurt just the same.

The magician's eyes widen further. "What's the matter?" Ange snarls. "Out of tricks?"

"No! No wait, how do you…?" Ange takes his head off before he can finish the question. And turns, to find Jamie and the Leventhal guard staring at her, horrified. There is nothing more frightening for a magician, she supposes, than seeing a force that none of their powers can stop.

"What?" she growls at them, as the overhead fire sprinklers erupt in a downpour, activated by the smoke and heat. Behind her, the severed head rolls on the floor. Jamie's eyes follow it, and he swallows hard. And he ducks, as something flashes at him from behind, blocked by the Leventhal guard — there's three more of them, blasting away, and Jamie deflects one with his bare hands, then sends an attacker flying through the air with a force shove…

"Go!" yells the guard. "I'll hold them, you take him and go!" Ange runs to Jamie but he's already moving, and they duck down an adjoining stairwell, feet fast on the steps.

"I need a wand!" Jamie announces as they descend. Hospital staff on the next floor down are scattering, or crouched frightened behind cover, having no clue what's going on. Ange wonders how the shroud will cover this one — an accidental fire? A drug addict gone crazy? The shroud is endlessly inventive. "Ange, I can't project without a wand or a staff! It's too close to me, I need some range!"

Ange rounds the bottom of the stairs and goes down the next flight. At the stairway elbow, someone has left some crutches. "How about one of them?" she says, indicating with her sword as she runs past.

"No, the end's rubber! It can't have an insulator." Hurrying desperately to keep up with bare, wet feet.

Ange heads down the next flight, past an old man climbing with a walking stick. She rounds the elbow, and is about to continue when she sees a man on the floor below aiming up at her with a gun. She flings herself back the other way and into Jamie, knocking them both to the ground as bullets hit the wall beside them.

"Guns!" Ange exclaims. And more loudly, to the man below them, "What kind of magician uses guns!"

"Hey, this is America bitch!" comes the reply, and several more shots. Ange looks at Jamie, who shrugs, and begins to climb back the way they came.

"No!" says Ange. "It's a trap, they'll have someone up the corridor with another gun, we'll get hit." Or she'll get hit, as Jamie is probably immune like most magicians.

Jamie grimaces, and extends a hand at the old man, now frozen in fear on the steps above them, leaning against a rail. The old man's walking stick flies into Jamie's hand, and Jamie looks it over, and finds the rubber stop on the end. "Damn it!"

Ange takes the stick, and slices off the rubber tip with her sword. "Better?"

Jamie takes it back, and points it over the rail. The air thumps, with a force Ange feels in her chest, and leaves her half-deaf from a sudden change in air pressure. From the hall below, crashing and banging, and general calamity. Jamie tosses the cane back up to the old man, and the cane somehow hooks itself onto the rail right beside his hand. "Thanks buddy! Sorry it's a bit shorter now, just get someone to glue it back!"

Ange rushes down the stairs, and peers into this hallway. Gurneys, hallway chairs and a trolley of hospital equipment have gone flying, scattered like in the aftermath of an earthquake. Ceiling light covers have come crashing down, and the armed magician is sprawled several yards away, unconscious, bleeding from the nose and ears. Further away, some hospital staff have fallen and are in shock, picking themselves back up. Shockwave, Ange recognises. In an enclosed space like a hallway, they can be devastating... but she's rarely seen one this powerful.

She darts to the fallen man, takes his gun, and gives Jamie a hard look as she passes him to continue down the stairs. "What?" he retorts. "You're good with swords, I'm good with shockwaves. Hey, I thought you didn't like guns?"

"Apparently I'm in America now," says Ange, rattling down the next stairs. "Nice to be reminded."

They make the basement carpark without further attack, and Ange runs between parked cars looking for her ride. "Wait, how did you get here?" Jamie pants.

"There," says Ange, spotting the motorcycle parking. She grabs her red Ducati, stands it, and grabs the keys from her pocket.

Jamie can't believe it, and stares. "But you just got here! How do you have a bike already?"

"Bought it after we played basketball." She throttles the engine, and it roars. "Best transport for assassins, get on!"

He climbs on, awkwardly, and doesn't know where to put his hands. "Where did you get the money?"

"I've got money," Ange retorts. "Hold on tight or you'll fall off."

She guns it, and they roar between rows of parked cars toward the exit, where boom gates await parking tickets. "Did you pay?" Jamie yells in her ear. Someone shoots at them from over the roofs of cars, bullets crack and whine off concrete walls, and shatter car windows. Ange dodges past a car waiting at the exit, runs up on the sidewalk to miss the gate, then roars up the ramp and jumps onto the main road with a bounce before turning left and screeching off.

"Yes of course I paid!" Ange yells back, sarcastically. "It was right on the top of my list!"

The road is full of cars and Ange weaves between them at high speed, throwing glances over her shoulder to see their pursuers. Sure enough, there's a big black chevy chasing them, with someone leaning out a window with gun in hand. Jamie sees them too.

"Go go!" he yells. "Don't worry about the guns, I can stop that!" From behind come gunshots, and Ange senses repeated, sharp tingles of energy as Jamie blocks them. It's a simple shield spell — the golden rule of magical combat is that magic can stop velocity, but not mass. Having little mass, bullets stop easily. Having larger mass, swords and clubs are much harder to stop, despite much lower speed. Thus it's much easier to kill magicians with old weapons than new ones.

Ahead the road is blocked by a bank of cars waiting at a red light. Ange looks at the sidewalks, but there are construction boardings on both sides of the road, and the sidewalks are blocked by rails. There's no other way through.

"Hang on!" she yells. "We have to go back or they'll ram us!" She hits the brakes and turns hard… and sees a black shadow crossing the road, and suddenly the canyon between buildings is blocked by the spread of wings. Big dragon feet slam on the chevy's roof, claws smashing windows and grasping. The huge wings pound the air, and the chevy lifts from the road in a hurricane of downdraft.

Ange laughs and whoops, punching the air, as Gia carries the chevy around the corner and banks sharply, gaining altitude. Turning her bike again, Ange can see down that road, as Gia crosses the elevated FDR Drive at five hundred feet, out over the Manhattan River, and drops the car.

"Wow!" says Jamie, awestruck. "I don't believe it! I've always wanted to see one! Is he friendly?"

"To me?" Ange says grinning. "Sure. To people who annoy me, not so much." Ange's mobile phone rings in her jacket pocket. She answers.

"*Hello Ange, it's Meisha!*" comes the voice. "*I take it this is Gia? Eli says you mentioned him, we'd all just love to meet him! Why don't you introduce us?*"

Ange turns to look at Jamie. "Can they see *everything* from their tower?"

"Pretty much yeah."

Ange and Jamie roar into the underground carpark beneath the Leventhal building, and the toll gate mysteriously rises for them. As soon as she's down the main ramp, a couple of men in suits indicate politely that she should head for the central elevators, where another several men insist that the bike will be safe, and that they might want to take the elevator to the roof. At the top floor, a wide corridor holds another two employees, both women, who escort them with clicking heels to the stairway to the roof.

It's a helicopter pad, of course. The surrounding view of mid-town Manhattan is extraordinary, and a strong breeze is blowing. The pad has about twenty people on it, and Ange feels a hum in the air, a faint tingle but deeper, like embedded magic. The rooftop is separately shrouded, she realises. Which means that no one from any of these surrounding buildings can see what goes on here. Useful, considering what Leventhal might get up to, on top of his tower.

The crowds are not watching her, however. They're watching the skies, and the surrounding towertops for another glimpse. "There! There he is!" one shouts, and Ange sees him too, a flash of wings and tail, darting behind the Chrysler building, heading north-west to Central Park.

"Gia!" she shouts. "Stop showing off and get down here!"

People turn to stare at her, and Ange sees Leventhal, Meisha and Croz amongst them. Then Gia comes, with just the occasional, leisurely flap, and dives at some point beneath the rooftop until he vanishes from view. And then appears, abruptly, right on the edge and slowing to drop onto the pad at just the last moment. The crowd gasps, and Ange runs to him, and hugs his big scaly head as he puts it down to greet her.

"I thought you'd left me!" she cries, suddenly in tears. And senses in his posture that he's not entirely comfortable with all these people around. She glances behind, and sees everyone coming closer for a look, a few of them far too trusting for their own good.

"Don't crowd him!" she tells them, wiping her cheeks. "He's not a dog, he doesn't like to be patted by strangers. He's a flying, fire-breathing killer, and about as cuddly as a chainsaw."

Which is overstating things a little, but it's what a lot of wide-eyed dragon lovers need to hear upon meeting one for the first time. From the look in many eyes here, it's the first time for quite a few, at least at this range.

"Ange!" exclaims Meisha, face alight in a way that says she can 'see' Gia just fine. "How did *this* happen?" Dragons are often solitary, and mix mostly with each other. They and humans have had bad history, with dragons generally getting the worst of it… and dragons, it's rumoured, have long memories. Most humans consider themselves lucky to see one a handful of times in a lifetime. Friendships between the two species are rarest of all.

"I went hiking in the Alps when I was a kid," Ange explains. "I was stupid, I went wandering, the weather closed in, I got lost. Gia found me and flew me out. We've been friends ever since." She scratches his jaw as he looms behind her, considering this array of bite-size people before him.

"He's not my pet, he lives his own life and sometimes I've not seen him for months. But he always comes back."

Leventhal looks amazed. And deeply thoughtful, braced on his cane. Surely a man who's lived two thousand years isn't surprised by much, but he looks surprised now.

Ange stares at him. With Gia at her back, surely she could kill him now. And everyone on the rooftop, if Gia wished it. Gia senses her anger, and bristles, the ridge down his neckline raising, neck arching. Across the rooftop, a silence descends. Leventhal raises his hand, a gesture for calm.

"Come now friend," says Leventhal to the dragon. "You don't wish to harm me. And you know, I don't think the girl any longer does either."

Gia considers him, creeping slowly sideways, his huge head angling for a better look. A blast of heat from his nostrils sweeps the platform, and Leventhal's employees turn to shield their faces, or perform fast spells. The hot air whips Leventhal's suit and tie, but he only smiles, as though finding it bracing.

"You might want to take this collar off me," says Ange. It's a rush, sometimes, to be friends with the magical world's most deadly killer. Gia won't kill on demand, but will when it suits him. Usually it suits him when she's being threatened. People who forcibly put collars on necks are not universally appreciated by humans or dragons.

"You're not his master," says Leventhal knowingly, not taking his eyes off the dragon. "As you said. He is his own dragon, and the autonomy of dragons must be respected."

"And their allegiances," Ange says dangerously.

Leventhal walks slowly to Gia. Gia regards him warily. "Oh I know dragons. I've known many, in my time, and been friends with some. They align themselves with forces beyond what you and I can see. They are sighted, like humans can be sighted. And this one, I think, has not brought you here to kill me. He's brought you here for some other reason entirely."

He stops before Gia, and leans on his staff. And reaches out a hand. Gia growls. It is a sound like impending death, a snarling vibration. About the rooftop, Ange sees all notion of cuddly, friendly dragons vanish from the faces of those watching. But Leventhal does not withdraw his hand.

Time seems to slow. And Ange realises that if Leventhal is so unafraid, probably Gia has as little chance of killing him as she does. Suddenly she finds herself desperately hoping that he doesn't try. Gia senses her change in mood, and swings his head to look at her. Then extends his muzzle to Leventhal, for a cautious sniff. Leventhal places a hand on his jaw, not a pat, just a contact. Like shaking hands.

Gia snorts, and steps back to Ange's side. Ange feels her heart restarting, and her face is hot with shame. She might have got Gia killed too, he'd only been reacting to her emotions. If she was angry, he'd be angry too. He might have struck at Leventhal and not survived, and then she'd have killed her last best friend as well. She puts an arm around his neck, and rests her head on his jaw in apology.

"Good," says Leventhal, looking at them both. "Wisdom is learning to be responsible for your actions. Do not use your friend to get you out of a situation that you yourself created. Obviously he's not interested in your revenge quest, or he'd have helped you try to kill me before."

"Why then?" Ange asks sullenly.

"Because you wanted to come, and he loves you," Leventhal says simply. "And because he knows, I think, that events are unfolding in New York, Angelina, and that you belong here now. If you stay, and work for me, I will show you why."

CHAPTER FOUR

A 40-ish, thin, bearded man named Michael Stanthorpe leads Ange down two flights of stairs and into a wide office floor. Leventhal Tower is like office towers everywhere, with central working spaces where men and women stare at screens, and talk into phones. They seem entirely preoccupied in their work, and unaware that a dragon just landed on the roof of their building.

"There are nearly ten thousand people working in this building," Stanthorpe tells her unasked, walking quickly. Ange follows, hands in pockets, looking about with sullen interest. "Most on the upper levels are on our side of the shroud, but quite a lot of the lower levels are not. We try to recruit the best people, and the best people are not always magical, difficult though some of us find that to accept."

"Can Leventhal pull them across the shroud?" Ange asks. Some workers look up from their screens to stare at her, and a few whisper and point to others.

"Yes he can," says Stanthorpe. "It's one of the wonders of being Eli Leventhal."

"Recruiting innocents to fight his war."

"Dear girl," says Stanthorpe, turning past the elevators, "every person on Earth is in this war whether they happen to be aware of it or not. Especially if they live in New York. Now as you'll know, Leventhal Holdings is a financial services corporation, that means we do lots and lots of really cool things with money."

"I didn't ask," Ange growls.

"Yes, your total lack of enthusiasm is quite the charm. But Eli told me to fill you in, so I will." He seems totally unbothered by her attitude, and confident that his wit can defeat her sniping without effort. His suit looks expensive, black with pin-stripes, a neat collar and a perfect, red pocket square. Ange thinks he's probably gay. "As you'll see, everyone is very busy today — why, we've had the Fed announce interests rates, one of our European competitors acquired a stake in a corporation *we* were eyeing, so that's got a few of us a bit peeved, and our legal team is scrambling to prepare for trial next month in the case against City Hall."

Ange frowns. "The Mayor is prosecuting you?"

"Yes, well his office is. He says we didn't pay our taxes, which is nonsense of course, but proving it against that fiend will be something else. And the Mayor uses magic to cheat in court, while chivalrous Eli refuses. It drives our lawyers up the wall."

"Sure," Ange says drily. "I bet Eli never uses magic to cheat in business either, and he got all this wealth fair and square."

Stanthorpe stops before a door, and confronts her. "Yes," he answers her succinctly. Then he opens the door and beckons her in.

Within, between several desks and broad windows, sit or stand several men and women, surrounded by computer screens, various mobile phones and pads, taking notes, pointing and discussing. The office walls are not decorated like a typical office — there are military photos, pictures of men in camouflage, posing for the camera. A few of them look like they've been taken in Afghanistan or Iraq. Two men Ange immediately spots as ex-military, one wiry with blonde hair and a scarred cheek, the other big and powerful, sleeves rolled up, a tattoo visible up one forearm.

The blonde man is tossing a baseball one-handed as he watches the screens. He glances up to see Ange, and without warning hurls the baseball at her head. Ange sways aside and pulls her sword in a single motion, as behind her glass shatters, and someone shouts warning. The blonde man grins, unbothered by the sight of an angry, sword wielding Ulani, and clicks his fingers at the bigger man. The bigger man snorts, forks a ten dollar note from his pocket, and hands it over.

"More impressive if she caught it," he says.

"Nah mate," says the other. His accent is broad Australian. "That sword takes two hands, catching it wastes a hand she could be using to take my head off." He tucks the note into his jacket pocket. "Sorry 'bout that Princess. Nice reflexes."

"Angelina," Stanthorpe says drily. "This is Stew Bickel." Indicating the Australian. "And Helios Hernandez." The bigger man. "They head our Response Division." He looks down his nose at the two men. "She's charmed, of course."

"Say that sword's a beauty," says Bickel. "Can I see it?"

"You've got eyes, you can see it," Ange tells him, sheathing the blade.

"Hey magic man," says Bickel to Stanthorpe without missing a beat, "you can magic that right up, huh?" Pointing to the smashed glass in the door frame, with a baseball sized hole in it.

"For the thousandth time," says Stanthorpe, "this isn't a children's movie. No, I can't just *magic it up,* magic allows the manipulation of elemental forces, and elemental forces are much better at breaking things than putting them back together. The glass will be replaced, out of your budget."

Bickel winks at Ange. "Whole building's crawling with accountants. You know what it needs is more tall, hot Italian girls with swords..."

"Hey Stew," says Hernandez, "pay attention to your poor bloody assistant." Stew looks about, at the spectacled woman on the phone behind him.

"Al says he can get you an address in half an hour," she tells him. "But it'll cost us two Yankees tickets. Front row."

"Police corruption," says Hernandez, shaking his head.

Bickel looks at Stanthorpe. "We can swing that, yeah?"

"Two Yankees tickets seems a fair trade if it gets us that address," Stanthorpe agrees. "Now Angelina, please stay here and familiarise yourself with operations. You may find this more your speed than all that boring money business that goes on elsewhere in the building."

He leaves, carefully opening the door and stepping over shattered glass. On the phone, Bickel's assistant promises the baseball tickets. To a policeman, Hernandez said?

"Whose address are you after?" Ange asks, peering at the screens on the tables. There are a lot of maps and New York streets, and various databases that might be running IDs, licence plates, etc. Ange has seen a bit of that, it's the same procedures the police use when they're searching for someone. Assassins sometimes need to find people too.

"The guys who tried to kill your buddy J-Mac." Ange frowns... then realises. J-Mac, James MacDonald. Jamie. Americans and their Hollywood nicknames. "We've got some guys running IDs off the bodies you left behind. We can't do all of that ourselves, but lucky for us we've got lots of friends in the NYPD."

"Yeah, but so does the Mayor," Hernandez adds in his deep, bass voice. "So we gotta be careful who we ask. Al Kerpowitz is an old friend, guy deserves some good seats."

"Captain of Eleventh Precinct," Bickel explains. "Hey, where is J-Mac? Is he okay?"

"He's upstairs getting changed," says Ange. "He wasn't happy being dragged across town in his pyjamas." It occurs to her that these men like to talk. Possibly if she asks them, they'll tell her about Tori MacDonald, and what happened to her two years ago. But it doesn't feel right to go behind Jamie's back like that. "You were military?"

"Green Berets," says Bickel, pointing at Hernandez. "Australian SAS." Pointing to himself. And he points to three others in the room, with, "French Foreign Legion, Navy SEALS, and British Royal Marines."

"And NSA," the spectacled woman volunteers. "Which means I'm the only one here who's actually any use."

"Spies," says one of the other men, making a face. The spectacled woman smacks him on the head as she passes.

"Probably right," Hernandez concedes. In Ange's line of work, she's gotten to know military special forces units quite well, as many of the magical ones take up similar lines of work to hers once they're civilians again. For hand-to-hand fighting, she'd take Green Berets or Royal Marines. SEALS for the more technical stuff, difficult locations, hard to reach targets. For sheer physical and mental toughness, Special Air Service, any day of the week.

"Oh I forgot," she says, and pulls the pistol she recovered from her pocket. "I took this off one of them. Maybe you can trace it."

"They'll have removed the serial number," says Hernandez, "they use magic to clean guns down real good, make them hard to trace."

"Can trace the magic though," says Bickel, coming about the desks to take the pistol from her. He ejects the magazine and inspects it in several lightning fast moves. "Andy, take this down to Chenko, would you?" As the tough-looking guy named Andy comes to do that, with a playful wink at Ange on the way. Ange wonders for the hundredth time why it is that all the men who like her and flirt with her are crazy and dangerous, while the nice civilised boys avoid her like the plague. And suddenly, with all this odd male attention, she's realising that her hair's even more of a mess than usual, what with magical assassination attempts and motorcycle escapes. She reaches into her pocket, and finds her plastic comb is melted.

"Caspita!" she mutters. "Anyone have a comb I could borrow?"

"Whoa!" says Bickel, taking the lump of melted plastic from her fingers. "Nice one! Say Beast, look at this!"

He tosses the ex-comb to Hernandez, who whistles. "Takes a lot of volts to do that," he observes. "Which one was that? The headless guy in the hallway, or the guy in J-Mac's room?" They've seen photos of the crime scene, she realizes… if you can call it a crime.

"The one in the room," Ange confirms. "He teleported to the end of Jamie's bed and did a lightning charge immediately, I had to jump on the bed to stop it."

"What, and he hit you?" Bickel looks incredulous. Much of the room is now taking an eye or an ear away from their other work to listen in. "With ten thousand volts?"

Ange nods. She can't help it, she's quite enjoying this bit. "Yeah. I'm sure I've got holes in my clothes somewhere from electricity entry and exit points."

"Does that hurt?" Hernandez asks.

"No. But it makes a mess of my hair." The spectacled woman detours toward her, still talking to someone else on the phone, and pulls a small ladies' hair brush from a pocket. "Thank you," says Ange.

"I'm Katie," the woman whispers with a smile, so not to interrupt the person on the phone, and goes back to her computer screens.

Ange runs the hairbrush through her fringe, and it sticks fast. "Merda! Che disastro." Tugging hard to get it out.

"Looks like you'll need a steel horse brush to sort out that bird's nest sweetheart," Bickel observes helpfully, going back to his work.

"Full on Italian nightmare," Hernandez adds. Ange glares at them.

It's actually very interesting to watch the Leventhal Holdings Response Division in action. Ange learns that this office of ten people is just the headquarters, that the entire division has hundreds of people spread across smaller offices in New York. And they don't just respond to Togova activity, they also deal with magical nasties and disturbances, from vampires to werewolves, to instances of spells gone awry and medical emergencies. In the half hour Ange spends waiting for Al the policeman to get them the address, she sees them coordinating responses to a hex on someone's car that's causing everything to crash into it and every passing bird to crap on it, to a petrified taxi driver the medicos couldn't wedge out of his cab because his hands were locked on the steering wheel, to a report of rogue punks on the subway making female travellers' clothes disappear.

Most of the people needing help are not connected to Leventhal Holdings in any way, they're just regular New Yorkers, and most of them shroud-blind. Other New Yorkers who are not shroud-blind will see the problem, and call the Response Division. Apparently it's quite well known, like 911 for magicians. The shroud-blind in New York are about ninety-five percent, she learns, meaning only one in twenty people on the street have any clue what's really going on. In London and Milan, the rule of thumb was ninety-nine percent. New York appears to have a curiously high percentage of magical folk… but she sensed that the moment she slid from Gia's back in Central Park.

She learns further that Response Division shares a lot of its work with the regular emergency services — the police, fire department and the ambulances. Each of those services have their own magical people who coordinate with Response Division, but they also have to do their regular non-magical jobs as well, so coordinating a response to magical problems would otherwise be hit and miss. Response Division provides that central coordination service, so that getting help isn't just a question of 'knowing a guy' in the police, as it was in London or Milan. There if you didn't 'know a guy', and have his phone number available, you were usually on your own. Here, it's more organised. In spite of her cynicism, Ange grudgingly admits to herself that it's a damn good idea. And she wonders why it isn't copied elsewhere.

The person who *should* be coordinating all of these magical services, of course, is the Grand Magister who sits in City Hall. But Mayor Riley is the man in charge of the Togova Alliance, and the Togova don't do that. *Libero Venenatis,* they call it — Free Magic, in Latin. And it's what the Togova are all about, the freedom of magical folk to do whatever the heck they like. Which might sound nice to some people, but in reality just means the Togova are filled with ambitiously powerful magicians who feel that the rules should not apply to people like them. Or that there should be no rules at all.

Eli Leventhal, on the other hand, is leader of the Shtaal Alliance, and the Shtaal Alliance are all about rules. The Response Division seems a good advertisement for them, Ange thinks... but too often it seems to her that the choice is between magical tyranny and magical anarchy. She doesn't want to live under a set of strict rules laid down by a Grand Magister like Leventhal any more than she wants to live in the total absence of magical rules under Mayor Riley. Why can't there be something in the middle?

"What happens if a Togova phones you?" she asks Stew Bickel in a quieter moment, sitting on a chair by the windows and fighting with her uncooperative hair. It really needs a complete wash — when it gets like this brushing and combing alone won't do it.

"Happens all the time," says Bickel. "Good opportunity to get something out of them. Recruited quite a few spies that way."

"Against Mayor Riley?"

"Yep."

"And what happens if Riley catches them spying?"

"We send someone around to collect them in a plastic bag," says Hernandez.

The door opens, and Andrew Crosby strides in. "G'day Croz," says Bickel. "What's up?"

"You're up," says Croz. "Got that address, we're leaving."

"Us two? Hang on, how did you get the...?"

He looks around, and Katie-the-ex-NSA-agent taps her phone. "I passed it on, you were busy." Bickel shrugs and gets up.

"Her too," says Croz, with a dark look at Ange. "Eli's orders."

"Great," says Bickel. "Get to take the expensive Italian out for a spin, huh?" Ange is about to retort when she remembers what car Croz drives. She gives Bickel a mock smile as she gets up, to say 'very clever', and gathers her sword.

"Hang on," she says, as the obvious occurs to her. "You can't fit three people in a Ferrari."

"Can," says Croz, striding out. "You'll see."

They're barely out the door when Jamie comes running up, out of breath in a good shirt and pants. With his clothes at a Leventhal-standard of fashion, and his hair brushed nicely, he suddenly looks like an uptown private school boy, not the lower-middle class kid from Queens that Ange first met. It suits him, she thinks, in that he looks very good in it… and yet somehow it doesn't suit him at all.

"Croz, I'm coming with you."

"No you're not," says Croz, and keeps walking.

Jamie hurries to keep up. "Eli's orders. He said I could come."

"Don't lie to me."

"I'm not lying!" Croz just looks at him, still walking. "Look, they tried to kill me, okay? I'm coming too, you can't stop me!"

"Wanna bet?" They stop by the elevators, and others waiting at the doors find somewhere else to stand. "Kid, you've spent the last two years on the wrong side of the shroud. Your brain is still rearranging itself, you're having memory flashes, I've seen people have seizures recovering from that stuff. You'll be clear in a week, so be patient, and let us handle it."

"Ange!" says Jamie. "Let's go on your bike!"

"I don't know the address," says Ange.

"We'll follow them! You said yourself, motorcycles can get through traffic better, even that Ferrari can't outrun us."

Croz and Bickel look at Ange. Croz looks grim, expecting the worst, while Bickel is just curious. She *wants* to say yes, Jamie is the only person she knows in New York she is completely certain she likes. And she trusts

Jamie a lot more than she trusts Croz or Bickel. But liking someone means being concerned for them, and so...

She fidgets, and looks down at her boots. "I'm sorry Jamie. I don't think it's a good idea."

"Oh come on!" The elevator opens, and they file in. Croz puts a hand on Jamie's chest when he tries to follow. "Croz, what if these are the same people who killed Tori? What if they're trying to finish the job, huh?"

"Then we'll deal with it," Croz assures him. "Now go, I'm not dealing with this now." The doors close, and Ange gives Jamie an apologetic look before they seal completely.

The elevator begins down. "Good lookin' boy that J-Mac, don't you think Angelina?" Bickel suggests.

Ange rolls her eyes. "He's a nice boy, yes. He might be the only nice person I've met while I'm here."

"If you'd said that after just meeting me, Stew and Eli, that'd be fine," says Croz. "But you've met Meisha. And that makes you a bitch."

"Screwing her, are you?" Ange replies. Croz turns a deadly stare on her, which Ange returns.

Bickel steps between them. "Y'know, if we could just get to the ground floor without someone getting killed, that'd be great."

Down in the carpark basement, Croz leads the way to his Ferrari. He hits the unlock on his keys, and the machine flashes, all lights at once. It has to be magic, Ange decides as Croz folds the passenger seat down. It's a racing seat, they're not supposed to do that, but this appears to have been customed. Ange peers in, and...

"That's not supposed to be there," she says. Behind the front seats, are two small rear seats. Just benches really, with no leg room or comfort. "Enzo Ferrari would be rolling in his grave." She pulls her head out again. From the outside, it's clearly a two-seat car. Back inside, and it's a four-seater. Or two and two-halves, really. "Bigger on the inside than the outside. Magic."

"Eli did the whole custom job for him," says Bickel. "Pretty cool, huh?" It seems like the kind of thing only Grand Magisters could do, Ange thinks. Multi-dimensionality is serious magic.

"Well I'm not sitting in the back," Ange declares. "I'm the tallest one here, you could barely fit a dog in there."

"Perfect for you," says Croz. "With that collar around your neck."

Again Bickel steps between them before it gets nasty. "Hey hey," he says, with a hand raised at Ange. "Just be a sport and get in the back seat, huh? Then maybe we can arrange a sparring session when we get back, and you two can settle it properly."

"The collar stops me from hurting Leventhal employees," Ange mutters, climbing awkwardly past the folded seat. "Lucky for you."

"I'll see if Eli can disable it for a few minutes," Croz growls, marching about to the driver's seat. As he climbs in, he looks over his shoulder at her. "And if you damage that upholstery, I swear I'll put a bullet in you."

"I'm an Italian in a Ferrari," Ange retorts, "like that's going to happen." Even stuffed in the back seat with her knees up around her ears, she has to admit, Croz has nice taste in cars. "Lucky you don't drive a Porsche, I'd set it on fire."

In the passenger seat, Bickel laughs. "I like this girl."

"I'm happy for you," Croz mutters, and revs the engine.

Five minutes later, they're stuck in Mid-Town traffic. Croz has to shut off the engine so they won't run out of fuel before they get there. So it's not the most *practical* car, Ange reflects. But practical isn't everything. Her magic-sense feels a faint buzz coming from somewhere. Probably the multi-dimensional craziness, she thinks.

"Bit suspicious these guys just happen to rent an apartment within teleporting range of Jamie's hospital ward the day before," Bickel suggests as they wait for the traffic to move.

"Someone tipped them off," says Croz. "Someone who was keeping an eye on Jamie, and knew he was a threat, and wanted him removed before he started working for us again."

"You think Riley?"

"It's illegal," says Croz. "The High Council won't allow a move against an unsworn person. We only registered Jamie with the Council today, but DeLalio rented that apartment two days ago, so whoever tried to kill Jamie was breaking Council rules."

"You think that matters to Riley?" Bickel asked.

"I do. Riley's not sloppy, even he doesn't mess with the High Council.

That's old magic, as powerful as he is. When he kills magicians he does it by the book."

"Wait," says Ange, "who are these DeLalio people? The ones who tried to kill Jamie?"

"One of the guys you killed," says Croz. Ahead, traffic starts to move, and he guns the engine with a rumble. On the sidewalk, pedestrians stare. "DeLalio house, they're registered on the magical lists, only small though. No registered address, but our cop friends ran credit cards, found an address in Brooklyn. In exchange for some baseball tickets."

"Which kinda proves why I always say magic is overrated in investigations," says Bickel. "Government registries are useless, to find people you need good old fashioned police work."

"So if you can prove they were acting on the Mayor's instructions," Ange says slowly, "you can prove the Mayor broke the High Council's rules about killing the unsworn?"

"That is the idea," says Croz. "Which would drop Mayor Riley in the shit for a change."

"Wouldn't that be nice," Bickel agrees.

They finally reach the Queensboro Bridge, and make better time through its rush of grey steel girders. Then an offramp, and a right turn, Ange struggling to see where they are with her head down beneath the low roof.

"So what's it like to fly that dragon?" Bickel asks, giving an amused look at her discomfort.

"No one *flies* a dragon," Ange replies. "They don't take commands, they're too big for reins, and they're nearly as immune to magic as I am. They occasionally let people be passengers, but that's all."

"Stuck with you across the North Atlantic," Croz remarks. "Poor dragon."

Ange frowns at the back of his head. Croz's insults are usually more cutting. This one feels forced. Immature, even. Then it dawns on her. "You're jealous!"

"Yeah that must be it," he deadpans.

"You know, if you're *very* good," says Ange, "I might let you pat him. Of course, you might not survive it, but that's half the fun with dragons." Croz says nothing, glaring at the road.

"Jeez," says Bickel, "this is like being back in high school. No, *primary* school. So why'd you give your boy a girl's name, huh?" Ange blinks at him. "I dated a Gia once. Nice Italian girl, grandes tettes." With his hands at his chest. Ange rolls her eyes. "That's my only Italian."

"And it's wrong," Ange retorts. "*Una tettona!*" She makes a suitably crude show of big hands to her chest.

Bickel grins. "What'd I say?"

"It's just wrong, trust me." She takes a breath. It's actually a little embarrassing. "When I first met him, I thought Gia was a girl. And by the time I realised, he'd gotten used to Gia, so…"

"That's a pretty big animal, girl!" Croz laughs. "How d'you miss something like that?"

"I didn't look, okay! I just thought… we had this connection, and I thought it felt like something between girls."

"Well *that's* very sexist," Bickel remarks. "When exactly did you decide you'd never have any male friends?" Ange scowls.

"You thought you were in a My Little Pony cartoon, didn't you!" says Croz. "Just a cutesy girl and her pretty blue pony, only with bigger teeth. Man, girls are all the same."

"Bet you had a shock when you actually thought to look, huh?" Bickel adds. The men laugh as Ange fumes. Bickel catches her eye in the mirror and winks.

Brooklyn is busy, an endless sea of bricks and concrete. Some neighbourhoods look quite nice with their tree-lined avenues, busy shopping strips and the occasional park, but as they join a road beneath an overhead trainline, it becomes grimmer and uglier. Still, Ange knows better than to judge these city books by their covers — some of the poorer neighbourhoods in Milan and London were safer, from a magical point of view, because the locals did their own security, and didn't take crap from anyone. And some wealthier neighbourhoods had become havens for wealthy magicians who attracted unsavoury minions.

"You're a receptor too?" Ange asks Bickel as he directs Croz toward the address.

"Yep. Fourth Realm. Maybe not as potent as you Ulani, but it does the job."

"Did you know before you joined the SAS?"

"It's not much of an advantage," says Bickel, and "Left at the next lights," to Croz. "I mean even you've noticed magic doesn't help your endurance much, right? SAS are all endurance, we're skinny runts compared to these American big boys. But you drop those guys behind enemy lines, they're begging for extraction in three days so they can come home and munch some protein bars. Three *weeks* later, we're still there. Left here."

They turn left at the lights, and growl in low gear between rows of parked cars and featureless three-storey brownstones that look more like warehouses than homes. "I ran a four-minute-mile at age fifteen," says Ange. "So it helps endurance quite a bit."

"Hell girl," says Croz, "we'd all clean up at the Olympics if they'd let us. Big deal."

"SAS endurance isn't a four-minute-mile," Bickel adds. "It's a marathon with eighty pounds on your back every day for a fortnight with no sleep or proper food in 110 degrees. You try that, you find magic doesn't help you much, trust me. Just up here Croz, this fugly thing beside the vacant lot."

"This one?" There's a van parked out front, and a sedan pulled suspiciously onto the sidewalk. "The cops will get him for parking like that if they're driving past…"

Ange feels a massive tingle, like hot and cold flushes. "Massive magic!" she exclaims. "Right from that house, something nasty."

"You felt it?" asks Bickel, craning around in his seat.

Ange nods vigorously. "There's another one! Someone's spelling something big."

"Let's go," says Croz, and pulls the Ferrari up behind the illegally parked sedan. Bickel thoughtfully folds the seat for Ange as she wriggles out, then pulls back his sleeve to reveal a curious-looking wristband, leather with a metal ornament of some kind… and with a flash a staff weapon appears in his hand, with a blade on one end and a scythe/hook at the other, like a miniature Japanese naginata. Another tingle, and Croz is suddenly carrying a very large axe. Ange blinks, never having seen that magic before, especially used by receptors.

Croz walks straight into the tiny front yard, up the steps, and smashes through the door with a single kick. Bickel follows, then Ange at the rear and drawing her sword.

"DeLalio!" Croz bellows as he strides down the central hall. "I challenge DeLalio, we are Leventhal!"

Into the main room, and he and Bickel abruptly duck, as a shockwave blasts back up the hall, shattering windows and popping eardrums. But Bickel keeps moving, as yells and crashes erupt, and Ange enters to find Croz already having buried the axe in someone's chest, and now smashes another cartwheeling across the kitchen table, as Bickel blocks a swing from another's polearm, cleverly reverses to hook it from his opponent's hands, then completes his weapon's full spin as the blade slices, and blood sprays.

Which leaves one man standing, in the rear extension room overlooking the small backyard. He's young, wears a good suit, and is standing over some bodies. He looks familiar. Mathew Palmino, Ange recognises. Mayor Riley's assistant, from that day in the bookstore. He'd given her Jamie's number.

He raises a short staff at Croz, who ducks beneath the kitchen bench as flames roar forth like a flamethrower. The flames pivot across to Bickel, who is exposed, but he extends his weapon in a side-on stance, and the flames part on either side of him, as though divided by a wedge-shaped shield. Croz leaps the bench as the flames stop, rushes Palmino, and swings. Palmino smiles, and disappears with a flash, the axe passing through empty air.

"God damn it!" shouts Croz. And he looks down at the bodies Palmino was standing over. Ange looks at the three men Croz and Bickel have just killed. They're maugies, magical augments, with interlocking armour plates where skin should be, and short horns on their heads, like demons. But the armour hasn't stopped Croz and Bickel, which tells Ange something about the calibre of receptor employed by the Leventhal Holdings Response Division.

"Hey," says Bickel, also looking at the bodies at Croz's feet. "I think that's DeLalio. And wife. Jesus."

The bodies at Croz's feet have no skin. Just flesh, and lots of blood on the floor. "Interrogation," Croz says grimly. "He kept them alive, only just killed them — must have been what Angelina sensed. Can you trace him?" Looking hard at Ange.

"Teleporting, sure," says Ange. "I mean, he can't have gone far, more than a hundred yards isn't safe in a city."

"Great, let's go." Croz rushes back past her, with Bickel following. Ange goes too, with a final stare at the awful sight on the floor. What a way to die.

By the time she reaches the car, she finds Bickel already in the back seat, both his and Croz's weapons vanished. She hits the front seat with a grateful look to Bickel — he's military trained and efficient, waiting for her to climb in the back would cost time. Croz roars the engine, and fights the awful turning circle to get them out onto the narrow road.

"Which way?" he asks Ange.

"No idea, but I'd guess back toward Manhattan?"

"Why?"

"You didn't recognise him? That was Mathew Palmino, Mayor Riley's assistant."

Croz gives her a hard glance, and brakes abruptly at an intersection. "Riley's got a lot of assistants."

"I met him a few days back, he tried to chat me up. He'll be heading back to City Hall, right?"

"Right," says Croz, with an edge of excitement as he accelerates away from the intersection, parked cars flashing by. "If Riley sent him... hell yeah, let's get this guy."

He takes a left, and accelerates again. "Anything?" Bickel asks her.

"Not yet. Slow down a bit, no need for it when we don't know what we're chasing." Croz slows several gears, and the engine whines down in protest. "How do you make weapons appear like that? You're just receptors."

"It's the Leventhal network," says Bickel, pulling his sleeve to show the wristband again. "It's charmed, Eli makes them. It makes a link to the armoury in Leventhal Tower, and we get our weapon of choice when we want it. Saves us having to carry polearms in Croz's Ferrari, scratches the leather." Plus the bigger ones wouldn't fit, Ange thinks.

"Anything now?" Croz asks her impatiently.

"Not yet." They stop at an intersection, as cars pass. "You're sure that was Mr and Mrs DeLalio on the ground?"

Bickel nods grimly. "Bit hard to recognise, but yeah. Riley's goons covering up their dirty work — let them kill Jamie, then kill *them* to cover their tracks."

"Still think there's no difference between Togova and Shtaal?" Croz asks her.

Ange says nothing. Then, "There!" as they accelerate once more. A faint tingle, now moving. "Turn left. He's moving, I think he's got a car."

"How can you sense him?" Bickel asks. "Is he doing magic?"

"No, but he's just *done* big magic. It leaves residuals." Croz weaves past cars on another narrow road, and stops at a busy highway, four lanes of traffic. "Turn right." There's only a small gap, but Croz floors it and the Ferrari howls into a lane like a scalded cat. "Up ahead, I think he's stopped at the lights."

Sure enough, there is a big bank of cars waiting at traffic lights ahead. "Damn," says Croz, "should have brought Meisha."

"Why?"

"She's a techno-mage, she could get us any light we wanted."

"Sure," says Bickel, "could have put her in the boot."

"Wouldn't fit," says Croz.

"Lucky for Meisha." A black Corvette rams a car ahead of it in the queue, and makes space to dart out and dash for the lights in a cloud of white smoke.

"He's seen us," Croz says gleefully, "here we go!"

The Corvette dodges through the intersection, is nearly smashed by a truck, other cars skidding to miss it. Croz cuts between them in pursuit, as the Corvette dodges slower traffic ahead. Croz changes gears fast, and the acceleration presses them into their chairs, impossibly fast. Ahead, the Corvette brakes hard to turn, seeing half his lead disappear in a flash.

Croz laughs like a lunatic. "He just looked behind and wet himself!" The Corvette screeches across oncoming traffic and up a side road, Croz following much faster, and with only a little oversteer. "Look at that handling, go baby!"

"But I mean," shouts Bickel with white knuckles against the Gs, "if this was a Tesla we'd have caught him by now!"

"Do *not* mention that word in my car!"

The Corvette is just ahead of them now, and suddenly the Ferrari thumps and shakes as though it hit something. "Shockwave!" shouts Bickel. "He's spelling us!"

"He's got no line of sight," says Croz, "he's got nothin'!" In desperation the Corvette weaves about several slower cars, then skids right up an intersection. Croz nudges his tail with the Ferrari's nose, and the Corvette spins out completely. Croz slams the brakes and pulls across the road ahead, then around and in front of the other car. Ange finds her window winding down, and suddenly Croz's pistol is levelled past her nose, and she ducks. He fires repeatedly, punching the Corvette's windshield full of white holes. Ange opens the door and rolls out, staying low with sword drawn until she's alongside the stalled Corvette, then stands ready to smash in the driver's window. But the driver's seat is empty, the headrest peppered with bullet holes.

"He's gone!" she calls to Croz, who is now out of the car with pistol braced on the roof. "Teleported again!" Then she feels something burning down the front of her shirt, reaches and pulls out a spent cartridge. It burns her fingers, and she tosses it. "Ow, thanks a lot."

On the road, cars are slowing down to see, occupants staring at the wealthy black man with a gun, the tall Italian girl with a sword, and the two crazy looking cars in a cloud of white tire smoke. What the shroud will eventually make of *this*, heaven knows. Even getting back into the Ferrari, three people where only two can fit, will probably knock someone out cold.

"If he teleported again," calls Bickel from the rear seat, "you could trace him again."

"This felt like a big one," says Ange, looking around. "We showed he wasn't safe on wheels, I think he teleported back to Manhattan."

"Dangerous," says Bickel.

Croz makes a face, and holsters his gun. "Riley's got beacons in lower Manhattan, he can home in on those. Dammit. Now we've got nothing."

"There's Palmino's guys we killed back at DeLalio's house," Bickel offers, but Croz shakes his head.

"Just goons, they'll be untraceable."

Ange sheaths her sword. "You think shooting would have got him?" Indicating the well-holed windshield.

ANGELINA

"Sometimes when they're distracted," says Croz. "But mostly I wanted him focused on me while you slipped out and cut his head off. Come on, we gotta get back before the cops arrive, hopefully the shroud will stop them following us."

CHAPTER FIVE

Mayor Riley trots up the stairs at City Hall, amidst aides and police guard, smiling and waving to bystanders who take photos. He stops to shake some hands, and to kiss a baby — the election was last year, there's not another for three years, but a good politician never stops campaigning. Waltrip introduces him to a new intern, pretty with red hair, whose name is Daisy.

"You're a passive?" he asks her as they walk up the stairs.

"U-huh!" she says brightly, clutching her little bag, her dress suit still with hangar folds from the store. "My magic tutor said I drew power from Eleventh Realm. My parents are shroud-blind, but I've known what you are since I was about five! And of course I just knew I had to come and work for you."

"Well that's excellent Daisy," he says cheerfully. He can see why Waltrip recommended her — she's got that lightly activated consciousness that's exactly what he's after right now. He can sense it on her like a beacon, not too hot, not too cold. And the fact that her parents are shroud-blind is always good, for this line of work. "I'll just hand you back to Waltrip, and he'll make sure you settle right in. I'll catch up with you later, good luck!"

"Thank you so much Mr Mayor!" she gushes. "It's a wonderful opportunity, I can't tell you how much I'm looking forward to it."

In the grand old circular lobby, there are more people — a big real estate representative who wants to talk to him about a new development on old railways land, the Washington guy about the funding for the new subway line, and the network people who have set up a room with cameras and lights for a TV interview.

He shakes hands with them all, and puts them into his aide's hands to finalise times and schedules, then excuses himself to go upstairs to Palmino's office to see how the repairs are going. Outside the office door, Mindy is waiting, looking impatient.

"Hey Mindy," he says. "What's up?"

"The workers only just got here," Mindy complains. "They should have finished by now, but now I have to reschedule everyone on this floor because they'll be making a racket…"

"Mindy that's fine," Riley assures her with a smile. "I have faith in you. Make it happen." She growls in exasperation, and stalks off, heels clacking as she dials her phone.

Riley goes into the office, and dials his own phone, taking a seat.

"Hello, Godwin," he says. "Yes, our scheduled meeting tonight. I'm afraid I'm going to have to reschedule. Well, I've had a small problem with my assistant." A pause. Some builders, the source of Mindy's displeasure, are hauling tool boxes into the room, thumping them down on the broad, mahogany tables. Another man lugs a pneumatic drill. It's going to be very loud. "Well, the problem is that my assistant is no longer available, and he has rather a lot of what we've talked about stored away in his head. Yes. Yes Godwin, I have heard of computers. I'll make certain his replacement has too."

Riley glances at the wall alongside. There, embedded in the brickwork like some macabre work of art, is the visible half of Mathew Palmino. His left shoulder is completely exposed, the elbow out, though the arm is across his body, the left hand disappearing once more into the bricks. The line of the wall makes a vertical slice just inside his left eye, wide with astonishment. One leg protrudes from the wall to the knee, and part of a shoe, splayed out before him. He was sitting when he teleported, probably driving that noisy black Corvette he loved so much.

"Yes Godwin. I'll have my secretary call you to arrange another time, thank you for your understanding."

Riley disconnects. A builder brings a chisel and hammer across to

Palmino, and searches for a place to insert it. His lips purse in a silent whistle.

"He's dead, right?" he asks the Mayor, cautiously.

Riley has to laugh. "Oh yes, very much so. Just be careful not to bring down the entire wall, I think he's managed to put himself half through one of the support columns."

"Yeah, I can see that. Hey Billy, better get some jacks for the ceiling, this could take a while."

Riley shakes his head in disbelief, and walks for his office. He's told Palmino many times, teleporting was something even *he* did sparingly, and not without extensive controls. Manhattan is a giant forest of materials best not teleported into. He's told apprentices before that there's a *reason* he's lived so long, and it's not by using magic recklessly. But do they ever listen?

He walks to the big, old windows overlooking City Hall Park, and dials another number. The New York City Police Commissioner answers. "Oh hi Dave, it's the Mayor. Look, my little thing with Eli just took another turn, I just lost my most promising assistant."

"I'm sorry to hear that, Mr Mayor," the Police Commissioner says cautiously.

"Oh I swear Dave, these young people, they're so full of life and energy and rampant stupidity. Anyhow, he was onto something before he bought it — this James MacDonald kid, he's back with Eli apparently."

"I'm sorry, James MacDonald?"

"Before your time Dave, not to worry, ask someone about him. I know some of Eli's guys in the police have been keeping an eye out for Mr MacDonald, so I'd like that stopped now, if at all possible."

"I'm… yes of course, I'll see to it. He's a magician?"

"A very powerful young magician. Let's just say I have a personal interest in him."

"Of course, thank you for alerting me."

"And there's a new girl in town you should also be aware of. Angelina Donati. She's Ulani, you see, and I thought I made it plain to Starace that there should be no Ulani in New York."

"Do you want me to keep an eye on her too?"

"Um no. If at all possible I'd like to find a way to have her killed. Do you think you could manage that?"

After three more calls and a meeting with his finance people, he trots down some stairs and through a doorway only a magician can open, and into the basement beneath City Hall. In a secure room off the corridor, well insulated for sound, he finds Waltrip, clad in a white apron, just placing a bloody cleaver back onto a side table with its companions.

"Just in time," he announces, and unscrews the head of the person face down on the gurney from the clamp holding it in place. It comes away, now separated from the body, blood dripping into the drain, and Waltrip passes it to Riley by its red hair.

It's Daisy the new intern, eyes wide and mouth open.

"You know I wish you'd drug them before you do that," says Riley, examining the head with professional interest. "When they scream for so long beforehand, it leaves a mark."

"Well the drugs are worse," says Waltrip, wiping hands on his apron. "They get into the hypothalamus, contaminate the final potion. You want good longevity potion, it's gotta be drug free."

Riley shrugs. "Who's it for this time?"

"Calloway, the hedge fund guy. You wouldn't believe what he's paying."

"Enlighten me."

"Three and a half percent of yearly income." Riley whistles, handing back Daisy's head as Waltrip laughs. "Mindy talked him up a full percent, she's amazing.

"And to think the Times still thinks I struggled for election funds."

"You'd think these passives would learn," says Waltrip, taking the head to a circular saw and securing it in a new brace. "We can't harvest shroud-blind because of the High Council, and we're not going to harvest receptors or magicians, obviously. But still the passives come, like moths to a flame."

"She received a first class American education, my friend," says Riley as he leaves. "Twelve years of everyone telling her she's special. Probably turned her brain to mush."

Waltrip laughs, and fires up the saw.

CHAPTER SIX

"**R**emember," says the Leventhal employee who shows Ange into her new apartment that evening, "it's just a loan."

The apartment is on the lower part of Central Park West, directly overlooking the park. It's fourteen floors up, on the corner, with windows facing east and north. And it's big, for a Manhattan apartment anyway — a living room, open kitchen, and a separate bedroom into which another Leventhal employee takes her suitcases, newly brought from the hotel. Ange presses her face to the windows, and peers out. Mamma Mia!

North and south, overlooking the park, is an endless cliff wall of stone and brick. Not far north is the Museum of Natural History. South, the huge, imposing building fronts of Mid-Town, containing somewhere in their midst the bulk of the Leventhal Tower. All aglow in the deepening night. Directly below, the roads and paths of Central Park are alive with winding lights.

No kidding this apartment is a loan. Ange has money, but she's so far off affording this, it's not funny. It's fully furnished too, nothing fancy, but modern and comfortable. So much better than a hotel room.

"Don't I need to introduce myself to the landlord or something?" she asks the employees as they return from the bedroom.

"No need," says one, handing her the apartment keys. "You've met him, his name's Leventhal." Of course, Ange thinks. Stupid of her. "So be nice to it, and please, don't let any dragons in here."

They leave without further bother, probably quite peeved at the unfairness of it all — this new girl who nobody likes, getting treated like a princess for reasons no one but Leventhal can understand. Well. Ange deposits the Thai takeaway she's bought earlier on the kitchen bench and rummages for a plate and cutlery. And sits, considering the view, and wondering exactly why Leventhal *is* being this nice to her. Considering, as everyone keeps reminding her, she did try to kill him only yesterday.

Well the Central Park location is obvious. She's friends with a dragon. Gia needs a big space to land in and still not attract attention, even shrouded. No doubt Leventhal is very curious about Gia. As to the rest of the stuff, with Starace and the Ulani, and the reasons she ran away... her mood sours as she eats. Probably he knows. It's hard to imagine Leventhal doesn't keep tabs on the Ulani, one way or another. Both he and Riley, the world's two remaining Grand Magisters, have many old connections back in Europe. And Europe, like much of the world, is these days either Togova, or Shtaal.

Her phone rings. She doesn't recognise the number, except that it's local. Unsurprising — aside from Leventhal, Meisha, Jamie and Croz, who does she know in New York? "Ciao?"

"Ciao bella! Angelina, mi sei mancato. Scendere e dire ciao."

Ange's eyes widen in disbelief. But it doesn't last long, because truly, she's not surprised. She takes her plate, puts the phone to her shoulder, and keeps eating as she strolls to the windows. Down below, on the sidewalk opposite by the park wall, is a broad figure in a dark coat. Bearded and strong, a phone to his ear, looking up at her.

Ange takes another determined mouthful. "I'm eating," she says.

"Angelina." Starace can speak English well, if pressed. "Come down and say hello. I've come a long way to see you." Looking up at her. Something about seeing him down there, alone and asking for her company, makes her feel something. Something strong.

She takes another mouthful, and swallows more than just food. "I didn't ask you to come."

"Angelina." There is no bravado, no command in his voice. Humility. Perhaps even emotion. That's new. "Please. I've missed you."

Ange descends by elevator, and smiles and waves to the lobby securityman, then another smile to the doorman as he opens the door for her. She gets a tingle from each of them, nothing big, but Leventhal guards his properties well, and these security will deter at least casual trouble. To deal with the more serious kind, the whole building will be charmed — Ange has seen it done. Possibly it wouldn't stop a very determined Mayor Riley, but it would take a full scale magical attack... and if he does that in Leventhal's territory, Leventhal will do it in his, and then it's the kind of nasty, full scale war that Grand Magisters traditionally don't like. The most powerful magicians are builders of empires. They'd rather kill their opponents *without* trashing all their lovely possessions, if at all possible. A knife in the back, a poison in the cup...

At the door, Starace is waiting for her. Ange steels herself, and offers her cheek, but Starace hugs her instead. A strong embrace, and fatherly. *Then* he kisses her cheeks, Italian style, and steps back to size her up.

"Si guarda bene," he says with approval. He's a little taller than her, and much broader, with a trimmed beard and heavy brows. A powerful bear of a man, with an Ulani sword at his hip.

"Of course I look good," Ange sniffs in English. She's reluctant to speak Italian with Starace. Starace will claim her if he can. Has always claimed her. She loves to speak her native tongue, but with Starace it feels like slowly slipping back into the old straightjacket, to be controlled by his ideas, his goals, his power. Starace is the master of House Ulani. Some claim him to be the third most feared man in the magical world.

"Angelina," he says with an affectionate smile, hands on her shoulders. "We are surrounded by *altrui*. Not all of them speak Italian. Let's not make it so easy for them."

Ange sighs. "Bene. Prendiamo un caffè."

The only nearby place for a coffee is a Starbucks. Starace wrinkles his nose at the coffee, but drinks it anyway, settled at a small table in a corner. It's strange to see him here, amidst comfortable New York decor, and not the old courtyards and alleyways of Milan. New York is old for an American city, but it positively shines with squeaky newness compared to the old cities of Europe. Some Europeans, from powerful institutions that trace their lineage to well before America existed, never quite lose their disdain of the New World.

"I'm sure we could do better in Little Italy," Starace says of the coffee.

"It's fine," says Ange. "And I'm not travelling to the end of Manhattan for some coffee." They speak Italian, at least. Ange thinks that should be enough for even this man who hates to travel. Starace looks around, at the students studying on their laptops, the old well-dressed folks returning from a concert at the Lincoln Center, the office workers just now finishing up for the day, returning home for a few hours sleep before doing it all again tomorrow. A far cry from Italy, with its two hour lunches and long weekends. She can feel the lecture coming, the 'how can you bear to be away from home?', and 'the Ulani need you, and you have a greater duty'. Etcetera, etcetera. Ange became accustomed to fending off these lectures while in London, often twice, sometimes three times a year. Though usually it was not Starace coming to deliver it himself.

"You fly here?" she asks with a wry smile.

Starace represses a shudder. "Never. You know we have resources."

Teleporting, he means. It can be done, from here to anywhere in the world, if you have massive facilities, and friendly magicians to do the magic for you. No small thing, given that the killing of magicians is the main reason the Ulani exist. But these days, many say, the Ulani are more interested in controlling than killing, and many magicians will do anything if frightened enough. Or paid enough.

Starace removes a small lead case from his pocket, and puts it on the table. Within, though he won't open it here, will be an amulet of some kind, safely neutralised within the lead. Something drawing power from Third Realm. Its effect is to create a vacuum of magic, negating the powers of any other Third Realm drawer. It allows an Ulani to be teleported, by a magician, where normally the magic will not work on Ulani. It would also allow a magician to do whatever else he wanted to that Ulani… if he did not fear the wrath of that Ulani's friends.

"You know I hate those things," says Ange. "It's like kryptonite."

Starace frowns. "It's like what?"

Ange smiles in disbelief. "Oh come on, you're in the home of the comicbook superhero, and you don't know what kryptonite is?"

Starace waves his hand. "I'm Italian. I don't follow this American nonsense." Ange sighs. "And you?" Starace asks her. "Dragonback?" She smiles more broadly. "You're crazy. How long did it take you?"

"Oh, a few days. Ireland to Greenland, then Newfoundland and down from Canada."

"How do you survive, strapped to the back of a dragon for a few days? Over the freezing North Atlantic in autumn?"

"Bring lots of warm clothes, lots of food and water, and hold on tight." She shrugs. "I even brought a few bags. Dragons carry whole cow carcasses sometimes, eat them on the wing. They can go halfway around the world without having to land, stay airborne for days, even sleep in the air for short bursts."

"Still crazy."

"And we stopped a few times on container ships," Ange adds. "For necessities. It's dangerous for me to fall asleep while flying in case I fall off, but if I sleep under his wing, the shroud covers me too. So I'd unroll a sleeping bag on top of a cargo crate, and the crew couldn't see either of us."

Starace smiles and pats her hand on the table. "You were always the adventurous one. Do you remember, you used to climb out of your bedroom window when you'd been locked in there for being naughty? And Louisa would be putting your dinner on a plate to take up to your room, and be passing the table and find you already sitting there eating? *Angelina!*" He does a high falsetto of Louisa.

Ange grins, remembering that well. "Well I was hungry."

"It was a four floor drop beneath your bedroom window. You gave Louisa a heart attack, you were only seven. And the time you talked Luigi and Giancarlo into spying on the graduations."

"And we were caught immediately," says Ange. "It wasn't a good hiding spot."

"No, but you were determined to see what the examinations looked like. I was very proud, every Ulani child should break some rules. It shows character." He grasps her hand. "Angelina, come back with me just for a few days. Come back and complete your graduation at least…"

Ange rolls her eyes. "Starace, not this again…"

"To make it official! To tell the world at least who you are, and that you have arrived!"

"You know I'll pass." She looks him hard in the eyes. "I would have passed three years ago."

"I know," he says. "But the tradition, Angelina… surely that does not mean nothing to you?"

Ulani graduation, the *cerimonia*, is traditionally held when the student turns seventeen. There are tests of lore, and stamina, and fighting technique. For each student it is different, depending on his or her strengths or weaknesses. With Ange, all were expecting a grand test indeed. Until one morning, just after her thirteenth birthday, they awoke and found her gone.

"I'm not going to be the Master of House Ulani," Ange says firmly. "For the thousandth time. I won't be your heir. I refuse."

Starace had told her, on her thirteenth birthday. He'd expected her to be happy… thus proving that he'd never really understood her. It had horrified her, to be stuck in that place, shackled by tradition, year after year for the rest of her life. No husband, for the Master of House Ulani could have no equal. She could have children, if she wanted, but she could not love them and rear them as a normal mother would. They would belong to the House, like all Ulani, and raised by the House, as one amongst equals.

"Angelina," Starace says sternly. "I know it was difficult for you. You have no family history with the Ulani, an outsider, and the *legato* are always tough on the outsiders. Especially an orphan. And I'm sorry I could not be there to help you more, I could not be seen to show favoritism…"

"I learned to take care of myself," Ange says shortly.

Starace grasps her hand more firmly. "But you know you were always my favorite."

Ange's heart thumps harder. His eyes are so sincere. She wants badly to believe him, this man who is the closest thing to a father she's known. The Master of her House, the ruler of her destiny.

"Because I was your best fighter," Ange says sullenly. "Because you saw value in me. For the House."

"Yes." Unapologetically. "I cannot deny it. I am the Master, and it is the greatest honour to be the Master of the greatest House in all the world.

I take it so seriously, Angelina. But I cannot have an heir who is just a good fighter. She must have style, and she must have spirit. I saw those in you, from the day I first came to collect you from the sisters in the orphanage." He smiles, eyes twinkling, and looks at her hand in his. "You had a grip on you, even as a little girl. The grip of a warrior. You grasped my hand, just like this, and I knew even then that you were special."

"They're bastards," says Ange. "The *principali*. They don't want a woman as Master. They want Pietro, he's always been their golden boy. They'll fight me every step, and you."

"The ones that matter are with me!" Starace says earnestly. "Angelina, don't you worry about the others! I can handle them, you know that they don't dare to defy me! I chose you, not Pietro, and they'll accept that if I tell them to."

Ange snorts, and sips her coffee. Parts of her childhood she loves. But the Ulani are not a soft and nurturing people. They are competitive, and as a child the bullying and teasing was relentless. In time she overcame it, by becoming the biggest bully of them all against her tormentors... and grew to hate herself for it. From what she's seen, amongst the senior Ulani, that behaviour doesn't change when they grow older. The only reason they don't bully Starace is fear. In the early days of his leadership, the Ulani legend goes, Starace killed three fellow Ulani in various squabbles and duels. If she becomes Master, surely there will be more.

Killing evil things and dark wizards she can manage. To kill Ulani, over politics, it would have to be for some cause she really, truly believes in. And this cause, she just doesn't. She loves many people in the Ulani, but as a House, she wishes they'd all just grow up. And to think they call *her* the child for running away.

"I'll think about it," she says. She doesn't really know why she says it. Except that she's feeling lonely, and a little lost and confused. And Starace's grip on her hand, and the affection in his eyes, touch a place in her heart that has been touched by too few.

"Excellent!" Starace's eyes gleam. It's more than she's given him in a long time. "You do not need to decide so soon. I have pressured you enough. But it would mean so much to me, Angelina. And to others. You know the ones. They miss you too."

Ange nods, and swallows more coffee to cover her emotion. She does know the ones. A few of them came to visit her in London from time to time, to remind her she was not as alone as she imagined. Good people. Stupid House.

Starace's eyes drop to the thin steel collar. "That magic works on you?"

"Apparently," Ange says drily. "I barely feel it."

Starace chuckles. "Trying to kill Eli Leventhal. That's my Angelina. I could have told you what would happen, if you'd come to me first."

"I wouldn't have believed you."

"No," Starace sighs. "No, probably not. We're immune to *most* magic, Ange. Grand Magisters don't do *most* magic. They're different."

"How?"

Starace shrugs broadly. "We don't know. No one does."

"One of the Oxford professors I knew said he thought Grand Magisters drew power from First Realm," says Ange.

Starace smiles. "Every cheap magical expert claims to be drawing power from First Realm. First Realm is dead, Ange, the world has not seen its influence for the best part of three thousand years. I think the best theory is that Grand Magisters are multis, they draw from several Realms at once, only they're much better at it than most multis."

"I don't know," Ange says doubtfully. "There's a girl who works for Leventhal, Meisha Wing, she's a lawyer. She won't say it, but she's obviously a multi — she's blind yet she can still see in colours and emotions, and she's also a techno-mage."

"Ah," Starace nods. "Techno-mages are usually Eighth Realm, something to do with silicon that connects with Eighth. But blind sight... that's very rare. I'd have thought Fifth Realm, Fifth is more emotional, lots of telepaths are Fifth. Fifth and Eighth is an odd combination."

Ange nods. "She's very powerful, but it's a completely different feel than Leventhal. I don't know. Meisha's power just feels very clear to me, very obvious. Leventhal is... murky. I don't see how he can be a multi if I get so little from him. I mean, he's obscenely powerful. If he's drawing from multiple Realms at once, he should ring like a bell."

Starace frowns, thinking about it. "Well, you did always have the strongest sense of any of us. Like I said, Grand Magisters are a mystery, even to Ulani."

"Could I be a multi?" Ange asks.

"No," says Starace, smiling. "You asked this before."

"Yes but I'm different!" Ange insists. Starace sighs. "You said yourself I'm different. And there's Gia, he and I just have this connection, it's the strangest thing, right?"

"All Ulani are Third Realm," says Starace, with finality. "That's all. The Great Founding was done by magicians working for the Pope, it was all Third Realm magic Angelina. It simply won't work with anything else, and that's what makes us special. And as for Gia… dragon magic is even more mysterious than Grand Magister's. They don't play by our rules."

Ange sighs, and gazes at her coffee. Starace grips her hand. "Look, I know young people always feel they're different. They always feel left out and unusual. The thing is, it's normal to feel that way. You have a special gift, it's true, but it doesn't make you some kind of freak."

"So how many other thirteen year old girls have been groomed to be Master of House Ulani?" Ange retorts.

"Angelina. You're very special, it's true, but there have been special Ulani before. And truly, being a girl makes no difference, with magic." Ange is unconvinced. Starace's power is not *all* magic, he's huge. With swords, it does make a difference. "So how much will Leventhal pay you, with this job he's offered you?"

Ange frowns. "You're spying on me?"

"I'm the Master of House Ulani, I spy on everyone. Is it true?"

Ange shrugs. What's the harm? "There's a job," she admits. "It was an offer I couldn't refuse. Not much money, but the apartment's free."

"He is an interesting man, with an interesting organisation. You could learn from him."

Ange frowns. "But we're Ulani. We're not supposed to be friends with any magicians. They hate us."

"And where better to learn about your enemy than at his side?"

CHAPTER SEVEN

Ange gets off the Leventhal Building elevator at the lowest level, well beneath the car parking. There are Leventhal Holdings people everywhere, all in their best suits, the men with red handkerchiefs in their jacket pockets, the women with flowers. They hustle in the wide hallway with bright bouquets, or bottles of champagne, and talk on their phones, coordinating movement.

Ange walks along the hall, seeing more of these groups lined up against the wall, rehearsing names and double-checking pictures on their phones. Ange wears her best black dress — side cut so that the diagonal hem leaves her left leg more exposed than the right, and high, soft leather boots. The jacket is a nicely cut number with a belted waist, and silver embroidery that she found on a Fifth Avenue stroll two days ago, and goes perfectly with the dress. Just because she's now an employee, doesn't mean she has to dress like the others. She's probably now the youngest employee for any big Mid-Town firm in all New York. God knows how they'll explain it to anyone on the other side of the shroud. She thinks they're hoping the shroud will encourage them not to ask.

"Angelina," says Michael Stanthorpe, directing traffic in the hall. He's looking particularly stylish in his pinstripes and a red bow tie. He looks her up and down. "Black is the new black, apparently. Very fetching."

Ange nods to the big steel reinforced doors beyond. They look more like something you'd find in a secure military facility than a New York tower basement. "Can I go in?"

"Oh Angelina, the inner sanctum?" Stanthorpe clucks his tongue. "I don't know. There are a lot of people arriving who won't be pleased to see you."

"I just want to see it. I've never seen a long-distance beacon before." Starace asked specifically if she could take a look. But she's *not* doing his bidding, she tells herself firmly. It was a friendly request. And she is genuinely curious herself. No harm done by looking.

Stanthorpe glances quickly about, to see who else is looking. "Look... just for you, Angelina. But only if you promise to be fast in and fast out. You are coming to the dinner tonight yes?" Ange nods. "Then you'll be seeing all these people anyway, it's not like Eli's keeping you a secret from them."

Lights above the big doors flash green, and the mechanism clanks open. A senior employee emerges, guiding two people in traditional Chinese robes, each carrying bouquets. Two junior staff walk behind, holding the new arrivals' overnight bags.

"Go on now," Stanthorpe urges, "hurry in!" And calls out, "One coming through, Sarah!"

Ange goes through quickly, and finds herself in a holding room with another set of doors before her. The door operator — Sarah — closes the big steel doors behind her with a clank, then opens the lighter doors ahead, with a misgiving glance at Ange.

Ange goes forward... and finds herself inside an enormous, silver plated cavern. It's huge and entirely spherical, perhaps thirty yards wide in any direction, like standing inside a giant silver ball. She's on a circular walkway that goes around the sphere's circumference at what would be the equator. The walls of the sphere gleam with metal plating, and protruding into the precise center of the sphere directly before her is the arm of a separate walkway, ending on a circular platform.

Above and below that platform, equally spaced, are big steel orbs, several feet wide, held in place by steel beams protruding from the giant chamber's north and south poles. Those orbs are glowing now, and beginning to crackle with dancing electricity.

To Ange's left, about the encircling platform, are more welcoming committees, each a senior Holdings employee with two juniors, waiting with bouquets. To Ange's right stand Leventhal himself, with Croz, and several others.

"Next is Lewis Adabe and his assistant," says Croz, reading off a computer pad. "Assistant is unnamed." And looks up at Ange. "What's she doing here?"

"Ask her," says Leventhal.

"What are you doing here?" asks Croz.

"Questo e quello," says Ange with a shrug. "Qua e là." Croz looks drily at Leventhal, who smiles. "How much power does it use? Does it draw from the main grid?"

"Oh this and that," Leventhal repeats what she just said. "Here and there." Ange smiles back. No surprise Leventhal speaks Italian. She supposes that if you live over two thousand years, you pick up a lot of things.

"We're back to full power," says an employee beside them, with a radio headset on his head. "Preparing to charge." He glances at Ange, as though wondering if they should do this in front of her.

"Charge," Leventhal confirms.

"Put the call through to Mr Adabe," Croz confirms. "Go when he's ready." Another employee puts in a call on her mobile. Suddenly the two orbs above and below the platform begin to crackle. Ange can hear generators whining, a great, building howl somewhere nearby. The crackling becomes intense. Blue lightning begins leaping between the orbs, engulfing the central platform.

"Mr Adabe confirms," says the woman with the telephone. Ange squints against the blinding light, as the crackle of artificial thunder echoes off the spherical walls. Suddenly a dark flash amidst the light, and smoke.

"Power down!" shouts the man with the headset, and the blue lightning stops, the generator howl winding down. On the platform, rising from a crouch, are a pair of African men — Mr Adabe and his assistant. Adabe wears a western business suit — his assistant, traditional African robes. Both men walk from the platform, a little shakily. The beacon is not a teleporter — the magicians have to do that themselves. The beacon merely guides them, creating an electrical charge so steady, and so plainly artificial, that it cannot be mistaken for anything else. Such a powerful beacon makes accurate teleportation possible, and relatively safe for powerful magicians, over many thousands of kilometers, by giving magicians something to aim at. Prior to modern technology, attempts further than a few hundred miles were usually fatal, however powerful the magician, due entirely to the difficulties of aiming. If they didn't materialise in solid rock, they could appear thirty thousand feet in the air, and suffocate or freeze before they even hit the ground. And contrary to popular mythology, magicians can't fly, with or without broomsticks.

Starace must have used a beacon like this to come from Milan, Ange thinks. She knows they're usually much smaller than this one, big enough for only one person at a time. This one is enormous, and the central platform looks large enough to hold six or seven. It must save an enormous amount of time, gathering magical people for large events like the one planned tonight.

"Mr Adabe," Leventhal greets his new guest with a smile, and shakes his hand.

"Mr Leventhal. An honour, as always."

"Mr Adabe, this is my personal assistant Mr Crosby. And over here is Ms Fueglo, who will escort you to your personal car, and will accompany you to the house and make certain all your needs are met for the duration of your stay."

Ange steps aside as Fueglo edges past to shake Adabe's hand, and present him with the bouquet. Abade notices Ange, and does a double take at her sword. And walks on, following Ms Fueglo's escort, the junior suits taking a carry bag from Adabe's assistant.

"You can go now," Croz tells Ange. "Before one of our guests thinks we're trying to have them assassinated."

"Bouquets," Ange chortles. "How very wizardly."

"Get out." Croz points at the doors, menacingly.

"Make me," says Ange.

Leventhal thumps his staff against Croz's chest to stop him from advancing. "Angelina," he says, "please recall that in any fight against my employees, you will be immediately immobilised."

Ange snorts, and looks Croz up and down. "It's the only chance they'd have," she observes, and turns to leave.

"Eli," says Croz, "disable that collar for just a minute. She needs to learn some manners."

"Angelina!" Leventhal calls after her. She pauses. "And remember that for the duration of this dinner, the collar will protect every one of my invited guests as well."

Ange rides her Ducati out to Queens, and parks in Jamie's driveway. She's wearing leather pants under her black dress, and a leather jacket over the top. The worst thing about the bike, however, is the helmet pressing down her always rebellious hair. She has to resist the urge to play with it now as she walks to Jamie's porch, as that usually makes it worse.

Jamie opens the door before she can knock, and greets her with a smile. "Hey, Angelina." He looks good in a suit and tie, and has a leather jacket of his own to wear over the top.

"Jamie please," she scolds him, "it's Ange." And kisses him on both cheeks, Italian style. Like a total geek he messes it up, and makes it awkward. Americans!

"So why 'Ange'?" Jamie asks. "Angelina's a nice name."

"You know what Angelina means?" Ange says sullenly. Jamie blinks. "Little Angel."

Jamie tries not to laugh. Ange wants to be angry, but finds herself grinning at his efforts. "I guess when you were a cute baby they didn't know how big you'd get."

"I got teased for it, I prefer Ange. It still means Angel, in French."

"Jamie!" comes a shout from down the hall. "Is that Angelina?"

"Yes Ma!" And beckons Ange inside with a wry smile, and whispers, "Just remember she's shroud-blind…"

"I know!" Ange whispers back with a scowl, then brightens to a smile as they reach the kitchen.

Jamie's mother is dark haired and pretty for a forty-ish woman. The kitchen smells delicious, of something baking, and Mrs MacDonald wears an apron. On a kitchen bench are the makings of cookie dough, and trays of fresh baked cookies.

"Oh Angelina!" she exclaims, coming over. "So nice to meet you…" and she makes a much better job of Italian-style kisses than her son. "My goodness, aren't you tall! And so pretty, you could be a model."

"I'm so glad everyone thinks so," Ange replies. It's the standard nice thing to say to a freakishly tall girl. If only they knew how completely unglamorous the lives of most tall girls are. "It's very nice to meet you Mrs MacDonald. This kitchen smells delicious!"

"Would you like a cookie? I baked them special, just for you."

"For me?" Ange is astonished.

"Mum," Jamie complains, looking embarrassed. "Ange is Italian, I'm not sure she likes cookies."

"Nonsense, of course I like cookies," says Ange, and selects one from the tray Mrs MacDonald holds for her. Jamie's discomfort is too much fun. She bites, and… "Wow! That's really good!" They really are delicious, all politeness aside.

Mrs MacDonald beams. "Well here then, take some more! Look, I'll wrap some up for you kids, it's a long ride to Connecticut. You'll get hungry."

Jamie has explained the plot to Ange — his mother thinks they're going to a dinner with Ange's uncle, who is wealthy, and lives in Connecticut. With the shroud-blind, lies are unavoidable, for the shroud is the biggest teller of lies there is, and is always believed. They talk for another five minutes, which is fun partly because Mrs MacDonald is lovely, and partly because the other part of the tale is that Ange is Jamie's well… not-quite-a-girlfriend. It's a second-date, as Jamie has told it, which if Ange thinks about it is sort of true. Hopefully this date won't see quite as many people trying to kill them as the first, but she's certainly not going to mention that to Jamie's mother.

"Sorry about that," Jamie says as they go to the bike. "She was kind of excited to hear I had a girl coming over…"

"Don't apologise for your mother," Ange scolds him, and gives him a light punch on the arm to go with the helmet. "I think she's wonderful, any boy should be lucky to have a mother like her."

"I know, she's great isn't she?" Jamie agrees with a grin as he examines the helmet. "She just comes on a bit strong, that's all."

"I'm Italian," Ange laughs. "Trust me, that's *nothing*. So are you safe out here?" Looking up and down the street, at rows of identical wooden houses and porches.

"Turns out I've had three Leventhal employees as neighbours for the past two years," says Jamie. "Eli's been keeping an eye on me."

"Ah." Ange doesn't think that sounds quite as nice as Jamie makes it.

"Say, this is a 916, yeah?" says Jamie, examining the bike. He doesn't like to dwell on questions of safety, Ange has noticed. Any conversation that might drift too close to old memories, and Tori, he quickly diverts. "I was too busy to notice the other time. Classic bike."

"Yeah, sorry about the pillion seat. I didn't buy it with passengers in mind."

"How much?"

"Twelve."

"Twelve thousand? You can afford that?"

Ange shrugs. "Sure. It's good money to be freelance Ulani."

"Man," says Jamie. "Everyone's got more money than me."

They talk about the bike for a few more minutes, then get on. It's not a particularly big bike, and for two riders at six-foot-one, it's going to be a bit of a squeeze. Amusingly, Jamie is a bit shy with his hands.

"You'll have to do better than that or you'll fall off!" Ange shouts above the revs of the engine. "Here!" She takes his wrists, and puts his arms more tightly about her middle. "Now tell me which way to go, because I have no idea how to get there!"

It takes them half an hour of riding through increasingly light traffic once they leave the Connecticut Turnpike at Norwalk. The final roads through rural Connecticut are pretty in the late afternoon, with sunlight and dappled shade falling through the trees. Ange sees cows on green pasture, and wonders if Gia is coming out here for food.

Jamie tells her to go left at a nice little town, and a mile further on she sees a big two-storey mansion on the left, with a European-styled slate roof amongst pretty ash and cedar trees. She slows at a turnoff, bumping on the gravel until they reach big iron gates. Two men on duty there recognise them and wave them through.

The mansion grounds are all manicured lawns and gardens, as pretty as any old European estate. There are many expensive cars parked in the big U-shaped driveway before the mansion's front columns, men and women in expensive clothes mingling, being greeted by Leventhal employees. Ange does not want to park her bike out front, and so takes the extended driveway around the back, where big rose gardens and stone pavings extend onto the lawns. Ange bumps across the grass, not wanting to leave the bike by the road where someone can knock it over. She parks on the edge of the rose garden paving, and they look around at more guests mingling, or arriving from cars parked further back.

"Have you seen an event this big?" Ange asks as they remove helmets and jackets.

"No," says Jamie, which surprises her. She'd thought this kind of gathering might be typical for Leventhal Holdings. "I've only been here a few times, Eli uses it for Shtaal meetings. But those were North American meetings, this is global."

There are a lot of foreign outfits, for sure. The Asian guests look especially striking, Chinese in their colourful silks, Indonesians in batik shirts, Japanese in kimonos. There are many Africans, with bright, less restrained colours. Indians in saris, kurtas and turbans. And many Europeans and Americans. Ange wonders if she'll find some old enemies from home, and is glad she brought her sword, even if the collar will prevent her from using it. Lacey had a teddy bear she still hugged for comfort, even at eighteen. Ange has 23 inches of Japanese steel.

"Hey look, it's Ren." Jamie points, and beneath an oak tree, Ange spots Meisha in a nice blue dress. With her is a young Chinese man with long hair in an old-style topknot, wearing a traditional long coat over a western suit, and a sword at his hip. "Meisha's boyfriend, he must have come with Master Yu. Master Yu is Jade House, they're…"

"…the biggest in China, I know," says Ange. "Hold my boots please?" As she pulls them off, then tries to wriggle out of her riding pants. Jamie watches with amusement. "Enjoying yourself?"

He grins. "Hey, if you want me to look somewhere else I will." Ange rolls her eyes, trying to make certain the dress comes down to properly cover what the pants leave bare. Maybe pants under a dress wasn't the best idea. "Here, give me a foot." She presents a foot to Jamie and he crouches to pull the pants off one leg at a time. His hand rests briefly on her bare thigh to do it, whether on purpose or by accident she can't tell... but suddenly her mouth is a little dry, and her heart beating harder. "Takes a long time with these legs."

"Shut up." But she's grinning, and struggles into her boots as Jamie gives them back, feigning impatience. "You know, you don't have to wait for me."

"Girls say that," says Jamie, "but I don't think they mean it."

"Oh, and you're an expert, are you?"

When she finally straightens, Jamie has put both jackets and her pants over one arm, helmet in hand, and presents his other arm to her. "M'lady."

Ange raises her eyebrows and takes it. It does seem the formal place for it. "Grazie mille," she tells him, and they walk along the garden pavings toward Meisha and Ren.

As they approach, Ren and Meisha kiss. "Maybe we shouldn't bother them," Jamie murmurs.

"Nonsense," says Ange, pulling him onward. Meisha turns as though hearing them, despite being thirty yards away, and waves. "Is my hair okay?"

"Why, you want to take another half an hour to fix it?" Ange elbows him hard.

"Hello you two," calls Meisha. "Did you have a nice ride?"

"Very nice, thank you," says Ange. Introductions are made, and Ren takes Jamie's helmet so his right arm doesn't get sore. Ren, Ange notes, is *very* handsome, with wide Chinese features and gentlemanly manners. His accent is broad New York, and she learns that he's as American as Meisha is. His Grandfather was Meisha's magic tutor, hired by Meisha's wealthy parents to nurture her gift. They became childhood best friends, before Ren won admittance to the Jade House Academy in China, run by the Yu family, where he has since become a favorite of old Master Yu himself.

"Must be hard, doing the long distance relationship?" Ange suggests.

"It is," Meisha sighs. "I see him so rarely these days. But we'll make a decision soon, I think."

"She should come to China," Ren says confidently. "Master Yu has great respect for her."

"I'm not Chinese, Ren," Meisha replies. "I'm American. As are you."

Ren makes a face. "These nations are just names. The names are new, but magic is old. Master Yu says magic is important, not names."

"Master Yu is an old fashioned Chinese gentleman," Meisha explains to Ange, grasping Ren's hand. "Old fashioned as in ninth century."

"He's not that bad," says Ren, smiling. "He's even accepting women apprentices now."

"After eleven hundred years of refusing, sure," Meisha says drily. Ren looks around as someone over by the rose garden waves to him.

"I'm sorry," he says, "I must go. Master Yu promised to introduce me to many people. Angelina, very nice to meet you. Jamie, so good to see you again." Jamie smiles, and looks uncomfortable. Ange guesses that the last time he saw Ren, Tori was probably present. Ren kisses Meisha goodbye and leaves with a wave.

"Well he's a bit dreamy," says Ange to Meisha.

"I know," says Meisha. "How lucky can a girl get? I mean, aside from him being on the other side of the world."

"Well take it from me," Ange assures her, "he looks good enough to wait for."

"Guys," says Jamie, "I'm right here."

"Oh poor Jamie," Meisha teases, "are you feeling neglected?" She grasps Jamie's arm, as Ange takes the other, and they walk back to the mansion. "Ange, I can't believe you missed an opportunity to bring your date on your dragon!"

"Hey," says Jamie, "in her defence, a Ducati 916's nothing to sneeze at."

"Well as I keep telling everyone," says Ange, "he's not my dragon, and he'd get very bored as my private taxi service. And secondly, he has this habit of stopping for fast food on the way, and then you end up covered in cow blood... it's not really that glamorous."

Someone stops Meisha, and she excuses herself to talk. "Jamie," she says as they part, "remember to take Ange around the front way, so you can be introduced."

"Introduced?" Ange asks Jamie as they continue on.

"They do things the old fashioned way here," Jamie explains. "You'll see."

At the front door a butler takes their leathers and helmets. Then, in the pretty little ante-room, they join the back of a short queue through the main inner doors. Everyone in the queue is a couple, as she was warned she'd need a date... and there's only one person at Leventhal Holdings she'd wanted to come with. Within the doors is a beautiful old central room with a very high ceiling. It has been arranged like a ball room, with many dining tables laid for a grand dinner beneath gleaming chandeliers and expensive wall paintings. It's milling with people, talking as a string quartet plays Mozart in one corner. Directly ahead, the queued couples stop at another pair of Leventhal aides, a woman with a computer slate, and a man with a very loud voice.

"Mr and Mrs Adams!" he bellows to the room, and there is some polite applause from more servants and aides who seem positioned to do exactly that. Mr and Mrs Adams nod gracefully, and enter the grand room to mix with the rich and powerful.

"Ah," says Ange. "Introductions. Very quaint."

"Mr Ali, and Miss Mirza!" bellows the man, and the couple before them sail off into the crowd to more applause.

"Why does the man get introduced first?" Ange asks as they step forward.

"Are you going to be difficult all night?" Jamie replies. The woman with the computer slate taps something, then shows the loud man the screen.

"Mr James MacDonald and Miss Angelina Donati!" bellows the man. All conversation in the room stops, and faces turn to stare at them. There is no applause from anyone.

"Yes," Ange answers Jamie's question, coolly. "Yes I believe I am."

People part before them as they walk, with dirty looks at Ange, and darkly curious ones at Jamie. All of Ange's good humour vanishes, as she feels the tingle of a hundred magical stares pressing in around her. She feels jumpy, like someone might try to put a knife in her at any moment, and her hand itches for a naked blade. Why on earth did Eli insist she attend this nest of vipers anyway? She'd only finally agreed because Starace had said she really ought to try fitting in, and because she hasn't been on a date in so damn long...

A man with a big smile and a different American accent intercepts Jamie, and shakes his hand, ignoring Ange even though she's standing right there. He offers to introduce Jamie to others, and Jamie looks to be thinking of excuses to get Ange included. "You go along," she tells him coolly. "You go be with your kind."

And she stalks off, adjusting the sword at her waist, searching for the ladies bathroom in the hope of fixing her hair. Out of the main room and down a hall she finds a bathroom and enters. It's full of over-dressed women, crowding the mirror. Conversation dies as she enters. Ten pairs of dark-rimmed eyes stare at her beneath a thicket of false lashes and elaborate fringes. The air smells so thick with perfume it's hard to breathe.

"Ulani bitch," one mutters, turning back to the mirror.

"'Strega omicidiala," Ange replies, taking her place at the mirror's edge. The woman there leaves rather than rub shoulders with her, as though she's toxic.

"I beg your pardon?" another woman insists. "What did you call her?"

"I called her a murdering witch," says Ange. "Because that's what you all are." Most of them leave, with a clatter of heels and a storm of dark stares and muttered curses. Suddenly Ange has the mirror mostly to herself. She smiles drily as she takes her new comb to her hair, thinking how many other women would love to have this mysterious power of hers, to get the ladies bathroom all to herself on a busy night out. Or mostly to herself.

"You stay away from that boy," says one of the two women who remain. She's American too, but again Ange can't place the regional accent. California, maybe? "He's a good boy, and his sister was one of our best. He deserves better than the likes of you."

"I think he can decide that for himself," says Ange. "He's not your pet."

"You're one to talk, with that collar around your neck," the woman sneers. "You're Eli's pet bitch but you still walk around like you own the

94

place. Why he didn't just stamp on you like the vermin you are, I'll never know."

"Alexis," says her companion, a younger woman, more over-dressed than most. "Alexis, she's not worth it."

Alexis… and suddenly Ange places the face and name. Alexis Rhodes, the CEO of Blue Sky Mutual in Philadelphia — Michael Stanthorpe has taken some time to explain who all of Leventhal's key allies are in America. Rhodes is unofficially ranked number three, a powerful magician who would certainly be far more powerful than any magician in Italy, and probably in all Europe. But American money, and proximity to Leventhal, brings her here.

"There was a big company in Rome," says Ange, brushing her disagreeable fringe. "*Illustre*, they sold insurance, they looked and talked a lot like you. All Shtaal Alliance, I'm told they're the good guys." With dry irony. "Respectable business people, employing thousands, donating millions to charity. They were friends with all the politicians. Then the Ulani discovered they were using one of their charities to do transfiguration experiments and organ harvesting on homeless people. We stormed them, and we killed all the leaders we could find. One of them got away. She's still alive, and I regret that every day."

"You think you're scary with that collar on?" Rhodes snorts. "We know what it does, you're like a dog with no teeth."

Ange stops brushing and stares down at her. "Teeth don't grow back," she says dangerously. "But collars one day come off. And I'll remember you."

Rhodes glares, and storms out, her younger assistant following. "Don't go in there," Ange hears her say to someone on the point of entering. "There's a *terrible* smell." Ange goes back to brushing. Just a few more hours, she tells herself. Just try not to kill any of them for a few more hours…

A stall behind her flushes, and Meisha appears. She puts her cane on the bench beside Ange, and washes her hands. "Not all of us are murdering witches Angelina," she says quietly. Her glasses are on her head, her sightless eyes unfocused in the mirror, and obviously upset.

Ange does not want to reply honestly. She knows she'll regret it, and she does not wish to hurt Meisha. But neither can she stand to censor herself, on something she has seen so much of, and feels so strongly about. So many horrors, so many atrocities, by those who abuse their power simply because they can.

"Most, Meisha," she replies. "Most that I've seen."

Meisha's lips purse thinly, and she makes a gesture with her hands, and murmurs something. Ange feels a tingle, then a flash of warmth, and her hands are dry. Meisha takes her cane, and taps to the door. A squeal of hinges, and Ange is finally alone. She exhales hard, and leans on the bench. Come to the expensive party, Angelina. You'll have fun, Angelina. Should have brought Gia, she thinks. *Then* I'd have fun.

An hour later it is dark outside, and the social mingling continues. Ange sits alone at her table, sipping the sparkling fruit juice that is all the waiter will serve her, in spite of her request for wine. And probably a good thing, she thinks darkly, given that she does not truly want to have impaired judgement or reflexes here. She does not want to lose her hearing either, so she can't listen to music to pass the time. She browses the internet on her phone instead, and reads about '21 Ways to Know that He's Really Into You.' One of those 21 should surely be that he doesn't abandon you at parties, and she hasn't seen Jamie all night.

Someone stands at the seat beside her, and her hand goes to the hilt of her sword without even looking. The newcomer gives her a very strong tingle. "Miss Donati," says a deep voice, and she looks. An older black man, wearing a hat indoors, with sunglasses on top. "Mulberry Watson. I run Accord Entertainment. You might have heard of Velvet Records."

Ange nods. "I've heard of you. You signed Crew-Z and Alicia King, yes?"

Mulberry smiles. "That's the one. May I?" In Ange's opinion there hasn't been another great pop artist since Prince, and most of what she listens to, other teens haven't heard of. But talking to a guy who signs pop stars and funds TV shows and movies seems like more fun than the rest of her night so far. Mulberry Watson is Leventhal's number two ally, she recalls from Stanthorpe's lectures, and even more powerful than Alexis Rhodes.

"Sure, why not?" she says. Mulberry sits, and looks completely unbothered by her reputation. The strong tingle gets stronger. "I had no idea before I joined Leventhal Holdings that the head of Velvet Records was a magician."

"A magician's life has been good experience for dealing with singers and actors," he says, leaning back in his chair and crossing one leg on the other. He's very laid-back, and speaks slowly, with purpose. His voice is musical, almost hypnotic. "The other day a young rapper demanded more money, because he was the 'biggest thing since Eminem'. Unfortunately I couldn't tell him that I briefly managed Beethoven, when he and I were friends in Vienna in the year eighteen hundred. And Ludwig van Beethoven was certainly bigger than Eminem." Ange can't resist a smile. "Now you're far too pretty a young lady to be sitting here all alone. Where did your date run off to?"

"I've no idea," says Ange. "He was ambushed as soon as we came in. I gather he's quite famous, though no one will tell me why."

Mulberry smiles, selects a half-empty wine glass from the table and sips it. "Tori and Jamie were the talk of the town. Magical twins, you see. It's quite rare. Tori was quite outstanding, James a little slower. But sometimes boys, you know, we take longer to develop. While girls can shine so bright so young." With a meaningful look.

Ange smiles warily. "And you didn't try to poach Jamie, once Eli let him go shroud-blind?"

"Ohhh," Mulberry drawls, with a slow shake of his head. "No, we don't poach from Eli. Eli is good, but Eli is also very firm on rules and etiquette. I won't even poach you, my dear, though I'd love to make you an offer. Word is you were Starace's favorite. Some say you still are."

This, Ange thinks, is not a man to be taken lightly. And he's fishing for something. "And why do you think we're here tonight?" Ange asks him.

"Something big," says Mulberry. "Something very big. I've not seen a gathering this large in a long time. And now, Eli recalls Jamie from across the shroud, and recruits you, a young Ulani who strikes fear into most wizards, but not Eli. I would say something is up, Miss Donati." He leans forward, and lowers his voice. "Do you know how Tori died?"

Ange gazes at him. She thinks she should really hear it from Jamie, and not go behind his back like this. But if she waits that long, she might be waiting months. "No," she murmurs, and leans forward herself. Mulberry smells of Old Spice aftershave, and cigar smoke.

"There is a research library," he says, in a low, quiet rumble. "Somewhere in the New York Library. It's magical, and only Eli's trusted few can gain access. Word is, Tori was doing some research on her own, some very advanced things that few fifteen year old magicians could dream of attempting. But while she was researching, someone broke in, and killed her.

"Now that library is one of the most heavily charmed locations in New York. Anyone with hostile intent, toward any member of Eli's inner circle, should have been detected. Even I, for all my age and powers, could not hope to enter that place with intent to murder. Which raises two possibilities. One," and he raises a finger, "it was an accident, and young Tori MacDonald was playing with forces she could not control. Given that she was under the direct tutelage of Eli himself at the time, this seems unlikely, as he would have known about it. Or two," and he raises another finger, "someone immensely powerful found a weakness in the charms. Possibly even Mayor Riley himself. But this too seems unlikely, as those charms are set by Eli, and Eli's magic is intensely sensitive to other Grand Magisters, and Riley is the only one of those."

Ange frowns at him. "So if neither of those is likely…"

Mulberry raises his eyebrows, and shrugs. "A great mystery. And this mystery is a part of the reason young James is now so famous. Everyone loves a mystery."

"Except Jamie," Ange murmurs.

Mulberry nods. "Except poor Jamie. They were devoted to each other, Tori and Jamie. He was just devastated to lose her. He blames himself to this day for not being there. Some losses cannot be made right with time. Even magic cannot return a missing limb." Ange thinks of Lacey, and grasps the peace symbol at her throat.

Dinner is long and expensive, with many courses. Jamie returns, but looks subdued, even moody. Ange wonders what the people he's been talking to have been saying. He stabs at his food, and makes only a little conversation. With her senses under assault from this many magicians, Ange's mood is little better, and they eat far more than they speak.

Finally Eli stands from his table, and bangs his fork against a glass. The room quietens to the chimes.

"Greetings to you all," he announces. He has a strong voice for a smaller man, and his speaking manner is animated and assured. Ange wonders if he's ever been an actor, he has that knack of projecting himself to fill a large room. "And what a pleasure it is, to see so many of us here together, in this great alliance to preserve all that is good and great about our magical world, beneath the one roof tonight.

"Many of you may have guessed that there is only one matter that could cause me to invite such a great assembly. I know you all have your busy lives and interests to attend to, and there are other, simpler forms of communication. But tonight, I have a matter that I feel can only be addressed by a full house in person, face to face. And that matter is of course a matter of Realm Law."

A knowing murmur of voices about the ballroom, with many soft 'I told you sos'. Ange flicks a glance around her table. Aside from Jamie, they're mostly Leventhal people whom she doesn't know. They watch Eli curiously. Grand Magisters don't make pronouncements on Realm Law very often. Some are recording Eli on their phones. Ange wonders if the shroud will erase the footage.

"Now a lot of you know," Eli continues, "that I was good friends with the great Ashkir. For you youngsters who've been busy watching shroud-blind TV instead of studying…" he pauses for chuckles, "…Ashkir was a great Somali wizard, who died in 1061. It was he who defined the Twelve Great Realms as we understand them today. Now I know there's still some in this room who will argue about that… I urge you youngsters, don't listen to them." More chuckles. It's obviously an old argument. "Ashkir was a genius. He was alive, as near as anyone could get him to say, since at least fifteen hundred BC. Egyptian Empires, Greek Empires, Persian Empires, he saw them all. He rode with Alexander the Great, as a younger man. He studied with the great old magicians of the age. And in his later years, he devoted himself to defining the different Realms of magic.

"You see previously... and I am old enough to remember this quite well... we didn't know there were twelve. It was debated. We knew there were different kinds of magic, but we didn't know the system by which those kinds all worked, and related to each other. But Ashkir applied scientific principles, when science was still this crazy new idea arising in Europe. It's hard to make scientific principles work in magic, but he managed it. And he simplified all the existing law of the day, and organised it into what we know today — twelve Realms, three for the receptors, five for the magicians, two for the passives, and two vacant. Since then, of course, Third Realm was converted by the Ulani from a vacant Realm into a receptor Realm, to become their exclusive domain."

About the room, dark looks fall on Ange, and soft muttering. How the Ulani did it is one of the magical world's greatest ongoing mysteries. Starace has always told Ange that not knowing how it was done, and continues to be done, only makes the Ulani more unpopular still. "The Realms' strength waxes and wanes," Eli continues, "and when one advances, the other recedes. Now we know how to recognise their powers, and how they work to oppose each other, like magnets of different polarity.

"Some of you may also have heard that Ashkir wrote a prophecy." He gazes around at them all, champagne glass in hand. Everyone has heard of the Ashkir Prophecy. "His prophecy was, that as different magicians of different Realms continued to fight, then eventually their numbers would thin. You see, magic requires a sender and a receiver. There is the Realm, an alternative dimension we lack the language to describe. And there is us. People. Magicians, receptors, passives. The sighted three. Ashkir said that eventually, the power of the Grand Magisters would become concentrated among too few of us. Magic needed a diversity of power at this end, he said. The human end. Eventually, he predicted, that diversity would end, and magic would end with it. The bubble would collapse, the connection broken.

"Everyone laughed at him. Many still do. At the time, there were hundreds of Grand Magisters... though perhaps none quite as powerful as now. With passing years, there were fewer. Today, there are two. We all know who is most recently responsible for this reduction." Growls of agreement from those listening. "Though Mayor Riley wasn't the first Grand Magister to start killing other Grand Magisters. He's only been the most recent, and the most skilled.

"Lately, I have been feeling a great change. I have spoken with many of you about this. The most powerful of you have felt it too, and agreed — Realm Shift is upon us. Sometimes the Realms rearrange themselves. Those once ascendant, take a decline. Some swap polarities. Those who draw power from Sixth Realm today, are happier than those drawing from Eighth Realm." Nervous smiles, and sideways glances.

"What I have invited all of you tonight to hear, is that I disagree with this assessment!" He raises his voice, and the room is hushed. "This is not Realm Shift. What I feel approaching, is Realm collapse!" Gasps. Hands go to mouths. "My friends, it is my most learned conclusion that my old friend Ashkir the Great was correct in his most controversial prophecy! Magic as we understand it, is in decline! And at the present rate of decline, we have but five years left, until magic upon this Earth disappears for good!"

CHAPTER EIGHT

In the pandemonium that follows, Ange finds a quiet corner to stand in, and watches the show. A cluster of great magicians, heads of formidable houses, stand in a circle about Leventhal and argue, with much waving of hands and red-faced agitation. A few women are sobbing, comforted by their shell-shocked friends. Many others have stormed out of the ballroom, while others sit alone and look stunned, or talk in furtive, horrified groups.

Ange thinks it's the most entertaining thing she's seen in her life. All of these power-mad fools, about to lose their powers. It's hysterical. They're hysterical, with their tantrums and nonsense. It serves them all right, and she stands for the better part of an hour, a drink in hand and sneaking desert snacks from abandoned tables, just watching the nervous breakdowns. A few times she takes out her phone to film them, when a particularly funny outburst occurs — a man kicking chairs, or a woman throwing her shoes at a waiter who dared offer her a drink at the wrong moment. What children, the lot of them. And she wonders why Eli chose to break it to them like this, all at once, rather than quietly behind the scenes, as magicians usually would with any big news.

Eli manages to free himself from the arguing group. Shortly after, her phone buzzes with a text — it's Meisha, summoning her to an upstairs room. Ange finishes her drink, and strolls that way.

The room is at the end of a long hallway, and is guarded by a pair of magicians with official-looking staves. Within the doors, she is surprised to find a grand bedroom, and that instead of the large gathering of Leventhal employees she'd imagined, it is only a few of them. Leventhal sits by a window with his cane, while Meisha sits on the edge of the huge, four-poster bed. To her left by the door is Croz, scowling at everyone, while Michael Stanthorpe argues with Leventhal. Stew Bickel is also here, looking very uncomfortable in his dinner suit. By Leventhal's shoulder is a woman Ange does not recognise — black and heavy-set, with her hair in corn-rows at the front, and braids at the back.

All conversation ceases when Ange enters, Stanthorpe backing away from his conversation as though worried he shouldn't speak in front of her. Ange eyes them all warily.

"Angelina," says Leventhal. "Have you seen Jamie?"

"No," she says drily. "And it's odd, because we were getting along great as we usually do, and then some magicians took him aside and said some things to him, and he's barely spoken since."

"Eli what's she doing here?" Croz growls.

"The same thing you're doing here," says Eli. "Or Jamie, when he gets here. I want people I can trust."

"You think you can trust *her*?" Croz looks astonished. "A week ago she tried to kill you!"

The door opens again before Eli can reply, and Jamie enters. "Um, hey," he says uncertainly. "Got caught up." Ange puts her back to a bed post and looks at him suspiciously. Jamie won't meet her eyes, and stands near Croz by the door.

"Eli it was reckless to announce it like that," Meisha says quietly. "It's going to go around the world now, and it'll be chaos. Everyone's upset." Ange smiles darkly.

"It had to be done," says Eli. He looks watchful, not upset, not even especially worried. As though judging them, to see their reactions. Is he doing that to everyone? Is that what he's up to — seeing who's with him and who isn't? "If I only tell the other Masters, they'll keep it quiet and do their own thing in private. Powerful magicians are dangerous when they're frightened. They need others to keep an eye on them. Better that everyone knows, and all at the same time, so we can all keep an eye on them together."

His hard stare settles on Ange. For a moment, his eyes bore into her.

"Eli, you know the problem as well as I do," says the black woman that Ange does not recognise. "This could be reversible. You know the magical theory as well as I do, how they say we could shift the primary magical influence upon this Realm from the current twelve Realms to some alternative set…"

Eli slams his cane down on the floorboards, and the whole room shakes and booms like the inside of a drum. Dust clouds down from the ceiling. Everyone stares. "Not while I'm alive," he pronounces, in a very clear, dark voice. "The risks are catastrophic. You know them as well as anyone Shawna."

So this is Shawna DuBois, Ange realises. Leventhal Holdings' effective second-in-command, named by some as the third-most-powerful magician in New York. Her nickname is 'Smiley', because she almost never does.

"Many will insist that we try," says DuBois. "Eli we're talking about institutions that have lasted thousands of years. Entire histories and traditions that…"

"You talk to *me* about histories and traditions?" Eli retorts. "Magic had the potential to be the light of hope for the world. For a while I believed in that too, but then came Riley, and all of his kind. He wasn't the first, I know, but he is the most skilled, and the most ruthless. This development will destroy him. And it will destroy everyone else as well, or everyone magical, myself included. But it will all be worth it, if it removes Riley and all of the Togova from the face of this planet, and leaves the rest of its inhabitants in peace."

"Eli." Croz appears to be struggling with powerful emotion. Ange is astonished. "Eli, you'll die."

"So what!" Eli demands. "So what! I never planned to live this long, I thought it would last as long as it lasts, and I'd be happy to go when my time was done. But Riley shows no sign of dying, he's younger than I, and he ages more slowly. At our current rates I'll be gone in a few centuries anyway, and he'll still be here. Possibly for many centuries more. Possibly for a *millennia.*"

He stares about at them all. "This is my one true chance to be rid of him. I've tried to face him in battle, I've tried to move great armies against him. But his defenses are always too strong, and his armies are somehow always more powerful. We cease fighting, and everything around us is destroyed, while only us two remain standing. He intends to out-wait me, you know? What's a few hundred more years to Riley, when the reward is a thousand years free of any challenger, and happily killing any new threat who looked to rise to his level before they came of age? This is my one chance to realise my dearest dream — a world without Riley, and without the Togova. And I will not squander it."

"Even if you bring the entire magical world down with him," Stanthorpe says drily.

"A net victory Michael," says Leventhal, with a jab of his cane. "And you know it."

Two thousand years old, Ange thinks as it dawns on her. Leventhal is so old that when the magic stops, so will he. Magic is his life support, and Riley's. And every other magician who has dramatically outlived a normal lifespan. He's not just announcing the end of magic. He's sentencing all of the most powerful magicians in the world to death, and demanding that they do nothing to stop it.

"That's why you recruited me!" she exclaims, staring at him incredulously. "You're about to declare war on the entire magical world! You're looking for people you're sure will stand with you, because you think most of your trusted allies are going to stab you in the back!"

Silence for a moment. Eli watches her. Watches them all.

"You'll lose your powers too," says Bickel from behind her. "We all will, receptors, passives, magicians, everyone."

Ange shakes her head with an angry smile. "I don't care! I wouldn't *need* these powers if there weren't so many evil wizards who needed killing! I'll get a job and have a nice life like most ordinary people. I don't *need* to be special."

"Amen," says Jamie, and Ange turns to him. He looks uncharacteristically serious, leaning against the wall with chin in hand. "Damn right." Ange smiles at him, and he smiles back.

"They won't all turn on us," says Eli. "We will find allies. But there will be dissenters. I believe that we can find enough supporters to keep the alliance strong, and prevent Riley from any great magic to shift the alignment of the Realms. He's sure to try, and by my best judgement, he's far more likely to kill us all than succeed. But Riley would much rather the whole universe die than he lose power. We must prevent him from the attempt.

"I need to know who else is with me. You must declare yourselves now, so that I know. Many who I had previously relied upon will now find their judgement compromised. I know I ask much of you."

His gaze settles on Meisha, who sits quietly on the bed, looking sad. For Meisha, no more magic will mean no more sight. Eli has been given a death sentence, but Meisha has been sentenced to life in the dark.

"Oh Eli don't be silly," she sniffs. "Of course I'm with you. You wouldn't have invited me here if you didn't already know it." And Eli smiles at her with real affection.

"Same," says Croz, his voice tight. Croz is an orphan like her, Ange recalls. For him, Eli is the father he never had, and is now about to lose.

"Sounds like a fight," says Bickel, laid-back as always. "I'm in."

Ange looks at Jamie. He must be something quite special that Eli invited him here, for this. Just looking at him, she receives another sharp tingle, like goosebumps up her skin. "Hell yeah," he says. "I can handle being normal again. If we'd always been normal, Tori would still be alive."

Stanthorpe takes a deep breath. "Well if everyone's going to plunge head first off the cliff, fashion demands I join them. And I'm nothing if not fashionable."

Eli turns to look at DuBois. "Shawna?"

"Of course Eli," says DuBois. "I'm with you." Eli takes her hand, and squeezes. DuBois is a long lived magician also, though nothing on the scale of her boss. This end will be hers as well, though she might get another decade before the ageing truly kicks in. It's a lot to give away, when you were expecting centuries.

Everyone looks at Ange. "Well," says Ange. "Mr Leventhal. *If* you're completely serious, and this isn't some kind of wizardly trick…"

"No trick," Eli says sombrely.

"…then I have completely misjudged you," Ange finishes. "That was stupid of me, and I apologise. I was born with these powers, but I've never yet found a cause I can really use them for. Until now. *This,* I can fight for."

She walks before him, unslings her sword, and kneels to bring herself just below eye-level. For the first time, Eli looks faintly amazed. Ange puts her scabbard point down on the floor between them. "My sword is yours," she says fiercely. "Tell me what to do."

Eli's first task for Ange is to work on the security detail for the big court case that's been dominating Meisha's days. The City versus Leventhal Holdings, it's called, and the details escape her — save that Mayor Riley's people say Eli didn't pay his taxes properly, and Eli's people say he did, and now it's going to court. Ange doesn't really understand what this has to do with a long running war between the world's two most powerful magicians — after all, how much damage could a win for Riley cause, in a court? Eli Leventhal is the other most powerful magician, and that ruling would hardly strip him of those powers, right?

Nonetheless, she gets up early, does a few hundred sit-ups, pushups, planks and others, then goes for a dawn run around Central Park, which at her speeds would certainly set Olympic records against the men. Then she stretches, showers, and catches the subway south.

The train is full of early morning commuters, heading to the financial district in suits, checking their phones, sipping their coffee. None look at her, meaning those who aren't shroud-blind are doing a good job of hiding it. Ange hangs on a support pole and scrolls her messages — she's on the Leventhal message service now and there's an endless stream of them. A magical artefacts seller in the Bronx has been broken up for selling dangerous charms, anyone having bought one is advised to hand it in to senior management after one trinket turned a girl's pet cat into a hellbeast that tried to eat her neighbour. This message is followed by a helpful note from Michael Stanthorpe, who handles most personnel issues — **transfiguration is dangerous kids! Don't turn your pet cat into anything the Marine Corp couldn't kill without magical help!**

Another message says that love potions are not allowed on company property, after several 'improper incidents'. Ange now knows what Leventhal office workers must gossip about in their lunch hour, the mind boggles. Yet another message advises employees not to feed the pixie that has somehow gotten into the tower ventilation system. Which is actually less funny than it sounds, because what gets called a 'pixie' as shorthand could actually be any number of transfigurations gone wrong, magicians have been messing with new forms of life for so long they've created all kinds of nasty spinoffs, many of which should never have been created. A lot of them are so old, like dragons, that no one can remember who created them.

At a dark tingle, Ange looks up from her phone, and sees a cloaked figure at the end of the carriage. The face is invisible within the folds of a hood, save for a bony jaw, and sharp fang protruding past a lip. The dark tingle gets worse. Ange gives the hooded figure a look of deadly contempt, and goes back to her phone. Of course they're watching her. In places where Ulani are unwelcome, 'they' always do.

She gets off at Canal Street, as all Leventhal employees know not to use the subway south of that. South of Canal is the Mayor's territory, save for some isolated pockets. Leventhal's people are fairly safe in most parts of the city, but unlike most powerful magicians, Riley is not concerned with territory. One small part of the city is all he reserves for himself and the Togova alone — Canal Street down to Battery Park and everything in between. Down here, every Leventhal employee watches their step, and never ventures at night.

A brisk walk down Broadway brings Ange to the courthouses opposite little Foley Square, and she trots up the huge stone steps and waits for security to scan her. They do, and the metal detector shrieks and hollers at the sword on her back. But the guards wave her through, because in yet another amazing oddity of the shroud, the shroud-blind won't hear the detector if the object causing it is magical. But others in the huge lobby do hear the alarm, suited figures against a wall, watching the people who enter and talking into mobile phones. Ange feels the tingles coming at her from everywhere as she walks through the traffic, and wonders what it is about the profession of law that draws the magical like moths to a flame. Or like flies to manure, Starace had once put it, and she smiles as she searches the signs for her courtroom.

She finds it upstairs, with lawyers gathered against a wall by the waiting courtroom door. There's no robes here like she might have expected in London or Rome, just suits and briefcases, and a lot of people talking and exchanging papers. Ange sees Meisha, minus her sunglasses, and heads for her.

"Ange!" says Meisha, as though genuinely pleased to... see her? She's not looking at her, but just past her, disconcertingly. "Good you're here, this is Wallace, Emily, Ashton, Rani and Mujiber — guys, Angelina." Ange exchanges polite greetings with the wary lawyers.

"So, um, what do I do?" Because she truly has no idea. She's seventeen and she's good at swinging a sword, but most of what she knows about the law comes from watching TV shows, or hanging out with people who've been in jail. In her work, it happens.

"Well," says Meisha, rummaging in her briefcase for more files, "we've got a guy coming in today who's kind of special. He's an independent expert and he's going to testify for us, that means he's a witness for the defence."

Ange nods sagely. "So... wouldn't I be better off staying with him?" she suggests. "I mean, if he's your witness, you don't want anyone to hurt him, right?"

"Oh no, we've got people looking after him," Meisha assures her. She finds the papers and hands them to a fellow lawyer. "But he's shroud-blind, you see, so it has to be discreet."

Ange frowns. "You're worried Togova would hurt a shroud-blind in this court? Wouldn't that be kind of obvious to the High Council?"

"Sure, they *would* prosecute Riley's people if they hurt a shroud-blind here, it's too obvious. But as I'm sure you of all people know very well, Angelina, there are other ways to get to the shroud-blind."

The underworld, she means. That means everyone unaligned with magical houses, which in practise means vampires, wraiths, werewolves, every nasty magical, inhuman or half-human creature going. The High Council only polices those who can be policed, and the underworld are rarely that. Meisha seems to be implying that using the underworld to kill the shroud-blind is the kind of thing only Togova would do — in Ange's experience both sides do it, and the High Council makes a show of investigating but ends up catching no one. But she doesn't think it's the time to mention that, given her ongoing argument with Meisha.

"Are you expecting an underworld attack in *here*?" Ange asks with disbelief. Everything looks far too civilised for that.

"Oh Angelina," Meisha says pityingly. "You really have no idea." Her phone rings. "Just sit in the visitors' gallery behind me, and I'll fill you in as we go." She answers the phone before Ange can ask further questions.

A further procession of lawyers comes up the corridor, and files past the waiting Leventhal group and into the courtroom. Ange stares. At least half of them are maugies — magical augments, or worse. Several have scales, and one is bright blue, walking openly through the court hallways, only seen by those with the sight. Which in this building, Ange thinks, might be about half. Here beside the blonde woman leading them walks a tall, thin humanoid with ebony skin with reflective hardness, and ridged brows like a humourless statue.

"That's a Chayavak," Ange murmurs to no one in particular. "They're telepaths."

"U-huh," says Rani, one of Meisha's companions. She's tall and brown, though not as tall as Ange, and wears an Indian-style nose stud. "They're originally Indian, the name comes from Hindi. Shadow Walker — Chaya Vakara."

At the tail of the group comes a hulking figure, with a huge barrel chest and a thick forehead. Red eyes glare within huge, curled horns to either side of his head, and his half-cloven feet are unshod. He stomps with a cane in one huge fist, and Ange smells something between burnt ash, and cow hide.

"They brought a stone demon to a courthouse," Ange observes flatly. "What the hell?"

As he passes, the stone demon glares at Ange, nostrils flaring… and the vision flickers, to reveal a bald headed, big-chested man, walking with a cane. This is the disguise, what the shroud-blind see — Ange sometimes gets glimpses of both the disguise and the real thing. Then back to the bull-headed beast, as he passes into the courtroom. Ange feels a shiver. She's never seen a stone demon before, and has no particular desire to get into a fight with one. She doubts her blade would do more than scratch that natural armour… and stone demons are smart, despite appearances, and use magic like magicians.

"He goes by the name of Marshal," Rani says drily. "Mike Marshal. He has the full resume, service in the marine corp, twenty years at law. It's all nonsense, the Mayor fixes it up for guys like him." Where do they all live when they're not here, Ange wonders?

She takes her seat on the left, in the visitors' gallery behind Meisha. She doesn't like that, she'd rather sit in the rear with her back to the wall, where she can view the entire chamber and not feel threatened. She also doesn't see how Meisha can tell her what's going on, given she's going to be paying attention to the case, and can't just turn around and chat with visitors.

All of the Leventhal people sit here on the left side, while the Mayor's wild array sits on the right. All up and down the aisle, opponents in the long magical war sit and glare at each other. Her phone buzzes, and she answers it. It's a message from Meisha, but when she opens it, the space is blank. Then writing appears.

It's a bit like the Cold War says the text. **All our forces on this side, all their forces on that side, we try to counter each other without actually firing a shot.**

The words appear as fast as speaking, too fast for even the fastest texter. Ange shoots a look at Meisha, but can see only the back of her head, as she calmly arranges files, fingers tracing on the labels in braille. Her phone is nowhere in sight. Ange texts back as fast as her thumbs can manage, which is pretty fast.

That you Meisha?

It says so on the phone, dummy. Better yet, this only counts as one text on my phone bill.

Ange grins. Meisha is a techno-mage, of course. She texts back. **Cool wat u want me to do?**

We want to know the second you sense any unusual magic. Emily can mostly block their telepath, Rani's the best with mind control, and we've got most of those angles covered. But you can sense magic that even we might miss, and today with a shroud-blind testifying, it makes us paranoid.

Because Riley's people will try to rig the trial, Ange realises. It's not a jury trial, so they can't just manipulate the minds of the jurors and cheat that way. But they could manipulate the mind of the judge, if no one stops them. Or they could do it to the people testifying, and make them say things they don't mean. Or they could transform evidence, or any number of things to change the outcome of the trial. But...

Y U have to win? she asks.

Because if Eli's found guilty he'll go to jail Meisha replies. **For quite a long time.**

And he'll go? Because he doesn't have to, Ange is quite sure. He's a Grand Magister, he can play this game of manipulation just as Riley can.

Yes. Meisha says nothing more. She can hear Meisha's accusation in that one word, telling Ange how badly she's misread him.

Ange selects a wide-eyed, astonished emoticon, then a smiley face, and sends. I'm amazed and pleased to hear it, that means. It's an apology, of sorts. And Meisha turns, and gives her a little smile. She hasn't touched her phone, Ange notes. She must be seeing these texts in her head. She remembers Meisha's painting, the colours and shapes. Meisha must really live in a world of her own, and if she can draw from technology, and 'see' those visuals spread across her own inner mind... wow. Rather than having a disability, Meisha probably notices much more going on in the world than just about anyone. No wonder Eli finds her so valuable.

Two hours later, Ange is hideously bored. Even the sight of a stone demon and his friends arrayed behind the prosecution in a New York courtroom can't make this interesting — all those exciting TV shows and movies are lies, she thinks, listening to one lawyer after another drone on about something so technical it might as well have been in Chinese. Then again, tax law isn't like a murder trial, maybe those are more interesting. Patience has never been her strong point, and if she has to listen to another hour of this, she'll eat her leg.

Stew Bickel gives some relief by sitting alongside. Ange rolls her head toward him, with a 'kill me now' look. Bickel smiles, as someone else from Response Division goes and taps Meisha on the shoulder, and whispers in her ear. Ange glances back, and sees Bickel's buddy Hernandez escorting a thin, bespectacled man to a seat before the row of journalists from Wall

Street Journal and business TV shows. Bickel and Hernandez are running personal security for this guy then. Meisha wasn't kidding when she said he was important.

Now Riley's team has noticed, glancing back at the new arrival. Ange sees some whispers and nods... and a flash of magic, a shiver across her right cheek, answered immediately by a flurry of defensive shield spells around her. Ange finds herself staring directly at Mike Marshal, the stone demon. The human-disguise smiles drily, seeing how she immediately looks his way. They're testing her, she thinks. She pulls up a leg to adjust her boot on the bench, allowing a glimpse of the throwing knife sheathed in there. The stone demon snorts, a sound like air from a bellows.

"Nice boots kid," Bickel whispers. Ange smiles... and abruptly feels something odd to her left. She looks. A young man sits there, his suit untidy, his hair a bit long with his fringe drooping on stylish spectacles. Looking at him, Ange is increasingly certain. There's a sense coming off him that's not quite right. A disharmony, like a painting where all the brush strokes are going one way, then in one small spot suddenly twist the other. Out of place.

She texts to Meisha. **Whose on my left?** She means 'who's', of course. Damn autocorrect.

Adrian Rampelly, he's one of us. He's a law student, came recommended from my old professor at Columbia, he's here to observe. Why?

Feels weird, strnge mgic. It's frustrating trying to keep up with Meisha, her thumbs rebel at trying to make all those letters, and given how she's often texting in and out of Italian, she's grown to despise and avoid English predictive text.

Oh he's got some unusual charm passed down from his grandparents. Peruvian I think, goes back to the Incas. Michael Stanthorpe looked at it, said it was different magic but no problem for us. Hmm. Well, thinks Ange, Stanthorpe is one of Leventhal's best. If he thinks it's okay, fine. Adrian Rampelly gets up and leaves, and the weird feeling fades with him.

At a pause in proceedings, Meisha stands. "Your Honour," she says, "at this point we'd ask the court's leave to invite our expert witness to the stand, Mr Christopher Mills."

The judge peers at his notes. His name is Melzer, and Ange thinks he looks scared. No guesses why. He swallows nervously. "Uh, Mr Mills, yes. From Mills and Associates, the accountants."

"That's correct Your Honour," says Meisha.

"Your Honour," comes Riley's head lawyer, Ellie Gold. She's blonde, with a pinched and pointy little face and a butt so skinny Ange thinks it must be painful to sit. "We'd like to call a ten minute recess?"

"Very well," says Melzer, and bangs with his gavel. "Ten minutes." He gathers his files and leaves in a hurry. Sighs and conversation in the court as the spell of proceedings is broken. Ange glances over her shoulder once more, and sees Mr Mills getting up with a word to Hernandez. Hernandez murmurs something into a microphone, and Bickel puts a finger to his ear.

"Bathroom break," he tells Ange. "You go, be discreet."

Ange gets up and edges past him, then strides along the aisle. Ahead, Hernandez is also rising, with a glance her way. On her left as she walks, Ange feels waves of dark magic, clutching at her. Ahead, several journalists watch her closely. She wonders how many of them are *not* shroud-blind, and if so, who they really work for. Fancy sitting in this courtroom, and not having any clue what's actually going on.

"He's got no clue what's going on," Hernandez murmurs to her as they walk together in Mr Mills' wake down the hall outside the courtroom. "He thinks I'm just a Leventhal assistant, not a bodyguard."

"Probably just as well," says Ange. "If he could actually see what's in there, he'd never testify."

"Oh he might," Hernandez mutters. "But not for us."

Ange gives him a sideways look. "Hard to work for the good guys, si?"

"So you think we are the good guys now?" Hernandez replies.

Ange smiles. "Touche." Since Eli gave his speech about being prepared to die to see bad magic vanish from the Earth, yes, she does. And if he tries to backtrack, she'll hold him to it, somehow.

Mr Mills vanishes into the men's toilets, and Ange and Hernandez wait outside the door. "Shouldn't you go in and check it first?" Ange suggests. A man in a cleaner's uniform exits the toilets as she says it, and gives a little nod to Hernandez. "Ah, got it." The cleaner strolls away, pushing his little trolley. "How do you keep spies alive here, on Riley's turf?"

"With great difficulty," says Hernandez. "But the judges are mostly with us, so it's not *that* hard. They're just scared."

"How are you going to explain following him to the toilets?" Ange asks as she thinks of it. "If you're not a bodyguard?"

Hernandez pulls a leather wallet from his pocket, and flips it open to reveal Mr Mills' drivers' licence. "He dropped his wallet." Ange raises her eyebrows — that's smooth work from a guy who looks as subtle as a sledgehammer. "I'll go in and return it to him, just give him a minute to do his business. Then I'll stay to do my business, and you follow him back to the courtroom, real casual."

Again, Ange gets that odd sensation, of something out of place. The sensation of Adrian Rampelly's Inca charm, Meisha said. But here? No, she recalls — he left, just after she mentioned it to Meisha. Did he come here? The bad feeling gets worse.

"Go in now," she tells Hernandez. He frowns at her. "Just do it!"

Hernandez sees the alarm in her eyes, and does so. No sooner has he gone in than Ange hears a yell, and feels a sharp flash of chills. She dashes after Hernandez, pulling her sword… and finds him before the urinal, confronted by a big, dark shadow, lifting a man one-handed in the air. The dangling man is Mr Mills. The dark shadow looks at them, and grins, a gleam of sharp white teeth, pointed ears and indistinct form. Blood drips onto Mills' shoes, and puddles on the floor. The shadow drops him, and he falls in a bloody, lifeless heap.

With a yell Hernandez produces a bladed staff from mid-air with a flash, and swings hard. The shadow blocks with an armoured forearm, and smashes Hernandez aside on the counter. Ange follows, and the shadow takes one look at her and teleports with a flash.

"Yeah you better run," Ange mutters, and crouches by Mr Mills. The shadow must have had a knife in that fist somewhere, because Mills is very dead, a horrible wound driving up into the brain. He looks astonished, as though just before he died, he caught a first glimpse of the thing that the shroud had denied him his entire life. What a thing to realise just before you die, Ange thinks. That your entire life has been wrapped in a lie.

"I got him," Hernandez gasps, crawling back to Mills, holding what are probably broken ribs. "I got him, is he okay?"

Ange gets up in a fury, strides to the toilet stalls, and smashes open the one shielding the strongest chill. Hiding within is Adrian Rampelly, huddled on the toilet seat. "Give it here!" Ange yells at him, and levels her blade at his neck. Rampelly whimpers, and fumbles in his jacket until he produces a jade amulet on a leather necklace, shaped like an eye. Ange snatches it. "What's the range? How far does it block?"

"I don't... I don't..." Ange puts the point to Rampelly's neck and prepares to run him through. "No! No please, I just... twenty yards! It's just twenty yards!"

"Figlio di puttana!" Ange races away, stuffing the charm into her pocket as she passes Hernandez, who is trying desperately to revive a corpse.

Out in the hall she passes Bickel on his way to help. "Ange what's wrong?"

"Twenty yards!" Ange yells as she runs. "He's right here, I can smell him!"

"Angelina!" Bickel shouts after her. Then, "Son of a bitch," as he runs after her.

Ange races along hallways, dodging lawyers, cops and others, sword in hand. Several guards see her running, and shout, drawing pistols. Ange turns a corner, hits the stairwell door and rattles down the stairs at speed. Shroud-blind guards and cops may follow for a while, but the shroud will reassert itself at some point, especially if she catches the shadow she's chasing. She just has to hope they don't shoot her first, this crazy woman sprinting through the halls of justice.

She exits on the next floor down, and stops, turning her head like a dog sniffing the air. Bickel nearly slams into her from behind, running from the stairs. "Twenty yard range," Ange explains, "he was on this floor or the one below, Rampelly's amulet broke the damn teleport barriers, gave him a way in."

"Ange he'll be headed basement," says Bickel, "there's nothing we can do to catch him here."

"Like hell there isn't." She ducks back into the stairwell.

"Angelina!"

Ange ignores him, and descends fast to the basement carpark. She runs between parked cars, slides over a bonnet, and hears cops yelling 'there she is!' and coming in pursuit. No matter, she can practically smell the trail ahead, slick and foul, and following it makes her skin crawl… yet she can't turn away. Ahead is a bank of elevators, with people standing and waiting. Ange hits the doors, slides her sword between them, then heaves them apart with raw strength. Waiting people exclaim, while those who can see what she is quickly back away. An alarm sounds, and the whine of a descending elevator halts.

Ange stares down into the empty shaft below… and gets a nasty, dark shiver. This is certainly it. "Angelina!" yells Bickel, catching up. "Don't go down there, it's suicide!"

"For you maybe," says Ange, and jumps.

CHAPTER NINE

She falls a few yards, then hits the concrete floor, and pulls a small flashlight from her coat. It's one of those things she's learned from long experience never to leave home without, and it lights the walls of the elevator shaft around her well enough. But one of those walls is not concrete, but a rusted sheet of metal. She grabs it, and it lifts away far enough to reveal a passage within. Before she can think twice, she squeezes inside, and the darkness engulfs her.

The tunnel within is small and dank. Ange has heard of the warren of tunnels under Manhattan, old subways, old and present utility trenches for power and telephone lines. Sewers, where the rats scurry and darker creatures lurk. But this tunnel looks nothing like those. This looks rough, with none of the machine-perfect edges of those man-made necessities. This looks like it was carved by hand, for a specific purpose.

She holds the flashlight against the sword hilt, which she grasps in turn with both hands. It's an improvised posture, one she invented herself in imitation of the cops on TV who entered dark spaces with flashlight braced beneath their pistol. It works similarly with a sword, though if she has to swing fast, she'll probably lose the light. She doubts that a pistol would be more than annoying against what she's chasing.

She's gone fifty yards before she notices the tunnel angling sharply down. Her footsteps and breathing echo, and her light dances disconcertingly against the shadow ahead. The air smells bad, thick and unpleasant to breathe. It occurs to her that this might not have been the smartest idea. She'd been half expecting Stew Bickel to follow her down here, do the chivalrous, crazy thing like the former Special Air Service guy he is, and back her up. But he hasn't, and Stew Bickel is no coward. Food for thought, perhaps.

Stone rumbles underfoot. There's a subway line nearby. Suddenly there's a hole in the tunnel floor ahead, and she pauses, and shines her light into it. A glint of water below. Then she hears something splash. A sewer?

She lies flat, and sticks her head into the gap, swivelling the flashlight around. Sure enough, she's at the ceiling of a sewer, and the smell is foul. A concrete footpath lies on either side of the trickling dark water below, and she swings down and over one-handed, dangles for a moment, then drops herself onto it, sword ready. Shadows leap away from her as she swings the light, but it's just the illusion of movement. She feels an unpleasant chill from ahead, and presses on, with increasing certainty.

Another sheet of rusted metal covers a patch on the sewer's side, and she pulls at it. It tingles her hand, charmed and probably invisible to any shroud-blind sewer worker passing by. This passage too seems rough. Too much work for picks and shovels, surely there are magic spells that can bore holes through rock? This rock looks like something has eaten a hole in it.

The tunnel widens out, and Ange sees a red glow. Soon the glow is strong enough that she can turn off the flashlight. The ceiling and walls arc apart, and become caverns, separated by natural stone arches. Red light casts shadows, glimmering as though from lava in the bowels of the earth. But these are not natural caves, she thinks, turning her head to look up and about as she walks. These arches were made to *look* like natural caves, as though whatever made them was nostalgic for an old home. Some jagged rock has been left overhead, to hang like stalactites. But who or what would build such a thing?

Several more steps, and she passes beneath a stone arch, and stops. Before her is a smooth floor, checkered black and white with tiles. Upon the cave walls are golden artefacts, picture frames of idols, candle holders, incense burners, flickering red lamps. Is this a... a place to live? Or is it what it looks like — a shrine to gods unknown?

Before an altar crouches a black shadow, with arms, legs and wings.

The wings are draped about it like a cloak, spread upon the tiles. Engraved on the altar before the winged figure is a single eye, full of menace. Ange has not seen its like before.

About her, in adjoining caverns, she senses movement. The shadows come alive with rustling wings and narrowed eyes. The kneeling figure slowly rises, wings pulled back to flow like a cape. It turns, and in its hand is an elaborate silver staff. The black of its shape is a coat of some kind. This is not some animal. This is intelligent, with religion and prayers, and weapons, clothes and decoration. The smell here is bad but not foul, alien rather than uncivilised. A thick and musty smell, like a city girl might smell entering for the first time a barn filled with farm animals. Cloying, almost overpowering.

The winged creature pulls a gleaming silver sword from a sheath within its cloak, and holds both staff and sword crossed before it. Crouched, with deadly intent. Ange backs up, sensing movement all around. There is only a faint tingle here, and the prickling of hairs on her neck is mostly adrenaline, and no small amount of fear. Whatever they are, they don't cast magic, they're just the product of it, like so much else in the world. Suicide, Bickel said, before she jumped down here. Yeah, she thinks, looking side to side as she backs up. There's at least twenty of them, and there are passages down these caverns that she cannot see, from within which comes further movement. Suicide, maybe. Blades gleam on all sides, and hooks, and other weapons. And black eyes, glinting.

She hits her flashlight on full power, and sees them flinch back, shielding their faces. Then she runs like hell. Claws and wings rustle and clatter behind her, a rush of fast pursuit, and she runs into darkness but for the lurching glare of her flashlight, then hits the metal sheet over the entrance and crashes it aside so hard she hurts herself. Then she's in the sewer, and running back the way she came… and here ahead of her come swarming a mass of different dark figures with weapons, coming at her along the footpaths. Behind her, black winged shadows crash through the protective metal plate, and she sees that the hole in the ceiling she came down from is the only escape.

She runs at it, straight toward the black wave before her, and glimpses crude armour, dried flesh with protruding bone, like corpses brought to life but with the speed of any living man… and she puts on a desperate burst of speed, and leaps straight up just as they reach her. She grabs the lip of the hole, and hauls herself up and over, standing just in time to be confronted face to face with a huge, snarling animal head with fangs the size of her hand.

Ange screams and lashes, stumbling backward and tripping on the lip of the hole. She rolls, and with a snarl the beast is on her, and she gets a cut on its jaw to save herself from fast decapitation, but is knocked sprawling and dazed by a blow from its paw. She rolls up as it comes at her again, and… wham! wham! wham! the tunnel erupts with the deafening sound of automatic gunfire. The animal shrieks and staggers, trying to turn but its hindquarters aren't responding. A dark figure approaches from behind, only a silhouette against Ange's flashlight that she dropped by the hole, and stands over the faltering animal with a heavy rifle to his shoulder. Two more earsplitting rounds, and the animal dies.

Ange stares at the suit, and the lean figure holding the gun. He has nightvision goggles on his face, protruding like alien antennae, and he's all business. "Stew?"

"You hurt?" asks Bickel. He didn't abandon her — he went to get his gear, like a true professional would. Probably in his car, god knows how he got it past the courthouse security.

Ange's heart is galloping fit to burst, and her head pounds in unison. Yes she's hurt, but not badly enough to mention, and with the adrenaline she can barely feel it. "No."

Scrabbling and scraping from back at the hole to the sewer. Bickel turns, and in the light of Ange's fallen flashlight, she sees the corpse-like creatures pulling themselves up, arms gripping the concrete, armour bolted straight through naked bone. Bickel pulls up his goggles, aims and blows one's head off. Then a second, pieces of bone spinning away. A third shot removes a skeletal arm at the shoulder, and its owner falls back through the hole. But more are replacing them, blocking the way.

"Use a grenade?" Ange suggests, suspecting he'll have some.

"A grenade in a tunnel is like a shell in a shotgun barrel," says Bickel, and picks off another. "We'd shred ourselves as bad as them. We're cut off, we have to go that way." He briefly indicates their backs, away from the courthouse. Deeper into the tunnel.

"You're kidding," says Ange. She's beginning to understand what this place is. It's another city, an endless warren of new and old tunnels, woven together to make a living space for all manner of horrors. This is why Riley doesn't take and defend more territory — he only needs this, because this is where his powerbase lives, underground. "We won't last five minutes down there."

"Oh, *now* that occurs to you?" Bickel blows another head off, and flips his goggles back down as that scrabbling horror takes Ange's flashlight back through the hole with him, plunging them into darkness. "Stay behind me, and fire this only in the direction I tell you to, understand?" Ange feels a pistol pressing into her hand, and she grabs it. "*Understand!*"

"Yes! Si, yeah, I got it."

"Let's go, back up."

Ange backs up, as Bickel fires round after round. The things coming through the hole make no noise aside from the rattle and scrape of bony limbs and metal on concrete, a sound like a hundred armoured rats running in the dark. Flashes from Bickel's rifle light the tunnel, flash-framing the scene, an increasing pile of corpses, glinting weapons, splayed limbs. Ange counts twenty shots before Bickel pushes past her and runs, and she runs after him.

She's blind now, following him by sound alone. Behind them, above the pounding of their boots and the gasping of breath, she hears the clank and rattle of pursuit.

"Left," says Bickel, "watch the fork." And she nearly hits the wedge between this and the forking tunnel to the right. From that direction she feels something chilling that makes her blood run cold, and is glad Bickel's gone this way.

After a few minutes of running, Bickel slows to a walk, and murmurs 'hold here' before stopping — a necessary precaution in case she runs into him with her sword. Ange crouches. There is no clatter of pursuit now, not even a distant echo.

"They're not chasing us," Ange murmurs.

"Yeah great," Bickel mutters. "That means we're now in the territory of something they're scared of."

"Can you kill everything down here with bullets?"

"Those are dakran, already mostly dead, all offence and no D. Dumb things can usually be blown away. The smart ones use charms and defensive spells, guns are less use. The really smart ones cast spells themselves. This way."

Ange follows in the pitch black, skin crawling at the thought of what might be out there, trusting only that Bickel's technology will see it first. Then a metal clank as Bickel steps on something steel.

"Ladder," he tells her. "It goes down. I'm first."

"Wait!" Ange hisses. "I need light, I'm a sitting duck up here if I can't see!"

"Use your phone."

"If I use it down here, I'm going to lose it. I need that phone, it's got stuff on it."

Bickel presses something small into her hand — a cigarette lighter. She flicks, and a tiny flame appears. Bickel shields his goggles, and she sees the hole in the ground, like a manhole shaft, and the ladder. "I'll call if it's clear."

He descends, rifle raised in one hand to keep clear. The hole looks like a tight fit. Ange stares around, at the few short yards of light cast by the flame in her hand. Something whispers nearby. The flame flickers. Fear stabs at her, and she forces it down desperately, swallowing against a dry mouth. She got herself into this, and fear is a luxury she can't afford. Typically, with her skills and confidence, the fear doesn't register. But down here… this is not her place. Down here there's no room to move, fight and swing, and she can't defend against what she can't see.

Something growls, and she looks down the tunnel… and sees nothing. A mad scamper of feet, closing fast, and she gets to her feet and takes a fighting stance, one-handed with the lighter out in front… and sees a charging shape enter that circle of light, big and catlike, coming at her like a bowling ball in a tenpin alley. Ange jumps and slides down the ladder, shouting a warning to Bickel below. Then her boots hit ground, and Bickel fires up past her as the big animal above snarls and thinks about coming down after her. Gunfire convinces it otherwise.

"Found out why the dakran won't follow us here," Ange says breathlessly.

"Come on." Bickel leads her down what looks like a proper access tunnel, with concrete walls and ceiling. The lighter goes out, and she flicks it again, desperate to see as the darkness crowds around. Again the ground thunders, a train going past real close. They reach a steel door, and Bickel fumbles with a lock. It doesn't work, and he backs off and kicks it, once and again.

"Here," says Ange, losing patience, and puts full force into a front kick as Bickel crouches aside. The door smashes open, and wind rushes in. It's a subway tunnel, and another train is approaching, a glare of lights and squealing wheels. It rushes past — there's three lines, all headed one way in Manhattan style, slow, fast and express lines to handle the crowds. "Shouldn't be too far to walk to a station," she shouts over the noise.

She steps out, and there is a narrow walkway along the wall, relatively safe from trains. "Right," says Bickel, and she turns that way. And freezes, as winged shadows drop from holes in the tunnel ceiling, and land with evil grace across the tracks. Another train approaches, lighting wings, limbs and gleaming weapons in silhouette. "Dammit," says Bickel, and puts five rounds into one, with no apparent effect. His magazine clicks empty. "Reloading!"

The shadows sprint at them. Ange parries the first and spins fast to slash him from behind, then blocks a second with force that slams her into the wall. She bounces, loses her footing and rolls. Slashes at another's leg, then rolls again as a polearm stabs the place where she'd been. She dodges around a signal pole, parries another, drives a boot into a leathery midsection, uses that body as shield from another while surprising a fourth with a lunge and cut across his face.

And a horrid glare and blaring horn tells her she's fought directly into the path of the next train, and flings herself aside in the wind of its passing. An attacker stabs at her as she rolls up and sways aside, grabs the spear and throws it and its wielder straight into the train side. The winged shape bounces off in a spinning contortion of wings and broken limbs. Ange backs up to the far wall, yet another train coming, the shadows flapping aside. One lands on the wall above her head, and climbs down at her like an insect. That's not fair.

She sprints across tracks, back to Bickel who has abandoned his rifle and is now fighting with his bladed staff, fending off four of them and having less success than her. Ange drives her blade through one's back, pulls clear and spins low to take her beneath another's retaliation, taking his leg off in the process. The others flap aside, shrieking.

"Go!" yells Ange at Bickel, who runs up the tunnel without having to be told twice. Shadows flap, run and leap after them, spreading across the tracks as Ange runs half backward, trying to keep them away. They're wary of her, and she pulls the pistol from her pocket to make them moreso, but bullets they see coming have no effect, she can see them flashing as they strike shield spells and disintegrate.

Bickel finds another hole in the wall and scrambles through. Ange turns to follow and glimpses a shadow flying straight at her, and raises her blade just in time to be pinned against the tunnel wall, fighting desperately against the thing's inhuman strength to keep its sword from her throat. Then she recalls her pistol, and puts it up under the thing's chin.

"Block this!" she snarls, and blows the top of its head off.

Then she's half running, half crawling through a low tunnel, whacking her head on the stone and cursing both its height and hers. She's gasping now, and exhausted, and just hoping that Bickel knows some other way out. Finally they emerge into a low cavern about a large pool of dark water. Deep in the water, there is a bright glow. It must open into the East River, she realises.

"Gotta swim," says Bickel, somewhat less exhausted than her. He's limping, she notices for the first time, though it's too dark to see why, and she's lost the lighter. He folds the blades on his staff, and she realises he didn't teleport it into his hand like before — Eli's magic doesn't reach down here, Bickel must have brought the staff in as well.

"How far?" Ange gasps

"No idea. It's this or nothing, if we keep fighting through, every crawly critter under the financial district is gonna find us." To underline his point, an awful, echoing shriek sounds from down the tunnel they've come from. "You a good swimmer?"

"It's not my favorite. I'll manage."

Bickel nods, secures his folded staff in some unseen holster beneath his jacket, and dives in. Ange sheaths her sword, takes a deep breath, and follows. The cold water hits her with a crash, and then she's kicking after Bickel's heels. There's a hole in the wall further down, it looks concrete, like a retaining wall. She kicks harder, as the pressure converges on her ears, making them hurt.

They reach the hole together and swim inside. It's brighter here, but the visibility is poor and getting worse as they near the river. Ange is half expecting steel bars to block their path, but there's nothing, probably they're not the only ones to use this passage. But the tunnel continues, on and on, and her lungs start to ache, then to burn. Panic threatens, and she lashes harder... and realises that Bickel is no longer with her. She looks, and he's just behind, and struggling, unable to get any force in the kicks of his injured leg.

Ange grabs his collar and kicks and strokes as hard as she can. The burn turns to real pain, light headed and frantic. And then there's brightness around them as the tunnel ends, and she thrashes upward. They break the surface amidst boardwalk pylons, gasping sweet air. The traffic on neighbouring FDR Drive is music to Ange's ears, and the chatter of people above their heads.

When she has some oxygen back in her system, Ange strokes carefully to the rocky shore, and helps Bickel to crawl from the water. "You okay?" she asks him.

"No," he says. "I lost my best gun. You owe me another."

"And now my damn phone's dead," Ange mutters. "Wonderful."

CHAPTER TEN

Ange enters the top floor meeting room in a borrowed grey jumper and some men's jeans that she's had to tighten with a borrowed belt to stop from falling to her ankles. Borrowed sneakers and socks, and a borrowed phone to replace her now waterlogged original, she's beginning to see why many Leventhal employees keep a locker in the tower, filled with spare clothes and gear.

Leventhal Holdings employees sit around the long boardroom table, with soaring Mid-Town views on two sides. All of Meisha's legal team are here, plus Hernandez and two others from Response Division. At the far end are Leventhal himself, and Croz. Croz gives Ange a dark look from behind his laptop, texting on his phone even now. As one of Leventhal's personal assistants, he's required to monitor many things at once.

Ange limps to lean against a windowsill rather than sit, as there are no seats available close to the head of the table. That, and the cuts and bruises on her back are making it painful to sit. Everyone is very quiet, and Eli sits not at the table's head, but away from its corner, his chin on his hand and staring at nothing.

Finally he sighs. "I don't see what else I could have done. Mr Mills' testimony could have greatly damaged the City's legal case. There was no one else. We looked... we did look, didn't we?" His eyes search the table. The others nod. Except Hernandez, who won't meet his eye. The big man looks morose. Mills was under his protection. "We looked for some other way. We had all the bases covered, but then a traitor…" He takes a deep breath. "On some other issue I might have expected it, but on this…" He trails off.

"Eli I'm so sorry," Meisha says quietly. "If I hadn't invited Adrian to observe proceedings, none of this would have…"

Eli makes an abrupt gesture. "Don't be silly Meisha, of course it's not your fault. We recruit top legal and magical talent constantly, and we ease them into our operations constantly. Rampelly being there was procedure, procedures that I signed off on. If it's anyone's fault it's mine." He exhales hard, and gazes out a window. "This is why I hate to use the shroud-blind in our dealings. They are so defenceless against these perils. That poor man."

He looks genuinely upset. Nothing Ange has seen of Eli so far has done more to dispel her doubts as this.

Stew Bickel enters the meeting room. He wears a tracksuit, and limps on crutches. Everyone watches as he levers awkwardly through the doors.

"How's the leg?" Croz asks him.

"I get to keep it," says Bickel. "Apparently they don't grow back." He comes around the table the long way, headed for Ange. There is nothing of the good humoured, laid-back joker about him now, and his lean, scarred face is set hard. Ange watches warily as he approaches, and stops close. "So," he says to her. "Why'd you try to get me killed?"

"I was chasing our murder suspect," Ange retorts. "Only no one told me what was down there. I mean, does *anyone*, outside of Leventhal Holdings or Mayor Riley's top people, know what's down there? That place is like the nine levels of hell! Why didn't anyone tell me?"

"Because when we tell them," says Croz, "and they're new to the company, they tend to run away."

"Do I look like the running type?" Ange glares at him. Croz meets her gaze without expression. "No offence, but I'm almost certainly the best close quarters fighter here…"

"Is that a fact?" Croz interrupts.

"Yes it is, and as your best fighter, I'm going to need to know things about the enemy before I get sent in to fight them!"

Croz is about to continue his objection, loudly, but Bickel cuts him off. "No she's right. About the fighting, she's got crazy skill, I wouldn't have lasted two minutes without her. Problem is, I shouldn't have been down there at all, because she shouldn't have gone. I told you to stop. I told you it was suicide to go down alone. You ignored me. Why?"

There's something disconcertingly hard and straight-forward about the question, put like that. "I thought I could handle it," she says defensively. "If I'd known…"

"If you'd done what you were told, you wouldn't have needed to know."

"Yeah well I don't work like that!"

"You listen to me," says Bickel, and swings on his crutches to get right in her face. Ange has long thought herself invulnerable to dressing-downs, but this is an SAS dressing-down, and the intensity is on a whole different scale. "I don't care what you are, or who trained you, or what you think you know. You may be the best swordsman in a thousand mile radius, but you're also a spoiled kid with daddy issues who ran away from home rather than deal with it. You operate alone because you've only faced enemies who you can defeat alone. This enemy, you can't. Do you understand that?"

Ange just blinks at him, unable to think of anything to say.

"You still haven't learned the only thing that actually matters," Bickel continues. "That *you* don't matter. Not to the world, not to Riley, hell, not even to this cause. None of us do. Individuals, against *that*, just crumble and disappear. What beats *that,* is teamwork. Leventhal Holdings is a company. A company is a team. People who work together have a place in this world. Those people matter, because they make themselves matter, and they make the world notice.

"Not everyone here has your sword skills, but some of us have things that you don't. One of them is experience. In this environment, I have it, and you don't. So the next time you ignore my instruction, and go charging into something I've told you not to, we'll be through. I'll have no further association with you, and Eli can do with you whatever he likes from there. Are we clear?"

Ange's first reaction is hostility. It's her first response to everyone, when challenged or threatened. And then she realises that she'd be dead if it wasn't for Bickel, just as he'd be dead if she hadn't fought with him in the tunnels. Like he said, they'd saved each other, and gotten out alive, where alone they each would have died. And he hadn't needed to come after her. He'd known what he was heading into, but he'd come anyway. She hates owing people, but there it is, undeniable.

She takes a deep breath, and looks at the ground. She knows what she has to say, but that doesn't make it any easier. These words have rarely passed her lips in all her life. "I'm sorry," she mutters.

"I didn't ask if you were sorry," says Bickel, in just the same tone. "I asked if we were clear." Ange nods, still looking at the ground. She's not going to apologise again. Bickel puts his fingers beneath her chin, and makes her look at him. Then slaps her cheek, just hard enough to startle her. Suddenly the smile is back, tugging the corner of his mouth. "You got potential kid. Try to live long enough to live up to it."

After swearing never to head south of Canal Street again, the following afternoon she's called back down there. But if there's one place an Ulani can feel safe south of Canal, it's Little Italy.

"So Leventhal tells the world how magic is about to end," says Starace, "and you believe him?" They sit in a little upstairs apartment overlooking the best Italian butcher in Manhattan. The owners are Ulani friends, and delighted to allow them the upstairs room, and two cups of excellent black coffee. On the street below, the sidewalks are thick with tourists and locals, and the queues out the door of a famous pizzeria have to be seen to be believed.

"He wasn't faking," Ange snorts. "He was completely real." Starace gives her a skeptical smile. "What's his advantage? Why should he make up a story like that?"

"Because he's planning something," says Starace. "Some kind of end game. So he says the end is coming in five years... so a lot can happen in five years. Maybe he wants to find out who his true friends are, maybe catch out some of his rivals talking to Riley. Then he can destroy them. My guess is he's suspicious of several of his own Shtaal alliance, and is looking for an excuse to do away with them."

Ange sips her coffee and looks out the window. The brown brick walls of Little Italy are hardly pretty, but the life on the streets is fun, and on a bright spring afternoon it seems as though nothing could ever be amiss in this town. But she's tired of Starace not listening to her. It reminds her of why she left.

"Fine," she says. "It's all a plot. What will the Ulani do?"

"If it's all a plot, we will do nothing," Starace replies with an expansive shrug. "The question is, what will *you* do?"

"If it's all a plot," Ange says blandly, "I'll be very careful." Starace smiles. He knows her too well. He knows what she'll think of the end of magic, and the man promising to bring it about. He's not fooled for a moment.

"Angelina," he says. "The end of the Ulani would not bother you even a little?"

"Of course it bothers me," Ange says shortly. "But the Ulani were created for a purpose, to stop the excesses of wizards. If we're not going to do that, then what are we for?"

"We do not exist to commit suicide."

"You would still be alive." Ange smiles sourly. "You'd just be normal. Like everyone else out on those streets. And you don't like it any more than the magicians do."

"You would miss it too," Starace says slyly. "You pretend that you don't care, but you've always been different, Angelina. So much have you embraced your difference, you couldn't survive as a normal person any more than Mayor Riley could."

"The difference between you and me," Ange retorts, "is that I've been friends with normal people. I'm not scared of it like you are."

Starace shrugs. "Anyhow. I hear that you had an adventure yesterday?"

"Yes, I learned that the southern end of Manhattan is crawling with unofficial tunnels that link the official tunnels — the subways, the sewers, et-cetera. But of course the unofficial tunnels are magically made, so the shroud hides them from city workers who might stumble across them. Except for those on our side of the shroud, and they are far too smart to head down there." Another sip. "Smarter than me, anyway."

"And what lives in them?"

"An army. Mayor Riley's army. I've never seen such an evil swarm. Everything you can think of, and a lot you can't. God knows what they all feed on, it's not like they're preying on innocent New Yorkers, the shroud might hide disappearances from most, but not from Leventhal, and Leventhal says those disappearances are few. The creatures are not seen very often. It's like Riley's hoarding them, in case of a war."

"It's already a war," says Starace.

"A cold war," Ange corrects, recalling what Meisha said in the courtroom, and the standoff of magical powers. "I mean a hot war. The day when they all come pouring out and engulf this city for good."

"And the dead man," Starace presses with a frown. "The accountant. The shroud says it's a heart attack."

"A traitor," says Ange. "A law student, his family was being threatened, somehow the background checks did not find it. He wore an amulet that made a breach in the defensive charms, and allowed an assassin to teleport into the bathroom and kill the accountant there."

"Devious and determined," says Starace. "This legal case is a bigger deal than you think. Leventhal values his reputation amongst the normal people, as you so charmingly call them. He believes in laws and rules. The shroud will prevent his company from being dismantled by magical deception, but it will not prevent non-magical actions. If Leventhal Holdings is found guilty, he could lose everything."

"Or be forced to use magic to trick his way around his precious laws," Ange says solemnly. "I know. He's a man of principle. If they force him to destroy his own principles, in full sight of everyone, then everyone will stop believing in him. It would be like forcing the world's greatest policeman to break the law to save his own skin. And then he's lost."

Starace nods with appreciation, pleased to see how well she understands. "It sounds like you're coming to like him."

"I'm coming to understand him," says Ange. "It's not always the same thing." Although in this case, she does not add, it probably is.

"And I hear you've been seeing quite a lot of a certain boy," Starace suggests. Ange just looks at him over the rim of her cup. A warning look, though not aggressive, and not angry. Just a flat refusal to discuss it. Starace spreads his hands, and smiles. "Angelina. Of course, it's your life.

Just remember that when thoroughbreds and donkeys breed, they make infertile mules."

"The only donkey here is you," Ange mutters. Starace laughs.

Ange gets back late from Response Division duties, and is making fettuccini carbonara in the kitchen when the doorbell rings. She takes her sword from the back of a kitchen chair, but the hallway monitor shows her it's Jamie, so she relaxes and opens the door.

"Hey," he says, with a forced smile that tells Ange something is wrong. "You're here."

"Yes. I'm here." She pushes the door fully open. "You hungry?"

"Oh no, I just wanted to…"

"No no, come in. Have some food. You do eat pasta?"

"I have to say yes, right?" He closes the door behind him. Ange smiles and heads back to the kitchen, turning down Vivaldi on the speakers.

"No no," she says, "you can be an uncivilised person if you wish." She goes back to mixing eggs, cream and cheese while pasta boils.

"Smells good," says Jamie, looking about the place. She doesn't have much furniture here yet, but she's adding more every few days. Jamie sees the open bottle of red on the kitchen bench. "Wow, wine, pasta and classical music. You some kind of foreigner?"

"Isn't everyone, in this city?"

"You know the wine's illegal? You're underage."

"Not in *my* country, amico mio," says Ange, and sips a little from her own glass.

"Seriously? You can drink at seventeen in Italy?"

"Sixteen," says Ange. "And this apartment is Italian territory, I'm having it declared. You want some?"

Jamie makes a face. "Don't like it much."

"Suit yourself, there's juice and ginger beer in the fridge, glasses behind that door. So what brings you here?"

Jamie pours himself some ginger beer. "Well, I just kinda wanted to…" He takes a seat at the bench. Ange cuts some pasta from the saucepan and bites it. Another minute, she thinks. "The other night. At the mansion. I got dragged aside and... well, I might not have been the best date."

Ange shrugs. She's not going to say 'that's okay', because she was kind of pissed. But it was an awful if eventful night, and a lot of people had a far worse time than she did. In the grand scheme of things, including nearly getting killed yesterday, it doesn't seem like a big deal.

"You see," says Jamie, with a sarcasm she hasn't heard much from him until now, "I got pulled aside to be informed of their latest theory. 'They', of course, meaning all the magic folk, the ones you love so much in this city. They think an Ulani killed Tori. You know how she died?"

Ange feels a twinge of shame. Here's her chance to hear it from Jamie himself, but Mulberry Watson already told her. She nods.

Jamie exhales hard. "Everyone does," he mutters. "Anyway, the charms in that library were unbreakable. Not like your courtroom bathroom stuff the other day, I mean permanently unbreakable. But someone got in. They think only an Ulani could have penetrated that magic."

"And killed her with a sword," Ange finishes. "Was she killed with a sword?" Jamie stares at her. Then swallows, and shakes his head. "We kill with swords, Jamie. It's kind of a thing, with us. We don't do quiet assassinations, we kill to make a point, and we let everyone know about it."

"They think she was researching some dangerous secret the Ulani want hidden. And your friend Starace had her killed for it. You're still friends with him, yeah?"

Ange blinks at him. And closes her eyes with her head back, repressing a curse. "Jamie, you don't believe these people? You think I'm here to... what, finish the job?"

"No!"

"Because they don't like us being friends, you know that right?"

"Ange no! Of course I don't think that, I just... she was my sister, Ange! And I've been away for two years, and now I'm back, and I don't know who to trust, and..."

He's upset. It gives Ange a lump in her throat, and she sits opposite, and takes his hands. "I talk to Starace," she says. "He wants me back. I don't want to go back. That's all it is." She's not entirely sure that's true even as she says it. She wants it to be true. Doesn't she? "Jamie, I left the

Ulani because of what they do to each other, not what they do to others. To non-Ulani. Ulani don't just kill people like that Jamie. They really don't. And certainly not in New York, because we're not welcome here, almost no one except Eli actually wants me here."

A little pain must have shown in her voice, because Jamie squeezes her hands back. "That's not true. I want you here." Ange smiles at him. "And Stew… god, I was talking to Stew today, he doesn't shut up about you."

"Stew Bickel thinks I'm a dangerous lunatic who's going to get him killed."

"Exactly, and he loves it. The guy's nuts." Ange laughs. Jamie glances at her saucepan. "Hey, is that done?"

Ange looks, and swears, rushing to the stove. "Overcooked pasta!" she exclaims. "There's nothing worse than overcooked pasta!"

"I'm pretty sure there's several things worse."

"There's not, and it's your fault for distracting me with your big brown eyes." She drains it in the sink, dumps it back in the saucepan, then turns on the heat under the sauce once more, stirring.

"You think I have big brown eyes?"

"You do have big brown eyes." Ange risks a grin over her shoulder, stirring. "Look in a mirror. So will you trust my cooking? I mean it's not as good as your mother's, I'm sure…" And she stops, feeling a pleasant sensation, like a summer breeze on a hot day. She gazes out the window, a smile spreading across her face.

"Ange?"

"Oh look who's back! He wants to meet up… damn it Gia, why can't you come *after* dinner?"

"Gia's here?" Jamie asks with excitement.

"Yes, and my pasta's going to get cold."

"I can warm it up for you when we get back, better than a microwave."

"You don't put pasta in a microwave, are you mad?"

"I said better, I promise!" Jamie is up and urging her along. "Come on, let's go!"

They run across the road and into Central Park. It's only eight, and there are still plenty of people running or walking along the main paths near the road, lit with light. Like all foreign visitors Ange has heard the stories about Central Park having once been dangerous, but it seems those days are long past now. Riley's hoards aren't welcome up here, save for the occasional dingy hangout near the rivers, and Shtaal allies keep all Mid-Town and Central Park clear of unwanted visitors.

Ange heads for the wide expanse of grass known as the 'sheep meadow'. There are a few people sitting around on the grass in the cool spring evening, but not many, and she jogs for a spot where there is no one within a hundred yards. Once there she eagerly scans the skyline beyond the trees, searching for that familiar silhouette.

"Hey he's shrouded right?" says Jamie.

"Of course, all dragons are." All magical creatures for that matter. But if a vampire strolls down Fifth Avenue, the shroud will disguise him as a normal person, that being the simplest thing. Dragons are the size of small airplanes, but behave more like birds, and can not be credibly disguised as either. And so the shroud simply makes them invisible, that being the only working solution. Most dragons seem aware of their status with the shroud-blind humans, and are careful not to abuse it. Though not all dragons are friendly, and when the occasional aeroplane goes missing, some magicians get nervous.

She turns, sensing movement behind her, and here across the treetops glides a forty-foot wingspan as silent as air. Gia descends, flares with a great rush of wind, and bounds athletically onto the grass. Ange runs to him and hugs his neck.

"Hello Gia, how are you? You don't mind if I speak English do you? The new boy doesn't speak Italian." As Gia peers over her shoulder at Jamie, turning his head one way then the other to consider him.

"Um, hi," says Jamie, standing quite nervously, eyes wide. "Why is he snaking like that?"

"Oh he's got excellent side vision, but his forward vision's not great, it's the way his eyes are offset." She whacks him on the jaw a few times. "Hey Gia, this is my friend. You met him briefly before, his name's Jamie. He's a nice guy and he's very pleased to meet you."

Gia doesn't go straight to Jamie, but circles to one side, as though checking him out. Jamie looks even more nervous now.

Ange grins. "What are you doing, Gia?"

"Wondering what I taste like?"

"I don't know why people think dragons will eat them," Ange complains. "We've hardly any meat on us, we're not worth the effort. If dragons kill people they usually don't bother swallowing."

"Oh that makes me feel much better." Gia is such an impressive sight up close, Ange has spent so much time with him yet she's still in awe. He's dark blue fading to black, but the membrane of his wings is streaked red through orange. His body's about twice the size of a big horse, though his arched neck and rudder-like tail give him a far greater presence. He circles back now, checking out Jamie with his other eye.

"Oh you imbecile!" Ange laughs, and runs at him. Gia springs back like an enormous puppy, and again as Ange tries to swat his nose. "You don't have to check out my male friends, I'm not bringing them to you for approval you big goat!"

Gia lunges and uses his head to bowl her over, and stands over her gloating for a moment before jumping back once more as she aims another swat. Jamie watches incredulously as they play, ending finally as Ange 'submits' him with a headlock, the huge dragon sliding to the ground with her hanging about his neck.

"Come here," Ange beckons to Jamie, and rubs at Gia's eye ridge. That eye closes with pleasure, and the other remains fixed on Jamie. "Kneel down and say hello."

Jamie does so. A huge gust from Gia's nostrils blows his hair back. Ange gives the dragon a whack on the brow.

"He's just playing with you," she explains with a grin. "He does it to annoy me, he thinks he's like my dad, checking out my boyfriends and making me all uncomfortable."

"Really," says Jamie, eyebrows raised. Ange blushes a little. Jamie leans, and rubs Gia's nose.

"A bit higher," says Ange. "Near the nostrils is a bit sensitive." Jamie complies. Gia manages to look somewhere between amused and content. "Now a couple of things," Ange continues. "First, he's not an animal, so don't stare and don't suppose you're smarter than him. It's a different kind of intelligence, I doubt he's that great at maths, but he certainly understands what I say to him, even if he doesn't get the words."

"How does that work?" Jamie asks curiously.

"I don't know. Ulani are sensitive to magic, and dragons are magical. He uses that somehow to communicate, but I've no idea how."

"Plus dragons are kinda telepathic, aren't they?"

"Yeah," says Ange, rubbing Gia's eye ridge once more. "Something like that. Oh here," and she swings off the little backpack she's brought especially. She rummages for a moment, then pulls out a bag of marshmallows. "Here you go, favorite."

Gia raises and opens his mouth, revealing huge teeth. Ange pours the whole pack in, and smoke rises from Gia's nostrils. "He melts them in his mouth," she explains. "It started as a joke, because I thought I'd toast marshmallows on his breath. But I gave him one and he loved it."

They talk for a long time, just sitting on the grass with Gia, who seems to follow the conversation in that outsiderly kind of way that dragons do, like lurkers on some internet forum who like to observe but rarely join in. Occasionally Ange will sense a burst of energy from him at some point of conversation, usually in response to some emotion or amusement between them. She even shows Jamie where the saddle sits, on the odd occasion she's flown with him, and the big straps that fit about the chest plate.

"I'd love to go flying with him," says Jamie.

"It's actually pretty damn dangerous," Ange admits. "There's not a lot to hold onto, and I mean, the saddle's got straps, but he can turn so fast that they snap. I can sense what he's doing before he does it, so it's a bit safer, but I wouldn't recommend it for beginners."

"And he's so much bigger than us, and his hide's so tough, he might not notice we'd fallen off until we'd hit the ground."

"That too," Ange admits.

Gia eyes Jamie's outstretched sneaker near his jaw. He opens his mouth, and flicks at it with a huge tooth, prodding Jamie's toes. Jamie grins, and looks at Ange.

"He doesn't like your shoes," Ange explains. "Doesn't like plastics or rubber much, synthetic things, guess he hates how they smell. Cotton, wool or leather he likes though, gives me a look like I haven't bathed in weeks if I wear anything else. *Hates* perfume. And mobile phones are worst of all."

As if on cue, Jamie's mobile sings, an incoming text. Jamie pulls it out to glance at it, and Gia growls, eyes narrowing. "Ooops," says Jamie, not especially worried, and puts the phone away. "Sorry." Gia nudges his shoe again, apology accepted. "Just my Mum, she's wondering when I'll be back."

"Well answer her," Ange scolds him. Jamie blinks, and looks at Gia. "Don't worry about him, he just whines a lot. Gia, it's Jamie's mother. His mother wants to check on him, okay? Don't be rude."

Jamie retrieves the phone, and Gia just watches, a little amused, a little unimpressed. Jamie texts, then puts the phone away. "Thanks Gia." He nudges the dragon back. "I think phones are pretty annoying too, but not all of us are telepathic. Here, can I try something?" He kneels upright. "Let's see if he can receive anything from me. Any kind of thought or image."

"It's not going to work," says Ange, lounging against Gia's neck, her head by his ear. "Magicians don't connect with him, a few have tried. He doesn't get a signal, it's like he's on a different frequency."

"Like you?"

"Well yeah."

"And other Ulani? Have they tried?"

"Yep." She smiles smugly. "Just me. He can't hear anyone else."

"Well then." Jamie closes his eyes, takes a deep breath, and seems to concentrate. Gia just watches him, with lazy interest. Jamie opens his eyes. Gia yawns, a flash of devastating teeth. "Nothing huh? Okay, maybe wasn't strong enough. Try this."

Again he closes his eyes. Ange feels Gia's easy breathing stop beneath her cheek. And he raises his head, forcing Ange to sit up, and gazes at Jamie with great curiosity. Jamie opens his eyes, to find the dragon staring down at him. He grins. "You get that?"

"What did you send?" Ange asks in amazement.

"Well," Jamie says, a little awkwardly. "I thought maybe if I thought about something we both know in common… I mean, me and Gia. So I… well, I thought about you."

Ange stares. "Me?" Jamie nods. He's blushing. "He only really receives anything with an emotional connection, I mean he can get images and things from me, but only if I feel something strongly about…" And her jaw drops open as she realises. Jamie looks at her helplessly.

Ange realises it's now or never, and she's never been good at 'never'. She crawls to Jamie, puts both hands on his shoulders, and kisses him. It feels so nice, as though time has slowed to a crawl, and suspended them both in some beautiful other place. She'd thought it might be awkward, given the mess he makes of kissing cheeks Italian style, but somehow the awkwardness has vanished. He kisses her back, and his hand is gentle on her waist. The other hand goes to her neck, and runs through her hair, and she thinks she might just die and go to heaven.

A rustling brings them back to the world, and they look up to find that Gia has shifted, and now covers them both with one huge wing, tail and neck curling protectively about them. They grin. "You know," says Jamie, "that's one magnificent pet you've got here."

"I keep telling you," Ange scolds him. "He's not my pet!"

"I was talking to the dragon," says Jamie. Ange gapes at him, and slaps his arm, and kisses him once more.

CHAPTER ELEVEN

Mayor Riley waits atop the stairs of City Hall for the motorcade to arrive. It's raining, and only a few photographers have ventured out to see the Mayor of Paris's official visit with the Mayor of New York. New York is home to the United Nations, after all, and there are far bigger foreign visitors to photograph than the Mayor of Paris, who is only here to sign a 'sister cities' agreement and exchange a few artworks between major galleries.

The motorcade is not big, just two black cars with official city registration. Riley's staff greet them with umbrellas, and Riley himself breaks protocol to trot down the stairs in the rain to shake the French mayor's hand as he exits the car. The photographers like that and snap shots of Riley getting wet to greet his guest at the bottom of the stairs instead of the dry top. They go quickly back up the stairs together, and pose for more photographs with a handshake and lots of smiles. A couple of questions from a Times journalist, and they go inside and settle into the meeting room, with big chairs before an old fireplace, and windows overlooking City Hall Park.

For the first twenty minutes Riley and Mayor Jean-Luc Le Fevre discuss the official reason for the visit — the sister cities' agreement, and the loan of some French paintings to the Met Museum of art. It's the kind of soft fluff that the media likes, France doesn't have much more than soft fluff to offer these days. Riley recalls when that wasn't true, when la Grande Armée marched on Prussians and Russians and Austrians and laid them all to waste. What grand days those were, great masses of soldiers, rows of guns and steel marching through cannonfire. Now here they sit, two men who were both around in those days, and discuss trinkets for tourists.

When they're finally done with the nonsense, Le Fevre looks at Riley with eyebrows raised. Riley nods, and Le Fevre waves his hand. Instantly two French shroud-blind assistants fall to the floor unconscious. Riley's people drag them out a door, to lie on a sofa until needed once more, and the shroud will take care of the rest when they awake.

Riley waves his glass. "Mindy, pour Monsieur Le Fevre some more wine, will you?"

Mindy does that. "My dear," says Le Fevre in appreciation as Mindy does so. "You know, it is not bad. For Californian."

Riley smiles, nursing his own glass. "So, Jean-Luc. Your investigation." It is the real reason he's here, of course. Jean-Luc Le Fevre is one of the senior Councillors of the High Council. The High Council is the final word in magical justice, and has been for twelve hundred years. Anyone who breaks a serious enough rule, answers to them.

"Yes," says Le Fevre. "The boy. MacDonald. Someone tried to kill him. Was it you?"

"Come now Jean-Luc," says Riley. "He was sworn to Eli at the time. And you know I'm under no obligation to answer that question, contests between magical families and alliances are not the High Council's business."

"Yes, but the assassination attempt seems to have originated *before* MacDonald was sworn to Eli," says Le Fevre, and sips his wine. "Eli has traced the attempt to the DeLalio family, who are now conveniently dead. Killed, it seems, by your former apprentice, Mathew Palmino, who is now also conveniently dead."

Riley shrugs. "Teleporting youth. It's like young men and duels, back in your day Jean-Luc. It's always thrilling, and often fatal."

Le Fevre smiles. "Eli suggests Palmino was acting on your instruction. If he had information on MacDonald's location in that hospital *before* he was sworn to Eli, and passed that to the De Lalios, that would be a breach, my old friend, and most assuredly the High Council's business."

Riley nods. "Yes. Yes it would."

"So you deny any involvement?"

"You are the investigator, Jean-Luc." He smiles his most charming smile. "Investigate."

"I will," says Le Fevre. "Have no fear."

"Well then," says Riley. "If you'd like a place to start, why not try this? Eli's closest ally in America, Mulberry Watson. The head of Accord Entertainment."

"Yes of course," says Le Fevre. "A powerful man, nearly seven hundred years old himself. Wasn't he born in the Niger Delta?"

"Yes, Ijo tribe," says Riley. "Haven't they produced some amazing magicians?"

"Indeed. I believe he had a degree from the Sorbonne University in the fourteenth century, before it became fashionable. Fluent French speaker, France can take some credit for his interest in things artistic. Though he did spend a lot of time in Italy with the Medicis, going to the opera and running his trading empire."

"And then he came to Detroit in the sixties and did the whole MoTown thing and became an American musical institution," Riley agrees. "Crazy lives we wizards lead."

Le Fevre chuckles. "And what involvement does Mulberry Watson have with young James MacDonald?"

"Well not with *James*, exactly. With his sister Tori."

Le Fevre raises his eyebrows. "The one who died? The mysterious murder?"

"Yes."

"Are you suggesting that *Mulberry* killed her?"

Riley laughs. "Oh no, I don't enter into these whodunnit guessing games. There's only one person in our community I'm sure *didn't* do it, and that's me." Le Fevre looks skeptical. "No really! It really wasn't. I mean the girl was powerful, and could have become truly great, but you know the young, they can go any which way. I was betting she'd be the cause of problems for Eli before she caused them for me. Better to leave her where she is."

"And so the same with James MacDonald?"

"Exactly," says Riley. "He's a young, confused boy. Who knows what trouble he'll yet throw up? He's more Eli's problem than mine, for the moment."

"But not the young Angelina Donati?"

"No," Riley says grimly. "Ulani are always trouble. And this one in particular."

"Yes I hear. My spies say Starace wanted her to be his heir, to take his place as the Master of House Ulani in time. A first, for a woman. Evidently she found this idea disagreeable."

"She may still come around, given the chance," says Riley. "Starace has come to New York repeatedly, to persuade her. And Starace hates to travel."

Le Fevre smiles. "So naturally you're trying to have her killed?"

Riley levels a good natured finger at him. "And you can't stop me."

Le Fevre holds up his hands. "It is not the High Council's business. She is still Ulani, and now works for Eli — in either case the girl is fair game. And yet I see she is still breathing."

"Yes," says Riley, unhappily. "We've announced a big reward for her head, but when our best killers hear *who* they're being asked to kill, they mysteriously lose interest." Le Fevre smiles. "You go and talk to Mulberry about James and Tori MacDonald. Because I'll tell you this for free — my late assistant Mathew Palmino? I checked his phone records, after we dug his phone out of that wall. He was talking to Mulberry Watson a *lot* before he died."

Le Fevre smells his wine for a moment, thinking hard. "Interesting," he says finally. "And Eli's other thing? The end of magic? You wouldn't be intending to do anything about that, would you?"

Riley spreads his hands wide, like a man with nothing to hide. "Who me?"

"Yes, that's what I thought."

"The question, mon ami, is not what *I* intend to do about it. The question is what *you* intend to do about it. You, and all the High Council. Sit back and watch magic die, and everything you've worked and built toward for more than a thousand years come to an end? I think not."

Le Fevre smiles, and says nothing.

Ange rides her Ducati to Jamie's house after work, and puts it in the empty carport. The MacDonalds don't own a car, and Mrs MacDonald takes the train to work. Ange goes through the side gate and around the back, into a tiny rear yard. The rear door is open, and in the cramped corridor beyond is a door with a poster of a bearded wizard with pointy hat and long beard, shouting, 'You shall not pass!' at anyone thinking of entering.

Ange knocks on the door. It doesn't feel right that Jamie's house should be so small given that he now works for Leventhal Holdings, as she does. Her own apartment is bigger than this entire house, and that in central Manhattan. But Jamie's 'employment' remains unofficial, unlike hers, as he's still in school and living with his mother. How do you explain to a shroud-blind mother why her dear but otherwise unremarkable son is suddenly working for the richest man in New York? And so Jamie has a bank account, which is filling up fast, but can't be spent on anything that his mother would notice.

Jamie doesn't reply, but Ange can sense magic — Jamie's magic, a familiar, gentle tingling. She knocks again and enters, and finds him lying on his bed, music on his headphones, staring at a string of paperclips that hover above him. As she watches, another one lifts from his desk, and goes to join the string. It approaches, then clips onto the end of the chain, but the whole chain slips and changes shape, then nearly falls. Another clip becomes unattached, and he swears, gesturing with one hand to try and rejoin the broken chain.

"Bouna sera," Ange tells him with amusement.

"Hey." His eyes don't leave the floating paperclips. "Just a minute. This is really hard."

"It doesn't look very hard."

"Sure. Well I think swordfighting looks easy too." Ange huffs impatiently, and waits. Surely it's not too much to hope that her besotted new boyfriend might be happy to see her? And might find the prospect of having her in his bedroom for the first time more exciting than a bunch of paperclips? "They don't know whether to behave as a single string," Jamie explains through gritted teeth, "or as individual clips. So I have to control all of them, and they keep trying to run away... it's a nightmare."

The chain of clips comes back together, but now a new break opens up.

"You know, I could come back at a better time?" Ange suggests.

"Yeah could you? I really gotta practise this."

Ange realises he's teasing her, and swats the paperclips from the air and jumps on him as he laughs. She straddles him, and they kiss with what feels to Ange as much like relief as excitement, as she's been thinking about doing this all day. But now it starts to get heated, and her heart starts hammering in a way that feels too much out-of-control for her liking, she's too accustomed to telling her body what to do to feel comfortable when that relationship is reversed. And her body is now telling her to do things that she's pretty sure are unwise at this point, and Mrs MacDonald will be home shortly, and...

...she slides off him, reluctantly, and puts her head against his shoulder. Jamie accepts that, his arm around her, and they wriggle to get comfortable on a mattress too small for a pair of 6-1 teens.

"How was work?" he asks her.

"Fine. I'm still alive. How was school?"

"Fine." Drily. "I'm still alive."

"Eli says I should go back to school at some point. Finish year twelve."

"Well Eli's very big on education," Jamie reasons. "Would you like to?"

"I'm a little busy saving the world." Her fingers interlock with his. "But sure. If I had the time."

"You're so lucky you can work instead. I offered Eli to drop out and work for Holdings, but he insisted I stay and finish my exams. I guess another magician isn't as useful to him as an Ulani."

"Well he's not exactly short of magicians," Ange says affectionately. "Don't take it personally."

"I don't." He smiles. "And I can't disagree that you're pretty amazing." He kisses her again. That lasts for long enough that when she puts her head back down on his shoulder, she can hear his heart thumping in her ear, much faster than normal. He looks at her, and sees her listening, with a smile on her face. "You hear that?" She nods. "That's all you, girl."

Ange takes his hand and puts it on her left ribs beside her breast. "Feel that," she says. And, "Not *that,* that!" With a stern grin as his hand wanders. "Faster than yours."

Jamie shrugs offhandedly. "Sure. Well I am pretty hot."

Ange laughs. "Yes you are." And stretches to kiss him once more.

A key rattles in the front door down the hall. The door opens, and Jamie rolls his eyes. "Great timing Mum."

Ange gives him a soft punch, reprimanding. "She lives here too, and she works hard to pay for this place."

"Jamie!" calls his mother from the hallway. "Are you home?"

"Yes Ma!"

"Hello Mrs MacDonald!" Ange adds, and makes no attempt to move as footsteps come down the hall. Jamie looks at her in mild consternation, making to get up or be a little less intimate, but Ange just snuggles against him and makes moving impossible.

Mrs MacDonald appears in the doorway, and blinks at them. "Oh hello Angelina!" With dawning delight. "Oh don't you two look adorable! No no, don't get up, I shouldn't interrupt you kids snuggling. I'll just close the door for you."

She does that, and the footsteps retreating back up the hall are irregular. Like she's dancing. Jamie laughs.

"Why so surprised?" Ange asks him. "Every mother thinks every girl his age should be madly in love with her boy." She puts her head back against his shoulder. "I wish I had a mother. My life's been all men and boys. Except for Lacey. That's one reason I loved her so much, she let me feel like a *girl* for a change."

Jamie gives her a squeeze. "I'm the opposite. Dad disappeared so early, so my life's been all Mum and Tori. And Mum's not exactly quiet, and Tori was worse." He puts his hand at his chin. "Women up to here, I tell you."

"Hen-pecked?" Ange suggests, and pecks at him with her fingers.

"They're not hens, they're pterodactyls. Here, you still haven't seen Tori, have you? I'll show you Tori, it's about time you two met."

He gets his laptop off the desk, and they sit up on the bed as Jamie opens a video file. The video is of two girls trudging through the snow in

Central Park. One is Meisha, and she's holding the other, younger girl's hand. Tori, Ange recognises her from photos. Whoever is filming is doing it on a phone, hiding behind a tree.

"Tori was a snowball fiend," Jamie explains. "I mean she set up the worst ambushes, and she was a deadly throw. We thought we'd get her back."

On the video, someone shouts, 'Now Meisha!', and Meisha runs. Tori squeals as snowballs pelt her from all sides, the vision blurring as the phone holder joins in the throwing. But Ange can still see snowballs exploding just short of their target as Tori force-blocks them... but there's too many. Then someone runs into screen and grabs her, and shoves a big handful of snow down her coat — it's Croz, Ange recognises with astonishment, laughing and playing with the rest.

Then the phone holder runs at her to join in, and suddenly a close up of Tori, pretty with big dark eyes like Jamie, and flushed from laughing so hard, her beanie covered with snow. "Jamie!" she yells at the camera. "No, don't film my moment of defeat!"

Ange laughs, it's impossible not to. "She was a terror," says Jamie. "She deserved it. She put a bucket of snow above the door in Croz's office after this, and spelled it to hover there until he walked in." Ange looks at him, and his eyes are wet with tears. She hugs him, and puts her head on his shoulder. "I haven't looked at this in ages. I still don't know how it's on my computer, I had no memory of any of this for two whole years... I thought the shroud would erase it from the hard drive, but maybe it was there all along and just invisible to me."

"Jamie?" A question has been puzzling her for a while now, but there hasn't been a right time to ask. "Why did you want to become shroud-blind when..." And she stops as she notices something. On the paused video, dislodged from beneath Tori's jacket by the commotion, is a red gemstone on a chain about her neck. "What's that? Is that a vestigium?"

Jamie nods, frowning. "She's had that since... actually I can't remember who gave her that. But I remember her wearing it."

Vestigium are magical amulets, typically gems or crystals, which can be spelled to permanently activate them. Adrian Rampelly's Peruvian amulet in the court house was one type of vestigium, creating a magic-free bubble within which teleportation magic wouldn't work. Most vestigium have to be targeted at particular types of magic in order to work. Others can be used to store information, or to block certain types of spells, or anything a magician can think to 'program' them with.

"That silver clasp is familiar," says Ange, peering closely at the screen. Pity Jamie didn't use a better smart phone, the picture quality isn't good enough to see more clearly. "Starace uses one like that to let magicians teleport him."

"It blocks all Third Realm magic?" Jamie asks. Ange nods. "Like kryptonite for Ulani, huh?"

Ange smiles, remembering how Starace hadn't understood that reference when she'd made it. "They're not common, and the Ulani like to keep it that way. Do you know where this one is?"

"No," Jamie admits. He looks bothered.

"What's wrong?"

"We shared everything. I mean, all magical stuff. But I can't remember her sharing anything about that gem. And now I'm wondering if that's just because my memory's still not all back yet, or if she was keeping things from me..." He quits the video. "I want to find that gem, maybe it'll have some clues about what she was doing before she died. It's not in her things she left at Leventhal Holdings, Croz gave me all of those. But she studied with Mulberry Watson sometimes, I know she kept some stuff there."

"You know where?" Jamie nods. "Great, let's go!"

"Um, yeah," Jamie says uncertainly. "There's just one problem."

The problem is that Mulberry's Fifth Avenue apartment building, which he owns entirely, is tonight being used for a huge showbiz industry party held by Mulberry's company, Accord Entertainment. Alcohol is being served (in very large quantities, Ange guesses) and New York State law means that absolutely no underage people can be admitted. Jamie, of course, has a plan to bust in anyway.

Ange has suitable clothes, and goes home first to change, but Jamie is another matter. She meets him at a Fifth Avenue Armani outlet, which in

Manhattan closes at nine like everything else. He keeps her waiting half an hour, but rather than being annoyed, Ange is pleased because it gives her a chance to check all the clothes out first. When he arrives, she doesn't have to contend with his shopping-novice ways, and simply marches him to the best smart-casual stuff in the store. Best of all, Jamie accepts her greater expertise without much argument, so that when they leave, she's strolling up Fifth Avenue on a busy Friday night with a truly well-dressed and handsome boyfriend. Whereas if she'd left it to him, he'd have probably bought that ghastly blazer he liked, and she'd have been grinding her teeth all night at the missed opportunity...

"Holy crap this is expensive," says Jamie as they walk north through a thick mass of pedestrians, looking down as though not recognising himself. "Don't know how I'll explain it to Mum."

Ange shrugs. "You can keep it at my place."

Jamie looks at her suggestively. "Keep my clothes at your place?"

Ange smiles, and holds his arm as they walk. "Sure, why not? What was so important that it kept me waiting half an hour?"

"I'll show you in a minute."

After some blocks walking through increasingly crazy crowds, they see a portion of sidewalk opposite Central Park has been closed off with rope and red carpet, and is surrounded by a cluster of picture-snapping paparazzi, onlookers and autograph hunters. Limousines are pulling up, and fancy-dressed people emerge to shouts from the crowd, and a storm of camera flashes.

"Mulberry always knew how to throw a party," says Jamie.

"We could always try another night," Ange suggests.

"No. With everyone busy downstairs, upstairs will be pretty deserted. It's probably easier tonight." Ange looks up, and sees that the tower is about thirty floors — smallish for this part of Manhattan, but made of beautiful bricks with stylish decoration, from back in the day when people made skyscrapers that were pretty and not just functional.

"Or you could just *ask* Mulberry for Tori's stuff," Ange suggests.

"I did. Only that vestigium you saw isn't in the stuff he gave me, which makes me suspicious. And I don't know where else it could be."

Which makes Mulberry Watson a suspect in Tori's murder, Ange thinks grimly. Which would in turn make him a suspect in the attempt on Jamie's life, at the hospital. "So how do we get in?" she asks.

Jamie takes her arm and leads her across the road — with the sidewalk closed ahead, pedestrians are walking around the limousine entry zone on the road. Men with dark glasses are watching that temporary 'sidewalk' carefully, and Ange doesn't think it's just to make sure people don't get hit by limousines.

On the opposite sidewalk, Jamie pulls a small lead box from his jacket, and opens it. Ange feels a little dizzy, and blinks hard. She has an odd buzzing sensation, very different from the tingle when she detects magic, and not very pleasant. Within the lead box is a red gemstone, much like the one they're seeking of Tori's. Ange's eyes widen. It's a vestigium, and to judge by the effect it's having on her... and the buzzing fades as she thinks it, to be replaced by an odd sort of numbness.

"It draws from Third Realm?" she asks Jamie, and he nods. "Close it!" With something approaching panic, as the numbness spreads. Like the slow descent of blindness, her powers are being blocked.

Jamie closes the box, and the sensation returns with a rush. The roar of conversation from the passing hundreds and thousands of people, the growl of cars, the blare of horns, the wail of a nearby siren... it's nearly overwhelming. She takes a deep breath, and Jamie puts a hand on her arm to steady her. "I'm sorry," says Jamie. "But if we're going to get in, we have to teleport. And my magic won't work on an Ulani, unless your magic is blocked first."

"Where did you get that?" Ange asks incredulously.

"A friend owes me a favour," says Jamie. "I'm sorry, I promised I wouldn't say. I'm only borrowing it."

"You know that if Starace finds you've got that, he'll kill you? In fact, any Ulani who discovers any non-Ulani with one of those is supposed to kill them."

"Oh," says Jamie with a nervous grin. "And?"

Ange gives him a light punch on the arm. "There, I tried and failed. But Jamie, don't mess around with these things, they're dangerous! Blocking the powers of big magical people and houses, they don't like it much."

"Do you want to come with me?" Jamie presses. He looks at her very closely with those big brown eyes, and Ange knows it's going to be a real struggle to say no. Even considering what it will mean.

She exhales hard. "Si. Whatever, yes. Can you do it safely from here?" She looks across at the building.

"I can feel everything from here, at this range I get this mental map, I can place us to less than an inch."

"Including people?" Ange asks nervously, as Jamie opens the box once more. Again the unpleasant buzzing, and the spreading numbness. "Because I wouldn't want to rematerialise inside another person, either."

"Really?" Jamie teases. "Some of those people are really famous, might be fun to be inside them."

"Have you seen an old horror movie called 'The Fly?'"

"No, why?"

"Probably just as well." She represses a shiver, and Jamie puts his arms around her. His embrace feels stronger than usual… or rather, she's now much weaker. She's still very fit and strong, but with her powers gone she's just a regular athletic girl. And Jamie's still a powerful magician, and in this state could do anything to her that he liked. No wonder magical houses will kill rather than let others have the power to do this to them. "Damn I hate it," she mutters. "Being powerless."

"I did it for two years," Jamie says sombrely. Ange looks at him, nose to nose. "If magic ends, it'll all be like this. For all of us."

"At least we won't have to do it alone." She kisses him. And feels her stomach abruptly flip-flop…

…and with a jolt she's falling, then hits the floor barely a foot beneath her, and flails for balance. She hits a wall with each hand, and finds they're squeezed into a tight space… with lots of conversation, noise and… flushing toilets? She looks behind Jamie, and sure enough, the toilet is right behind him.

"You teleported into a toilet stall!" she hisses at him.

"Sure," says Jamie, reaching past her to change the latch to 'occupied'… and just in time, as someone rattles the door. "The upper floors are all shielded, but Mulberry can't shield the lower floors with a big party on because he's got so many magical guests."

All of the voices around them are male. "You teleported me into the *men's* toilets?"

"Was hardly going to drop into the women's toilets, was I?"

Ange rolls her eyes. "Jamie there's no room in here! You could have teleported us into one of these walls…"

And she stops as something tingles across her cheek, and she senses the arrival of several new magicians. They're sending out active pulses of magic, as though searching for someone. She points, and raises two fingers at Jamie.

Jamie nods. "They're looking for us," he whispers in her ear, as other conversation echoes loudly — several party goers having a raucous chat by the urinals. "They know someone teleported in, but having an Ulani here should block them from sensing either of us."

"Merda," Ange mutters, as she grasps the other reason why Jamie wanted her to come. "You might have explained that a bit more before we came."

"I thought it was obvious. I gotta stay close though." He wraps his arms around her, his body pressing hers from behind.

"Yeah, I don't know if you need to be *that* close."

"Better safe than sorry."

She hushes him, finger to his lips over her shoulder as she senses the two new magicians come closer. Being magically resistant, her body should be making Jamie as invisible to their scanning attempts as she is. Someone rattles the door again.

"Yeah wait your turn buddy!" says Jamie.

Ange senses the magician move away. Then they both leave the bathroom. "They'll be watching the exit though," she says. "Looking for anything out of place, like a girl leaving the men's room. Now what?"

"Hey, you ever wanted to be a man?" Ange stares at him… and then realises what he's suggesting.

"You're not going to use that vestigium again are you? Because I really hate that…"

"No no, I don't need to cast a spell on you. Just them."

Ange points out the door. "Jamie, some of these are serious adult magicians. Are you sure you can…?"

"Of course I can, come on." He closes his eyes for a moment, his hand on the stall door. Ange feels a sharp, deep chill. Then, "Let's go. Act manly."

He opens the door and they walk out. No one sees two people exiting the stall, though the urinals are full of well-dressed men against the wall. Ange blinks, having never seen that in person before. And resists the urge to grin like an idiot as men shoulder past her, use the drier, all without a second glance. Jamie's got them all fooled, she must look like any other guy to them.

The toilet door opens onto a crazy dance floor. Loud music booms, and several hundred guests dance and drink and shout conversation over the noise. Immediately Ange spots some famous faces, singers and actors, all signed to Mulberry's company. And there by the bar, she spots Alexis Rhodes, Eli's ally who exchanged threats with her at the big party the other week.

"Crap," says Ange. "Some big Shtaal Alliance people are here. You're not going to fool them with magic."

"We just need to make the stairs over there." Jamie nods across the room. It's so packed with people, getting there might take a while. And with so many of Mulberry's people, and even Eli's people here, they're going to get recognised.

Ange grabs his arm. "Let's dance," she says, and hauls him into the crowd. With a swordfighter's footwork, dancing comes naturally to her. With Jamie, not so much, but he copies her as best he can, and two people gyrating and bobbing amid a mass of gyrating, bobbing people become almost invisible in the crowd. They manoeuvre through the bodies as they dance, and Ange abruptly finds herself dancing beside the rapper Crew-Z, whose new album is just all over the radio, and then his girlfriend Gwenda Lane, whose line of fragrances they'd just walked past in a Fifth Avenue window display.

And then Crew-Z is dancing with *her*, somehow, and that's ridiculous fun for about thirty seconds… she gets no tingle from him, no doubt he's shroud-blind and has no idea who Mulberry Watson really is, and that this party is crawling with magicians. But Gwenda Lane looks very unimpressed at this tall, Italian intrusion, and Ange slides away before she creates some tabloid incident… and suddenly her arm is grabbed from behind, and she nearly smashes the assailant's nose back through his face in surprise…

"Hey there!" a white haired man in a pink jacket yells above the racket. "Which agency are you with?"

She blinks at him. "Agency?"

"You're a model, right? I'm a talent agent, but I haven't seen you around!"

In this place, people see a girl standing 6-4 in heels, of course they think she's a model. "Actually I'm not!" she replies. "Just a regular girl!"

"Really?" The man produces a business card with a near-magical flick of his wrist. "Well if you'd like to change that, give me a call! You'd have to go on a pretty strict diet, but we can help you with that!" And Ange reconsiders her decision not to smash his nose through his face, but she takes his card, and tries to smile graciously. "Oh, and great sword too! You wouldn't happen to be Ulani, would you?"

"I've heard of them, but no," says Ange, and retreats, searching for Jamie and cursing beneath her breath. So many magical people, she didn't pick that the agent was magical before it was too late. She spots Jamie by the stairs, now just nearby, and jogs up the first flight as he joins her.

"That guy was a passive," she tells Jamie as they climb. A couple are kissing drunkenly on the stairs. "He might give us away, I can't tell."

"Tori's room was on the seventh floor," says Jamie, taking two steps at a time, his face determined.

He's more out of breath than her at the seventh floor, and they walk along a hall between apartment doorways. "Strict diet!" Ange is complaining. "I've got no spare fat, he wants me to lose *muscle*! I'd be a walking skeleton!"

"You'd be a walking coathanger," Jamie puffs. "You'd last two seconds in a fight, and I'd stop wanting to kiss you. This door here." He tries the door, but it's locked. Then he tries some spells, for no better result.

"You really wouldn't kiss me if I were skinnier?" Ange asks, watching the deserted hallway.

"Why do women do this self-abuse?" Jamie murmurs, peering more closely at the lock. "Don't make this about me, most men think women are nuts on this stuff."

"That's really comforting Jamie, thanks."

Jamie smiles. "You sound like Tori. I can't get the door open Ange, I'll have to teleport."

"They'll see it," Ange warns. "I don't know if I can shield you, I mostly block magic that's directed at me."

"I'll chance it. I'm pretty sure I know where Tori left her stuff, see you in a minute." And with a flash of black smoke, he's gone. Ange rolls her eyes and leans against the wall, abandoned by her date at a party once more.

The elevator dings, and two women appear up the end of the hall. Ange immediately strides toward them, to hide the doorway she was waiting in front of, and not give Jamie away. With a sinking feeling, she sees that one of the women is Alexis Rhodes' blonde assistant who was with her boss in the bathroom at Eli's country house.

"I thought it was you," the blonde says coldly. Her friend is black, skinny in a blue dress. Both have venom in their eyes. "Where's James? I don't trust you alone with him."

They block the hall, and Ange stops. They have to tilt their heads to meet her eyes. "His name's Jamie," says Ange.

"Where is he?"

"None of your business."

"What have you done with him?" the black girl demands, pulling a wand from a handbag. They both do.

Ange smirks. "You think that's going to work on me?"

"You're so smug," the blonde girl sneers. "I bet you were that smug when you got your English buddy killed. Leading her to dinner with a guy Eli was trying to kill, you might as well have painted a target on her yourself. Though if she was anything like you, I bet she deserved it."

Ange can't recall making a conscious decision to swing, but suddenly Eli's collar has her convulsing, falling against the wall and sliding to the floor. The women stare, astonished. Then laugh hysterically.

"Oh my god! That's so precious!"

Past the painful convulsions, Ange has rarely been so furious. As soon as she has control once more, she goes for her sword… and is sent convulsing again, falling and rolling face up on the floor.

The blonde woman steps on her chest with a painful stiletto, and points her wand at Ange's face. "Poor little bitch, can't break her collar! You tried to swing at me, didn't you? This won't do any damage, but I bet it'll hurt." Electricity erupts from her wand. She's right, it does hurt.

"Hey!" comes a familiar voice from behind, and the women turn. Croz hits the blonde with a right hook and she flies, rebounds off the wall and sprawls motionless.

"Oh my god!" screams her friend. "I can't believe you hit her! You hit a girl!"

Croz puts a big knife to the other girl's throat, and she backs against the wall to try and escape it. The knife is huge, the kind of thing you'd use to skin a moose. "Some of my best friends have been killed by girls," Croz growls. "I see you pointing that wand at another Leventhal employee again, let alone a defenseless one, I'll cut your head off. Understand?" A short, fast nod. "Run."

The girl runs. Croz puts the knife away, and extends a hand to Ange. "Here."

Ange is too furious to breathe. She hates helplessness above nearly everything, and the collar turns any attempt to do what's right, into something wrong. She tries to strike Croz, and is immediately convulsed by the collar. It's truly painful now, and her teeth grit as her back arches.

"Hey," says Croz, annoyed. "Don't be stupid, take my damn hand."

As soon as the convulsions stop, she starts them again. It's not hard. She could kill anyone right now, if the collar let her. Herself included, maybe. Now the pain gets awful. She snarls against it, heart racing, fighting to breathe.

"Angelina!" Croz kneels by her, grabs a fistful of collar and tries to stop her convulsing. "Damn stupid girl, you stop that. What do you think you're going to prove?"

Ange glares at him as the collar releases her once more, saliva frothing at her mouth. And tries to headbutt him, with a defiant glare past the pain... which lasts only until she starts screaming, only there's no air in her lungs and no sound comes out.

"Goddamn *idiot!*" Croz shouts, genuinely alarmed. "You trying to kill yourself, is that it?" He straddles her, and pins her to the ground with a hand down hard over her mouth, keeping her looking at him through the pain. "You think you've had a hard life? Huh? You think this proves how unfair it is? Poor little you, huh?"

His eyes stare into hers, with hard intensity. This time when the collar releases her, she lets it, and just gasps. "You had a place to call home. You know who you are. But you left it. That's your choice. I had *nothin'*. Just this company, and Eli, and some good friends who've got my back because I've got theirs'. My part of Chicago's where if the shroud-blind don't shoot you, the vampires will eat you. Sometimes I think I'd prefer the damn vampires, they don't rack up the same bodycount. My daddy got shot three times before he finally died, and my mommy was a crackhead who abandoned me 'cause I didn't mean as much to her as her next score. She ODed a year later, and I've never learned any more about her because honestly, I don't care.

"If it weren't for Eli, I'd have probably gone the same way. Now you come here, and you try to take away the best and only thing I got. And now you're miserable 'cause it didn't work out for you? Well boo hoo for you. I've seen a thousand people worse off than you. So get your shit together, 'cause I'm sick of this spoiled brat crap."

With a flash, Jamie rematerialises on this side of the door. "Croz? Ange!" He runs over, staring at the unconscious blonde on the floor. "What the hell happened?"

"Mean girls being mean," says Croz, getting to his feet. "You know, I once heard a woman on TV say the world would be more peaceful if women ran it. Funniest thing I ever heard."

"Ange." Jamie kneels at her side, all concern. Ange ignores him, and climbs slowly to her feet. The fury is still there, but she can't hit Leventhal Holdings people... and would never dream of hurting Jamie. She smashes a door with a kick, then another, making a huge hole and sending splinters flying. Then she slumps against the wall, tears streaming.

"I think I killed her, Jamie," she gasps. "I think I did."

"Who?" Jamie points at the blonde on the floor. "Her?"

"No! Lacey. I knew it was dangerous, and she wanted to go, and I should have said no, but I didn't and she died! I killed my own best friend!"

"No you didn't, don't be stupid." Jamie holds her while she sobs. "There's no way you could have known, the odds are crazy! She'd have as much chance of being hit by lightning, you're being stupid."

Jamie looks at Croz. Croz watches, expression softening. Realising, perhaps, that her reasons for being upset are somewhat better than he'd thought.

"You get what you came for?" Croz asks him.

"Yeah. I think so."

"Good. I'll cover for you."

"Thanks buddy. What is it with big parties that everyone's so excited when they start, and in tears at the end?" Croz snorts, and checks on the unconscious blonde girl. "You need help with that?"

"Nope." Croz flings the woman's limp arm, then lifts her easily over his shoulder. "First thing Eli taught me — always clean up your own mess." He walks to the elevator.

CHAPTER TWELVE

One of the perks of working for Eli Leventhal is that he's got friends working in every major public building in Manhattan north of Canal Street. One of them lets Ange and Jamie into the New York public library through the Fifth Avenue entrance after midnight, and they walk down the quiet entry hall, footsteps echoing off the high ceiling.

The main library chamber is gorgeous, with high vaulted ceilings and a whole upper floor balcony running around a solid wall of books. Reading desks across a wide floor make rows, and the decoration in the stone reminds Ange of a church. It's lit only with nightlight, and shadows fill the alcoves between shelves.

"Here," says Jamie, striding to the center of the reading floor. "It's supposed to be here." He extends a hand, and his short staff appears in it with a flash. In his other hand, he holds the red gem he recovered from Tori's belongings, but it gives no sign. Jamie closes his eyes and concentrates, murmuring to himself. Then opens his eyes. Nothing. He frowns, and looks around.

"You're sure that's it?" Ange asks, wandering about the book-filled walls. There's something here, she can feel it. A faint prickling, like background radiation.

"Well, it's where I heard it would be."

"Heard from whom?" She looks around. If it opens from the middle of the floor, it'll have to be some kind of magic portal, she thinks. She wonders if an Ulani will be any help at all.

"People," says Jamie.

"Ah." She's always found the vagueness of magicians annoying. They never bother explaining. "Jamie, can I ask you something?"

"Sure."

"Why did you want to be shroud-blind? After Tori died. I mean, the shroud made you believe she was killed in a car crash. That hurt just as much, surely?"

Jamie says nothing. Ange knows it's painful, but right now she's thinking of Lacey, and it hurts like hell. "I should have been there Ange," he says after a long moment. "She asked me to come, that night. But I was pissed at her... I got jealous of her sometimes. She was so much better than me, at magic. Everyone said so, everyone knew she was going to be a big deal in Leventhal Holdings one day, or beyond. And she'd been teasing me about something earlier. And she wouldn't tell me what was going on over the phone, so I said either tell me what you're involved with, or you can go on your own. And she hung up on me."

He wasn't trying to escape Tori's death, Ange realises. He was trying to escape his feelings of responsibility for it. Ange thinks of Lacey, of how she invited her to come along to that pub. She knows exactly how it feels.

"And I think of how annoyed I got with her," Jamie continues, his voice strained, "and how I wished sometimes she'd just leave me alone. And now that she has left me alone, there's nothing I wouldn't give to have her back here as annoying and bossy as she liked."

Ange crosses the reading floor to him, and grasps his hands. Immediately she feels it, like a jolt of electricity. Jamie's eyes go wide. "Whoa! You feel that?"

Ange nods, astonished. "What *is* that?"

"Well, I don't know what *you're* feeling, but I'm feeling some kind of... portal?" He looks at her hands on his, which are in turn holding his staff, and Tori's vestigium. "I think you're completing some kind of circuit, like an electrical circuit. No don't let go!" As she thinks to test that theory. "Sometimes it doesn't come back. Just don't fight it. Just..."

Something changes.

Everything changes.

And it feels like the world has been flipped over.

Ange blinks around. They're not in the New York library anymore. They're in an attic, with old wooden floors and rickety roof beams. Around them are many shelves, full of books. Daylight shines through the attic windows. Ange goes to one, her boots squeaking on the floorboards, and peers out.

"Um, we're on a mountain," she says. Her voice holds only mild disbelief, because she doesn't really believe it. For an Ulani, this isn't possible. "It looks like we've teleported."

Jamie joins her. The mountains are beautiful, if a little desolate, and covered in pine trees. A pair of women walk up a dirt road, leading a donkey. They wear old coats and headscarves, and look cold. The attic is cold, far colder than the library had been. From the women come snatches of distant conversation, not in English. Ange and Jamie frown at each other. "You're the linguist," Jamie offers.

"Having two languages doesn't make me a linguist," Ange retorts.

"Russian?" Jamie wonders.

"No!" Ange scolds him. "It sounds nothing like Russian, use your ears."

"Well sor-ry for growing up in Boston," says Jamie, pulling out his phone. Which is a good idea, Ange thinks, and pulls out her own. "I get no signal, what about you?"

"Um…" A bar appears, as her phone finds a network. Then **Welcome to Turkcell**. "Turkey," she says. "They're speaking Turkish." Her phone tells her the time and date. "And it's tomorrow, early morning."

"So it's the same time as New York." Jamie turns and looks at the shelves of books. "And this is Eli's secret book collection. How cool is this?" But he's not smiling or excited. This is where Tori died. Or so they've heard.

"Why?" Ange demands. "Why would he keep a stash of books in Turkey? And how is this even possible? To teleport that distance takes a huge energy beacon, or we'd…"

"Be dead, sure." Jamie peers at the shelves. A lot of the books seem quite old, but not all. Everything is well dusted and maintained. "That magic didn't feel like teleportation to me. Teleporting is violent."

Ange nods. "Yeah, it felt…" and she realises she can't explain it, to someone who doesn't have her powers. Maybe she should cut Jamie some slack about being vague. "It felt different."

"I don't think we've actually left New York." Jamie pulls a book and peers at it.

"How...?" Ange tries to gather her thoughts. "How can we still be in New York?" She points out the window. "I'm pretty sure we're in Turkey. Unless we're in two places at once."

"Exactly," says Jamie. "Realm shift."

Ange blinks. "Realm shift?"

"The Realms are alternative dimensions, right? We can't see them or interact with them directly, we only know they exist by the magic they generate... or rather, by the forces that magicians interpret as magic. Like trying to guess who the guy is in the toilet stall next to you by how bad he smells, or what noises he makes, even if you can't see him."

Ange grins at him in disbelief. "You know, that's the *worst* magical analogy I've ever heard. Yuck."

"You're welcome." Jamie puts the book back, and moves on. "But the alternative dimensions do exist. There's been theory for a long time that the most powerful magicians might be able to bring a bit of that dimension, into this dimension. It makes an overlap, two different places, existing in the same place, simultaneously." He puts his two hands flat, one atop the other. "It's called Realm shift. I've never seen it before, but if anyone can do it, Eli can."

"Like Croz's Ferrari?"

Jamie frowns. "What about his Ferrari?"

"It's a four-seater inside. Bickel says Eli did it as a custom job."

"Wow," says Jamie. "It was a two-seater when I sat in it. But yeah, I guess Eli could pull that off. It's only a small thing. He'd have had to borrow space from another dimension to do it."

Now Ange is feeling the disbelief. She'd thought it must be some kind of illusion or trick. But if Jamie's right, this is real. And she's actually in Turkey... and not. She stares out the window, at the beautiful mountains. "So it's limited to this attic?"

"If we try to leave it," says Jamie, "I guess it'll collapse, and we'll be back in New York."

"And what if someone here tries to get in?" Thinking of who might have tried to hurt Tori.

"Yeah," Jamie murmurs, looking around. "I got no idea. Have to ask Eli." He peers along a row of shelves. "Most of these books aren't in English."

"English is a very recent language," Ange reasons. Jamie is walking with Tori's amulet held up before him, scanning the rows of books for some kind of response. "Lacey said English is only about four or five hundred years old. Most of this looks like Greek, Latin and Arabic, they're all much older."

"And Chinese," says Jamie, pointing as he walks. "Lots of Chinese. Should have brought Meisha."

"Meisha speaks Chinese? She was protesting how she's American, *not* Chinese."

"You don't know the Chinese magical community much, do you?" Ange shakes her head. "If you have Chinese parents and you do magic, you speak Chinese. They've got the oldest tradition of all of us."

Tori's red gem suddenly begins to glow. Jamie presses it along the row of books, back and forth until it glows strongest... but still not strong enough.

"It's on the other side," says Ange, and they go around to the next aisle. Jamie runs the amulet across the spines of a row of old books opposite where they'd been looking. The gem glows red on one in particular, and Jamie pulls that book from the shelf. It's black and plain, small and ordinary looking. It doesn't look especially old, as Jamie opens the cover page.

"This is Latin, right?" says Jamie.

Ange nods, pointing to the page. "This looks like the author's name. Umm... Asclepius. Sounds a bit familiar."

"It should," says Jamie, very seriously. "That's the name of an old Greek god."

Ange is astonished. "You know the names of old Greek gods?"

"I know this one. It's the pen name of the great wizard Ashkir. What's the bet Tori was researching the Ashkir Prophecy?" He stares at Ange. "Oh my god. What if she knew it was coming? What if she'd guessed that magic was about to end, and someone didn't want her to know any more?"

A phone call to Croz tells Jamie that Eli has left the party, and can be found at a big old church in Mid-Town. It's a catholic cathedral that would not have been out of place in Milan, but is nestled here amongst the high towers of steel and glass. The new and the old, the mystical and the commercial, all jostling together for space.

It's nearly two in the morning, and the side door is locked, but a gesture from Jamie solves that. They enter, and walk down the central aisle in that great, silent hush that only a deserted church can make. Down the far end stands Eli, gazing up at the huge stained glass windows in the shape of a giant flower. Beneath the windows, Christ, on a crucifix, looming above them all. Eli talks in a low voice with a priest, and Ange puts a hand on Jamie's shoulder.

They wait, and Ange bows her head and crosses herself. "Didn't know you were Catholic," Jamie murmurs.

"I'm not," says Ange. "Just Italian."

The priest leaves, and Eli glances at them. They walk to him, and he gazes up at Christ on his cross.

Ange can't resist to ask. "Did you know him?" Jamie elbows her. Evidently it's the wrong thing to ask.

"Don't worry Jamie," says the old man. "She doesn't know the rule."

"What's the rule? Don't ask Eli about Jesus?" Jamie gives her an 'oh my god' look. "Scared you'll have to tell me he didn't exist?" Jamie facepalms.

"Of course he existed," Eli says mildly. "And of course I knew him. Which is exactly why I won't discuss it."

"Why not?"

Eli smiles, and indicates where the priest has just departed. "Even the priests ask. Everyone wants to know what he was like, from someone who actually knew him. But all these years, the faith has been shaped by the word, from the book. Do you know why the word is so important?"

"Tell me."

"Because it is all people have. No one lives today who was there. Except me. Were I to talk, then I would replace the word, and the book, which would become irrelevant. So I shall not talk."

"Hang on," says Jamie, "most people wouldn't know you'd talked, because most believers are shroud-blind. They couldn't accept that you were there even if you told them."

"And there are many senior in the church who are *not* shroud-blind," says Eli. "As Angelina knows, being of an order created by the church long ago." Ange nods, remembering the priests who came calling on Starace. "If I have struggled for anything in my life, it is to keep the fates of the magical and the non-magical separate. To combine them brings no good to anyone. And I will not change the fate of this institution, built on faith in the word, by speaking of things that would destroy that faith."

"You can only be a good Christian if ignorant?" Ange asks drily.

"Faith is not ignorance," Eli says firmly. "Faith is faith." Gazing upward, as though remembering an old, admired friend. "And even magicians can have it. So what brings you kids here?"

"Why do you have a secret library of books in Turkey?" Jamie asks him. "And why can you only get in with realm shift?"

Eli gazes at him intently. "Every senior magician in my organisation knows about the library, Jamie. That's why the entry portal is in the New York Public Library, where anyone can access, with the right tools and permissions. You got in." Jamie nods. "Why?"

Jamie dangles Tori's vestigium. "I recovered this from her workroom at Mulberry's. It holds memory of all the latest stuff she was reading and studying. Why would she store so much on here?"

"Because the shroud often melts computer drives when you try to store magical information on it," says Eli. "Including phones, now that we have computers in phones. The shroud hides some information more vigorously than others."

"Tori was studying very advanced stuff, wasn't she?"

Eli nods, frowning. "She was."

"Like the Ashkir Prophecy."

Understanding dawns in Eli's eyes. He takes a deep breath. "And like I told her at the time," he says heavily, "I will not discuss the Ashkir Prophecy beyond what I've already said."

"You're scared someone will try to reverse it," says Jamie. Ange recalls what Shawna Dubois said to Eli at the mansion in Connecticut, following his announcement. "That someone will try to save magic. How is it done?"

Eli's expression goes hard. "This is a secret that I guard with my life, Jamie. I ask you to respect that."

"What if she already knew it was happening two years ago?" Jamie retorts. "What if she knew that Mayor Riley knew, and that he was trying to reverse it? Because she *despised* that man, she kept telling me how one day she was going to kill him personally… what if she went into that library to find out how to stop him?"

"Jamie…" Eli begins.

"Because you wouldn't talk to her about it!" Jamie blazes. "Like you won't talk to me now!"

"Eli!" says Ange in alarm, sensing a building rush of magic up the church's far end. In a rapid series of flashes, three men and two women appear beyond the pews, amid drifting smoke. Eli gazes at them, unsurprised, one corner of his mouth twisting upward.

"Well met, Monsieur Le Fevre," he calls, his voice echoing off the vaulted ceiling. "And friends, High Councillors all. Welcome to my city."

"Oh come now Eli," says the portly, balding man leading the new arrivals. He wears a bureaucrat's suit, as do they all, and his accent is thick French. The Mayor of Paris, Ange recalls, in the shroud-blind world. She vaguely recalls a newspaper article on his courtesy visit to New York, something about trade and sister-city relationships. Apparently that wasn't the *only* reason he came "I do not think that the city is *all* yours?" He walks down the aisle, and points at Jamie. "I have come on High Council business, to investigate the case of young Mr MacDonald here." His fellow bureaucrats follow behind him, in close formation. Ange feels something odd about their approach, not so much a tingle as a static buzz, but uneven. Like a radio signal that keeps fading in and out.

"Ah," says Eli. "Jamie, Angelina, this is Jean-Luc Le Fevre. A senior High Councillor. A magical institution that I created, you may recall." Le Fevre smiles drily. "And how goes the investigation, Jean-Luc?"

"Ongoing," he replies. "It is too early to say. You must wait to find out, as the rules say. And even you must play by the rules, Eli. Even you."

"I know," Eli says evenly. "I *wrote* those rules."

The buzzing and surging sensation gets worse, grating Ange's nerves like fingernails being drawn down a blackboard. "Eli," she says in a low voice, warningly.

Eli holds up a hand to her. He knows. Ange puts a hand on Jamie's shoulder, and draws him back several steps as the five High Council officials arrive at the front of the church, and spread in a half-circle about them, with Le Fevre in the center.

Eli gazes about at them all, with a small, almost-smile on his face. As though something has just happened that he was somewhat expecting. He's leaning on his short staff, Ange sees, though she can't recall him having it when she and Jamie entered. "Jean-Luc," he says, almost reproachfully. "You did not really come to New York about Jamie's case, did you?"

Le Fevre's smile is tight. "Eli. You are not a stupid man. You knew how the news of Ashkir's Prophecy would be received by the magical world. You must have expected this."

"The High Council is not the magical world, Jean-Luc," Eli says warningly. "The High Council is just another institution. I should know, since I created it. And what I create, I can destroy."

"I don't think so Eli. We practise the oldest magic, older even than yours. Not even Grand Magisters can oppose us. Some have tried before, and failed, as you recall."

"I do recall," Eli agrees. "But I am not them."

A flash of smoke, and a short staff appears in Jamie's hand. Eli glances at him, then at Ange, and gestures with his eyes that they should move back further. Neither does. Ange's hand itches for her sword, but now is not quite the time.

"We will not let the Ashkir Prophecy stand, Eli," Le Fevre warns. "It cannot stand."

Eli laughs, with real amusement. It's the first time Ange has heard him do that. "Well you can't stop it, Jean-Luc. Any more than King Canute could stand on the beach and turn back the tide. He was a wizard you know. Intensely vain man. Never *actually* stood on a beach and forbade the tide to come in that I know, but having met him I can understand why people might think he would."

"The High Council will not allow magic to die!" Le Fevre thunders. He's quite upset, his big cheeks flushed red. "The decline of magic is reversible, and you know it. Now we have asked you to assist us in this reversal, and you have refused." Ange blinks. It's the first she's heard of it. Eli has not been sharing the High Council's distress with everyone. "Now we ask you again. Politely."

Eli sighs, and rubs his forehead. "You know, there are times I think my Ulani friend here is right. We magicians really are the biggest bunch of fools." He smiles to himself. "And I'm the biggest fool of them all. I mean, I helped create the High Council. Third century and thirty, by the Christian calendar, I was wandering the streets of this brand new capital that Emperor Constantine had built for himself — Constantinople, he called it. And it looked so impressive, and promised this new age of Christian law... and I thought, wouldn't it be nice if there were laws for wizards? Wouldn't it be nice if they had to answer to someone, for running around and doing all the nasty, stupid things that people with too much power and no responsibility will do, to those who can't stop them."

He glances at Ange, and winks at her.

"And so, the High Council," he continues, with a grand gesture to all five magicians before him. "No more murders of the shroud-blind... or, well, *less* murders. But it can't stop the wars, because no one will agree to *those* powers, or stop all the other horrible little things that we magicians continue to do to each other. And of course you never consider it your mission to actually help *ordinary* people, oh no. Just to perpetuate the same old tyrannies that we always have. And now it leads us here, to this. The choice between the evil wizard who will save your bacon, and the good one who won't."

"We take no sides in your little war with Mayor Riley," Le Fevre huffs.

"No? You've met with him, yes? What did he tell you? 'I can save magic, but first you have to get Leventhal out of the way?' That is what you're here to do, yes?"

"You have no right," says Le Fevre, "to stand in the way of the preservation of the magical race!"

"Oh, a *race* are we now!" Eli's eyebrows arch, dangerous anger in his eyes for the first time. "A *superior* race, perhaps? And that would make you the most superior of them all, would it?"

"Says Mr Leventhal from his ivory tower, the seventh richest man in the world…"

"And I've paid back every cent I've earned with jobs and donations and investments!" Eli shouts at them. "When have the rest of you parasites ever done the same? Sucking on the blood of your so-called inferiors, at least I built my ivory tower with my own two hands!"

"You think yourself so much better than your own kind?" Le Fevre snorts. "Every magician has his weakness. And the old magic of the High Council can find even yours, Eli."

They produce staves, each with a flash of smoke, and place them end down on the church floor pavings. The uneven buzz in Ange's ears, and on her skin, becomes a pulsating throb. Atop each of the staves is a small metal container, built into the wood. The High Councillors' faces look very hard and determined.

"Oh," says Eli, nodding and looking at each in turn. "I sense… hydrogen!" He points to the first staff with his own. "The simplest element, the foundation of any good elemental trap."

An elemental trap. Magical power flows through the natural elements, converting their energy into some other form. The old magic can make a shield, Ange has heard, comprised of a series of elements particular to each magician. In the right combination, these make a trap, that will neutralise a magician's powers, and render him vulnerable. Vestigium alone cannot work on Eli, or on any Grand Magister, as no one truly knows which Realm his power comes from.

"And a vacuum!" Eli continues, pointing to the next woman. "Good choice Elaine, vacuum can block conductivity in the right combination. And Jean-Luc, yours is clearly uranium, the radiation is obvious. And lastly silicon, and… oh, this is a hard one." He closes his eyes for a moment. "Deuterium! Very interesting."

"We've had two thousand years to analyse your magic," Le Fevre says heavily. "This pattern, arrayed against you, will block access to any of the natural paths that you might use. Combined with the old magic, the shield will be impenetrable. It's over, Eli. You must concede."

"Eli!" Jamie hisses. "Eli you have to leave!"

"Oh my boy," says Eli, with tired amusement. "They don't want me to leave. They want me to die."

"This does not concern you boy," says Le Fevre. "Only him. We do not even require him to help us in saving magic for all humanity. He only needs to stop plotting against us. We will not join you in this insane suicide pact, Eli. And we will defend ourselves against you."

Now is the time to draw her sword, and Ange does so. "Eli, I'm immune," she reminds him. "Give the word and I'll cut them down."

"No Angelina. This magic is as old as that of the Ulani. You're not immune to me, and you're not immune to this." He raises his staff crosswise before him, his face set hard. "This fight is mine alone." And he gives her a faint smile. "Though you can have whatever's left."

Le Fevre raises his staff at Eli. "Allez!" he shouts. A huge wall of light erupts across the five raised staves, in a great arc before the church seats, and a deep bass hum that Ange can feel rattling her bones. Flickers of lightning dance between the five Councillors, then flash forward, and strike Eli's staff. He stands braced, staff crosswise, lightning strikes feeding outward towards its ends.

"No!" yells Jamie, and raises his own staff. A great shockwave rebounds off the wall of light and his staff disintegrates in flame and ash as Jamie staggers for balance.

"Angelina!" shouts Eli, face down as though to protect his eyes. "Shield him! You can defend him, but do not attack or it will kill you both!"

Ange shoves Jamie behind her, and feels immediately hot as the energy coursing into Jamie is absorbed by her instead. She grits her teeth against the burning pain, and holds her sword and opposite hand before her, attempting to establish some kind of barrier.

The great arc of light continues to grow, brighter and stronger, circling around Eli as he stands before the altar. Within, Ange sees it converge on him like a colossal weight, driving him to one knee, his staff raised like an umbrella against a hurricane.

"Now now now!" screams Le Fevre, and the wall begins to crackle and burn. Within, the circle turns to a firestorm, and for a moment Ange loses all sight of Eli, consumed by the unimaginable energy. Le Fevre laughs hysterically, for the sheer joy of such power. Ange can barely believe her deafened, blinded, crackling senses. She's never seen anything like it, nor even imagined such a thing was possible. And then she sees, beneath the sheeting flame, Eli's feet, and a hand tracing a circle about himself near the floor as he crouches.

Gravity shifts, and for the briefest moment, everything in the church seems to fall toward the middle, benches and pews leaping across the stone, the altar falling, soundless in the din. A howling gale erupts, and the flames swirl and scream, electricity blinding as it strikes the walls. Then the flames are gone, replaced only by Eli, standing behind what appears to be a black void of nothing, as large as he is. About it, reality itself appears to bend, and with a sensation approaching nausea, Ange realises that time within the church is slowing, the closer to that hole one stands. The five councillors stare at it, wind whipping their clothes and hair. A candle holder leaps into it, and slows briefly before vanishing. Behind it, Eli stands calmly, head down and not looking at it. But he looks sideways, at Ange.

"Get down," he says, and though she cannot hear him, she can read his lips well enough. She throws herself on Jamie, and covers him. With a final gasp, the black hole expands, and Ange can hear the entire church grinding and groaning, trying to fall into that black annihilation. Pews lift off the church floor and fly at Eli, and abruptly the blackness is gone. The wind stops, and benches, books and broken glass fall and clatter to the floor. A sudden silence, save for the creaking of roof timbers, far overhead. Of the five councillors, there is no sign.

Jamie pulls himself out from under Ange and crouches, staring in disbelief. "Holy shit."

Eli leans heavily on his staff, breathing hard. Ange moves carefully to his side. "You nearly lost this entire church, didn't you?" she gasps.

"This entire part of Mid-Town," Eli mutters. "A near thing. But it was the only way." He turns and looks at Ange. "The backlash has finally started. This will be just the first."

"And you're going to stand in the way of the entire magical world?" Ange asks in disbelief. "All of them desperate not to lose their powers? Eli that was the High Council! If you've lost the High Council..."

"You must have faith, Angelina," Eli says quietly, and turns to gaze up at Christ on his cross. "We have friends in this fight yet."

CHAPTER THIRTEEN

Ange doesn't like the Mercedes dawdling down Broadway in the heavy midday traffic — they're approaching Canal, and with the sidewalks swarming with tourists and locals alike, the possible threats are many. But Eli Leventhal is no one's easy target, and he has Croz and Bickel in the car with him, a second Mercedes packed with Response Division commandos, plus her trailing them on her Ducati.

The lead Mercedes goes left along busy Houston, then right into Little Italy, Ange keeping a wary lookout from side to side through parked cars and delivery trucks. Here the roads are lined with cafes, markets, gelato stores, restaurants, all with Italian names in fancy signs to attract the tourists… because the locals, of course, don't need the advertising to know what's what. Little Italy gives way to China Town, and suddenly all the signs are Chinese, and there's duck hanging in the butcher window, and live crabs scuttling in baskets before the seafood shop, and every second face is Asian.

Parked cars and pedestrians make a narrow bottleneck ahead, and Ange roars past the two Mercedes to get there first, peering past vans and into blindspots between shops in case of ambush. A couple of policemen by their squad car nod to her as she passes — friendly cops, keeping an eye out. Behind her the Mercedes pulls up outside a nondescript restaurant, and Bickel gets out, holding the door open for Eli, Meisha and Croz as the second Mercedes parks across the street. Ange pulls the bike around and comes back to park beside some scaffolding that covers a neighbouring facade. A couple of tough-looking Chinese kids come to keep watch over it, and wave away the fiver Ange offers them, phones and cigarettes out, preparing for the long haul.

Ange pulls off gloves and helmet, and walks to where the rest of the gang have vanished into the restaurant, several more locals taking up guard at the doorway. She's admitted with a nod, and passes quickly by the dining area through a back way that goes into the kitchen. Chefs scramble by roaring hot woks, far too many and far too frantic to account for the small number of diners in the restaurant. Something important is afoot, no doubt.

Beyond the kitchen is a small room with just one large, circular table. There the restaurant's owners, husband and wife, bow and shake hands with everyone, smiling nervously and showing guests their seats. They are suitably awestruck with Eli, and nearly as much so with Meisha, holding her chair for her, making certain her chopsticks are perfectly aligned, while Meisha thanks them with her usual charm. Ange takes a seat at Meisha's side, hanging her sword on the chairback, and smiles as a shy girl of perhaps ten approaches to pour some tea, but with eyes only for Meisha. It occurs to Ange that in this part of town, among those with the sight, Meisha is a rock star.

"Yo Ange, where's J-Mac?" Bickel asks her.

"At school," Eli answers for her. And gives her a stern look. "Like every seventeen year old should be."

"Yes, but I get to be with you instead," Ange says sweetly. "So I can learn from the wisdom of my elders."

"Listen here young lady," Eli begins, and Croz groans. "I've been alive for a very long time, and I've seen a lot of people succeed, and a lot of people fail, and the common factor in all of those successes is education. Now you can ignore this lesson at your peril, but..." And he's interrupted by shouting and commotion from the kitchen.

"Oh thank god," says Croz, as they all rise from their chairs, and Eli reaches up to whack his assistant on the back of the head.

First through the kitchen door is Ren, deadly handsome in a nice suit and a sword not unlike Ange's own. His eyes too are only for Meisha, and

Ange realises why the chair on Meisha's other side remains empty. Second through the door is Master Yu himself, the most powerful magician of all the great Chinese masters, and the restaurant owners stammer and bow as though in the presence of royalty… which Ange supposes is close to the truth. Master Yu thanks them, and shakes hands warmly with Eli, with a genuine smile. To everyone else he nods and smiles, and they all take their seats, with Ren at Meisha's right side. Her right hand, and Ren's left, remain under the table, Ange notes with amusement.

"Master Yu," says Eli, as the owners hand out menus with trembling hands, and a crowd of chefs watch on anxiously from the kitchen door, "so how is the teleporting beacon in the Chinese Embassy?"

"It is adequate," says Yu. "Though nothing like as impressive as your own monster. We have to come one at a time, and the time between recharges is more than ten minutes."

"And Mr Ren can do his own teleporting over those distances?" Eli asks, looking at Ren. Ren blushes.

"He can," says Yu. "He is most accomplished. Like your Ms Wing." He looks at Meisha, then to Ange. Master Yu's age, Ange hears, is about twelve hundred years. To the uninformed, he looks a young sixty, hair still mostly dark, and wearing an expensive suit. He could be a visiting businessman, doing deals. Ange meets his gaze, and does not look away. Yu has the look of someone displeased, but hiding it well.

Meisha orders for them all in Mandarin with Ren's help, and the owners triple check before taking it to the kitchen. There all hell breaks loose, chefs shouting and much banging, chopping and clanging, while Eli and Yu make smalltalk. Then the family children and others are paraded into the room to say a shy hello, and bow, and have their cheeks pinched, before being trooped back upstairs to their homework. Expensive peach wine is poured for all but Ange, and the food when it arrives is as delicious as the smell in the air.

"Mulberry sends his apologies," says Eli as they eat from the selection. "He's in Los Angeles, there's some Hollywood deal or other, I forget."

"A new TV talent show," says Croz around a mouthful of noodles. "Starring some of his biggest singers as the judges."

"Oh wow really?" says Meisha. "Is that the one with Lucy Ray?"

Croz nods. "That's the one. Only they're all arguing over who gets to headline, and there's millions involved."

"Lucy Ray's a great singer," Meisha says promptly, "but I don't know about her as a judge. She's such a bitch."

Ren looks nervously at his Master. Master Yu roars with laughter, and gestures for Ren to relax. Ange sees Meisha's little smile, completely unsurprised. What an advantage in any social setting, she thinks, to already know a person's mood before you say something. Meisha will see it as a colour. "Young people and their entertainments today," Yu muses. "Do you know such things, Eli?"

"I'd rather have my ears cleaned with red hot pokers," says Eli. "A *talent* show, they call it. What misuse of the English language." Meisha and Croz smother smiles.

"The Chinese language is now misused in just the same way," says Yu. "Now there are dancing shows. Meisha, do you know these shows too?"

"I know of them Master Yu," says Meisha, "but I can't really appreciate what I can't see. I stick with the singing."

"And just as well you can't see them," says Yu. "These girls, they put on horrible shoes and they thrash about the stage like someone has put an electric eel in their underwear." Meisha smothers a laugh. "When I was a young man, near the end of the Tang Dynasty, my father brought me to court where I saw a beautiful woman perform a lotus dance in the traditional style. If I regret anything, it is that I was not born even earlier, that I could not enjoy more of the Tang Dynasty arts and dance. So much has been lost."

"Ange, I hear that you can dance quite well," Meisha volunteers.

Ange glances at Croz, who flashes eyes at her. Of course Croz told her, she and Jamie weren't as stealthy at Mulberry's party as they'd thought. "Sword fighting is basically dancing," she says. "Though my favorite dancing is Cossack dancing."

"Why does an Italian learn to dance like a Russian Cossack?" Eli wonders.

Ange shrugs. "Ulani and Cossacks are warriors. We're noisy too." Master Yu eyes her with continued distrust. "Ren, pass me those prawns? Yum."

"Anyhow, I was speaking of Mulberry," Eli resumes. "He protests he doesn't like LA, but I think he's had the Hollywood bug for a while. I can't stand that town."

"You're a New Yorker," says Meisha. "Of course you can't."

"In New York," says Eli, "whenever I meet some new ambitious person, I can speak at least five or six sentences before conversation turns to money. We can talk about how much the Mets suck, or how much the Knicks suck, or can you believe what beautiful old building is being pulled down to build some horrid glass monstrosity in its place."

"And then you try not to admit you're the one financing the damn thing," Croz adds.

"Shush," says Eli without missing a beat. Ange realises just how much like father and son Eli and Croz really are, the younger man endlessly teasing the older, with affection. "But in LA, whenever I meet such a person, the very first thing they say comes down to, 'By God aren't you rich, how can I get some of it?' Every time."

"This is like Shanghai," Yu agrees. "Just the same. Though I am glad I just run the Jīnmén school, and not a business empire. I spend all of my time thinking on magic. Eli, running your business looks exhausting."

Eli shrugs. "Money is a habit of mine, I acquired it young. The oldest Jewish cliche, I know, but in my case it's true. I've been involved with money most of my life, it holds no mysteries with me. Making more is as much a hobby to me as anything. Some old men play with cars in their garage. I play with money."

"An interesting hobby," Yu agrees. "If it has lost its mystery to you, what keeps you interested?"

"The conviction that I know better how to spend it than anyone else," says Eli.

Master Yu laughs and nods. "Mayor Riley. Politicians."

"Anyone. But him especially."

"And now, it seems, he has won the High Council to his side," says Yu. Silence at the table. Smalltalk is now over, Ange thinks. Now the business begins.

"Not all of the High Council," Eli replies. "Le Fevre is just one man. The Council's high table has ten chairs."

"And all of them afraid. Is there a man or woman amongst them who is younger than a hundred and fifty? When magic ends, they will die."

"At a more natural age," Eli growls. "We've all had a good run, Yu. I'm not going to let a bunch of cowards destroy the world because they can't let go of their unnatural privilege."

Yu holds up his hands, placating. "Eli please. We have been friends for eight hundred years. You know that I agree with you entirely. We have both been incredibly fortunate, moreso than we deserve. If it is needed that I die, to preserve goodness in the world, then I am honoured to meet such a noble end. But I speak not of what is right, but what is likely."

Eli looks unhappy, staring at his wine cup with a dark, brooding scowl. He glances at Croz. Croz nods. "He's right Eli. They're all turning against us. You're asking them to give up everything…"

"They'll lose everything anyway when Riley destroys the world with his madness," Eli snaps.

"Eli, people tell stories about bravery," says Croz. "Everyone has this idea of how brave they'll be, facing their death, or the loss of everything they have. Everyone thinks they'll do the right thing. I saw it growing up in Riverdale Chicago, I saw a Shtaal-aligned house get raided by Togova, I was watching from a rooftop when they dragged them all out into the back yard. And I saw these bigshot magicians who'd always bragged about how brave and good they were, sobbing and begging for their lives, offering everything they had. While the quiet ones with little power… they were brave, one of them spat in a Togova's eye just before he killed her."

"The more powerful they are, they more they have to lose," Ren murmurs.

"We should be leading by example," Eli mutters. "That was always the old tradition."

"Your problem," says Ange as she munches on a prawn, "is that you've never had to think about losing." Eli turns a dark stare on her. "The rest of us have. Receptors get beat up as a matter of business. We're used to it, even Ulani." Bickel nods, and even Croz doesn't disagree. "Meisha's very talented, but even she's got only a fraction of your power. I mean, the High Council used the old magic on you, an elemental trap wielded by some of their most powerful magicians working together, and still you beat them. Has that ever happened before? In the last thousand years? Two thousand?"

She looks at Master Yu, who purses his lips in thought. Clearly he knows that if it had been him, he'd be dead. "You don't understand losing," Ange resumes to Eli, "because you've never lost. The rest of us know that we're going to lose at some point, probably. We just hope we don't embarrass ourselves when it happens."

"Eli," says Master Yu. "As your friend. You must tell us what Riley is going to try. We know he's going to try some great magic to prevent the collapse that Ashkir predicted in his prophecy. I know that you do not wish the information to get out, but you must trust *someone*. If we know what he is going to try, we can stop it. And you're the only one that knows."

"Or some of us will go looking for answers on our own," Ange adds. "Like Tori. And it killed her."

Yu frowns. "Tori?"

"Tori MacDonald, Master Yu," says Ren. "Jamie MacDonald's sister." Realisation dawns on Yu's face. "She was researching the Ashkir Prophecy when she was killed."

"She hated Riley with a passion," Meisha says quietly. "As does Mulberry. I think Mulberry might have encouraged her, and Riley found out, and stopped her."

"And if you'd told Tori what she needed to know," Ange continues to Eli, munching another prawn, "she might not have gotten herself killed by looking."

"Hey!" says Croz with a dark stare. "Why don't you...?"

Eli interrupts him, a hand on his hand. "It's all right Croz," he says. "She may not be wrong." He takes a deep breath. "Realm Shift."

Ange frowns. "Jamie said that's what you did to the secret library room. Placed one dimension atop the other..."

Eli shakes his head. "That's one way of doing it. But just a small one. I speak of something much larger. Something that realigns everything. A reset button, if you like. Like the planet swapping magnetic poles, north becomes south and vice versa. Haywire, if it happened too quickly. Calamitous."

"You can do that?" Croz asks quietly.

"Oh no, no." Eli stares at the far wall. "We magicians don't control anything. Or not really. We direct it. We conduct the orchestra, we tell it what to do, but we do not actually play an instrument. The power itself comes from elsewhere. And this one, I'm fairly certain, will refuse to be controlled, if unleashed. It will play its own tune, and we will not like to hear it."

"Realm Shift," Master Yu breathes. "You speak of using First Realm to... to reposition?"

"But First Realm is dead?" says Meisha, puzzled.

"No more," Eli warns Yu. And Master Yu only nods, slowly. His eyes are wide, as though realising that Eli's silence was not so ill-advised after all. And that frightens Ange more than anything. Eli is the oldest magician still living. What old magic does he remember that others have forgotten? That could make even Master Yu turn pale and silent at the mention of?

"Well," says Yu. "You have told me something I did not know was possible. And so I shall repay you. We have information of shipments. Ordered by Mayor Riley, making their way from Chinese suppliers, to here in New York. Whatever he is planning, I think these shipments may have something to do with it."

"We've traced those crates all the way from the ports, and a few in through JFK, and they all end up here." Stew Bickel taps his finger on the wall screen, which shows a giant computer map of Manhattan. "The Municipal Building. Those crates are large, and the building doesn't have cargo elevators, so we're not sure how they're moving them in. Teleporting, maybe. Of course that's all Riley's territory down there so we've got no idea how much magic he's using, or what kind. It's all blocked from this range, even to Eli."

Eli sits against the edge of the desk in his office, and watches grimly. Everyone is here, Shawna Dubois, Bickel, Hernandez, Croz, Meisha and Stanthorpe. Ange and Jamie sit side by side on the far side of the conference table.

"Do we know what's in those crates?" asks Dubois.

"No," says Bickel, with a long glance at Eli. "Of course, if Eli would give us some idea of how you might go about changing magical polarity by using the dead First Realm, we might be able to make some guesses."

"I've said all I will," says Eli. "More information is dangerous."

"Eli," Dubois attempts, "I'm sure you can trust everyone here…"

"No more I said." Dubois sighs.

"Riley's building something," says Croz. "If it's as bad as Eli says, we have to stop him."

"Well it's obvious who has to do that," says Ange. Everyone looks at her. "None of you can do it, that building will be so well charmed that any magical penetration will set off alarms all over south Manhattan. It's deep in Riley's territory, and you need someone who can move silently through it. That's me."

The following night, Ange waits atop the Leventhal Tower, with Mid-Town towers gleaming all around. A cool wind ruffles her hair, and she wears a long coat, and has ski goggles on one arm. At her feet lies the simple saddle she had made by a Milan leatherworker, a man who knew horses and was thrilled to adapt the design for a dragon, in exchange for a reasonable fee and a personal introduction.

Meisha hands her a pair of glasses. Ange looks at them, and sees they've got little laser projectors behind each lens. "These," says Meisha, "are for when you're inside. The building will be magic shielded, so we can't help you there. But I can get into the phone data network, and it'll send you messages on the glasses."

"They can't turn off the phone network?"

Meisha shakes her head. "Often technology keeps working where magic fails. Magic's good at manipulating natural forces, mobile phones are actually quite hard to stop. For most people."

She gives Ange a hug. Ange is surprised, and returns it with feeling. She and Meisha have had their differences, but Meisha doesn't hold grudges, and is genuinely kind and open-hearted. Ange is coming to realise how rare such people are in the world. And she glances aside on instinct, as a familiar shadow comes gliding across the forest of brilliant towers.

Gia lands on the pad with a rush of wind, and bounds. To Ange's surprise he comes not first to her, but pauses to look at Eli, who stands to one side and watches. Eli gives a respectful little bow to the dragon, who considers him curiously. No doubt sensing… whatever it is that dragons sense. Great power, certainly. He sniffs at Eli, who pats his muzzle. Then the dragon comes to Ange, and gives her a big nudge that would knock her over if he didn't know she'd hug him and hold on.

"Gia," says Ange, "this is Meisha. Be careful with her, she can't see."

"Oh he's so beautiful!" says Meisha, hands outstretched and grinning. "Hello Gia." And Gia nudges carefully at her palms, surveying Meisha with brilliant golden eyes. Ange turns to find Croz and Jamie watching. Croz looks sullen, and no little jealous, as she expected. Tonight, she takes no pleasure in it. The world feels even more dangerous than usual, and the tension of what she's about to do makes her wonder at the logic of driving away potential allies, and friends of her friends. If she's going to outlive her teens, she's going to need all the friends she can get.

"Boys," she says. "I need a hand getting the saddle on, the straps are a pain. Both of you, come on. Gia can't do it, he's all claws."

Croz approaches more cautiously than Jamie, who grabs up the saddle and huge long straps. Ange beckons impatiently to Croz, and presents him to her friend. "Gia, this is Croz. Please don't eat him, I think he has potential."

Gia puts his head low to consider him, crouched and curious. "Hey," says Croz, awkward and nervous. Ange smothers a smile. She's never seen Croz nervous. Suddenly he seems almost human. "Hey Gia."

Gia exhales a big gust that could incinerate Croz if he ignited it. Then submits to a pat on the jaw, and stretches his wings to full span, a good thirty feet across the rooftop.

Croz stares in amazement. "Wow. Just wow."

"Better than a Ferrari, Croz?" Meisha asks innocently.

"Maybe the only thing that is," says Croz. And joins Jamie and Ange in getting the saddle up onto Gia's back, and the dual straps fastened under Gia's front legs.

Once finished, they consider their work, while Meisha chats to Gia about her boyfriend in China, and asks the dragon if he's ever been to China, and what the dragons are like there. Having one-sided conversations with dragons is a learned art, but Meisha seems to have the knack of it, as Gia doesn't seem bored.

"Now if you get in trouble," Croz tells Ange seriously, "don't hang around, just get out. We know they've got nasty things guarding the secret floors. Seriously nasty. Just get what you're after and leave."

Not long ago, Ange might have made a cocky reply. Now she just nods, remembering what she found in the tunnels down that end of the island. "I agree."

"He'll hang around?" Pointing at Gia.

Gia puts his muzzle on Ange's shoulder. Ange smiles. "He'll hang around. He knows what's going on."

Croz looks at the dragon, then at her. "Right. Well. Good luck."

And Ange finds herself facing Jamie. Jamie looks worried. Worse than worried. Ange hugs him, and he grabs her back, hard. And he parts to look at her once more, trying to speak, but unable. Ange understands, and smiles. "See you soon, huh?"

He kisses her. And kisses her. Long and warm, atop the soaring tower, with all the night lit city murmuring and buzzing about them. Ange barely feels the chill. Until their lips part, and she realises that if she takes any longer to consider what she might be about to lose, she'll never leave. She jumps to Gia's shoulder, takes a handful of saddle and swings aboard. There, more straps go over her thighs, to keep her in place once the flying starts.

She glances at Eli as she puts her ski goggles on. He nods, just once. Ange nods back, and gives Gia a whack on the neck. "Let's go."

He moves so gracefully that she barely feels motion until the edge of the tower passes below them, a breathtaking plummet to street lights and late night traffic far below. Then the wind is rushing, and the tough leather of his huge wings flaps with a sound like a tent in a gale. He flaps once, then twice, and they accelerate, gaining height. So many towers, it's like a giant forest of light, and they weave past towertops and windows, north toward Central Park. The wind strengthens to gale force, tearing at her hair and face, and thank god for the goggles or she could barely see.

A wide bank, then away toward the Hudson, the huge long length of Manhattan Island stretching south before her, dark waters lit with blazing light. Ange laughs, and decides that there is nothing in all the world to compare with flying over Manhattan at night on dragonback. Nothing, perhaps, except that first kiss... and her eyes search for Leventhal Tower, but it's nearly lost amidst the swarm of buildings.

Gia flies south down the Hudson, toward the tight cluster of buildings at the southern tip that make the financial district. A helicopter buzzes past, heading the other way. And now they're passing the financial district, and across the dark water of Upper Bay she sees the Statue of Liberty rising on its small circle of light. Gia flies on, heading toward Staten Island.

"Hey Gia!" Ange yells above the wind. "The Municipal Building's back there! Where are we going?"

Gia flicks an ear to indicate he's heard her, but does not change direction. There is a moon tonight, and as Ange looks down at the water, she can see the faint shadow of Gia's wings on the silver lit water. Another shadow joins it. Ange blinks — *two* dragons. She looks rapidly about, and spots a second dragon flying not a hundred yards off Gia's wing. Also dark blue, with a flash of orange, like flame in the night. The other dragon flies closer, clearly the same species... and just a bit smaller? It's looking at her, and Ange waves — not all dragons are friendly, but Gia would not introduce her to a friend if the friend were a threat.

Suddenly the other dragon flaps hard, and climbs. Gia follows, with huge beats of his wings, and Ange feels as though her stomach has been left behind as she hangs on for dear life. They both climb, higher and higher, then circle and dive. Gia overtakes and snaps at the other dragon's wingtip, and Ange ducks as the tail comes close by her head. The other dragon zigzags, then swats at Gia's head as he ducks, and Ange yelps as he tears after... *her?*

Her! Of course! And Ange gasps with delight as she realises. "Gia you devil you! You've got a girlfriend!"

Gia and his girlfriend play in the night sky above New York until Gia senses that his passenger, while enjoying dragonflight, might not be handling the high-G manoeuvres quite as well as him. He levels out and flies straight, and the other dragon joins at his wingtip. They're quite high now, Ange sees, with a view far across New Jersey, then out to Brooklyn and Queens in the other direction. At JFK airport, a stream of golden dots where airliners queue to land. Another queue at La Guardia. A jet passes below them, running lights blinking.

Ange leans on Gia's neck near his ear. "She's very beautiful Gia," she says, looking at the other dragon. "Can I give her a name?" Whether dragons know or care what humans call them, she doesn't know. But Gia didn't seem unhappy when she called him by his name. "Bella. It means 'beautiful'. Do you like it?" He doesn't tip her off his back, so she guesses that's a yes.

She waves to the other dragon. "Hello Bella! Nice to meet you!" If she's not completely mistaken, the little toss of Bella's head, and the sideways angle of her golden-eyed gaze, suggests the feeling is mutual. "You have very good taste in men! We have that in common!"

Why Gia has introduced her to Bella, she doesn't know. A coincidence, that he was close enough to respond quickly to her desire to see him, and had Bella with him? Previously he's been gone for weeks and months. Lately he's been close, and now he has a friend. She remembers what Eli said about dragons sensing things in the magical world that elude humans. And about Gia bringing her to New York for a reason, and that reason certainly not being to kill Eli Leventhal. Jamie joked about her being Gia's pet rather than the other way around. Maybe that's not so far from the truth, she thinks. Circling up here in the night, she wonders at this dragon's perspective on the world — far-seeing, somewhat telepathic and undeniably intelligent. Shepherding the short-sighted, grounded humans through these broad waves and patterns of magical events that only dragons can see. Maybe humans aren't actually running this show as much as they think they are.

Gia descends, passing through some scattered cloud, and they approach the mouth of the East River, where the Brooklyn, Manhattan and Williamsburg Bridges make thick lines of traffic across the water. There, at the head of the Brooklyn Bridge, Ange sees the Municipal Building directly alongside City Hall, and in turn beside the tall, square courthouse. This is why she can't just walk in on the ground — this is the heart of Mayor Riley's territory, and access from the ground will be impossible for anyone unwanted. Eli has a helicopter, but it's noisy and easy for magicians to detect and stop. Gia is silent, and nearly as invisible to magic as she is.

Past the mad, bristling cluster of financial district towers on the left, then low above the looping tangle of roads feeding traffic onto the Brooklyn Bridge, and Ange unstraps her legs and prepares to move. Ahead, the Municipal Building is a real New York stunner, an early 1900s government structure from back when governments knew how to build pretty things. A forty-storey rectangle with columns and flourishes, and a gorgeous gold-tipped spire in the middle, like something off the top of an old Italian church.

Gia flares to a flapping hover, and bounds on the rooftop. Ange jumps off, and Gia keeps running, and soars off the edge and over the courts. Ange jumps down a level on the multi-level rooftop, then runs to a window at the base of the central spire, and pulls the goggles off her head, replacing them with Meisha's glasses from her coat pocket, placing the accompanying earbud in her ear. Bickel's intelligence is that the upper entrances aren't especially well guarded, given that magicians generally can't fly... and non-magicians even less. She breaks the glass, not caring if anyone knows she *was* here.

Inside is an office, with a locked door. She takes a moment to pick it, as a Milan burglar taught her. It had come in handy many times in Milan — the Ulani had many locked doors through which children were forbidden to go. By the time she was twelve, she'd gone through most of them.

Down stairs from the base of the building tower, and she's in a broad hall. It's art deco, 1930s style, and she feels like she's walking through a very old movie. She holds up her flashlight, not yet bothering with the sword, as she feels no tingle nor sense of magic here. Her boots are soft-sole, and she walks silently on the smooth polished floor.

"Hello Ange, nice work so far," comes Meisha's voice in her ear. *"Next stairs down on the left."* They can all see through the camera on the glasses, Meisha must have scrambled the signal somehow so it can't be traced to this location, as a regular phone might be. Especially if you're the Mayor of New York and all the police department's high tech toys are working for you.

Ange goes down the stairs. Suddenly she can see an image of the building displayed on the inner lens of her glasses — it shows the stairwell, and how far she has to go before she reaches the bottom. There's no way the glasses are doing that on their own, the image is far too good for current technology. Meisha must somehow be making the lens projectors do that.

"You should work for Google, Meisha," she whispers.

"They couldn't afford me. Level 28 is the administrative level, there's no one listed as working there."

Ange stops at Level 28, and picks the lock. Even as she does so, she can feel her hands buzzing, as though she's gone to sleep on them. "It's charmed," she whispers. Which is why they don't have regular alarm systems here — the magical ones are enough for most purposes. But magical deterrents won't work on her, nor spot her as she slips through.

The door clicks open. The hallway just feels different. Darker, somehow. Chills sizzle up her arms as she steps through, and raises her flashlight.

Try the door.

The words appear on the lenses of her glasses. Meisha is not risking even to talk, sending her texts instead. Ange tries the first door on the left. It opens. Within, her flashlight reveals rows of shelves. They're partly covered in tarpaulins, and filled with what looks like old junk from someone's garage. Ange moves about the wall, shining a light down each aisle. It will be less safe down there, trapped between shelves. The air smells musty as she breathes deep to control her thudding heart.

They'll have been moving things. Boxes, crates. Try the next room.

Ange creeps along the wall, then around the corner. There is a mid-room door. From here she can see a window on the far wall, which should open onto a view of City Hall. Instead, it's boarded shut. Something feels cold, somewhere distant, in a way she's never felt before.

The door opens and creaks. More shelves. On the shelf immediately opposite are jars of formaldehyde. Within them float odd creatures, shrivelled, with heads too large and clawed feet. The unborn babies of something unpleasant, she thinks. Magicians long ago did experiments on human babies, spelling them to create new, augmented-human types. Some magicians still do.

She represses a shudder and closes the door behind her. She's halfway along the next wall when she sees that the shelves here only go a short way. The rest of the room is filled with boxes, covered with plastic wrap. Ange moves that way at a crouch, and now shines her light across them. The boxes fill the room, long and wooden, nailed shut. She turns her head so Meisha, Eli and all can see on the camera.

Open one. We have to know what's in them.

Ange pulls her boot knife, and slices the plastic cover. Then she holds the flashlight in her teeth, and sticks the blade into a lid near one of the nails. Some levering, careful not to damage the knife, and the whole corner comes up. Ange sheaths the knife and pulls. The lid creaks and groans, and she grimaces. When there's enough of a gap, she shines her flashlight inside.

The light reveals great bundles of metal wire, endless coils of it. Also, lots of steel rods. Ange frowns. She's not dumb, she knows that magicians planning great magic don't actually use bubbling cauldrons filled with odd bits of rare animals. Magic employs its own kind of physics, and physics, in this world, is best harnessed with engineering. What kind of engineering would all this be used to create?

Another crate. Need more information.

Ange turns… and hears a low growl. She freezes. A new sensation, a cold chill, makes its way up her left side. Whatever's making it wasn't here before. Ange pulls her sword, and holds the flashlight against its hilt, both hands together before her.

Ange?

"Something's here," she whispers. She creeps along the aisle, where boxes are stacked high and block her view. If whatever-it-is is inside the room, it will see her light. But she doesn't hear any doors open, and without her light she's completely blind. Why did they board up the windows? What lives on this private level that doesn't like the light?

Ange, Eli says try another crate. We need to see.

The chill on her left side is moving. Ange thinks whatever's causing it is coming down the main hall outside. That would make it less than ten yards away, but on the other side of the wall. Ange looks desperately around for another box — she can't have come all this way for nothing. She spots an available corner, puts the flashlight into her mouth and pulls her boot knife once more, unwilling to use her beautiful sword for something as crude as opening a lid.

A rush of horrid chills floods over her like nothing she's felt before. Ange backs off gasping, her back against a wall of boxes, and takes the flashlight from her mouth with her knife hand. It feels like a bucket of ice dumped on her head, only it slides slowly down her skin, like thick oil. Her heart pounds, and terror floods her veins. She doesn't scare easily. She does not think this fear is hers alone. It feels almost as though something else is radiating it, like heat from a sun, only cold and awful.

Ange? Ange, I can feel something through the connection… oh god Ange, you have to go! Go now!

Ange doesn't need to be told twice, and runs for the next connecting door. It opens, and the next room is filled with more boxes. She runs between them, and the boxes turn to high steel shelves reaching to the ceiling, holding all kinds of wire, screws and braces. Whatever-it-is is following her, she can feel the chill pursuing, the goosebumps on her skin that no amount of running will make disappear.

The aisle bends, and suddenly she's in a cul-de-sac, with rough plastic sheeting on all sides, covering great glass jars. Through a gap in the plastic, her flashlight catches the glimpse of a face in that jar, horrid and alien, fangs and red eyes. It's like nothing she's seen before, as insectoid as human. She knows most of the world's magical creatures, it's an Ulani's job to know. What the hell is the Mayor messing with in this building? A stab of cold terror threatens to turn her muscles to ice, and she spins, light searching the plastic-draped shadows.

Angelina! It's Eli! Turn off the light! It's hunting the light!

She spins again, and finds a hooded face before her, fangs and evil eyes just like the heads in the jars… only living. A skeletal hand snatches her wrist. Ange screams and swings, connecting with nothing and running, only running in desperate terror. She hits the door to the hallway as the pain begins, crawling up her arm from the thing's icy grip.

She sprints into the hall and it's like her arm is on fire. Another ten strides and now the pain is stabbing her stomach like a blade, making her stagger.

ge.. you ha.. t..to..vator..

The letters break upon the glasses like shattered ice, and the earbud crackles with static. With a snarl something rushes around the corner ahead and charges at her — it's doglike, only twice the size, and fast. It leaps for her head and she slides beneath it, blade slashing upward, then gets up and runs once more as it howls and thrashes and slips in its own blood. Only she's lost the flashlight, and now runs in the dark, heading for that corner with nothing more than the certainty that the evil hooded thing is after her once more, light or no light.

She hits and bounces off the wall in the dark, trying to keep upright and run properly despite the pain that forces her to double over. Behind, the fast approaching snarl of another animal, and the rush of fast approaching claws. Ange spins to face it, and…

…with a crash the boards over the hall-side window are smashed inward, as Gia's head thrusts into the hall and jaws crunch the animal to pulp. Then a scrabble of claws on the building wall as he loses his grip and falls from the window. But he's left a rectangle of light to see by… and here, emerging from the very wall with no respect for doors, is the hooded face of death.

Ange runs, as the pain twists in her gut so hard that she would scream if she had breath in her lungs. More claws clatter behind her, two pairs this time, as the pain finally brings her to her knees, and she slides on the polished floor, trying hard to rise, and at least meet her end on her feet. Two dark shapes bound toward her down the hall, but she barely notices them — just the approaching shadow at their backs, moving as though floating. No walls, no sword, no thing, can save her from that. Just to look on it, she feels herself melting, and sinks to the floor once more.

The boarded window behind explodes about her, and again Gia thrusts his head past and into the hall. Flames blind her and sear her face, white hot, and blast the hallway clean. And stop, and though walls, floor and ceiling remain on fire, and the two charging animals are charred lumps, the black shadow advances, relentless.

Again Gia scrabbles to find purchase on the outer building, and slides. Ange senses her very last chance, drags herself to her feet, somehow retains enough sense to sheathe her sword, then jumps after him as he falls. Even falling to her death from twenty eight floors is a relief, after that. Even more of a relief is when Gia's scaled foot catches her barely yards from the ground, and he bounces down, then springs skyward once more with a rush of wind.

Ange is flying. Or dangling. She's delirious with pain, and feels only that, and cold wind. A glimpse of Times Square, bright lights about a giant cross on the ground. Then a helicopter landing pad, Leventhal Tower, and hands reaching up to grab her.

She's being carried, fast down stairs. Then a room, and a table, and she's laid upon it while people shout and hands grasp her limbs. Someone is shouting at her to keep still... she must be thrashing, so great is the pain she barely notices. She feels as though she's being impaled by a giant, red hot blade. Death would be better than this, this just has to stop, someone please, make it stop. She's screaming it, she realises, in Italian.

Then a building sensation of fuzzy static, pins-and-needles in her hands and feet, barely noticeable past the pain, save that her hearing disappears as sometimes happens in a great magic, like the pressure differential from diving deep under water. Then the world seems to fall in around her, and nothing.

She awakes to the odd sensation of someone holding her hand. Another hand is gently stroking her hair. She blinks her eyes open, and her blurred vision slowly comes clear on... Jamie. Kneeling alongside, looking very worried. She tries to smile, and say something, but her mouth is too dry and nothing comes out.

"Ange!" comes Meisha's voice, and then she's kneeling alongside as well, her unfocused eyes all concern. "Angelina... Eli! She's awake!"

And then Eli is there, and Croz, all looking down at her. The pain is gone, and she can't be sure if the moisture in her eyes is from that blessed relief, or some other emotion, at seeing so much concern on the faces of people she'd once thought her enemies. She'd thought living here, with these people, would be a lonely existence. But she was wrong about that as well.

"Angelina," says Eli, crouching by her head. He looks upside down, from her vantage. She's lying on a sofa in Eli's private office, she realises. "How do you feel?"

"Better," she manages. Croz hands her a glass of water, and Jamie raises her head so she can sip it. "The pain's gone." She rubs her stomach, expecting to find some terrible damage there. Everything feels normal, not even a lingering soreness. "I'm sorry I couldn't look in the next box. I didn't get enough information, did I?"

"You got plenty," Jamie assures her. And looks at Eli. "She got plenty, right?"

"I should never have let you in there," Eli says grimly. "If I'd known, I'd never have let you go."

"Well then, maybe just as well you didn't know. Here," she says to Jamie, "help me sit up."

He puts an arm around her, and eases her gently upright. And stays there on the sofa beside her, holding her, keeping her steady. Ange feels a little dizzy, a little nauseous, and utterly exhausted.

"What was that thing?" she asks Eli, now that she can look at him right-way-up. "All it did was touch me." She holds up her wrist, to look at where it grabbed her. There is a red mark on the skin, and she stares at it. They all do.

Eli gets up, and puts both hands in his white hair. "I've tried everything to avoid speaking of it. Everyone has forgotten, you see. Once it was known, these old things. These dead things. The dead Realms. The world has been a better place for that forgetting, and for centuries I've tried to keep it that way."

He takes a seat on a nearby chair, and looks at them all, with weary resignation. "First Realm is not empty," he says. "Nor is it truly dead. The other ten Realms of the twelve are separate realities. Alternative dimensions, to use the physics term. Think of them like rooms in a large house. But First Realm is not a room. First Realm is a hallway, connecting them all together. And it is a door, as all hallways lead to doors."

"Like a wormhole?" Jamie gasps.

Eli shrugs. "Yes, close enough." He manages a weak smile. "Perhaps all those science fiction comics of yours serve you well after all."

"And that lets you…" Jamie waves his hands, striving to find the words. Almost like an Italian, Ange thinks. "That lets you move between Realms?" Eli nods. "Draw power from multiple Realms?" Another nod. "Create passages between Realms that let you… let you stack them? One atop the other?"

"All of these," Eli agrees. "There are many uses. The old magic is almost entirely about the use of First Realm to combine powers and Realms together. That is why it seems to defy easy explanation. And that is why those who have forgotten the old arts, struggle to replicate those powers today."

"Eli?" says Meisha. She takes off her glasses, her sightless eyes wide with amazement, as though beholding some vision known only to her. "You draw from First Realm, don't you? That's why you're so powerful."

"Through the hallway!" Jamie breathes. "You could draw from all the Realms at once!"

Eli takes a deep breath. "Yes," he says shortly. "Riley too. We are the last two that do. It is the thing that makes a Grand Magister. The High Council still uses artefacts that draw on that old power, but the people who use it, who sit in the High Council, do not understand it."

"That thing in the building," says Ange. "It's not of this world. The Realms can't physically manifest in this world, it goes against…"

"I know. But First Realm is a passageway. Realm Shift allows the layering of realities, as you found in my library. But those two realities are just two simple places on Earth — the New York Public Library, and a little house I own in Turkey. I can connect two places on Earth quite easily. But I never, *never* contemplated using the passage to connect to somewhere else entirely. A physical connection, between Realms, layering reality from another dimension entirely. But it looks like Riley did exactly that, on Level 28 of the Municipal Building."

"And that thing?" Ange asks. "What was it?"

"I don't know," says Eli, with an exasperated shrug. His voice, usually so strong, almost cracks. Almost like… fear. "I don't know. Riley is talking to it, I suppose. Perhaps it will benefit from the great magic he plans.

Perhaps he will build a bridge, between its reality and our own. If they cross that bridge in force, whatever they are, then god help us."

"He wouldn't be stupid enough to think he can *negotiate* with it, would he?" Croz mutters. "Not even Riley would think that?"

"Maybe he's not negotiating with it," says Meisha. "Maybe it's negotiating with him."

Deathly silence in the room. Ange hadn't thought Meisha was capable of such horrible thoughts.

"So your power works on me," she says slowly, "because you draw through First Realm. Which means you really draw from all the Realms, including Third Realm, the Ulani Realm."

Eli nods. "That's a bit simple, but yes." And he looks at Jamie. They all do. Jamie looks a little stunned.

"What?" Ange asks. "What is it?"

"Do you really feel better, Angelina?" Eli presses. "Do you feel healed?"

"Yeah, it's amazing. Whatever magic you did, it worked perfectly." She manages a smile. "I could even get to like magic a little."

Everyone is looking at Jamie. Ange does too, questioningly. "Eli didn't do the magic that healed you," says Jamie. "I did."

CHAPTER FOURTEEN

Ange awakes on the sofa in Eli's office, beneath a blanket. She blinks through blurred vision, and finds her sword leaning against the arm rest, and her phone on the ground. She reaches for the phone, and it tells her it's nearly 1pm. A scroll through messages… there's voicemail from Jamie's mother.

The phone suddenly buzzes, and a new text appears, from Meisha. **Ange, now that you're awake, your dragon is still on the roof pining for you. Please go up and show him you're okay.** Ange smiles, and realises that her wrist still hurts. As does her head. Thinking is hard, her brain feels like wet cotton wool.

Eli's secretary produces a toasted cheese and bacon sandwich, and some good black coffee. Ange takes it to the side exit, then slowly up the stairs to the helicopter pad, her head pounding with every step. She pushes through the doors and it's a beautiful, half-sunny day, with patchy cloud making dappled light across towertops, and the vast sprawl of cityscape and rivers beyond.

Gia is here, lounging in a patch of sun, while Croz sits nearby, and several others Ange doesn't recognise. Gia leaps up immediately upon seeing her, startling the watching humans, who gasp.

"Oh sit down, sit down," Ange tells him, too tired for games, and leans on his neck as he eases her down on the pad. There she hugs him one armed, and kisses him on the nose. "Saved my life again, yes? What does a girl need with a knight in shining armour when she can have a dragon instead?"

She bites her sandwich, and looks at Croz and the other watching Leventhal employees. They're regular men and women in office clothes, sipping coffee or eating lunch. Just watching Gia, which is surely more interesting than anything else they could be doing at lunch, and she can hardly blame them.

"Half the building wants to come up and have a look," Croz explains. "But we remembered what you said about him not liking crowds. Everyone gets ten minutes, then they rotate and someone else comes up."

"Except Croz," says one of the watchers, sarcastically. "He's been up here an hour."

"Don't like it?" says Croz. "Get promoted." But he's smiling. The last time Ange saw him this happy, he was roaring after Mathew Palmino at the wheel of his Ferrari. "Besides, I found the secret." He produces a donut from his suit pocket, unwraps and tosses it to Gia. Gia snaps it from the air.

"Donuts?" says Ange, disdainfully. "Gia, you're such a food slut. And you'll get fat, you know that sugar's not good for you."

"You see those wing muscles?" says Croz, pointing. "He'll burn that off in two flaps. This boy's an athlete, athletes gotta burn sugar."

"Yes, well he has more of a protein diet. And dairy, if you count what's in the cow when he eats it." Gia sniffs at her sandwich. "What?" she retorts. "It's bacon, I don't care if you don't like bacon."

"He doesn't like bacon?"

Ange shakes her head. "I guess that's what happens when you eat the whole pig. Only half of it tastes nice. Cows are bigger, he can pull bits off."

"Yeah, try frying it first, Gia. I bet you'd make some serious crackling." Croz grins. "Man, when I die I wanna come back as a dragon."

"You believe in that stuff? Reincarnation?"

Croz's grin fades. "Yeah, maybe. Be nice, wouldn't it? If everyone gets a second chance?"

"Not everyone."

Croz snorts with approval, as he takes her meaning. "How you feeling?"

"Awful. But a lot better than I was. Do you know what Riley's building yet?"

"We're looking at it. Eli's got some ideas. Might take a while."

Gia puts his head against Ange's leg, muzzle down on the pad. Ange plays with an ear. "And you're okay with this? Ending magic?"

Croz shrugs. "We're not ending magic. It's ending itself." He frowns. "Hey, if magic dies out completely, that won't mean dragons die, will it?"

Ange sighs. "No. Dragons were made by magic, but they don't need it to live. Though there's a lot of nasty stuff living under the southern end of Manhattan that does. I won't be sad to see all that go."

"But the shroud will go. And if everyone can see dragons…"

"There's going to be a lot of very surprised people," Ange agrees. She pats Gia's head. "Poor Gia. They're going to be staring at you."

"They might do a lot worse than stare. They might get pretty scared."

"Yeah," Ange says quietly. "They won't like dragons taking cows. Millions of cows in the world, only a few thousand dragons, but still they won't like it."

"We got a complaint the other day from some sighted people who work in air traffic control," Croz adds. "They said they're aware of an increase in dragon activity around New York, and they say Leventhal Holdings is responsible, and dragons are a threat to aviation."

"Nonsense," Ange snorts. "Well, mostly nonsense. Airplanes fly in predictable lanes, dragons are smart, they just avoid them." And she frowns at Croz. "Wait, increased dragon activity? Did they say how many?"

"No, why?"

"In Europe the airports only ever complained about dragons when there were at least five or six in an area. And…" she recalls she hasn't told them yet, "…well, it turns out from last night that my boy here's been cheating on me. He has a girlfriend."

"Does he now?" says Croz, impressed. He plucks another donut from his pocket and tosses it to the grateful dragon. "Way to go buddy. Is she hot?"

"Very," Ange agrees. "Same species, Atlantic Blue. We flew together for a while last night. But that's only two dragons, and two very smart dragons who stay well clear of airports. Can you check with those traffic controllers again?"

"For what?"

"Check how much dragon traffic they're seeing. I didn't know Bella existed until yesterday, Gia's not great at conversation. Usually he goes flying for weeks and I'll barely see him, but lately he's been hanging around. And now he's got a girlfriend, and who knows how many other friends."

"You think he knows something's up?"

"That's what I'm guessing. Dragons can sense things that we miss. And not all dragons are so friendly, and Riley has this habit of attracting dangerous creatures. What if there are dragons out there who sense that the shroud is about to collapse, and they'll be in danger from frightened humans?"

Croz nods slowly. "We can't just ask him?"

Ange shrugs. "You can try."

Croz gets up and kneels, looking straight at the dragon. "Hey Gia. You can understand me, right? How about a sign? A nod? Or maybe thump your tail once for yes, twice for no?" Gia's golden eyes watch him lazily. He blinks, slowly.

"They like being all mysterious," says Ange, finishing the last of her sandwich. "Just because they get a general idea what we're saying doesn't mean they really understand the whole talking thing. You can guess if a dog's angry or happy by its body language, but good luck trying to speak that language back to it."

"You mean he's reading our mood more than listening to our words?"

"Something like that," Ange agrees. "Just talk to those controllers. Would be worth knowing if we've got lots of dragons coming. Especially if they're not all on our side."

"Yeah," Croz agrees, looking troubled. "Yeah. I'd better get on that." He gets up to go, and hesitates, looking at Gia.

Ange smiles. "Oh come on, give him a pat. He likes you."

Croz comes over, kneels, and pats Gia's nose. Gia snaps at him, playfully, and Croz falls flat backwards in shock.

Ange laughs. "That's a dragonish sense of humour. It grows on you, but not all at once." Croz grins in amazement, and fends off another thrust of Gia's snout as he gets up. And swats back at the dragon, taking a mock fighting stance, then swats again, like a boxer. Gia growls, and opens a wide row of teeth just to show what would happen if he was serious. Then puts his muzzle back down by Ange's leg.

"All those stories about knights slaying dragons in single combat," says Croz. "It's all crap, yeah?"

"Total crap," Ange agrees. "Just proves that knights were liars." Though with the shroud gone, today's knights wouldn't come after him with swords and arrows — they'd use fighter planes and combat helicopters. And even Gia can't survive that. For the first time, Ange truly wonders if she's doing the right thing, helping Eli to help magic die.

Croz claps his hands at the gawking employees as he leaves. "Come on people, lunch break's over! The only ones here with nothing to do are lazy Italian teenagers!"

They sigh, and reluctantly follow Croz to the stairwell doors... save for one girl who comes over with great trepidation and asks if she can just... well... you know... please? Ange looks at Gia. Gia blinks, with mild boredom... the dragon equivalent of an eyeroll. Given her permission, the girl pats Gia briefly, then gives excited thanks and scurries after her colleagues like a kid given a treat.

"Must be hard, just lying about all day being gorgeous," Ange tells him. She pulls out her phone again. "Now listen, I have to call Jamie's mother, okay? So just behave, it's important..." As Gia snorts and gets to his feet with a sinewy unfolding of limbs, tail and wings, and moves away to the edge of the pad where the view looks down Broadway to Times Square. Ange ignores him as he resettles himself, and dials the number.

"*Hello?*"

"Ciao Mrs MacDonald, it's Angelina."

"*Oh Angelina, look, thank you for calling. I was just a bit concerned because Jamie didn't come home last night, and he's not answering his phone now.*"

"He didn't come home this morning?" Immediately she's worried. Jamie performed the magic that healed her. That makes him like Eli — a potential Grand Magister... and therefore, logically, Tori must have been too. Which would have been a shock last night, and... damn her woolly headedness, she's been too slow and distracted to give it any thought.

"*I just... well Angelina, I don't mean to pry, you kids are allowed to live your own lives and make your own choices. But Jamie was with you all last night, wasn't he?*"

203

Ange blinks. "Um… yes. Yes, he was."

"*And were you using protection?*"

Ange claps a hand to her mouth. Takes a deep breath, and forces herself to calm. "To tell you the truth Mrs MacDonald, it hasn't come to that between us. Mostly we were out all night. Nothing more." She's a little panicked at the question, and fights the crazy urge to laugh at herself. The end of the world is approaching, and she's suddenly freaked out by her boyfriend's mother asking about safe sex.

"*I'm sorry Angelina, I just had to ask. And please, call me Jess.*"

"Um… si. Naturalmente, sure." And nearly smacks herself in the head with the phone for always reverting to Italian when she's rattled. "You haven't heard from him at all?"

"*No. So he's not with you?*"

"Oh," she says, feigning sudden recall, "I think I know where he is. Just let me see if I can find him and I'll call you back… it could take a few hours, his phone battery was nearly dead when he left." Oh the lies. She hates the lies, but again, with the shroud-blind there's no choice.

"*Thank you Angelina, I'd like that. Talk to you soon… and, um… arrivederci! Did I get that right?*"

Ange smiles. "Yes perfect, you sound like an Italian." Give or take every single vowel. "Arrivederci Jess." She disconnects, and calls Jamie. Sure enough, it goes straight to voice mail. She doesn't bother with a message, he'll know what she wants. Instead she calls Meisha. "Meisha can you find Jamie? His phone's off and his mother's worried. And he must have been a bit rattled last night, but I was unconscious…"

"*Of course Ange, just wait a moment.*" Because Meisha has mad ninja skills with magic and cellphones, and can trace them even when they're turned off. A moment's pause, then, "*Ange I'm getting his phone from down in the financial district.*"

"The financial district?" Aghast. That's Riley's territory, Leventhal people don't venture down there. "Can you find where? We have to get him out!"

"*Ange I don't think he's in trouble. I can sense him on the other end, he seems fine.*"

"You can do that?" It seems incredible. Unless Meisha can turn the phone all the way back on, which she's seen some CIA people do in the movies. If it's technologically possible, then a high level techno-mage can probably do it too.

"*Ange look, we'll try to get word to him, but anyone we send down there will be more vulnerable than he is, to be honest.*"

"I'll go." Even as she says it, her phone tells her another call is coming through. It's Starace. "Meisha, I'll call you back." She switches calls. "Ciao Nonno?"

"*Angelina.*" He speaks Italian, urgent and serious. "*Your friend Jamie is about to get himself into serious trouble looking for the person who killed his sister. I'm in Philadelphia, I've paid a visit to Alexis Rhodes, who I understand you've met, and…*"

"Wait wait wait!" Ange says incredulously. "Alexis Rhodes? She hates me! She hates *all* Ulani, what are you doing in…"

"*Angelina just listen. She hates Ulani but she values Jamie. She wants him to owe her, I'm sure she'd like him to work for her instead of Eli. That's why she contacted me, she doesn't want to go through Eli. She says she knows who killed Jamie's sister. And she can prove it, but you have to come in person, and you have to come alone. Now.*"

Ange thinks furiously. It makes sense — the thing that really made Alexis Rhodes angry with Ange was her friendship with Jamie. All the top magicians in Eli's alliance hate that Jamie, their golden boy, is friends with an Ulani… and now more than just friends. Rhodes won't want Jamie harmed. If this has any chance of making Jamie safer, given his current reckless pursuits…

"I'll be there as soon as I can," she says. "Less than two hours. I think." Because she doesn't actually know how long it takes to fly to Philly on dragonback.

As soon as she disconnects, Meisha phones. "*Ange, I'm coming to Philadelphia with you.*"

"Wait… how do you know I'm going to…" But Meisha is a techno-mage, of course. "You were listening in?"

"*I'm sorry Ange, but if you've just been phoning me I really can't help it, I access a lot of phonecalls without trying. I was in that bathroom when you had that first fight with Alexis, remember? She might not like you, but*" *she's always been nice to me, she made me a job offer once. I'll make sure you two get along."*

Ange thinks about protesting. Starace will be enough to make sure Alexis Rhodes behaves, surely. But then again, she doesn't trust Rhodes at all, and Meisha can see what people are feeling, whatever they actually say.

"Okay fine. Meet me up here in fifteen minutes, I have to put Gia's saddle back on."

It takes Meisha two minutes to go from fearful to exhilarated. They fly across the lower bay with the industrial sprawl of New Jersey to their right and the Statue of Liberty below, and Meisha gasps and shouts in Ange's ear.

"Oh my god! This is so amazing!"

Ange wonders what a blind girl would find amazing about flying, other than the rush of wind and the sensation of motion. "I can see all the way down the coast across the bay!" she shouts to Meisha. "And here's Staten Island right ahead, it looks very green! I can see the ferry just below!"

The roaring wind is cold, and Ange catches most of it, with Meisha clutching her from behind. The weather isn't great, with low broken cloud at two thousand feet. Gia keeps below it, flying in much the same way that old airplanes used to fly before modern jets — staying low at one hundred and fifty miles an hour, and navigating by sight. Ange thinks it might rain.

"Oh listen to his wings!" Meisha exclaims. "I can feel his wings catching the air!"

On the other side of Staten Island, Ange spots the I-95. Gia seems to follow it, a big concrete ribbon across the green, patchwork landscape of forests, fields, towns and industry, zigzagged with roads and power lines. Her phone's map tells her the I-95 will eventually meet the Delaware River, and the Delaware River leads to Philly. And she's surprised just how good her phone reception is at two thousand feet.

Meisha gasps again, and tugs Ange's shoulder. Ange looks right, and is unsurprised to find Bella coming in close to soar off Gia's wingtip. "That's her, isn't it?" Meisha gasps. "That's Bella! Hello Bella!"

Meisha must be able to sense her, Ange thinks, the same way she senses everything — with colour, motion and emotion. It sounds nice, but a tactical advantage occurs to her too — Meisha doesn't need line of sight to 'see'. Camouflage won't fool her, nor even hiding behind a wall. If you're close, Meisha will feel you... but in truth, it's not so different from what Ange gets with her magical tingles. But Ange will only sense magic at work, while Meisha will sense life, and thought.

Bella, Ange notices, is looking around, and not paying Gia too much attention. It gives her a creeping chill that has nothing to do with the wind. Increased dragon activity, the air traffic controllers said. Dragons would show up a little on radar, though only sighted controllers would see the blips. Sighted pilots couldn't report dragons on the radio, for fear of being thought mad, but they would make private reports to other sighted pilots, crew and controllers. There were enthusiast groups who monitored such things... and some, less enthusiastic.

Bella is Gia's girlfriend, sure. But is she also his escort? Suddenly Ange is wondering if this isn't like some old war movie, with two airplanes pressing their mission into unknown and hostile skies. She has no desire to see aerial dragon combat up close. Dragons may survive such fights, but human passengers probably won't.

The Delaware River is easy to find, wide and crossed with bridges. Gia cruises above it, and ahead on the right Ange sees tiny towers on the gloomy horizon, and the sprawl of suburbs around them. As they cruise, the towers grow slowly larger, until the entire right bank of the river is filled with Philadelphia suburbs and roads. It's huge and sprawling, but still only a little city compared to New York. Ange is struck by how big everything is, compared to Europe. So much wasted space, while European cities crowd every last centimeter. Finding Blue Sky Mutual is easy enough, it's a large tower in the center of the Philadelphia business district, with its name in lights and a convenient helipad on the roof.

"One hour and seventeen minutes!" Meisha shouts in Ange's ear as they approach. "Maybe dragons are the answer to America's transportation woes!"

"Great!" says Ange. "Write an article for the Times!"

Ange sees some people on the helipad waiting for them, then Gia flares, flaps twice, and settles with a bounce. Ange unbuckles and jumps off, then helps Meisha down. "Thanks Gia," she says, with a pat on his neck. "You mind waiting? We won't be too long."

Gia snorts, unfurls his wings once more, and bounds from the edge of the tower. Two flaps and he's away, heading for where Bella is circling beyond the towers. "Um, does that mean we're stuck here?" Meisha asks.

"No, I'd guess he's just hungry," says Ange. "He'll get a snack while we're busy." She turns and finds the Blue Sky Mutual welcoming party also staring at the departing dragon.

"That's quite an entrance!" says the young black woman leading them. She comes forward and offers her hand. Ange gets a pronounced tingle from her, prickling up her arm as she shakes her hand. "I'm Tabitha Cain, I'm one of the board members. Mr Starace and Mrs Rhodes are waiting, I'll take you to them. Ms Wing." With a curt nod at Meisha... which is dumb, because Meisha won't see it. "I'm sorry, but were you invited?"

"Yes," Meisha says pleasantly. "I invited me."

A dark stare from Cain. It's a reminder of how this relationship works — Leventhal Holdings can do what it likes, and Blue Sky Mutual can't stop them. It's also very un-Meisha-like — aggressive, and commanding. "Of course. This way please."

Tabitha Cain leads them across the helicopter pad, accompanied by three men in suits, then through a rooftop door. The whole arrangement is not quite as flashy as Leventhal Tower, the building barely half as tall, and as they descend from the rooftop, they walk through bare concrete halls. Alexis Rhodes will resent Eli his greater wealth, Ange has no doubt. She just seems the type.

"Ms Wing, it's quite an honour to have you here as well as Ms Donati," Cain offers, heels clicking on the concrete stairs. "You're quite famous outside of New York as well."

Ange smiles grimly, as she's been coming to that conclusion herself. Eli surrounds himself not only with trustworthy talents, but exceptional ones, and Meisha is a rockstar of the magical world far beyond just China Town. "Well thank you for saying so," says Meisha. "But seriously, who could resist a chance to ride on Angelina's dragon?"

"You know, some of our best magicians would love to meet you," Cain enthuses. "I'm sure they'd really appreciate it if you'd take a few minutes to tell them about your experiences with Leventhal Holdings while you're here."

"I was instructed by Eli to stay with Angelina at all times," Meisha says sweetly. "I'm sure I can meet with your people on the way out."

"Yes of course."

It's the first Ange has heard that Meisha checked with Eli before coming. Ange's phone buzzes. It's the heavy double-buzz of a text, and she takes it out. It's from Meisha. **Keep your eyes open. Something's wrong, she's trying to separate us.**

Ange texts back furiously as they descend some more stairs, hoping that their escorts won't realise she and Meisha are talking. **Whats her mood? Nervous.**

They walk across the upper executive floor of the Blue Sky Tower, and again it's like a cheaper version of the Leventhal Tower, glass walled office partitions on either side of the main halls... but the view of surrounding Philadelphia is from only half the altitude. Ahead, some men in suits are waiting.

Ange's phone buzzes again, and again Ange pulls it out. Tabitha Cain glances too, suspiciously. Meisha's stride is slowing, and Ange feels a building magical buzz, some of it resonating from Meisha. Something is badly wrong.

Angelina pull your sword, says the phone. **They're going to try to kill us.**

"Yeah I was starting to get that vibe," Ange mutters, putting the phone away. Just as calmly, still walking, she pulls her sword. Cain teleports in a flash, as do those with her. Ahead, in an open, central space between offices, waiting men pull guns.

"I've got the guns!" Meisha shouts, staff held vertically as the guns fire. Bullets hit her shield, several yards ahead of them, and fragment or ricochet aside. Glass walls to either side shatter and collapse, and doors splinter. A flash of magic, a simple force-shove, and small lead cases laid along the hallway floor spring open... Ange catches a glimpse of gemstones, and a buzzing wave hits her like a wall. She nearly falls, as numbness spreads... vestigium! Drawing from Third Realm, they'll remove her power and leave her helpless. Except that as the bullets snap and deflect off Meisha's barrier, she can feel the numbness fading. Meisha must be blocking the vestigium somehow, like the bullets.

"Stay close!" says Ange, advancing. "Keep behind me!" She moves at a jog, not to out-distance Meisha's shield as she follows. Half the men pull close-quarters weapons as she comes, the other half continuing to fire — eight in all, Ange counts. Two come at her at once, and Ange goes sideways to take one at a time. The first's attack is poor and she takes his arm off with the counter, then attacks the second with ferocity, forcing two parries and a fast retreat. Meisha's force shove hits him while distracted and blasts him through a glass wall, while Ange takes advantage of the others' astonishment to spin and lunge, impaling a third.

The guns cease and force shoves slam at them in return, but Meisha's defenses are back, while Ange feels only passing pressure. Electricity crackles over her from another attack, but with Meisha alongside, plus her own immunity, it barely even tingles. Another flings broken glass from a collapsed wall, but passing Meisha's barrier it reverts to blowing sand, showering them with a harmless hiss. A pause as the men stare, wondering how to breach these defenses.

"Ready?" Ange says to Meisha.

"Ready." She sounds very cool and calm. Ange has never really figured Meisha for a fighter, but it seems she's made a habit of underestimating people lately.

"Let's go." They can't move fast, needing to stay close, but there's limited room between partitions. Several men skip sideways, blasting at them from the sides while Meisha defends. Another pulls his gun again, figuring he's inside Meisha's barrier... but at close range Ange simply knocks it aside, drives a knee into his middle to double him over, smashes the hilt into his head.

Meisha brings the ceiling down on another's head, and his neighbour's gun magazine explodes, taking most of his hand with it. She fries him with electricity while he screams, and the last two teleport in desperation. Leaving Ange and Meisha standing amidst the suddenly silent offices. Ange looks at the smoke in the air, shoulders heaving, and wonders if it will set the sprinklers off. Meisha goes to one of the cases on the floor, and holds up a gemstone on a chain.

"We make a good team," Ange gasps. "You make that gun magazine explode?"

"There's a lot of chemical charge in bullets," says Meisha, peering at the stone. "Another reason why it's not wise to use guns around some magicians." There is a thumping and crashing from a nearby office. Meisha ignores it. "You seen anything like this?"

"Vestigium," says Ange. "Drawing from Third Realm. It was a trap, they had it set especially for me — those things to drain my powers, the rest to kill me if I somehow escaped their guns."

"Wow," says Meisha, turning slowly, as though scanning for things no other magician could see. "I'm so sorry Ange." She puts a gemstone into its lead case, then pockets it. Ange doesn't like that, but clearly they need to return it to Eli for analysis.

"Yeah." Ange doesn't know what she feels, except numb. Starace was in on this. Starace tried to have her killed. Having survived, that one fact still turns her entire world upside down. She doesn't know what to feel. Her brain can't process the information, leaving her baffled and blank. "Thanks for blocking the vestigium. When they first opened, I thought I was finished."

Meisha looks puzzled. "Ange... I'm not sure it's possible to block this many vestigium. I'm sure Eli could, but I'm not Eli."

"You mean... you *didn't* block them?" A mystified shrug from Meisha. "Well then either they screwed up and they're not drawing from Third Realm, or..." Or something very weird was happening. Again the banging and thumping from nearby. "What *is* that?" Ange wonders, and goes toward it.

Behind a shattered glass wall, the office is empty... save for one of the men who just teleported. His wrist disappears into the wall, where his hand has merged at the molecular level. The banging and thumping is him trying to pull it out, in frantic agony. Ange shakes her head in disbelief, and goes to him, putting her bloodstained blade against his arm.

"Need a hand?" she sneers.

The whole office thumps with a force blast that Ange feels in her chest, rattling the walls and breaking what glass remains. The man slumps unconscious, and Ange turns to see Meisha lowering her staff. "Please Angelina," she says reproachfully. "We don't let it turn us into animals. Come on, we have to go. I assume Gia will have sensed all of that?"

They retrace their steps, fast, and Ange leaps back up the stairs to the helipad... to find it empty. In the surrounding, overcast sky, no sign of dragons. But she can feel him, close by. Meisha follows, taking the steps far more carefully. "I think he's a few minutes out," says Ange, as cold wind gusts at her hair. "Why do you think Rhodes tried to kill us?" "She didn't try to kill *us*," Meisha corrects breathlessly, "she tried to kill *you*. I wasn't supposed to be here. I think the biggest question is why did Starace try to kill you?"

"He must have switched sides," Ange says helplessly, hands to her head, as though to try and keep her thoughts together. "Rhodes too, bloody cowards. Switched to Riley, to saving magic. They don't want to see their power end."

"If Alexis Rhodes has defected," Meisha says grimly, "then we need to get back as soon as possible. Eli's whole alliance could be falling ap..."

She's interrupted by a flash of magic behind them, and Ange grabs Meisha in a protective embrace as a roar of flames washes across the helipad. The intensity of them can only be Alexis Rhodes herself, and beyond the heat, Ange feels Meisha's own magic powering up to try something aggressive.

"No!" she shouts at Meisha as the flames fade. "Meisha she's too powerful! Stay behind me and defend!"

She turns into Rhodes' next electrical attack, feels her sword shudder as normally conducting steel refuses to accept the enormous charge, sending bolts leaping across the helipad to exposed metal beams, the stair railing, anywhere electricity is welcome. The crackling blast stops, and Rhodes stands tall and white-haired with staff extended, her coat whipping out behind at some new wind.

"How much did Riley pay you?" Ange shouts at her.

Rhodes smiles grimly. "He'll pay me my life. I'm three hundred and twelve years old, and if that old man in Manhattan wants to commit suicide, he can do it without taking me with him."

She whips her staff about her head, and the wind increases to a howling gale. Suddenly the clouds above are dark and swirling, as a huge tornado engulfs the Blue Sky Tower. Ange crouches low, Meisha holding onto her from behind as they yawn hard against the pain in their ears, and the sudden light headedness, hard breathing and plunging temperature.

"Ange!" shouts Meisha. "The air pressure! I can't stop it, it's too big!"

"Wait here!" Ange charges, and a big piece of stair railing breaks off and comes flying toward her. Ange ducks and rolls, and Rhodes flings a knife at her, nearly clipping Ange's ear as she rolls aside once more. The knife hits the helipad, then skids and comes back, twice as fast — propelled by magic or not, momentum is momentum and Ange clangs it aside with her sword before she's impaled. But Rhodes is laughing at her, circling away as the air pressure drops further, and even this little exertion has Ange gasping for breath.

"The great masters have been killing Ulani for a thousand years!" Rhodes shouts at her above the howling gale. "You think you're immune to everything? A vacuum doesn't care that you're in it!" It's too big, Ange realises — the magic creating a tornado is manifesting too far away from her for her immunity to block. Only when it's aimed directly at her will that happen... but this is aimed at the sky. Her head spins, and she struggles to keep her feet. If she passes out...

Fast movement behind Rhodes catches her eye. Dragon-shaped with wings tucked, ripping through the wall of wind and cloud with a dart-like, high-speed profile. Rhodes looks just in time to see the dragon falling on her, and screams as Gia smashes and smears her across the helipad, skidding to the lip before hurling what's left over the edge in several pieces. The wind fades, and black cloud dissipates like smoke in the breeze.

"If you're going to give that speech to a girl with a dragon," Ange gasps, "you really better watch behind you."

Ange straps herself then Meisha to the saddle, and Gia soars off the towerside, flapping in powerful beats to build up speed over highways, parks, and finally the smaller river beside the towers. There's lots of traffic as rush hour approaches, and a light rain mists on Ange's goggles. About the base of the tower she glimpses some commotion — probably people gathered about what's left of Alexis Rhodes, and wondering what did it, between bouts of vomiting. But whatever their improbable conclusions, they'll soon forget, just as they'll already be forgetting the huge tornado that formed around the Blue Sky Tower. She thinks it'll be too hard for the shroud to explain a dismembered company CEO on a downtown street, and after a few weeks it will settle for something mundane — like a car crash, for everyone to agree on. Like it did with Tori MacDonald. And suddenly she's thinking of Jamie, and wondering if they've found him yet.

"Why didn't she join in the first ambush?" Meisha yells in her ear above the wind.

"At close range I would have just killed her!" Ange shouts back. "Indoors there's no room! Outdoors, she's got the whole sky to play with!"

"Ange, I think we're in big trouble! First the High Council tries to kill Eli, then Alexis Rhodes turns on him! I think the Shtaal Alliance might be falling apart!"

Gia seems uncomfortable, tossing his head and snaking, then casting her displeased looks from the corner of his eye. It affects his aerodynamics, and makes the ride more treacherous. "What's wrong with him?" Meisha asks. "He feels unhappy!"

"He's only like this around magic he doesn't like!" Ange replies. "It must be that vestigium you're carrying!" Which makes sense, because she and Gia are in tune on so many things, and she doesn't like the vestigium either.

They rejoin the Delaware River, city sprawl on its left bank, green suburbs on the right. Ahead, Bella appears, holding something in her claws. As she comes closer, Ange realises it's the rear quarters of a cow. Bella lets Gia close right up, then arches her neck down and savages the hindquarters to tear off a leg. The rest she tosses into the air, and Gia lunges to catch. His head lowers as he eats, and Ange hears a lot of crunching and popping. Blood sprays on the wind, and Ange wipes some gore off her leg.

"Hey! Keep it out of the slipstream, please!" But she can appreciate what Croz said — Gia's wing muscles beneath her make the whole saddle ride up and down with his wingbeats, flexing with incredible power that will take a lot of food to satisfy.

"Ange! Eli says he's sent the helicopter! It'll meet us in a few minutes!"

Ange isn't sure if that will be a help or a problem, as she glances anxiously at the overcast clouds now low overhead. But Gia is still uncomfortable. "Great, we can unload this damn stone on them!" And she frowns. "Did he just send a text message to your phone?"

"Yes!"

"How do you even know how to read?"

"I learned just like you! I had trouble making out the shapes of letters in my head off a piece of paper, but when they were on a computer screen I found it so easy, they just lit up my mind! I think that's how I learned I was a techno-mage!"

"If someone could cast a spell that would give you sight, would you let them?"

"If it meant keeping my current powers? Sure! If it meant losing them, no way! I like seeing this way, losing it would be like you being struck blind!"

They pass over lakes on the inside of the final bend of the Delaware River, and an industrial estate on the island between lakes and river. A clover-shaped freeway overpass on the far bank, with four distinct leaves, filled with curling traffic and wet with recent rain. Grey veils of rain blot out the view of further suburbs, falling in patches. To the left upriver, a cluster of larger buildings, but nothing tall.

"That's Trenton on the left!" Meisha shouts. "Michael Stanthorpe's boyfriend is from there!"

"What does *he* do?"

"He's on Broadway of course!" Ange grins — a wealthy gay man in New York, of course Michael's going out with a Broadway performer. "The helicopter's just ahead! Stew's on board!"

Ange squints, and sure enough there's a little black dot just beneath the ceiling of clouds. It grows bigger, then swings about and cruises alongside them, ruining the windy peace with its thundering rotorblades. In the cockpit, the pilot is staring at them in amazement. In the rear, Stew Bickel waves out the window. Ange waves back, and points to the ground. Bickel gives a thumbs up.

"Gia!" she shouts. "Gia, let's get rid of this gemstone! We'll give it to the helicopter, okay?" And Gia folds his wings and plunges toward the ground with a speed that makes Meisha squeal.

He lands in a field near the highway, just past some big high tension power lines. The helicopter roars and thuds its way down alongside, as Ange and Meisha unstrap, and Ange helps the other girl to the ground. They walk to the chopper, Ange casting a glance skyward to where Bella circles, waiting for them.

"What happened?" Bickel yells above the helicopter roar.

"Damn witch tried to kill us!" says Ange, and recalls Meisha's sensitivities to that word, and regrets it. "Gia got her! They used these to ambush me, Gia doesn't like it so you'd better take it!" As Meisha hands the vestigium over. "And you'd better take Meisha too!"

"Oh but why?" Meisha protests. "I love flying with you and Gia!"

"Meish, Croz and I think there's other dragons around! We're not sure they're friendly!"

Bickel nods. "He told us! It's why Eli insisted we come to you!"

"In that?" Ange eyes the helicopter skeptically. If it was an army gunship, sure, but it's not.

"No way!" says Meisha, shaking her head. "If we get attacked, I need to be able to see! Or you know what I mean… the chopper's all engine and rotors, it blocks my sense! I'm staying with you!"

"Meisha, if we run into other dragons…"

"Where would you feel safer?" Meisha challenges her. "On Gia, on in that?" Nodding at the chopper.

Ange looks at it. "Si, okay," she concedes. "Stew, sorry mate!"

"Yeah thanks guys," he says sourly, and hefts the rifle in his hand. "Anywhere I should aim?"

"You won't get a shot off," Ange says confidently. "Dragons are too smart, they'll attack where you're not."

"Comforting."

Airborn again, Gia climbs back to altitude and speed well before the chopper, then waits with Bella for the noisy machine to catch up. Ange doesn't think he really likes helicopters any more than he likes mobile phones, but at least he can see how useful helicopters are. They leave the I-95 now and head off to the right, where Ange's memory says they should find Staten Island.

A shrill shriek sounds above the thunder of rotors. It's dragon-cry, and quite rare, used only in emergencies. This one didn't come from Gia. Ange looks, and sees Bella leaving formation on the chopper's far side, banking hard off to the right, an amazing silhouette against the drifting grey cloud. Gia is looking intently that way, and with his head turned, his entire aerodynamic shape is changed, forcing him to beat harder to maintain speed. Ange peers after Bella, squinting through her misty goggles, and sees the faintest smudge of a dot, low beneath the clouds. Or is it two dots? Then both vanish into cloud, and Bella follows, flapping hard and disappearing.

Ange waves at the pilot, and points at where Bella went. Then raises two fingers, the number of dots she thinks she saw. The pilot nods, exaggerated to be sure she sees. Gia is now looking back to the left, and drifts down and under the chopper for a better look. Ange realises her heart is thumping hard. What were those dots? Riley has choppers too, and probably more than just choppers... but even using the Air Force against them would be unwise, with Meisha here.

"Meisha! I saw two dots off to our right! You sense anything?"

"No! Are you sure?"

Gia swerves clear of the chopper, then flaps hard and shoots skyward. Ange clings on tight as suddenly everything is mist, cold and wet, and she can barely see beyond Gia's wingtips. Then they burst into clear blue skies, and the glare of sun from behind her left shoulder, low above a sea of blinding white cloud. Gia looks left and right, scanning that whiteness. Like a sea eagle above the water, searching the surface for any disturbance that might mean fish. Was something coming? Using the clouds for cover? The chopper is flying too close to the clouds, she realises.

"Meisha!" she shouts. "Meisha can you tell the pilot to dive?"

"No, I can't replicate speech on his earphones! I'll try to text Stew!"

Gia is looking to the right, and down, eyes fixed on a patch of cloud. Ange squints past his wing, searching. The clouds are too bright up here, and human eyes aren't made for the kind of telescopic distances dragons can see. Gia turns abruptly right, as Ange gathers a big double handful of leather on the saddle front, thankful for the buckles holding her and Meisha's legs to the saddle. Then she sees it — a swirl of cloud, something cutting through the white mist below. Like a fish through shallow water, only much, much larger.

Gia gives her a fast glance over his shoulder. "Yeah I got it!" she shouts at him. "Go, go, Meisha hang on!" And Gia flips over and dives like the world's worst roller coaster, and Ange is certain she's just left her stomach and last three meals somewhere behind. A rush of white cloud, then a huge, dark shape that flashes at them from the gloom, big wings and tail, all red and black. A smack! as Gia's claws make contact, then another fast bank that crushes Ange against his back, and then another... and dear god she doesn't know which way is up, she can't see the horizon and it feels like she's upside down and spinning, Meisha's arms clutching her like grim death. Another manoeuvre, then a dragon appears and streaks by just feet overhead with a hiss of wind as the tail passes above.

Another flip and turn, and Ange has completely given up trying to figure out what's going on when they burst into clear air beneath the cloud. Ange stares around desperately for the chopper, as her brain struggles to reorient itself to 'up' and 'down'... and there's the chopper, flying away to their right. The pilot is still hugging the clouds for cover, thinking that makes him safer. Against other human pilots he'd be right, but against dragons who are as comfortable in cloud as fish in water...

Suddenly a big dragon drops from the cloud directly behind the chopper, red with black patches. Gia flaps powerfully, heading for top speed. They're a hundred yards behind the red dragon, but the red dragon is closer still to the chopper. Ange measures its huge wingspan with her eyes, and compares that to the helicopter... good god it's enormous! That's at least a forty foot wingspan, maybe bigger. It'll swat the helicopter from the sky like a cat with a toy.

Bella erupts from the cloud directly above the red dragon and crashes straight into its wing. They fall together, tumbling over and over, striking and thrashing on the way down. Then Bella flares her wings and cuts away, and the red dragon does the same, only more slowly. It seems to have a rip in its wing, and isn't game to flap it harder in case the tear gets worse.

Gia is still flapping hard, and pulls up alongside the chopper, gliding as Ange feels him gasping air from the effort. Ange waves for attention, and sees the pilot looking. She points down, toward the ground. The pilot shakes his head, and points up, indicating the layer of cloud just above him. Ange shakes her head, points to the cloud, then at the pilot, then mimes cutting her throat. The pilot looks undecided.

A second red dragon appears directly in front, descending from cloud and coming straight at them. The chopper pilot dives frantically, and the red dragon lets loose a torrent of bright flame as it passes overhead. Gia turns hard to get behind the red dragon, as Bella circles across in front. Seeing it's outnumbered, the red dragon flaps into cloud and vanishes.

Gia turns again, and Ange searches again for the chopper, heart in mouth, expecting to see a flaming wreck falling to the ground. Instead she sees it still flying, heading lower. Gia flaps hard and dives after it. Coming alongside once more, Ange sees black scorch marks on the chopper's paintwork. It must have passed through the dragonfire too fast to catch alight... except she can feel a sharp tingle coming from behind her, and guesses that Meisha is doing something to stop the engine from burning. Either way it's an awfully close call, given the temperature dragonfire burns at, and the fuel in the chopper's tanks.

The chopper flies the rest of the way to Manhattan at treetop level, rising occasionally to pass over high tension power lines. Ange wonders if anyone has written a book on aerial warfare against dragons. Heck of a way to learn what not to do. Gia and Bella fly close off the chopper's flanks, watching all the way as the sun sets, and the lights of the cars make great white and red trails on the freeways below.

At Leventhal Tower there is no room for helicopter and dragons all at once, so the dragons circle while the chopper unloads Bickel, then flies off, Ange presumes to some other pad Eli owns for refuelling and to check the damage. Bickel stays on the pad as both Gia and Bella land, and gives Gia a hug even as Ange unstraps.

"Nice work mate! Saved my neck for sure!"

Ange helps Meisha down, but Meisha mostly ignores her, and runs to Gia to repeat Bickel's hug. "Thank you Gia! That was so scary!" Gia's nostrils flare as he sucks air — that final half hour was the equivalent of a middle-distance sprint. And he's looking very restrained, Ange thinks with affection, because she's really the only human he enjoys physical contact with, and now everyone's treating him like a pet dog, which makes him irritable.

Meisha goes to Bella, but...

"Meisha!" Ange cautions, running quickly to take her arm. "Meisha, probably best not to hug Bella, I don't know that she's even met a human before, on the ground." The other dragon does look nervous, with that uncertain head-snaking motion that dragons use to keep a moving object in sight. And she's favouring one leg, and Ange sees she has a bloody gash on her front thigh, just above the knee. "Oh look she's hurt... Gia? Gia, we can heal her. Meisha, you can heal her yes? Gia, tell her it's all right."

"I can heal her," says Eli, striding across the pad between the dragons, wind whipping at his white hair and tie. He extends his cane, and Ange feels not the usual deep chill, but a pulsing wave, like a cool breeze. Bella stops her snaking, and Eli approaches, holding up one hand to Bella's jaw. She lowers her head, and waits patiently as Eli points his staff at her injured leg, murmuring gently.

Then the pulsing stops. "She'll be fine," says Eli. "It's not deep, and it's clean." The wound still looks red, but the blood has congealed and is already beginning to scar and scab. It looks suddenly days old and healing, instead of fresh and painful. Bella tests her weight on it, gingerly with wings extended. Flaps hard, blasting them all with wind, then jumps a little as Eli backs up.

The leg takes her weight with evidently little pain. Ange has never seen a dragon look astonished before. Bella circles Eli, head down low and peering at him like he's the most curious little thing she's ever seen. She sniffs at him, and nudges his shoulder. Ange laughs, and Eli pats her nose, looking very pleased.

"Magicians have made many mistakes using magic to create new creatures," he says. "But dragons were not among them. You beautiful girl you."

CHAPTER FIFTEEN

"**E**dward Mandel," says Eli, sitting at the desk in his office. He's stroking his chin, and looking at the vestigium on its chain, lying before him. Ange leans against a window nearby, sipping coffee and feeling nothing of the gem's effects — Eli is blocking it somehow.

"Are you certain?" asks Meisha. There are frustrated Holdings executives waiting outside the door, with their files and discussion papers, trying to get in to see Eli and do the work that makes a New York financial corporation function. But instead, the magicians are taking over the office again. Ange has heard grumblings from sighted executives that it's a wonder Leventhal Holdings makes any money at all, with so many distractions taking their CEO's time. Heaven only knows what the shroud-blind executives make of it all.

"Very certain," says Eli. "Edward Mandel makes the best vestigium in all New York. These bear his signature — the very magic he charged them with. It cannot be disguised, not from me."

"So we have to take him down," says Croz. "Simple." Eli says nothing for a moment, gazing at the gem. Ange thinks he looks beyond sad. Almost... lost. And lonely. "Eli. I know he's an old friend. I like him too. He even set me up with the dealer who got me the best price on my Ferrari. But he supplied these to Alexis. Third Realm vestigium, very rare, Meisha says there were five of them. That's a big effort, the Ulani are the only ones who draw from Third Realm, and there's only one Ulani in New York and she works for you. For us."

Ange is nearly touched. But the look on Eli's face draws all her attention. It's the look of a man who is losing all of his friends, one by one.

"Yes," he says heavily. And draws a deep breath. "Yes. House Mandel must fall, of course."

"Now that's a *lot* of effort to go to," says Bickel. He toys with a big knife, twirling it expertly in calloused hands. "Five Third Realm vestigium." He glances at Ange. "I mean I know Alexis didn't like you girl, but bloody hell."

"Starace's the one who wanted her dead," Meisha reasons. "He did a deal with Alexis."

Croz shakes his head. "Alexis doesn't work for House Ulani. She joined with Riley, and so did Starace." He looks hard at Eli. "Which means that our second-most-powerful-ally in America joined with Riley, the High Council itself joined with Riley, and now even House Ulani have too." Eli says nothing. Croz leans forward. "Eli, we're losing. We're losing bad. We either attack Riley now, while we've still got some allies left, or we give up and let him do what he wants."

"My remaining friends will not abandon me," Eli says quietly.

"Sure," Croz says drily. "You thought that about Alexis. And the High Council. And…"

"Enough!" Eli shouts. The office falls silent. Croz does not look intimidated. He just folds his arms, and looks at his boss with exasperation. "We will attack Riley, but we need more time to plan. If we spend our strength attacking him blindly, we'll diminish ourselves and achieve nothing. You've seen the army he has beneath his feet."

With a glance at Ange. Ange nods. She has seen.

"Say Angelina," says Stanthorpe, "how *did* you survive five vestigium blocking your power?"

"Well they didn't think Meisha would be there," Ange explains. "She read their minds and sprang the trap too early. I wasn't completely surrounded by them *or* by vestigium, and even without my powers I can still run and fight, just not at the same level."

"Yes," Stanthorpe replies, "but you advanced *into* them. And Meisha can't block that many vestigium. And they were all powerful receptors to hear Meisha tell it, you couldn't defeat all of them without your powers, even with Meisha's help. Which means you still had your powers, yes?"

Ange shrugs helplessly. "I don't know. They must have screwed up. Maybe those five vestigium aren't as good as they thought. Maybe Edward Mandel made a mess of it."

Eli looks very skeptical, but says nothing. Stanthorpe looks curiously suspicious. Meisha, behind her glasses, typically unreadable. In truth, Ange has no more to add. She still can't believe that Starace tried to kill her, and is wondering if there's some way for a hostile techno-mage to fake his message to her. But Meisha has traced that call, and says it came from Starace's American phone, plus it just sounded like him, Italian mannerisms and all. Anyone faking that had to be a native Italian, and native Italians just don't upset the head of House Ulani unless they have a death wish.

"Eli," says Bickel, with an expert flip of his knife. "How do you want to do this?"

Mandel Associates occupy several floors of a major tower on Fifth Avenue, not far from the Rockefeller Center. Storming an office building in Mid-Town is no simple thing with the crowds and traffic, so Bickel calls in a favour from the New York Fire Department, who suddenly report a fire in the building.

Ange strides on Eli's right, Croz on his left with Hernandez and other Response Division heavies around them. Senior magicians form a phalanx, ahead and behind, striding along crowded Mid-Town streets to curious looks from passers-by. The last light fades from the sky as the Manhattan towers take over. Unsurprisingly they hit a green 'walk' signal at every crossing, a suited procession across the road before queues of waiting vehicles. Ahead, sirens wail and horns honk, as firetrucks roar across roads on their way up Fifth Avenue.

By the time they turn the corner past the huge old Rockefeller towers, the firefighters have already cordoned off the street ahead, and police are directing traffic down side streets. The lights of cluttered emergency vehicles make a dazzling sight, flashing off the streetside canyons. Bickel greets a waiting firefighter with a grim handshake, and explains the situation as the rest of the Leventhal contingent passes the barriers. A few firefighters move to stop them, but are told otherwise by their seniors, and Ange recalls Bickel explaining to her how some emergency departments have been stacked with sighted personnel, just for cases like this.

They approach the base of the tower, and Ange spots a lone figure walking up the center of the deserted road ahead. "Eli!" yells a familiar voice. Ange squints against the kaleidoscope of flashing light behind. The figure strides forward, unarmed but all threat, in jeans, hoodie and basketball shoes. Her eyes widen as Eli comes to a halt.

"Jamie!" she shouts. "Jamie, where have you been?" She runs to him, but Eli catches her arm. Ange stares at him in astonishment.

"Jamie," says Eli. His voice is tired, but wary.

Jamie stops on the road. His fists are balled, and Ange gets a cascading series of chills off him like an icy winter wind, full of power. As though he is seething with rage. "I went to see the Mayor!" he shouts.

Ange gapes at him. "Jamie, you *what?* Are you insane?"

"I healed Ange, after that thing grabbed her! That means I draw from First Realm, like you, like the Mayor! And like Tori! You have to draw from First Realm to get into your secret library too, without your permission! That's how Tori got in, and that's how I got in! There's only one other person who knows about that library and could have gotten in without your help, and I went to see him! And *he* says it wasn't him!"

"Well he's lying Jamie!" Ange retorts. "How do you think he got to be Mayor, if not by lying to everyone!"

"He says you've got that library so heavily charmed against him that there's no way he could get in!" Jamie shouts. "That only leaves one person who could have killed Tori!" With a flash, a short staff appears in one hand, and he points it menacingly at Eli. "It was you, wasn't it? You killed my sister!"

Ange waits for Eli's denial. And waits. And waits. Eli stands, leaning heavily on his staff, and looks small, old and tired. "Jamie," he says finally, with a heavy voice. "Jamie put the staff away, you cannot win this fight…"

A colossal bolt of lightning rips from Jamie to Eli, setting Fifth Avenue alight with silver fire. Eli deflects and it shoots to the nearest metal — firetrucks, police cars, street lamps, making sparks fly as officers dive for cover and thunder booms between buildings.

"Didn't you?" Jamie screams.

"She was too damn powerful Jamie!" Eli roars, shocked into animation. Ange stares at him in horror. "She was asking about Ashkir when she was still only thirteen! She knew, I don't know how she did, but she just *knew* magic was ending, and she was obsessed with it!"

"She *never* told me that!" Jamie retorts. "And she told me everything!"

"Because you were the reason for her obsession! You've a tumour Jamie, it's right here!" Eli points to the center of his forehead. "You and Tori were twins, you should have been identical in ability, but you were so slow! Tori thought something was stopping you, so she learned the spells and found the damn tumour in your brain. It's inoperable, medicine can't stop it, and without her magic to freeze its progress, you'd be dead in six months. She was keeping you alive, boy! And if magic died, so would you, and it made her frantic! She didn't tell you because if you knew the risks she was going to take for you, you'd never have let her do it!"

Tears stream down Jamie's face. "Why'd you kill her? You didn't need to kill her!"

"I never meant to kill her!" For the first time, Ange sees on Eli's face real grief. His voice trembles. "But she broke into my damn library, searching for the reversal to the Ashkir Prophecy, and I went in there to stop her... and she's just... I'd *never* seen a young magician so powerful at that age. In that place, that library, Realm Shifted and drawing from First Realm, the power just flowed through her like a river. We argued, and it got out-of-control, and then we fought, and... and I had to use all of my powers just to stay alive. And when I'm forced to use all of my powers, people die, and... and I just couldn't stop it!"

"You should have died!" Jamie yells, and another bolt erupts up the street, deflected again with a blinding thunderclap. "You should have let yourself die rather than kill her! You've lived for over two thousand years! She was *fifteen*! She had so much time left, and it's not fair that I have to spend it all without her!"

"You're right," says Eli. "It's not fair. Some people have a lot, others have very little. But that's what we're stuck with Jamie. She was trying to save you. I was trying to save the world. She was prepared to risk the world, to save your life. I wasn't — not for your life, not for her life, and not for mine."

"That's not your call!" Furiously. "You're not God!"

"No, I'm not. But yes, it is my call. Everyone else in this world is standing for themselves, and those close to them. No one stands for the whole world but me."

"Fraud!" Jamie yells, and blasts another bolt of lightning. "Living in your luxury towers!" The deflected bolt melts a street light, which crashes to the road. "Driving around in your fancy cars, claiming you're doing it all for everyone else!" A force blast sends bystanders skidding and grasping for supports, and firetrucks behind Eli skid several feet sideways. Eli blocks, staff crosswise before him. "You're a parasite, you live off the fears of others, you get them to worship you, and then you kill them when they get in your way! And you've got the nerve to say Riley's arrogant and greedy? You're just as bad as him!"

The fallen streetlight skids off the road and flies at Eli, who performs a vertical slice and splits it through the middle before it reaches him. The two parts crash into the building behind with an explosion of glass. Several cops fire at Jamie, as others yell at them to stop… Jamie barely notices, bullets exploding just short, as he elevates a parked, empty taxi and hurls it at Eli like a child's toy. Eli picks up a similarly empty delivery van and rams it, the two vehicles smashing in mid-air collision, then falling to the road with a crash, and a shower of broken glass.

"Jamie!" Ange yells, running out into the road, and is immediately grabbed by Croz and Bickel. "Jamie no! You'll push him too hard and he'll kill you like Tori!"

"Get the hell back here!" Croz snarls, hauling one arm as Bickel hauls the other. "You're not immune to either of them, you'll be a bug on their windshield!" They drag her back to the cover of the building doorway, where other Leventhal employees shelter.

Jamie sends a shockwave skyward, the huge glass walls of skyscrapers bending and rippling like waves on an ocean. And they break, an explosion of a billion shards, all of them raining down on Eli like a storm of daggers. Short of him, they hit an invisible, sloping wall, turn red hot and spatter into a huge, thick wall of molten glass. Eli builds the wall in seconds, then with a sweep of his arm lets forth a blast of cold, freezing the liquid glass solid as all Fifth Avenue gasps and exhales white plumes.

"You're kidding me," Croz mutters. Several magicians edge forward from their cover in the doorway. "No! Jamie's too powerful, stay down or die!"

Ange takes off running up the sidewalk to Jamie's side, keeping low behind parked vehicles, but Jamie's attention is all for Eli. With a thrust of his staff, water mains erupt to Eli's sides, giant plumes of water shooting skyward. Behind Eli, several firetruck water cannon turn on Eli's back. Water from the mains turns in midair, then combines with the firetrucks to blast Eli from all sides. Eli freezes it, and the ice wall builds around him, joining with the huge glass barrier to his front.

Jamie then points to the building to Eli's side, opposite the one holding Mandel Associates. He yells as the power channels through him, then the ground level windows blow out as a concrete support pylon explodes, fragments of concrete raining across the road. Eli stares up from within his prison of ice and glass, at forty storeys and thousands of tonnes of office tower above. Another concrete pylon explodes, and the building shakes.

"Run!" yells a policeman behind. "He's gonna bring the building down!"

"Jamie no!" Croz yells. "There are people in that building!" And he ducks as Eli blasts his glass and ice walls to flying fragments that Jamie deflects around him, staff held out to shield. The storm of debris passes, and Jamie sends another blast at the building's supports, only for Eli to block it, as the blast takes out a neighbouring facade instead, bringing down tonnes of masonry onto cars and sidewalk.

"I won't let you kill innocents Jamie!" Eli shouts, raising his own staff with properly threatening intent for the first time. "Don't make me stop you!"

Ange tears from behind the car parked to Jamie's side, and sprints at him. Jamie spins on her, staff raised… and seeing her, hesitates for the slightest moment. Ange hits him in a crash tackle, bouncing his head on the road as they tumble. And lies holding him, limp and unconscious, cradling his head in her arm. "Jamie I'm sorry!" she exclaims, checking him over. "Wake up, you hear me? Jamie, wake up!"

Down the debris-strewn ruin of Fifth Avenue, amidst shattered glass, concrete and ice, ruined cars, gushing water mains and shrieking car alarms,

ANGELINA

Eli takes off running toward them. He arrives in fair time for an older man, kneels and puts a hand on Jamie's chest.

"He's fine," he tells Ange. "But I can't risk him waking up, I haven't the power to restrain him without hurting him. Stand back." Ange doesn't move. "Angelina, I cannot be sure to teleport accurately with you this close. You do not block my powers but you certainly interfere with them, now stand back!"

"But isn't it dangerous to...?" Eli sends her tumbling backward with a force shove before she can finish, and she rolls as a lifetime's training has taught her... and Eli and Jamie vanish in a flash of black smoke.

CHAPTER SIXTEEN

Jamie is being kept in Meisha's office at the very top level of Leventhal Tower. Two magicians stand guard, but the door is not locked. Ange opens it, and there, seated on a comfortable sofa chair by Meisha's desk, with a view across Mid-Town's forest of towers at night, is Jamie. There's a slim gold collar around his neck, identical to hers. Ange can feel the faint throb of energy from it… and a static crackle of disruption. As though her own collar is interacting with his. His eyes are closed.

Ange goes and half-sits on the desk beside him. "Hey," she says quietly. "What does your collar do?"

"I can't leave the chair," says Jamie, not opening his eyes. "Or do magic. It paralyses me if I try."

"Unpleasant, isn't it?"

"Very."

"You draw from First Realm. Shouldn't you be able to break the collar?"

Jamie shrugs. "First Realm is a passage. It goes everywhere, connects to other Realms. That's the whole thing with Eli, he can draw from all Realms. He's had two thousand years to figure it all out, I've had… well, six, since I first learned I was a wizard." A pause. "Four, if you subtract the last two. Whatever Eli's done to this collar, I couldn't break it if I had years to try."

"Jamie." Ange struggles to control her voice. "I'm sorry about the tumour."

"Yeah. Me too."

"I don't…" She stares down at the floor. "I don't know what to do."

"You should do what you think is right."

"And what if I no longer know what's right?" she pleads. If magic ends, Jamie's tumour will kill him. Suddenly she knows exactly how Tori must have felt, facing the impending death of the most important person in the world. *And* the end of magic will probably end up killing Gia too, and Bella, and most of the world's dragons. Who is she kidding… regular humans are just going to coexist with dragons? Flying free over their cities, eating their livestock, dodging their airplanes? The fact that they've already *been* coexisting with dragons for centuries, unknowingly, won't count for anything. Dragons will be exterminated, or hunted down and drugged, defanged, de-flamed and put in zoos, chained to concrete floors beneath a low ceiling. Gia, she's certain, would rather be dead.

Jamie's eyes open, and fix on her. The anger there is controlled, and very real. "Then help me get this damn collar off, and together we'll bring this entire, shitty building crashing to the ground."

Ange stares at him despairingly. Hearing it put like that reminds her of all the reasons why Eli is right. "Jamie. You kill Eli, then Riley wins."

"So what?"

"So you haven't seen what I saw in the tunnels under the financial district. You haven't seen Riley's army."

"And what if he's only collecting those things because Eli's forced him to? Eli's powerful Ange, Riley needs an army to beat him."

"Good God, you really did talk to him, didn't you? Jamie, the man is evil."

Jamie's eyes burn. "He didn't kill my sister."

"No, but he would have, without blinking an eye. And he wouldn't be upset about it like Eli is."

"Poor Eli. It must be so hard for him." Bitterly.

"Jamie!" Ange kneels before him, to look him in the eyes. Searching desperately for any sign of the fun, mischievous boy she knew. "This isn't just about you! How many *other* people's sisters has Riley killed? How many has Eli saved? How many more will die if Riley wins now, and takes us all to whatever evil realm shift he has planned? You think he's doing that for the good of nice girls like Tori?"

"There are no girls like Tori," Jamie whispers. "Just Tori."

Ange hangs her head. Her heart wants him to convince her. If she can just put forward Eli's best argument, and Jamie can demolish it, then maybe she can follow her heart, and take the chance that Riley really can save magic in the world. But her head tells her that Jamie doesn't have an argument, only rage.

"Jamie, listen to me…"

"Ange!" He cuts her off, sharply. His voice trembles. "You say you haven't made up your mind, but you have, really. That's fine. You have no family. Your parents are dead, and you have no brothers and sisters. You don't know what it's like. You'll never know."

It hurts. The last man who had claim to being her family just now tried to have her killed. And she was secretly hoping that maybe Jamie would be her family. Or that maybe they could make one together, one day, when things were happier.

"I know that if Riley wins," she says, "then everyone who's ever been on Eli's side is in danger. And their families. You've still got a mother, Jamie. You forget about her? You think the High Council will stop him taking revenge on the shroud-blind now that the High Council's on his side?"

"Get out."

"What good's revenge on Eli if you get your mother killed in the process?"

"*Get out!*" he yells at her, then a convulsion, as his collar shocks him. Then silence, as he sits still in his chair, eyes closed, breathing deep. Trying to compose himself, and avoid further shocks.

Ange backs away, tears in her eyes, and leaves the office. That was a terrible thing to throw at him, the kind of thing a bully would say. For a moment, she hates herself… and yet, she doesn't think she was wrong to say it. Being what she is makes certain things necessary, and some of those things she despises. Despair threatens.

That night, Leventhal Tower remains abuzz with activity. Response Division are gathered, units from all across New York and surrounding areas, several hundred strong. They discuss tactics and possible ways to attack Riley's stronghold in the Financial District, focusing on the Municipal Building, and whatever apparatus it's holding for Riley's upcoming great magic.

Leventhal Holdings' senior magicians gather to discuss intelligence, and how they might penetrate Riley's various magical barriers to assaulting that region. Ange sits and listens for a while, but this isn't her territory, and both the magicians in senior management, and the receptors in Response Division, both know far more about this stuff than she does. After an hour of feeling like a spare wheel, exhaustion truly sets in, and she grabs some cushions off the upstairs sofas, and carries them with blankets up to the rooftop helipad.

Both Gia and Bella are still there, beautifully dangerous silhouettes against the blaze of city light. Meisha sits with them, an elbow on one of Gia's great clawed feet, gazing sightlessly across the humming spectacle of midnight Manhattan. She smiles at Ange as she plonks cushions and blankets down, enough for both of them.

"I'm surprised they're still here," says Meisha, patting Gia's foot. "You said they normally don't hang around too long."

"They know there's trouble coming," says Ange, settling behind Gia's front leg, as the dragon thoughtfully lifts his wing for her to duck under. "I don't know where they've been sleeping, probably someplace with mountains or hills. They like high places, so this won't feel too strange for a nesting spot." She puts her head against Gia's thick hide. "Why aren't you downstairs planning? I'd have thought they'd welcome your ideas."

"My skills are a little... specific," says Meisha. "Other people don't really know how to use them. Besides, I'm not much of a soldier really."

"You were great today."

"Without you there to block their weapon attacks, I'd have just teleported."

"And without you to stop their bullets," Ange adds, "I'd have run away. So I guess we made each other brave."

"Well you *are* a soldier. I mean, I trained in law. I think of all those years I spent with my head in those books, and now I look at myself here, in a time of soldiers." Meisha sighs. "I wonder if it was all worth it."

Ange shakes her head. "These are strange times, Meisha. In most times, in this city, I'd think lawyers are probably more valuable. Just maybe not today."

"As a soldier," says Meisha. "What do you think will happen? If we attack the Municipal Building with full force?"

"And Riley unleashes all his underground army on us? In his territory, with all his magicians to back them up, and all those defensive charms against us?" She doesn't think she needs to say any more. For a moment, there is only the sound of the wind, and the hum and honk of traffic from far below. A jetliner passes over, navigation lights flashing, and Bella lifts her head to look at it like a cat watching a passing butterfly.

"I think it'll look like something from the First World War," says Meisha. "When all the soldiers jump over the top of the trench and run into the machine guns. And none of them come back." Ange reaches around Gia's leg, and grasps Meisha's arm. Meisha smiles, and holds her hand. "I'm so sorry about Starace, Ange. I know that you loved him. In a complicated way."

"What colour is love?" Ange asks quietly.

"Love is strange," says Meisha. "It doesn't have a single colour, it's kind of a blend. I guess that's because there's so many different kinds."

"Kinds?"

"You know. Love between parents and children is different from love between men and women. Or even the love between an old couple who've been together fifty years, that's different from the love between teenagers. I don't see love as a colour so much, I see it as a depth. Two people will have a connection, and have their own colours for emotions, but those colours have depth based on what kind of love they have. It's hard to explain."

"Like seeing a movie in 3D," Ange suggests.

Meisha smiles. "Maybe, yeah. Of course, I've never seen a movie."

"Your life's probably interesting enough without them."

"I have music, I don't need movies." Meisha thinks for a moment. "I see love between you and Gia. It's very deep, and very strong, maybe because it's so simple."

Ange smiles. "Si. Simple love. I've never had much of that in my life."

"Between you and Starace... well I've never met Starace, so I can't really see his end. But at your end, it feels... fractured. Uncertain."

"And fading," Ange mutters.

Meisha shakes her head. "No, you don't always lose love like that, even if one person tries to kill you. You see it on the news all the time, these tragic romances. What you feel is rage, but that kind of rage is driven by love. It's so much more personal when someone you love tries to hurt you. Your rage confirms your love rather than negates it."

"You should have studied psychology instead of law," says Ange. It makes too much sense. "And between me and Jamie?"

Meisha squeezes Ange's hand. "Strong. But brief so far, and complicated. Very complicated."

Ange sighs. "Isn't everything?"

The dragons leave Leventhal Tower at sunrise, in search of food. Ange knows they won't go far, and uses an executive bathroom downstairs to shower, while secretaries rush to provide everyone with breakfast, ordered from an all-night delicatessen. Ange tries to check on Jamie, but that whole portion of the top floor is now blocked off by serious magicians with staves and defensive charms, and she doesn't feel like a big argument this early in the morning.

She has a sandwich and coffee at a workstation below the top floor with Michael Stanthorpe and several other top executives — Leventhal Holdings has dozens, though not all of them work in this tower, nor even in New York or the USA. They discuss profits, market movements and other technical stuff that goes completely over Ange's head, as she watches the morning news on low volume, and the sun peers through the neighbouring towers, splashing golden light across desks and computer terminals. Such a different life these people lead, all numbers and technicalities. She tries to imagine what it would be like, to wield a laptop instead of a sword. Meisha manages both, doing law and magic. So much of growing up and becoming an adult seems to be about learning to do lots of things at once, not just those things you'd prefer, or that you're naturally good at. Maybe Eli's right, and she should complete her education properly, and then think about a university. They're expensive in America, but she's pretty sure Eli will help her out.

And she smiles at her musings. As if any of them are going to live that long.

Mayor Riley's face appears on the TV. It brings ironic cheers from elsewhere around the office. One of the executives idly thumbs up the volume, but the Mayor is just talking about dull Mayor stuff — car registration, police and hospital funding, and some controversy over a city judge who said something sexist. He does it all very well, smiling and laughing with real charisma. The female reporter he's talking to seems to be having a great time.

"If only all these shroud-blind people knew," says Ange. The older men and women at the table glance at her. "How much magic he must have used to cheat and con his way into power."

Stanthorpe smiles. "Dear girl, Riley barely used any magic to get elected as Mayor. People voted for him because they wanted to."

Ange frowns. "Seriously?"

"Well, to be fair to the shroud-blind, they've no way of knowing that he'd harvest them all for parts if it suited him. But he's an excellent administrator, and quite a good Mayor... if you discount this whole... murdering and torturing people."

"And wanting to rule the world for evil," adds one of his friends.

"Yes," Stanthorpe agrees, sipping his coffee. "That too."

"They still should have realised," Ange insists, looking at the laughing, creepily-handsome face on the TV. "He's a slimeball."

"Perhaps, but no moreso than most politicians. And if there's one thing that Riley excels at nearly as much as magic, it's telling people what they want to hear. At that, he's a master, and there is no more important skill in politics."

"It's why Riley's so much better at politics than Eli would be," says Calvin, one of Stanthorpe's executive friends. "Eli would stink at politics, he's too honest. He'd run government like he runs Leventhal Holdings, he'd tell people exactly how much he had to raise their taxes and cut their pensions, and they'd hate him and call him a bad person. For being honest." He raises his eyebrows at Ange, like an adult will when inviting understanding from a teenager. Ange nods obligingly. "While the dishonest person, who lies and cheats and murders, is loved and elected by a large majority because he tells them the lies they all want him to say."

"They say that being honest is the greatest virtue you can have," Stanthorpe agrees. "But that's not quite right is it? *Listening* to honesty, when it's presented to you — that's the greatest virtue. But so few people do."

Ange has rarely in her life enjoyed lectures from adults. But these are good people, she thinks. And while she doesn't think she'll agree with them on everything, they're certainly worth listening to.

The TV news crosses to a reporter standing in front of the familiar building lobby. Calvin frowns and turns the volume up. "I'm standing in front of the Leventhal Tower, home to one of the world's largest financial services companies — Leventhal Holdings," says the reporter. "Now sources have told us that in just a few short minutes, special investigators from the NYPD will be arriving here to call on Eli Leventhal, one of the richest men in America. And hear this — our sources tells us that they may be about to arrest him on new charges of tax evasion."

Everyone stares at the screen, dumbfounded.

"Now viewers will recall that Leventhal Holdings has been the subject of City Hall's tax evasion case for the last year and a half... it's our understanding that these are *new* charges, based on new evidence that City Hall's hand picked investigating agents will be announcing to the media at a press conference scheduled for ten o'clock this morning."

Everyone at the table erupts to their feet, lead by Stanthorpe, and suddenly the office is in pandemonium. "I don't care how powerful the Mayor is!" Stanthorpe is shouting to no one in particular. "I'm going to kill him with my bare hands!"

Down in the Leventhal Tower lobby, the scene is crazy. Ange stands by a marble wall near the elevators, behind a line of Holdings employees, and watches as tower security deactivates the lobby security turnstiles so people can pass through. Eli stands with Shawna Dubois, and Meisha at his right, nearly lost amidst the crowd of his people.

On the far side of the huge, six-storey-tall glass walls that separate the vast lobby from the street, are crowds and crowds of media, with TV and photography cameras and big lights, all pressing close for a view. Uniformed police hold them back, and keep bystanders away, filling the road beyond with police cars and flashing lights.

It's all a show, Ange realises. Arrest warrants aren't supposed to be served like this, for people of any stature, let alone someone as important as Eli. The Mayor has timed this for maximum humiliation, before all the world's media, and now they're putting on this performance. Of course, there's no chance at all that the charges are real. No doubt the Mayor's people simply made them up. Probably they won't stand up in court, given the strength of Eli's legal team, and their outstanding ability to keep the courts from bending to Riley's will. Maybe Meisha could even prove that the evidence was fabricated, given long enough — and that would end with *Riley* in prison. But it won't go that far. This is just to keep Eli occupied, for the next couple of days. To stop him from launching any attack, or from being there to lead it. After that, if there is an after, the charges will simply go away, and being a Grand Magister, Riley can use the shroud to make everyone forget they were ever filed in the first place.

Ange looks at the men and women around her, standing on tip toes, trying to see. They're aghast, and worried, sighted and shroud-blind alike. Everyone is watching what comes next.

"He won't go now, will he?" someone is murmuring. "He can't go now. Not now."

Men and women in suits enter the lobby from outside. Some journalists come with them, hurrying with TV cameras. That's not right, Ange knows. It's against all police procedure to put on such a show for the media, incriminating a man who must be presumed innocent for now. So why are the police doing it like this, if it makes them look so blindly partisan? Like they're just Riley's lapdogs carrying out his personal vendetta? Surely it could backfire, and build sympathy for Eli, even among the shroud-blind?

"Eli Leventhal," says the head policeman, holding a piece of paper up for everyone to see. He stops before Eli, looming over the smaller, white haired man. Eli leans on his staff, his face expressionless. "I have here a warrant for your arrest on the charge of tax evasion. You have the right to remain silent. Anything you say can and will be used against you in a court of law. You have the right to an attorney. If you cannot afford an attorney, one will be provided to you by the state."

Smirks and smiles among the police at that. Ange is surprised at how badly she wants to hurt them. These are Riley's lackeys, not the regular city cops. If the regular cops made a habit of ignoring the law to do what Riley said, Leventhal Holdings would have collapsed years ago.

"Do you understand the rights that I have just read to you?"

Eli just looks at him. Of course he understands. And noble Eli, the great believer in law and justice under all circumstances, will have no choice but to go with him, whatever the cost.

Instead, Eli raises his staff. A deep thrumming fills the air, and Ange feels a magical chill of incredible power. The camera lights outside the windows dim, then go dead. Then the camera operators frown and look at their equipment, as those too go blank, and the red running lights flicker out. And finally, the air begins to chill, and a thick, white frost grows and crackles across the huge wall of lobby glass. It moves with steady purpose, covering the glass with crystals, blocking the view of those beyond like a coat of sparkling white paint.

Last of all, some of the people in the lobby suddenly look blank, staring ahead like zombies. The shroud-blind, Ange realises. By using magic on this scale, Eli gives the shroud no choice but to blank their minds completely. Soon they'll awake, and go about their day with no recollection of any of this. The journalists will resume their previous schedule, perhaps with newly invented memories to fill in this missing half-hour since the announcement of Eli's impending arrest.

But the sighted will remember. The suited cops all smile at Eli, quite broadly. The lead cop pockets his warrant, turns around and walks out. Eli also turns, grim-faced, and heads for the nearest elevator. Sighted employees watch him go with dumbfounded dismay.

It is done, Ange realised. The great man of fairness and principle has been forced to use magic to dodge the law, and save his skin, in front of all the magical world. Now everyone will see, and those who don't like him will conclude that he is a fraud. Lately, the number of magical people with reason to not like Eli Leventhal has grown very large indeed. The circle of Leventhal Holdings allies grows ever smaller.

CHAPTER SEVENTEEN

It's deathly quiet in Response Division offices all day. Ange wanders between desks and computer screens, looking at interactive maps of New York, and wonders where all the usual activity is. It's like the magical population of the city are avoiding them. Or, knowing something's about to happen, are holding their breath.

Upstairs, the big heads of Leventhal Holdings are planning. Ange sees them in Eli's office when she takes a break to go up to the rooftop to exercise and check on the dragons, men and women clustered about a central table, talking animatedly… but the blinds are partly drawn, making it easier to see out than to see in. On the rooftop, the dragons are absent, so she exercises and does sword drills alone, confident that the localised shroud will prevent neighbours from seeing. Gia and Bella's absence does not bother her, she can feel that they're close.

On her way down again, Bickel intercepts her, and beckons her into Eli's office. Her hopes rise, for maybe they've arrived at some brilliant plan that will save the day, or maybe there's something she can offer that will help. But in the office she finds only grim faces, and a series of images on a big, expensive display screen — key government buildings in the Financial District, Riley's strongholds. She tells them a bit about her and Bickel's adventures in the tunnels, and a bit more about Ulani powers, and where they allow her to sneak undetected by magic. And then she's dismissed.

"How's it going?" she asks Bickel outside the door. Bickel just shakes his head, grimly, and goes back inside. Ange's heart sinks. There's supposed to be some brilliant solution, surely? In the movies there's always a clear-if-difficult way to fix everything, something that a cast of heroic individuals can achieve. But Jamie is locked up in Meisha's heavily guarded office, and if the good guys do succeed in stopping Riley, that brain tumour will kill him eventually. How do you fix *that?* When doing the right thing will only hurt yourself and the people you care about the most?

In the late afternoon, as the tower begins to empty and the sun sinks low, downstairs security cameras show Mulberry Watson and some of his top executives entering the building. Ange heads upstairs, thinking this might concern her and Jamie, and waits by the VIP elevator for Mulberry's party to arrive. Some of Mulberry's senior magicians look at her with concern as they exit, but Mulberry heads straight for Eli's office. Eli greets him at the door, and some of his party remain outside, but Eli beckons Ange in. Ange goes, her nerves jangling at so many powerful magicians so close together.

"Eli," Mulberry says as soon as the door shuts behind them, "you have to call off this attack. People are saying you killed Alexis because she defied you. They're saying you sent your pet assassin to do it." He looks at Ange.

Eli sits tiredly against his desk. He looks worn, his white hair ruffled and tie askew, and older than Ange has ever seen him look. "Alexis was an old friend," he says. "I never turned on her, she turned on me. And my *assassin* was only defending herself, that trap was meant for her."

"I know Eli," says Mulberry, with that deep, serious voice. "But you don't have to convince *me.* You have to convince *them.*" He waves his hand out the windows, to the city at large. "I've been talking to them all day, trying to gather support. They saw you use magic to get out of legal trouble, they saw it on TV. You've never done that before, in anyone's memory."

"Oh I've done it before," Eli says wearily. "My memory is longer than most. But only when things are dire."

"Eli you can plan here all you like." Mulberry gestures to the maps and charts on the table, and the images of Riley's key buildings on the big screen. "But you won't have enough people following you to pull off any plan you decide. The numbers just aren't there."

Ange's jangling nerves get worse, and the tingles on her skin spread to become the involuntary drumming of one eardrum. Her left little finger begins to dance, all on its own. She frowns at it. It's never done that before.

Eli smiles tiredly. "So what would you suggest, my old friend? That we let Riley do his magic?"

"It's not a question of *letting* him, the people..."

"The people have no idea what they're asking!" Eli snaps. "The *magical people*, too, not the ordinary people, not the shroud-blind — they're the majority, but they don't get a vote, so let's not pretend this is a democracy! First Realm is a tunnel through time and space, Mulberry, it goes everywhere! And what Riley proposes to do is to reach into that tunnel the same way you'd reach into a sock, and pull it inside out. It changes *everything!* It could destroy everything! And even if by some chance it does not, it will bring about a new era of magic so dark and evil that all the old rules we've known and lived by for millennia will disappear... the *people*, they think they're going to preserve their power? No, the new power won't serve them, it'll serve the dark things, Mulberry, the old and evil things, the things that once were of this world as well, but now everyone has forgotten. Everyone except me."

He looks at Ange. Ange recalls the hooded thing in the Municipal Building, and shudders.

"These old things were here before?" Mulberry asks.

Eli runs a hand through his hair. "Yes," he says. "Yes, before even I was born. But I saw their aftermath, and I listened to the old magicians of that time. Ashkir, my friend, the Great Ashkir would have told them what that time was like. He'd have joined me against this folly."

Outside the office, in the hall beyond, Ange spots something odd — Meisha is talking to Croz, looking concerned, hands waving. Meisha rarely gets that animated. She's pointing to her phone. Croz pushes through the door, Meisha behind him.

"Eli," he says, "sorry to interrupt, but did you send Meisha a message telling her to go to Gershwin Associates on 7th Avenue to pick up some documents?"

Eli frowns. "No I didn't. But how could someone pretend to be me with *you* Meisha, of all people?"

Meisha steps from behind Croz and gazes at the room with sightless, yet all-seeing eyes. She looks… scared. "Eli? Eli, I'm being blocked. I can't get a sense for what anyone in this room is thinking…" And she points, straight at Mulberry. "It's *you!* You sent that message pretending to be Eli? But why would you…?" Everyone stares. Ange reaches for her sword.

"…want her to get out of this building?" Croz completes Meisha's question with a snarl. With a flash, his staff weapon appears in hand. "Unless you had something to hide?"

Then pandemonium, flashes of teleported weapons, lightning, fire and yells, glass breaking and furniture upended. Ange charges and is immediately immobilised by her collar, falling and convulsing as it defends the traitors in their midst. Past the collar, she feels the shock of a massive magic, and a blaze of blue light fills the room, then a series of teleportations. Then quiet, save for flames, and the hiss of overhead extinguishers.

Ange levers herself onto an elbow, and sees smoke, water spray and several motionless bodies. There is no sign of Mulberry and his people, they've teleported. The air shimmers blue, like an indoor swimming pool lit from below.

"Eli!" shouts one of the executives, and tries to help his boss up from where he crouches on one knee. A flash, as his hand grasps Eli's arm, and he's blown backwards into a wall.

"Don't touch him!" yells Dubois, as others help up the stunned man. "Don't touch him, he's been locked somehow!"

Ange stares as she gets to her feet. Eli is unmoving, face strained as though struggling against some enormous force. Crackling lines of light convulse across him, and in a growing sphere around him, like a bubble of energy.

"Where's that coming from?" Croz yells.

"Jamie!" gasps Meisha, and Ange is out the door in a flash, and running down the hallway to Meisha's office. A similar wall of blue light blocks her way, but she plunges in regardless. The pain is incredible, but it does not blast her away. She staggers to Meisha's door, her head pounding, every nerve on fire, and stares through the glass. Jamie sits calmly on his chair, in a glowing aura of blue light. Clearly this is what's immobilising Eli.

"Jamie!" she yells through gritted teeth. "Jamie what are you doing?"

"Angelina!" yells Dubois from behind. "Leave him, you can't reach him!" Ange tries the door, but the pain intensifies, and her vision begins to darken. If she passes out here, she'll die, as none of the others can venture even this far into the energy bubble to save her. She staggers back, and is grabbed by Croz as soon as she's out, the pain immediately fading.

"Shawna!" says Meisha. "The tower shields are down! That's what Mulberry did, he disabled the defensive charms!"

"Well we need to get them back up!" says Croz.

"Only Eli can do that," Dubois retorts. "We have to find some way to free him!"

"You can't!" Ange gasps in Croz's arms. "That power's coming from elsewhere, Jamie's just a conduit. The power's too great, it has to be coming from Riley himself."

"Oh no," says Meisha. "Jamie went to see Riley! He, Riley and Eli all draw from First Realm, Riley must have done something to turn him into a conduit to immobilise Eli! Which means…"

"We're under attack!" Bickel snarls, and takes off running to the elevators. "Full defensive deployment, now!"

Croz takes off after him, and others. Ange holds herself against a wall for a moment, steadying herself as Dubois talks fast into her phone. "This is Shawna Dubois to all Leventhal Holdings personnel. Leventhal Tower is under attack, I repeat, Leventhal Tower is under attack. Emergency mobilisation, get here any way you can."

"Shouldn't we tell them that Eli's down?" Ange asks as her head begins to clear.

"Absolutely not," says Dubois. "If they know that, they'll give up hope and then we're finished." There's fear in her eyes as she says it.

Ange heads for the elevators, and sees the doors ahead close on Croz, Bickel and some others, all heading down. Before she can follow, something hits the outer windows with a thud, then several more thuds. Ange stops, and peers into an adjoining office, which in turn opens onto a view of the city… and sees something black and winged hurtling straight at the glass.

"They're coming in the windows!" she yells, just before the body hits the glass and smashes through. Ange kicks open the office door, and finds a familiar winged shape unfurling from the office floor amidst broken glass and furniture. It hisses at her, and Ange cuts its head off. Against Ulani you have to do more productive things with your time than hiss, pal.

More crashes around the offices, winged shapes leaping through shattered glass, swords and other weapons flashing. Magicians blast them back and flames, electricity and projectiles rip across offices, smashing bodies into partitions, igniting others. Ange dashes to assist, but Dubois is there, decapitating one charging winged shape with a bolt of lightning, then crumpling another's chest with a powerful motion of her fist.

"We have to hold them here!" she yells at Ange. "If they reach Eli while he's defenseless, we lose everything!"

"They won't just be coming in on this floor!" Ange replies. "They can smash windows on any floor below us, then climb up! Or down onto the defenders on the ground floor!" Defending a thousand foot tower without heavy defensive charms to block flying assaults is nearly impossible, she was realising. Leventhal Tower has 62 floors, any one of which a flying attacker can break into. Organised defense is nearly impossible when any moment you can be surprised by an attack from the side or behind.

"The stairwells have defenses," says Dubois striding down the hall toward where Holdings employees are taking defensive positions around Eli's office. "Those will still be working." She smashes a charging attacker into the wall alongside, where Ange cuts him down.

In Eli's office, several winged attackers have smashed through the windows. Magicians fight them, and one attacker grabs at Eli, and is promptly incinerated in a flash of blue light. The others are killed quickly, and Ange checks the hall down to Meisha's office, and finds it's mysteriously free of fighting. Or not so mysteriously. Oh Jamie, what have you done? She can't believe he'd have done this on purpose. Mulberry may have turned traitor, like Alexis Rhodes, like so many others... but surely Jamie has not sold his soul to Riley on purpose, knowing all the people who will die as a result?

"Well that's something," she offers to Dubois through the smashed glass that used to partition Eli's office from the hall, as Dubois inspects the pile of ash that used to be a winged attacker. "They can't touch Eli either." Eli remains on one knee within that glowing sphere of light, as though frozen in ice.

More crashes and yells across the floor as new attackers dive in… and then a great roar of flame sears the air outside the tower windows, and winged shapes are tumbling burning from the sky. Gia flashes past the windows, and Ange yells in delight, running to see. He flaps hard past the Mid-Town towers, crushing another attacker with his jaws, like a bat hunting moths. Five of them pursue him, blades and spears raised, then vanish in flame as Bella torches them, swinging in behind to guard her partner's tail. They both turn back hard, wings stretched against the city skyline, Bella going wide as Gia comes back first… Ange loses sight of them on the tower's far side, then another roar of flame, and defenders on that far side are yelling in triumph as one, then the other dragon go whistling past.

"Now we've got a chance!" Ange tells Dubois.

"Get downstairs!" says Dubois. "We can hold things here! If there's a ground assault you'll be needed in the lobby!" Ange nods, and runs for the elevators.

It's the most surreal thing to listen to elevator music, in total calm isolation, while all about people are fighting and dying out of sight. It lasts until the elevator car reaches the lobby, and opens onto utter chaos, screams and yells and the roar of battle, as hoards of horrid creatures smash their way through the lobby walls and are electrocuted, incinerated or blasted apart by a line of defenders ringing the building's central core. The attackers are largely dakran, she sees, withered walking corpses with bolted-on armour and grinning teeth, but there are others there as well, evil-looking humanoids she can barely recognise.

The dakran are falling in droves, mowed down by concentrated magical fire so intense it makes New Year's Eve fireworks look dull, but the other humanoids are smashing new holes in the glass and sending their own magical fire into those gaps. Holdings employees duck or deflect, and dakran take advantage of the distraction to pour through unopposed.

Ange sprints at a breakthrough, and ducks low to cut through some legs, then up to take a head, then dodges and weaves through several more on instinct as friendly fire takes out others around her. Machine gun fire tears into more ahead, bodies jerking and collapsing as splinters of bone fly off, then a grenade blasts others to bits. Amidst it Ange sees a big human shape with a wand and a tail, crouched behind a shield spell against the new fire. Before it can rise and recover, she's on it, and splits it down the middle.

And Ange realises she's now treading on shattered lobby glass at the tower's outer wall, some distance from the inner defenses, with enemy pouring in around her. She retreats slowly, walking backward, taking arm, head then leg of those attacking as gunshots fell others, and lightning leaves others in jerking, smouldering heaps. Then a huge roar of flame outside, and Ange ducks instinctively as dragonfire incinerates much of anything standing on 7th Avenue.

It gets a big cheer from the defenders, as a big dragon shadow flashes overhead. "Don't relax!" Bickel yells at them, reloading his assault rifle behind the main defensive line, as others from Response Division do the same. "They're just probing us, this is just the beginning!" He glances at Ange as she steps back over shattered bodies, and gives her a wink, and a nod of approval.

"How the hell did Riley get his army up to Mid-Town?" Ange asks

"I don't know," says Bickel, calm and professional as he surveys the crazy scene. "We can't see much of anything outside, we've got people phoning in saying Manhattan's gone crazy, we've got civilians hiding in buildings, police shutting roads down, subways evacuated. My own bet is Riley's using the subways, but I don't know how he stopped the trains without us knowing it."

"It's pointless worrying about if we can't do anything to stop it," says Ange. Up the line of crouched men and women in suits, she's struck by the odd sight of Michael Stanthorpe with his red bow tie, marching up the line like a Sergeant Major in the age of Napoleon, shouting at his troops to hold their nerve and hold the line. "With Gia and Bella here, we've got a chance of holding them. We just have to hope Eli can break out."

Bickel shushes her, motioning that she should keep her voice down, but it's too late. "Where's Eli?" asks a nearby woman, her white blouse torn and dirty, her cheek bloody. She's scared and anxious, as are her companions. "Eli's going to save us, right?"

"Eli's fighting them on the top floor!" Bickel says loudly to the lobby.

"The tower's defenses were brought down, Eli's reestablishing them! Once they're back up we'll be protected!"

Up and down the line, men and women look at each other with renewed hope. Ange just looks at Bickel, not knowing what to think. Ask all these people to die fighting for a lie? Bickel gives her the hard, uncompromising look of a soldier at war. Ange rolls her eyes a little. She knows the drill, the 'by any means necessary' attitude. She just doesn't know if she believes it any more.

The sound of more fighting echoes down the big central aisle between banks of elevators — there's fighting on the lobby's other side, the Broadway entrance. "I'll go," she tells Bickel. "Keep those stairwell doors open, if we have to retreat the magicians can all teleport upstairs, but us receptors will have to run."

She takes off running down the big marble hall, and sees a similar situation on the building's far side — an insane wall of magical fire, only now there are big critters bursting through the glass, like great reptiles with big teeth, lightning and fire scarring their leathery hide. They tear into the defenders, bodies flying, and Ange sees others teleport in bursts of black smoke to escape. More gunfire brings down one creature, as Ange pauses at the hallway end — Hernandez nearby, and several others. But now the dakran are flooding across the lobby floor and into the space created by the charging lizards, and more defenders teleport before they're overrun.

Ange runs in and takes several down fast — dakran don't dodge or defend much, and have no regard for their lives, if you can call them living. But there's too many, and suddenly she's ducking and weaving backward to avoid being outflanked, and spinning now to defend another hacking at her head... but the dakran is sent spinning before the blow falls, and suddenly Croz is there with his bladed staff, laying about him and gaining her some space. They kill many, but others arrive fast to replace them, and now Response Division soldiers are backpeddling into the elevator hallway with yells of 'fall back!'

"Stew!" Croz yells up the hall above the noise, as Ange kills another two dakran coming at them. "We're overrun, fall back!"

They sprint for the stairwell door beside the elevators, as lines of magicians teleport and the defenses disappear. Ange comes second-last, dashing past Bickel who blasts oncoming dakran with his rifle, then follows. As they leap up the stairs three at a time, Ange feels the building sizzle of defensive charms, and pauses atop the first flight of stairs to see pursuing dakran blasted by massive electrical charges that turn the confined space into a death trap. Then a huge magical force hits the stairwell from outside, and the defensive charms begin to turn on each other, Bickel yanking Ange out of the stairwell as bolts shoot everywhere and bring part of the ceiling down.

"We've disabled the elevators," he tells her. "They can only take the building by climbing the stairs, so we defend them flight by flight. They'll knock out the stair defenses with magic, but that'll take time."

Further along the hall, someone exclaims, and Ange and Bickel look. On the windows on the outside of the building, dakran are climbing, gripping little grooves on the tower sides with bony fingers. "Only way up the building, si?" Ange tells Bickel accusingly.

"Bugger," says Bickel, staring in frustration. "Bloody architects."

Something flashes beside them and they spin, but it's Meisha teleporting in. "Ange I'm sorry," she says, "you're needed upstairs." She holds open the lead case in her hand, and Ange feels that awful, familiar numbness spreading once more.

She nods, and puts her arms around Meisha. "Do it," she says. A lurch and tumble of disorientation…

…and now she's on the top floor again, outside Eli's office. The blue sphere of energy has expanded, and is now protruding out into the hallway. Shawna Dubois stands before it, in Eli's line of sight, and pleads with him to fight it. Further away, magicians blast at more winged attackers, flapping through the shattered windows. It's looking desperate once more, and Ange runs to a window to look out.

"Where's Gia?" she shouts, staring out at the setting sun across the jumble of towers and flying shapes. "Why isn't Gia…" And then she sees him, a dragon's wings beating hard up Broadway… but this dragon is bright red and huge, this isn't Gia. The dragon flaps again, curving up and around to come back at the tower. Now it's familiar, as Ange recognises one of the two dragons that ambushed them on the way back from Philadelphia. And on its back rides a man, coat blowing in the wind. To look on this man gives Ange a horrid magical shudder worse than any mere human has ever given her before. "Oh buon dio, it's Riley! Riley's got a dragon!"

Worse, he's seen her, and is coming straight for her. "There!" shouts Meisha, and Ange looks high to one side. It's Gia, diving on the Mayor, wings folded back for maximum speed, teeth and claws bared with lethal intent. Riley sees him coming, and raises his staff.

"Oh no no NO!" Ange shouts, feeling that building rush of incredible force. "GIA NO!" A brilliant flash, and then Gia is falling, limp and tumbling, like a broken thing as he spins toward the ground. Ange screams. The dragon hits a tower with a lifeless thud, bounces, and falls from view.

Two dark attackers rush them from the side, and Meisha sends them spinning with a vicious blast. Ange senses movement behind and turns... only to find Jamie, wild-eyed, charging at her from behind and about to tackle them both over the edge. She spins through to kill him, but somehow her sword stops. It's not his magic that stops it. It's only her, looking in his eyes in that last split second, and realising that she just... can't.

He hits her, and then they're falling...

...and something lurches again, with the abrupt sensation of being elsewhere. They've teleported again, but still they're falling. Ange blinks against the howling gale, and instead of a New York street rushing up to kill her, she sees... a coastline. Far, far below, and shadowed with the sun setting across inland clouds, turning all red and orange. She's never jumped out of an aeroplane before, but she's flown on dragonback enough to guess that she's at about six thousand feet above the ground. There's no towers below, nor anything that looks like Manhattan Island, or anything New York. But the ocean ends quickly in another landmass, and she recognises Long Island, and knows that the water below must be Long Island Sound. Jamie's teleported them up the coast of Connecticut, far away from New York. Which is usually incredibly dangerous... only he's materialised them at six thousand feet to make sure they stay clear of the lethal ground.

She finds him falling nearby, arms windmilling in a way that tells her he hasn't jumped out of an aeroplane before either. He's reaching for her, desperately. The ground is getting closer fast, individual houses standing out, backyards, swimming pools. There's a beach down there, and a road, with cars moving on it. Jamie thinks he can teleport them down there from here, without the fatal drop... and how he's gotten them this far without a vestigium, she has no idea. But she has to take his hand, or in something less than twenty seconds, she'll make an Angelina-shaped hole in someone's roof. She has to take his hand, but all she can think of is Gia's lifeless body hitting that tower, and bouncing. Jamie did that. Or Riley did it, but Jamie helped. And there's not a million dead sisters that could make her forgive him.

But she can't avenge Gia if she's dead.

She reaches with her non-sword hand, and grasps Jamie's. Another tumbling dislocation, and suddenly they're falling again, from stationary three yards into shallow water with a splash. Ange surfaces with a gasp, glad she didn't cut herself on her sword. She splashes ashore, heart hammering and head spinning. Jamie does likewise, bedraggled and stunned.

"Wow," he says. "That's called hop-jumping, the old timers used to do it to teleport long distances. Never done it before." Ange stares at him. "Ange?"

"You killed Gia," she tells him.

His eyes widen in horror. "Ange, I... Gia's dead?"

Ange levels her sword at his neck, the point nearly touching. The collar Eli put on him is missing — removed by Riley's arrival, Ange thinks. Which must have freed Jamie, and allowed Riley to continue immobilising Eli by some other means. Jamie swallows, hands raised. Ange's eyes are wet with tears and salt water both. "You killed my last best friend."

"No. Ange I swear, I didn't mean this to happen!"

"You tried to kill Eli!" she yells at him. "You brought Leventhal Holdings down!"

"I went to Riley, yes! He... he did some kind of magic on me, I thought he was just scanning me! To make sure I wasn't rigged with some kind of trap! But I didn't... I didn't know he could do that to me, Ange, I... I was furious at Eli, and we fought, and... and I can hardly remember anything after that..."

He gazes at her desperately. Ange's hands tremble, and her sword point wavers at his throat.

"Ange I've no one left," he says. "You neither. Let's just go away together, huh? You and me, let's find some place and make a new life." She gives him nothing. "I'm not allied with Riley, all right?"

"You said you wanted to end Leventhal Holdings. You *told* me. And now you have."

"Ange." The dark temper is back in his eyes. The fury. "He killed my sister."

"Holdings employs tens of thousands of people," Ange says thickly. "And you ended them all, and let the most evil man in history win, and killed my last best friend in the world and a whole lot of new friends, because you were *angry*?"

"Like you were going to let Riley win when *you* killed Eli when you first got here?" Jamie yells back. "All because *you* were angry?" Ange's sword point falls. They stand together, soaking wet on the beach in the setting sun, and stare at each other. "Ange." He reaches a hand to her. "I lost Tori, but I found you. If Riley's big magic doesn't work, we might only have a few hours left anyway before he ends everything. Let's spend them together."

"Eli's not dead yet," says Ange. "Teleport me back there."

"No," Jamie says with certainty. "I won't."

"Is this really about Tori?" Ange snarls. "Or is it about the tumour in your head?"

Jamie's hand drops, and his eyes fill with pain. "You want me dead that badly?"

"If you won't take me back," says Ange, "then I'm wasting my time here."

She sheathes her sword and starts walking, waterlogged boots squishing on the sand. She does not look back to see Jamie, standing forlorn and lonely on the water's edge, watching her go. Then he vanishes, in a flash of black smoke.

CHAPTER EIGHTEEN

Ange walks in twilight through beachside suburbs. Her new phone is dead and waterlogged so she can't check maps to know where she is. She's never been this way before save that one time on her bike with Jamie, riding to Eli's mansion in the Connecticut countryside. That was along the Connecticut Turnpike, a huge freeway that runs all the way along this coast... and there's a train line that runs with it. So she walks inland, away from the water, in search of a car she can steal, or a train back to New York.

Out here, life continues. She passes corner stores, people buying things, getting a pizza, filling their cars with gas. They walk their dogs, or haul bags of groceries from their cars in preparation for a meal and an evening in front of the TV before bed. It's surreal to walk among them, and them with no clue that a power-crazed man a little to the south could be about to end the world in his quest to maintain that power. She had doubts before whether she should try to stop him, but that was because of the threat to Gia, and to Jamie. Now Gia's dead, and Jamie...

She tries to stop herself from crying as she walks, and is partly successful. Riley or no Riley, end of the world or not, she has to return to those few friends she has left. And if she can find a way to stop Riley in the process, then she no longer doubts that it's the right thing to do. At this point, she figures, what else is there to lose?

She boards a train at an elevated station near the freeway, and sits in sodden clothes with her sword on her lap. In this age of modern technology, it's amazing that she has no way of knowing what's going on in Manhattan, with its streets overrun by hoards of magical creatures, and dragons fighting aerial battles between its towers. But the shroud hides everything, and even those in the middle of it will soon emerge from their hiding places convinced that they've just survived an earthquake or a terrorist attack. And tomorrow they'll awake in their beds with likely no memory at all.

Ange stares out the window of the speeding train, at the flashing lights of passing buildings, and the great trails of traffic on the Turnpike, and knows she's most likely heading back to her death. There's no way that Leventhal Holdings still exists as a functioning thing — with Eli neutralised and Riley himself arriving, the tower had only minutes left to stand. Realising that, those magicians who had not yet teleported elsewhere would have quickly done so, and she can hardly blame them. But that might not include the receptors like Croz and Bickel, if they could not find a friendly lift.

Without Leventhal Holdings, Riley can do what he likes on the island of Manhattan. Monitoring the bridges and tunnels will be easy enough, and he'll know the instant an Ulani enters his territory. If she was smart, she'd get to a river's edge and try to get a boat across… but there's no guarantee that will work either, and boats on the water are slow and vulnerable. At this point she'd rather a straight fight, and blast her way in. Bella might try to find her if she's still alive, but that won't help her either — Ange doesn't want to ride her back into the city to meet near certain death at the hands of Riley and his big red dragon. With any luck Bella has flown far away, and Ange won't have to make a choice to risk the life of Gia's last love as well.

Dimly it occurs to her that she ought to be wondering how Jamie teleported her without a vestigium. His magic shouldn't work on her… only there was the time after that thing grabbed her wrist in the Municipal Building, and it was Jamie who healed her, not Eli, which shouldn't have been possible either. So Jamie's very powerful. Or Jamie draws from First Realm, like Eli, and could one day become a Grand Magister. He must have been certain of it, too, before tackling them both off the edge like that. Whatever. She doesn't want to think about it now, and it doesn't seem very important anyway.

Oddly for this time of evening, there's very few people on the train… though of course, most of the evening traffic will be heading in the other direction, she thinks. But her carriage is nearly empty when the train pulls into the Bronx station, and there's almost no one on the platform. Could the shroud be keeping people away from the city? Finding them other reasons to be elsewhere, without their awareness? Or could Riley?

Footsteps, then, as people enter. Six in all, three through the carriage doors ahead, and three behind. All wear dark clothes, and all carry swords. Ange gets to her feet, not especially surprised. She's too numb to feel particularly scared. The carriage narrows their options, forcing them to come at her one at a time. Also, they keep their hoods up so she won't see their faces, but that restricts vision and head mobility, which is never good for fighting. And she knows these people. If they think they can take her, they're about to learn differently.

"Only six," she says, drawing her sword as the train begins moving once more. "Tell Starace to stop insulting me." The Ulani say nothing. Starace must have truly joined with Riley, Ange thinks. He must be helping Riley's great magic to succeed. Otherwise why bother still trying to kill her? Knowing her so well, Starace will know that while there's breath in her body, she'll still try to stop them.

Swords come out in reply, and fighting stances are taken as the carriage rocks and sways. Ange skips back from the first two swings, then ducks low as the man behind cuts at her. The central pole blocks the sword as she stabs back and impales him. She leaps at the next man before he's ready, and kicks him flying into the windows, then uses the hand poles again to duck past the stabbing sword from behind, grab that man's arm, break it, kick him in the groin, then smash his face with her sword hilt.

Three down. She stares at the others with contempt, one way then the other, as bodies writhe and groan about her. The remaining three Ulani look wary, two on one side of the carriage, one on the other. One of the two pulls a pistol, and points it at her.

"Really?" Ange deadpans. "The proud Ulani warriors, using guns? You use that and Starace's finished, he won't be able to show his face in Italy."

"They'll have to find your body first," the man retorts, as Ange's hand goes to her throwing knife. Before she can throw, the gunman falls to a blow on the head from behind. The Ulani behind Ange also goes for a gun, but the man who knocked out the first gunman now throws a knife whistling past Ange's cheek, and that man falls with a cry.

Ange stares at the last, hooded man, brow furrowed as she tries to see. The man pulls back his hood, and lowers the handkerchief mask. A strong, handsome face, and longish, unruly hair. "Pietro?"

Pietro is the *other* great choice for Master of House Ulani, someday. With her gone, he is Starace's unofficial heir, and the obvious choice... if you happen to be a traditional Ulani man who refuses to have a woman as heir or Master. She'd thought Pietro was her enemy. Now this new astonishment.

Pietro smiles. "You still have friends in House Ulani, Angelina. Some of us remember what's right." The train slows as it pulls into a new station. "Your dragons are dead, but some of your friends still live. I've sent word ahead to the station. You'll reach Manhattan alive. Then, look to the skies." The train stops, and the doors open. "I cannot help you more, if I betray Starace further he'll root us out, and then House Ulani will be truly lost. Good luck."

He steps out into the night. Again, no one climbs aboard. As though somehow, the population know where this train is heading, and want no part of it.

Ange changes carriages, and leaves the fallen Ulani on the floor — dead or alive, it makes no difference to her at this point. The train enters the tunnel to take her below Manhattan, shuddering and squealing through the darkness like some living thing protesting its fate. Ange hangs on a ceiling strap, sword unsheathed, and waits. 'He'll root us out', Pietro said. 'Us'. More than just him, at least. She's not entirely pleased to hear it. Just when she'd thought she could erase that history from her life, Pietro reminds her that she still has something to live for. That some people will miss her if she dies, even though they are far away in Italy. Easier if she could just hate them all, she thinks. Hating is so much easier than loving. Loving hurts so much more.

The train squeals and grinds into Pennsylvania Station. Ange steps out, onto a narrow underground platform. Along the train's entire length, only a handful of people depart, when there should be hundreds. These all scurry for the escalators, with fearful glances. Neighbouring platforms are similarly empty, though noisy, as diesel trains roar beneath the low, black ceiling, engines idling at station, filling the air with diesel fumes. Empty trains block her view two platforms ahead. With a clank of carriages, the train moves. As it departs, it reveals the further platform. Ten people stand on it, in dark, grungy-looking coats, and dishevelled hair. A snarl of sharp teeth, and staring eyes. Vampires, her oldest enemies.

Ange walks to the nearest escalator, unhurried and calm. Two platforms away, the vampires do likewise, watching her. They've bladed weapons in their hands, makeshift and nasty, as vampires prefer. Ange has never understood the shroud-blind romance for these... things. Vampires are romantic the same way cocaine is romantic — people will glamorise it, but the reality is putrid and ugly. She's never met one that doesn't smell, and a diet of blood, often stale, leaves the most awful bad breath. Still some people become vampires on purpose, seeking powers and longer life, most of them sighted folk who ought to know better. In London Ange knew both vampires and cocaine addicts, but she only felt sorry for the latter.

She rides the escalator up amidst the rusty steel beams of Penn Station's ceiling. White light blooms ahead, and then she's rising into the station building. All the power is on, and all the store fronts open, but it sounds not of busy station bustle, but of echoing silence. Despite that, it's not empty. As she walks from the escalator, she sees that all the central floor around her, beneath the great display boards showing the arrival and departure of trains, is filled with dark, evil shapes, with red eyes and fanged faces turned in her direction. Waiting for her.

She stops before them, and surveys. At least sixty, she sees. Vampires, the dark winged attackers she still has no name for, a few dakran. Several other types of humanoid, some she has names for, some she doesn't. A few have staves, suggesting magical ability. The rest have close combat weapons, suggesting a preference for bashing and cutting. Well, Ange thinks. She's tired of running scared, and tired of living with the loss of dead friends. If she must join them, what better way than this?

She takes a fighting pose, and gives them a look of her most Italian contempt. "So," she says, with an inviting wave of one hand. "Who's first?"

Pop! Time with Stew Bickel has taught her to recognise the sound of a grenade launcher, and she hits the floor as all around her sounds pop-pop-pop-B-B-B-BOOM! And then a thundering concussion of explosions and hammering gunfire, battering her eardrums like a thousand jackhammers in a closed room. Bodies fall, fly apart, dive and run, as bullet fragments shoot about and tiles explode about the walls.

Then the gunfire stops, with remarkable discipline, and reveals carnage, bodies strewn about, many missing limbs. Many of those are struggling to rise, being hard to kill in the way of magical creatures, but explosive injury is different from mere bullets, and even vampires die when large enough pieces are blown off. A few of the winged things are rising from within the protection of shield spells, but now comes a roar of flame, and for the first time Ange sees some of the shooters emerging from the station's baggage claim window — two men lugging a flame thrower, and the winged things thrash and shriek, and try to fly with their wings on fire. Not so fire resistant as bullet resistant, Ange notes, watching as the distracted creatures are cut down by more gunfire. Then silence, but for the crackle of flame, and the slither of a few surviving bodies.

"Nice!" announces a voice, and a man emerges from behind a shop counter in casual T-shirt, jeans and assault rifle. "Real nice! Hey you, you're Ulani?"

"Si!" Ange replies, looking about as more shooters emerge from cover. "Yes, I am."

"Your buddy told us you'd be coming, said these freaks would try and stop you. Good thing they're so dumb, huh?"

"They don't see so well in the light," says a smallish woman, striding up to her with a rifle in hand. She wears army fatigues, and extends her hand for Ange to shake. "I'm Carla, that's Pat, and these are... well, everyone."

The shooters all look like regular men and women. Pat's a cop, NYPD currently out of uniform but with a police badge on his shirt, as are a number of others. One man wears the coat of a hotel doorman, another has a chef's jacket. One girl looks like a waitress, there's a skinny bespectacled guy in hospital scrubs, a number of construction workers and burly firefighters... about fifteen people in all, and armed to the teeth with modern and ancient weapons.

"We're New York," says Pat with determination. He's a big guy and no longer young, and looks like these days he might struggle chasing pickpockets down the streets. But he handles his rifle like he's used it before. "All sighted, lots of reservists and ex-military, a few just like guns. You worked for Leventhal?" Ange nods. "Ah, you're that one. We heard of you. Riley must be pissin' his pants about you, if he sent all these freaks to stop you."

"What happened to Leventhal Tower?" Ange asks, as others put bullets into the last slithering things on the floor. The slithering stops.

"Fallen," says Carla. "A lot of Holdings employees got out, they said Leventhal must have been taken out early, and when Riley arrived on his dragon they just got overrun. No idea how the tower defenses were disabled, Leventhal set those up himself, they were supposed to be impregnable." Impregnable to all but Eli's most powerful friends. Ange thinks darkly of Mulberry's betrayal, and wonders what it says about life that of all Eli's supposed flaws, the one that brought him down was that he trusted his friends too much.

"Damn cowards," Pat mutters. "Can't rely on wizards in a fight, something to be said for not being able to teleport when your back's against the wall." He hefts his rifle meaningfully.

"They'd all be dead if they stayed," Ange tells him. "It was hopeless, they'd lost before the fight started."

"You were there?"

Ange nods. "I was teleported against my will, about sixty miles north of here."

"And you came back?" Pat's impressed. "That's what we need girl, you can ride with us anytime."

"There were dragons defending the tower," Ange presses. "Any news on them?" Hoping against hope, certainly for Bella, and even for Gia, if maybe he was only stunned... but Carla's head shake confirms what she already knows.

"They're both dead on 8th Avenue," she says, "the Mayor's people are clearing them away."

"Both?"

"One atop the other," says Carla. "The first one died, and the second one wouldn't leave the body. Riley killed him there."

"Her," Ange whispers. "Killed her there. Their names were Gia and Bella. They were lovers, and they died for all of us." She takes a deep breath, and lets the anger fill her. In her life, she's found it more productive to be angry than sad. "So where's Riley now?"

"He's up top," says Pat, jerking his head at the ceiling.

Ange frowns. 'Look to the skies', Pietro had said. "Up in Leventhal Tower?"

"No," Pat says grimly. "Wrong tower."

It's surreal to see the streets around lower Mid-Town Fifth Avenue, at barely nine in the evening, with almost no people or traffic. Instead there are trucks, long lines of them, engines roaring. They form a barricade around the base of the block between 33rd and 34th streets, further reinforced by guards with staves and wands, and people carrying heavy equipment from the rear, and into the nearby open doors. Above them towers the Empire State Building, over 90 years old and still nearly the biggest, and certainly one of the most impressive to look at, as much an icon of the city as the Statue of Liberty or Times Square.

"They've been going for hours," Pat murmurs as they crouch by a window several floors up across the street. The lights are out in the office, so that no one will see them looking, and Ange is confident that her own immunity will stop anyone close to her from being detected by magic. "It's slowed down a lot now, I think most of the really big stuff is already up there."

"Earlier on," adds Carla, peering through military-issue binoculars, "they brought these big, covered pallets of stuff in on flatbed trucks. They put these small, steel things on them and then they just vanished. Biggest stuff I ever saw teleported, pretty amazing."

"The steel things are platinum," says Ange. "It's the densest metal you can get in large quantities, gives magicians a good marker that helps with teleporting. But to teleport everything at once off a flatbed, that would have to be Riley himself." She's not sure even Eli could do that. Eli has never said out loud that Riley is more powerful than him, but he's often given that impression. Turning Jamie into a conduit and amplifier of his power without Jamie or Eli knowing it, defeating Eli without even having to fight him directly, killing dragons with a single strike, and now this.

"Have to be pretty crazy to go in there," Carla adds, reading her thoughts.

Ange shrugs. "Born crazy," she mutters.

Someone raps on the door behind, and they turn. "Got someone here says she's your friend," says one of Pat and Carla's gang, looking at Ange. Meisha appears, hair amess, blouse and suit blackened and torn. Ange swears with relief and goes to her, keeping low beneath the window to hug her.

"Ange!" Meisha gasps. "I was so worried, I didn't know where Jamie took you!"

"Long story," says Ange. "It took me a while to get back, I came as fast as I could."

"And Jamie? Is he...?"

"He was fine last I saw him." Meisha seems to sense that she doesn't want to talk about it. "Where's everyone else?"

Meisha takes a deep breath. "Michael's dead." Ange recalls Michael Stanthorpe, striding up and down the defensive line of magicians, urging them to stand firm. She swallows hard. "Shawna's dead too, just after you left... I mean, after Jamie took you. She tried to stop Riley getting onto the tower, and he just... well."

"I know. Like he killed Gia and Bella."

Meisha takes her hand. "Stew's hurt, one of the others teleported him out, it looked pretty bad. Hernandez is dead. A lot of Response Division are dead, they just didn't quit, even when we magicians were running away." She looks ashamed. "I... I didn't stay when Riley came. It just seemed like such a pointless way to die."

"You did the right thing Meisha," says Ange. "Riley kills powerful magicians like swatting flies, with your powers you're so much more use alive, bravery has nothing to do with it."

Meisha nods, but she's unconvinced. "Ange, he's got Eli!" She points to the top of the huge skyscraper above. "Up there! And he's got Croz too, one of the others who... who left after I did said Croz just attacked Riley when he got off his dragon. Just charged him. And Riley knocked him unconscious with a wave of his hand, but he didn't kill him, I can still sense him up there, with Eli." Tears roll down her cheeks beneath the dark glasses. "I ran away. I didn't even see, he's probably my best friend and I ran away and left him there! I mean, I can't even remember teleporting, just suddenly I was gone, and I wanted to go back! I mean, I tried to, but I… Ange I was just so scared!"

Ange holds her as she cries. "I know. We were all scared. And if you'd stayed any longer than you did, Riley would have killed you, you're much more a threat to his plans than Croz."

"You wouldn't have run away. You would have fought like Croz did. Why am I such a coward?"

"You're not a coward Meisha," says Ange. "You're a nice, sensitive girl who everyone likes. I'm an angry, sullen, unpleasant girl who no one likes. You're more fragile than me because I'm a bitch. But that's not a good thing."

Meisha pulls back to gaze in the general vicinity of her face. "Oh Ange, you don't get it do you? You're my hero." Ange blinks at her in astonishment. "I'd give anything to be strong like you. And if you're going up there, I'm coming with you. You are going up there, aren't you?"

Ange smirks. "Of course I'm going up there. I can't let my fanclub down…"

She's interrupted by a huge vibration. It feels like she's standing too close to some big speakers at a concert, making her skin buzz and her teeth rattle. For a moment, everything in the room seems to slow, as though time itself is changing speed. Furniture rattles, the windows shake and the floor feels like an earthquake… only the shocks are too steady and even for a quake. More like some huge engine has just been fired up nearby, and is steadily thrumming away, making the whole city rattle.

Then the sound fades, and time resumes its usual march. Ange ducks to the window once more, and stares up at the Empire State Building. She can actually see the shockwave rolling away, rippling through the clouds like some enormous explosion in slow motion. That wasn't an illusion, that feeling of everything slowing. Space itself was bending, and space and time being physically the same thing, time was bending too.

"It's started," says Ange. "Whatever he had in the Municipal Building, it's now up there, and he's not wasting any time."

"What's up there?" asks Carla, staring fearfully upward.

"Doom," says Meisha. She gives her staff a twirl, grim and no longer fearful. "I guess if we're all going to die anyway, there's no reason to be scared of attacking. Let's go." With a huge flash of energy someone else teleports into the room.

"Oh, I could think of several reasons to be scared," says Mayor Riley, and blasts Carla flying out the window onto the street below. Pat's rifle crumples in smoke and melting metal before he can use it, then he screams as a burst of energy turns every drop of water in his body to steam. Ash and powder falls to the floor, then Meisha is hurled into a wall and sprawls. Ange charges, but is abruptly immobilised by her collar and falls convulsing to the floor.

"You know," says Riley, controlling the collar with barely a raised finger, "it's quite helpful of Eli to put that collar on you. It's really not as tamper proof as he suspected." One of the group in the corridor outside aims a rifle at Riley from the doorway. A wave of Riley's hand caves in the entire length of corridor wall, taking people with it. "You want to see what's going on upstairs? Let me show you what's going on upstairs."

CHAPTER NINETEEN

A nge wakes slowly. The air thrums with deep vibration, and the ground seems to heave and seethe beneath her, with a sensation much like sea sickness. She realises that her arms are above her head, and that she's sitting down, her wrists manacled to a wall. She must have passed out while teleporting. With Riley's power, it's not surprising.

She blinks to clear her vision, and it comes clear on a circular room. In the middle of the room, an elevator core. It's a skyscraper then, but not a big skyscraper, because the elevator core is quite small. Overhead, the ceiling is a dome of steel, and small windows ring the walls. No, she corrects herself — she's in a very big skyscraper, but right at the very top. The Empire State Building, in fact, just below the huge, steel spire that sticks into the sky like a needle.

Ringing the elevator core are a series of steel tubes. Each tube is wrapped with copper wire… and she recalls that night in the Municipal Building, what she spied in the box she opened. Lots and lots of copper wire. Hanging off it all, and making a spaghetti-like mess all over the floor, are electrical cables plugged into various power converters and adapters. Big electric generators whine, and the air is cold where windows have been opened to feed even larger power cables up from floors below. Everything whines and howls, and the rattling nausea comes in regular waves.

Technicians walk around the tangled equipment, many in overalls with insulated gloves, checking things. Further around one rounded wall, Ange spots Mayor Riley, talking animatedly with someone. He looks excited, hair neat and perfect, jaw well shaven. Like he's about to do a press conference to announce free puppies for all city residents. Stupid fools might fall for it too, Ange thinks blackly, and looks alongside.

Eli is there, just two yards away, similarly manacled and restrained. But there are gold bands around his neck, wrists, arms and ankles, some of them bejewelled and quite old by the look of them. In combination they give off a magical chill that makes Ange's left side numb. Eli's head lolls, with what looks like exhaustion. Beyond him, Ange sees Croz, and Meisha. Croz's face is bloody, his once-expensive suit burned and torn almost beyond recognition. Ange is surprised by the ferocity of the affection she feels to see him. Most men who walk and talk as tough as Croz don't actually measure up when the real pain starts. But Croz does. Like him or loathe him, he commands respect.

"Eli," Ange murmurs hoarsely. "Eli, are you awake?" A small nod, lips tight with pain. "What's going on?"

"The tubes are plasma," he murmurs. "Superheated. The copper creates a magnetic field. It's like a fusion reactor. Tokomak design."

Ange frowns. But Tokomak reactors don't work very well... and she realises. What doesn't work with technology, sometimes works with magic. Which is why Riley can make work with spare parts what leading science agencies can't with huge machines worth billions. "He's running superheated plasma around the top of the tower?"

"All the top levels," says Eli. "At least ten floors beneath us too. It's a massive concentrated energy signature. It creates a homing beacon for Realm Shift. Like a long distance teleporter, the energy is so big it gives the magic a target, lets it concentrate. Normally magical intensity tends to drift. This will put it all in one place. It acts as a capture net, letting magical energy build up stronger and stronger, until it tips and creates a cascade that flips everything."

"And either destroys everything, or flips the Realms," Ange finishes.

"Won't destroy everything," says Eli. "The universe is a big place. Just this planet. Possibly the solar system." His lips twist in some strange humour. "Hardly anything really. A pinprick."

Ange doesn't see what's amusing. "You can't move?" He manages a small shake of his head. "How can he immobilise you? I thought you were…"

"He's more powerful than me, Angelina," Eli says tiredly. "And he funnelled his initial strike through Jamie. Jamie's power, plus his… it's too much."

"Jamie's really that powerful?"

"Yes. He just doesn't know how to use it. But Riley does, he was using Jamie's power like a remote control operator flying a plane." Again the faint smile. "Old age and trickery beats youth and raw power every time, I'm afraid."

"Well why don't you use some of that old trickery and do something to stop this?"

Eli sighs. "I'm out of tricks, Angelina. I've never been as good at tricks as Riley."

"Absolutely you haven't been," says Riley, stepping over some power cables to come to them. He's positively brimming with enthusiasm. "You've too many rules, Eli. If you live for so long with your head filled with so many rules, it kills your sense of the possible! Open your mind, Eli! I'm going to need you to, if we're to pull this off."

"I'm not helping you," Eli mutters.

Riley beams. "As though you have a choice!" He squats opposite, balanced with his staff. He looks barely middle-aged at this range, Ange thinks. A young forty-five, in the way of those middle-aged men who age well. Well dressed and confident, she can see why people talk about all the women who think he's sexy — even as that prospect makes her a little sick. Confidence, power… and slightly creepy good looks, it's true… but women have thrown away their dignity and common sense for less. Worst of all, he's wearing Ange's sword in his belt, like a trophy. "I didn't want it to come to this Eli. My old friend."

"Spare me," Eli growls.

"No it's true! Look," Riley explains, with a glance at Ange to make sure she's included, "this whole mess basically boils down to this. I wanted to do what I like. You wouldn't let me. I didn't even want to do anything particularly *bad*, as you'd no doubt call it. But still you wouldn't let me, because good old Eli, you insist on *rules* for everything. Rules for this and rules for that. It doesn't work, it doesn't improve anyone's lives, you just like the order because you're scared of true freedom. And so I resisted, and you fought me.

"You think I *wanted* to build up all these armies? Waste all this time, fighting you, fighting your allies? I've got better things to do Eli, seriously. But you didn't leave me a choice, and now we come to this."

A huge shudder shakes the building, and Ange feels the nausea surge once more. The power is clearly coming from Riley, crackling and tingling across her skin. It feels like he's gathering it, and with each surge, the power here atop one of the tallest central structures in Manhattan continues to build.

"And you," says Riley, turning to Ange. "The Ulani with dragons. Dragons don't particularly like Third Realm, but here you are, bewitching that big Atlantic Blue into giving his life for you. There's something odd about you, girl. I can't put my finger on it. I know Eli knows what I'm talking about." Ange gives him a stare that could melt lead.

"Riley, we're getting real close to capacity," says one of his people, looking at his laptop.

"Yep," says Riley, and claps his hands. "I reckon we are. People! Come on, let's huddle!"

From around the far side of the elevator core, magicians come. One is Mulberry Watson, in dark glasses and stylish hat. Several others Ange recognises from brief encounters, but hasn't been in New York long enough to put names to. A number besides Mulberry are Shtaal allies and Eli's former 'friends', now gathering here before him to gloat, and drive home the scale of his failure and humiliation.

But the vibrations are getting worse, and a dull, green glow fills the air. As though the power of accumulated magic at the top of this tower is changing the visible wavelength of light. All of the magicians look anxious, and a few downright scared. They arrange themselves in a ring about the elevator core, parallel to the plasma tubes. They clasp staves, wands or favorite amulets, whatever they most prefer to project and receive power, a few murmuring words as though in prayer.

A final space remains at Riley's side. Jamie walks from the rear of the room to fill it. Ange stares in disbelief. Jamie won't meet her gaze, and takes his place beside Riley, clasping his short staff. He does however spare a glance at Eli, and it is filled with hate.

"It's not going to work!" Eli tells them all, raising his voice to be heard above the din. "You lack the control! You can accumulate energy, you can initiate the shift through First Realm, but you cannot control it! And that much uncontrolled energy will destroy everything!"

"We can control it!" Riley shouts back, and points his staff at Eli. "Or rather, you can!" A wall of light ignites between the circled magicians, so bright Ange has to squint. That light leaps from Riley's staff, and straight through Eli. Eli yells, straining against it, and Ange feels the most impossible surge of power, like a blinding light through her brain. It feels as though she's on fire, though without quite the pain, and everything sizzles and burns.

The roar in the room turns to a shriek, and suddenly Ange can see outside the tower, as though she's removed from her body, and looking across the vast sprawl of towers, rivers and suburbs. A huge wall of green light approaches, an imploding shockwave, new energy heading in, concentrating at its core. It races across roads, houses, factories and bridges, shrinking as it approaches, and bringing with it all the energy of many universes beyond this one. It is power beyond comprehension, and well beyond the capacity of even Riley to control... but Riley channelling the willing yet raw power of Jamie, and the unwilling yet great power of Eli...

The bubble collapses with a deep plunge into entropy, and time seems to stretch, and stretch, silent and breathless, as though the universe's very fabric is deciding whether it can take this strain without rupture...

...and snaps back with a crash, equipment exploding, sparks and flames flying as plasma momentarily escapes, then dissipates free of the magnetic containment. People fling themselves or are flung to the floor, covering their heads, and for a moment it feels like the tower might be about to fall. Then cold air erupts as magicians extinguish the flames, and throw debris aside where it's fallen on themselves or others. They get to their feet, feeling their balance, searching their senses to see what's changed...

"Oh good lord," says Mulberry, wide-eyed behind his askew sunglasses. He's staring at his hands as though he's never seen them before. He makes a light with one hand, and it is blindingly bright, and all shield their eyes. Mulberry laughs in amazement. "The power!"

Cheers and yells of triumph from others, quickly hushed by astonishment, as magicians feel the new world around them. Ange blinks blearily against the green-hued haze before her eyes, and glances at Eli. He looks in pain, head bowed and pulling at his restraints. The bands about his limbs are glowing bright blue, as though energized with some new force entirely. It does not seem to agree with him.

"It worked!" Riley announces. He looks out a window, at the great city beyond, all still intact in the night, an endless sprawl of lights. "By god it *is* possible!" He waves his hand before him, and makes a cascade of colours in the air. He laughs. "I can see so much more! It's *so* much more than I imagined!"

Ange looks at Jamie, standing quietly amidst the celebrations. He does not smile, nor join in the cheers and laughs. What did you think, she wants to ask him. That this would bring Tori back? That you'd be happier on this side than the other?

"Eli you old fool!" Riley laughs. "You knew this all along! You tried to resist it, I could feel you trying, but you *remember* this power, don't you, from all those years ago! And your memory guided us through! Thank you my old friend, we couldn't have done it without you. But now that we're here, I'm afraid your time is done. This may be a new world, but it's not big enough for the both of us."

He raises his staff, and points it at Eli. "You've been around a long time, and you've done some amazing things. You were my mentor for a time, and my hero. You shaped this magical world like no one else before you. If you speak your final request, you have my pledge that I shall honour it, within reason."

Eli smiles grimly. "Any request, honoured by you, would be ashes. I'm not interested in your charity, and while I'm not yet tired of this world, I'm sure as hell tired of you. Be done with it before I die of boredom."

Riley's brow furrows, a flash of real anger. Then he blinks, and shrugs. "Very well, as you will." He raises his staff.

Ange realises, quite strangely, that she's not going to sit here and watch this. It's an odd thought because there's no earthly reason why she should be able to do anything about it. But as soon as she thinks it, she feels very strange indeed. But good strange. She tears her manacles straight from the wall with a surge of power, and holds her hand out for her sword to leap straight off Riley's belt, and into her palm.

Riley fires as she steps into his path, and the incredible power doesn't even reach her. It hits a barrier, and sprays wildly about the domed room, sparking and exploding off metal roof and marble floors, sending onlookers diving and covering behind their shield spells. Ange angles her blade, and watches Riley's power spray roughly where she wants it, annihilating whole sections of tubing, generators and walls. Another slight angle, and she lets it flow down her sword, and pulverise her manacles, first hands, then feet. Such easy control, yet somehow, as though in a trance, she's not at all surprised at her ability to do it. Everything seems to be happening very slowly, and she feels oddly calm.

Riley stops his stream of power, and backs away, eyes wide. "No!" he exclaims. "No, that's not possible!"

Behind her, Ange can hear someone laughing like a maniac. Unbelievably, it's Eli. "First Realm!" he shouts between whoops of laughter. "I don't believe it! Angelina, you draw from First Realm too!"

"It's not possible!" Riley yells furiously. "Receptors can't do that!" He raises his staff again as though to fire, but thinks again, with real trepidation.

"Riley you young fool!" Eli laughs. "You haven't created your perfect magical paradise! You've created a monster!"

"She's just another Third Realm Ulani," Riley snarls. "Get her!"

Other magicians fire. Ange points and sends their bolts straight back at them, electrocuting several, sending others staggering. Receptors charge her with large weapons, and Ange dodges one thrust, spins below another, watching as the bladed staff swishes inches from her nose yet not feeling any particular threat. She can nearly count the notches in the blade as it passes. She completes the spin with an elegant drive of sword-through-face, then cuts back to remove an arm, then spins low to remove a leg, then leaps high to smash another spinning with a kick. She's always been good, but this feels insane. So much power and control, she's never imagined such control. Fights are always crazy, but now it's like she knows what's coming before her attackers arrive.

She carves through them with controlled carnage, bodies spinning, blood spurting, as enemies run, or flee, or fling themselves aside in desperation. Many teleport frantically and dangerously, while others strike at her with magical attacks from range, only to have those attacks rebound, killing themselves or their comrades instead. Mulberry teleports as she reaches him, her blade slicing through empty air, but the terror on his face is nearly satisfaction enough. Riley's female assistant hits her with a force shove that should have put her through a wall, but Ange spins through it and cuts her in half.

She spies Riley, watching with disbelief, and heads straight for him. "You know, I *like* this new world," she tells him with evil glee. "Thank you so much for this, I'm so glad I came." And Mayor Riley, the most powerful magician of the last millennia, teleports to avoid her blade.

Ange stops, in fighting pose amidst the sparking, smoking, bleeding chaos. And turns to face Jamie, the last one left, standing by the elevator doors and watching her. For a moment, their eyes meet. There is no fear in Jamie's eyes, and no anger, only sadness. Ange feels all blood lust and vengeance leave her, like a cool breeze blowing away the smoke. She gazes at him, and her sword lowers. Jamie nods once, and puts his hand on his heart. And vanishes.

Ange walks back around the elevator core, picking her way past debris, to where Eli is sitting against the wall and considering her. He's smiling, quite curiously. "These will be interesting times," he suggests.

"Tell me about it," Ange retorts, and begins removing his chains. "You think you might want to remove this collar now?"

"What collar?" asks Eli. Ange puts a hand to her throat, and feels only skin. She blinks at him. And recalls that when she swung at Mulberry, and others just recently in Eli's organisation, nothing stopped her. Eli smiles more broadly. "This is your time now, Angelina. And no power can hold you."

CHAPTER TWENTY

Ange sits in the passenger seat of the old Chrysler, and gazes out the window at the blaze of autumn leaves. They're in North Eastern Connecticut, nearing Massachusetts, and the forests across rolling hills are turning with the seasons, to every shade of red and gold and brown. Croz drives, and in the backseat Meisha tells him where to go with no need for a map.

The Chrysler is a far cry from Croz's Ferrari, but the need of the hour is to be inconspicuous. Besides, the Ferrari, like nearly everything else they own in New York, has been recently 'repossessed', or borrowed, by the new Shtaal Alliance under Mulberry Watson. The Ferrari is probably being driven by someone else, and Croz doesn't like to talk about it. Nor about the schmucks who are probably wearing his clothes, and living in his apartment. No matter, Ange thinks as she watches the passing trees. They'll all get what's coming to them, in time.

"...*hundreds of mourners attended the funeral of the late Eli Leventhal yesterday, following the tragic fire in Leventhal Tower yesterday that claimed more than a hundred lives,*" announces the radio. "*The mourners included leading business people, politicians and celebrities from around the nation and the world. Leventhal's good friend, New York Mayor Samuel Riley, spoke of Mr Leventhal's good works, his charities and his passion for the education of underprivileged youth...*"

Croz snorts with humourless laughter. He's smiling even less than usual these days, but that's mostly the swollen side of his face that makes any expression painful. The shroud is making up stories again, more elaborate than usual. Eli says the shroud has become more powerful too, like Ange, like everything and everyone else. Everyone, that is, except Eli. He's in hiding, until he gets his powers back, and his health. Something about the Realm Shift doesn't connect with him, and if he marches back into Manhattan and tries to reclaim his old place, Riley will kill him in a heartbeat. Rather than explain the reasons why he's hiding, the shroud has made up its enigmatic, magical mind to tell everyone that he's dead. If Riley gets his way, it'll be true. Or Mulberry, who's little more than Riley's lapdog now, and the grand Shtaal Alliance an 'opposition' to the Togova in nothing but name.

"It's beautiful out here," Ange observes as they pass through a little town. It doesn't look cheap, with big houses and huge, green yards amidst the trees. Gardeners rake multi-coloured leaves off the lawns and verges, and pile them into big plastic bins.

"Going to get real cold soon," says Croz. "See how beautiful you think it is then."

"I've spent months in the Alps in winter," Ange tells him. "I know cold."

"We'll see," says Croz, unconvinced.

"You know," says Ange, "the thing with you is you assume everyone's not as tough as you until proven otherwise."

Croz thinks about that for a moment. "So what's your point?" Ange grins.

"Croz, turn right up here," says Meisha, directing them into a narrow lane along a small gully.

A few miles further on they emerge from forest onto a clear hillside. Atop the hill are several big barns and a homestead, all with tall, pointed rooves. Big paddocks are closed with wooden fences, behind which roam a number of beautiful horses. Croz stops at a big gate, and Ange leaves the car to let them through.

"So pretty!" she says as she gets back into the car after closing the gate. Croz accelerates up the gravel drive toward the farmhouse. "Look at these horses, these are thoroughbreds."

"This is horse country," Croz agrees. "You see all the money in that town? Lots of breeding studs out here, a few guys I know in the city keep telling me I should invest." A pause. "A few guys I *knew*," he corrects himself.

"But horses don't have steering wheels," says Meisha.

"Exactly."

They stop at the farmhouse, and a middle-aged woman in working jeans and a flannel shirt greets them as they get out. "Hello there," says Ange, walking to meet her. "I'm Angelina, we spoke on the phone."

"Ellen," says the woman, and shakes her hand. She's got her hair in a bun, and has hands worn from working. At the screen door behind her, a pair of dogs bark at the strangers. "Oh shush you!" Ellen tells them. And to Ange, "I'm *so* glad to meet you. I was so worried when they didn't come back. And then I heard what happened… I'm so sorry. What a loss."

Ange swallows against the lump in her throat. "Thank you." She looks about at the hillside ranch. "He certainly picked a nice place for it."

"Well I'm not sure he did," says Ellen, gesturing for them to follow as she heads toward one of the barns. "The big female did the choosing, I think. Wasn't she the most beautiful thing? But your buddy was the big boy, yes?"

"That's right."

"I *knew* he had to have a human connection, and I knew it wasn't me. I mean, to trust some stranger with something like this, most dragons never would."

"Well normally they'll pick a high mountain," Ange explains. "I met him in the Alps, in Italy. But he needed to be near New York, and there's no big mountains nearby. So he picked the nearest place he felt safe… or Bella did."

"Bella?" Ellen asks with a sigh. "That was her name?"

"It's the name I gave her. She seemed to like it. The boy was Gia."

"Gia. Wow, Italian dragons, living in my barn. Who'd have thought."

"Well, Italian names," says Ange. "No dragons have countries, they go all over the world. They both must have really liked you. Dragons are a better judge of humans than any humans I know, they can just tell who to trust."

"Well they were both very polite," says Ellen, reaching the big barn door and pulling it open. "Didn't so much as sniff at my horses, even though I'd guess they're just meals on legs to a dragon. Scared the bejeesus out of them a few times though."

Sunlight falls through the barn's high windows upon bales of hay stacked tall about the walls. On the center of the barn floor, a huge pile of hay has been gathered in a big, wide pyramid. Atop the pyramid some colourful blankets cover the mound. The air smells of musty hay, horses, manure… and very faintly, of dragons. Ange's heart beats faster.

"Thank you so much for letting them borrow your entire barn," she says. "It must have been an inconvenience."

"Oh no," says Ellen, shaking her head. "It was well worth it, and they weren't here all the time anyhow. I've been a horse woman all my life, but good lord! Dragons!" Ange smiles, her eyes fixed on the blankets atop the nest. Ellen sees her looking, and smiles back. "Go on then. Be my guest."

Ange walks to the pile of hay and climbs up. The blankets smell incontestably of dragons, and two dragons in particular. She kneels, and gently lifts the blankets aside. There underneath, snug and warm, is a dark green and leathery egg. Ange's heart leaps with part excitement and part anxious fear. She puts her hands on the rough, warm surface, and feels a familiar magical tingle. Small and delicate, and speaking to her like an old friend.

"Hello there," she whispers to the egg. "I'm Angelina. I knew your mum and dad. Your dad was my best friend, and your mum was brave and proud. I'll tell you about them, when you're older. And I'll tell you who killed them, too. And then, when you're bigger? We're going to set the world on fire. And the people who killed your mum and dad are going to burn. All of them.

278

ABOUT THE AUTHOR

JOEL SHEPHERD is the Australian author of nineteen SF and Fantasy novels in four series. They are 'The Cassandra Kresnov Series', 'A Trial of Blood and Steel', 'The Spiral Wars', and 'The Dead Realm'.

He lives in Australia, is a keen cyclist and traveller, has a degree in International Relations, is a volunteer firefighter, and is currently learning Japanese. He has a podcast, creatively titled 'The Joel Shepherd Podcast', which can be found at his website, to which he intends to add more content when he finds the time.

Website; www.joelshepherd.com
Twitter; twitter.com/ShepJoel